A FATE FORGED IN FIRE

A FATE FORGED IN FIRE

A NOVEL

HAZEL MCBRIDE

DELACORTE PRESS

NEW YORK

Published in the United States by Delacorte Press, an imprint of Random House, a division of Penguin Random House LLC, 1745 Broadway, New York, NY 10019.

DELACORTE PRESS is a registered trademark and the DP colophon is a trademark of Penguin Random House LLC.

Hardback ISBN 978-0-593-97294-6
Ebook ISBN 978-0-593-97295-3

Printed in the United States of America on acid-free paper

randomhousebooks.com
penguinrandomhouse.com

2 4 6 8 9 7 5 3 1

First Edition

Map by Dewi Hargreaves
Celtic dragon art by DEWise / Adobe Stock

The authorized representative in the EU for product safety and compliance is Penguin Random House Ireland, Morrison Chambers, 32 Nassau Street, Dublin D02 YH68, Ireland, https://eucontact.penguin.ie.

For the little girls who were told to put their fires out.
Burn them all to the fucking ground.

AUTHOR'S NOTE

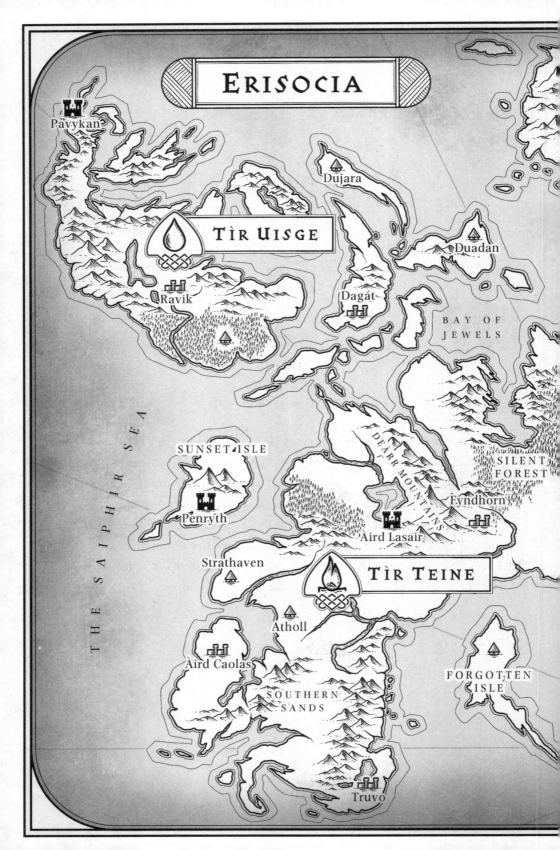

Pronunciation Guide

Many words used within this story are either inspired by, derived from, or direct translations of Scottish Gaelic. There may be variations in word choice and pronunciation due to different local dialects. There are unique sounds in Gaelic that are difficult to mimic using English phonetics. Therefore, it is recommended that readers access an online Scottish Gaelic dictionary to hear sound files of these words for accurate pronunciation and further learning.

CHARACTER NAMES

Aemyra	Eh meer ah
Adarian	Ah dar ian
Màiri	Maa ree
Orlagh	Or la
Pàdraig	Pah drec
Fiorean	Fee oh ray un
Lachlann	Loch lun

Laoise	Lee sha
Draevan	Dray van
Clan Daercathian	Dare cath ay an
Clan Leuthanach	Lay han och
Clan Leòmhann	Leeow an
Clan Iolairean	Yool er an
Solas	Soh liss
Gealach	Gee ah lach
Kolreath	Kol rey ath
Aervor	Air vor
Terrea	Ter ay ah

PLACE NAMES

Tìr Teine	Cheer Chey nuh *"ch" as in cheese*
Tìr Sgàile	Cheer Skal-uh
Tìr Ùir	Cheer Oor
Tìr Uisge	Cheer Oosh guh
Tìr Adhair	Cheer Ah air

(READER NOTE: To be completely correct in Scottish Gaelic, the addition of *an* or *na* should be used here, i.e., Tìr an Teine / Tìr na Sgàile).

Àird Lasair	Arsht Lass air
Àird Caolas	Arsht Coo liss

(READER NOTE: To be completely correct in Scottish Gaelic, the Àird would change Lasair to Lasrach and Caolas to a'Chaolais).

Caisteal	Kass jal
Penryth	Pen rith
Truvo	True voh
Saiphir Sea	Saf fire sea
Smàrag Sea	S mah rak sea
Deàrr Mountains	Jah-r Mountains
Beinn Deataiche	Bine Je tach

WORLDBUILDING NAMES

Dùileach	Doo lach
Sgillinn	Skil een
Beathach	Bee yo uch *ch as in "loch"*
Beathaichean	Bee yo eech in *ch as in "loch"*
Dorchadas	Dor ah chah diss *ch as in "loch"*
Breith-day	Brae-day
Copar	Cop air
Òmar	Aw mar
Seann	Sha ow-n
Cainnt	Kaa een ch *ch as in "cheese"*
Tùr	Toor
Athair	A her
Fèileadh	Fey ligh *"igh" is quite a unique sound, think of "ugh" as in groaning about something, but starting with an i.*
Cèilidh	Kay lee
Sgiath	Skee uh
Fearsolais	Fehr sol ish
Onair	On er
Chrùin	Croon
Beus	Bayse
A luaidh	A loo ay
A ghràidh	A gh rye

A FATE FORGED IN FIRE

CHAPTER ONE

As Aemyra crouched in front of the laboring mother, she came to the sudden realization that she only enjoyed having her face between a woman's legs when she was screaming out in pleasure, not in pain.

Aemyra had her own reasons for viewing childbirth differently than most women in Erisocia. Not least because her adoptive mother, Orlagh, had put her off the whole ordeal by beginning instruction in midwifery before Aemyra's first bleeding.

"Is it almost over?" Màiri moaned exhaustedly.

Extracting herself from the thin chemise and tightening her headscarf, Aemyra worked what she hoped was a reassuring smile onto her face.

"Not long now," she said, reaching for a clean rag to wipe her hands on.

The women of the capital city of Àird Lasair were said to have been created in the image of the fire Goddess Brigid herself, as revered for their strength as they were their beauty. Even still, Màiri was tiring.

When she let out another peal of excruciating cries, Aemyra bit her lip and hoped Orlagh would arrive soon. If her mother hadn't already been busy tending to a broken leg, she would have never come to assist this labor alone. Goddess knew she didn't have the bedside manner required.

Looking over her shoulder and out of the window to the busy street beyond, she wondered what was keeping her brother. She had summoned him from the forge to help hours ago.

"I think it's coming!" Màiri groaned.

Whirling back around, Aemyra lifted the chemise and gave thanks to Brigid when she spied a head full of dark hair. After a morning spent crouching on the cold floor, the babe had finally turned and Aemyra relaxed. She wouldn't need Orlagh's help after all.

"It's almost over, just keep breathing," Aemyra encouraged.

The sound of reluctant knocking alerted her to her brother's presence. Turning, she saw Adarian peering in through the window.

"Finally," she muttered.

Aemyra waved him in impatiently as she gently wiped the sweat from Màiri's forehead with a damp cloth. She was definitely going to need a drink after this, her knees were numb and her back stiff.

The door slammed shut and Adarian's cheeks flamed red as he got an eyeful of the miracle of childbirth displayed in front of him.

Màiri was too lost in pain to care.

Aemyra smirked. "Surely you've seen one before, Adarian?"

Gritting his teeth and squashing his broad shoulders through the narrow doorframe, he set the bucket of clean water he had brought with him on the floor.

"Not like that I haven't," he muttered, retreating hastily.

Before he could slip out of the house, Aemyra snapped her fingers. "Not so fast. I need more linens."

To his credit, Adarian didn't complain as he strode to the other room. While Aemyra may not have had the same affinity for midwifery as Orlagh, Adarian certainly didn't have the stomach for it. Most days they squabbled like they were still in cloots over who got to work the forge with their adoptive father, Pàdraig, instead.

Aemyra rubbed Màiri's arm encouragingly and noticed that the woman's skin was cold to the touch.

The weather had been overcast and damp for weeks, and the inside of the house smelled like it. Without thinking, Aemyra thrust her hand toward the hearth, fingers pointed directly at the peat. She loosed a tongue of flame that was decidedly too strong to belong to an average Dùileach.

When she saw Màiri's slack jaw, and the stern look in Adarian's eyes as he returned with an armful of linens, she knew she had displayed too much of her gift.

"I didn't know you had Bonded?" Màiri asked, her eyes agog.

Hearing Adarian's heavy footfalls behind her, Aemyra could feel her brother's disapproving gaze on her back. Many were blessed by the Goddesses, but few possessed her depth of power without Bonding as a way to amplify their elemental magic.

Except Clan Daercathian, the rulers of Tìr Teine. While most average Dùileach only had enough control to light a candle, the dragon clan had leveled battlefields with their fire.

"Uh, yes. Very recently," she muttered, praying to Brigid that another contraction would come on as a helpful distraction.

Adarian stormed from the house upon hearing the lie, a tinkling noise sounding as a cold draft blew through the doorway. Aemyra's gaze went up toward the low ceiling, where tokens made out of broken china, glass, colorful ribbon, and even a few silver sgillinn hung from the wooden beams to appease the air Goddess Beira.

She couldn't help but think that those silver sgillinn would be better spent to pay for a new door, but determined to focus on the task at hand, Aemyra resumed her ministrations.

Thankfully, Màiri seemed too tired to notice the stray lock of hair that had fallen out of Aemyra's headscarf.

"The Goddesses are discriminate with their blessings, but let us see if they have gifted this child," Aemyra said.

The conjured fire's warmth skittered throughout the damp room. Brigid was watching as they brought this babe into the world.

As the penultimate pain passed through Màiri, Aemyra watched the babe slither forward and couldn't keep the grimace off her face.

Màiri screamed so loudly that Aemyra felt her soul respond with an echo in the very part of her that understood what it was to be a woman.

A heartbeat later, the babe shot into her arms, already squalling.

The moment Aemyra caught her, for it was indeed a daughter, the fire in the hearth flared.

Blinking rapidly, Màiri raised her head and her eyes widened at the blessing. Aemyra deftly severed the cord and cauterized it in one fluid motion with her magic.

"A Dùileach . . ." Màiri breathed in awe as she reached for the newborn.

Finished wrapping her in the clean linens that Adarian had thoughtfully warmed with his own magic, Aemyra handed the little girl to her mother.

"Your first?" she asked out of plain curiosity.

Màiri looked up with tears shining in her eyes and nodded. "My grandmother possessed an ember, my mother and I barely a spark. I hardly dared to hope that one of our children might be Goddess blessed . . ."

With a nervous glance toward the glowing fire, Aemyra flinched as the door swung open again. This time the scent of comfrey and wild garlic accompanied light footsteps.

"You're late," Aemyra said with a wry smile as her mother bustled into the room.

In a no-nonsense fashion, Orlagh rolled up her sleeves to reveal smooth umber skin. Solas fluttered down from her shoulder to perch on a chair, his flaming tail a little too close to the wood for comfort. Aemyra eyed the firebird in trepidation, praying fervently to all the Goddesses that Màiri wouldn't bring up Bonding again.

"I knew you would manage well enough here in my stead," Orlagh said, setting her bag down and checking Màiri over with a practiced eye. "Judging by this bonnie babe and her contented mother, I was right."

"A Goddess-blessed Dùileach . . ." Màiri said in a dreamy voice, enthralled in familiarizing herself with her daughter's face.

Orlagh raised one shapely brow as she used her own gifts to cauterize Màiri's small tear. Relinquishing the afterbirth rituals to her mother, Aemyra washed her hands and made to scurry out of the house in search of a very late breakfast.

"Aemyra," Orlagh called out.

Pausing with one hand on the door handle, Aemyra turned. Orlagh's deep brown eyes were tired but filled with pride.

"You have done well," Orlagh said.

Solas flapped his tiny wings as if in disagreement.

Avoiding the penetrating gaze of her mother's firebird, Aemyra slipped from the house.

The bustle of the lower town assaulted her senses the moment she closed the door behind her. The scent of roasting meat and fried onions slunk up her nose and her stomach growled.

She didn't make it two steps toward the nearest cart before a firm hand pulled her off the sagging porch.

"What the——" she exclaimed, breaking the hold easily by twisting the large arm and whirling around to face her brother.

Adarian's eyes were on the stray lock of hair escaping from her headscarf.

"Cover that up. Now," he barked, his sapphire eyes darting nervously toward the other houses on the street.

Packed together as they were in the swarming lower town of Àird Lasair, Aemyra wasn't worried about anyone paying them attention.

She aimed a punch at her brother, which he easily dodged. "Don't tell me what to do," she retorted, but tucked the curl under the scarf anyway.

She strode off down the street, dodging puddles of filth and ignoring vendors attempting to flag their wares from carts, stalls, and even the backs of some horses.

Adarian, significantly taller and broader than she was, struggled to keep up as she wove her way through the crowd.

"What was that back there?" he asked between clenched teeth.

She smirked as they walked the cobbled streets. "It's called childbirth. Dangerous business. I suggest you keep drinking the contraceptive tonic Orlagh makes."

Adarian's skin flushed the true color of the hair he kept shorn and dyed with soot.

"You know what I mean, Aemyra. You are growing reckless," he muttered, pulling her into the shadows of a stinking alley. "Have you forgotten why you need to keep the extent of your magic hidden? Or do you simply not care anymore? Thank Brigid that Màiri assumed you were Bonded."

Aemyra rolled her eyes and brushed dirt off of her breeches. "Hormones make women in childbirth say and do things they won't remember the next day. It won't be a problem."

Adarian didn't look convinced and Aemyra didn't particularly like the way he towered over her now. She felt like it made everyone forget that she was the oldest. By a whole seven minutes.

"Just because your power outranks every un-Bonded Dùileach in Tìr Teine doesn't mean you should use it," he warned.

Aemyra smirked again. "I outrank most of the Bonded Dùileach too."

Lifting her hand, she summoned flames into her palm, the light illuminating their faces as her magic surged forth eagerly. Adarian moved to block the flames from the view of the street and Aemyra struggled to contain her fire to her palm. It would have been only too easy to let it pour out of her like wildfire until it covered the ramshackle buildings around them.

A cart rattled over the cobblestones, making them both jump, and she quickly extinguished the flames. Only the smell of smoke lingered in the air.

"But not the king or his sons," Adarian warned. "You're no match for a dragon-Bonded Dùileach. If they found out . . ." His jaw tightened. "Perhaps you *should* Bond if it will conceal the depths of your original gift."

Aemyra took one step toward him and he wisely backed away.

"What an *excellent* idea, Brother," she said sarcastically. "Bonding would be a great way to amplify my magic and make it even harder to hide."

Aware of the dangerous turn in conversation, she glanced down the alley in case a vagrant was crouched in a doorway unseen.

Adarian shrugged. "With your temper, you would do well with a chimera."

"Don't insult me," Aemyra hissed. "You know what beathach I deserve."

Adarian gazed at her flameless palm. While her brother also battled with keeping their gifts a secret, he had mastered an art of control that Aemyra could only dream of. With his lesser depth of magic, Adarian showed no sign of an inward struggle, whereas she always felt like a pot that had been left too long on the boil.

"The world is already on fire, Aemyra. We don't need you burning anything else down." Adarian sighed.

Her only response was a ferocious glare.

Adarian wiped a soot-stained hand across his face, his knuckles sporting fresh burns from the forge. It angered Aemyra just to see it. Not that she resented their parents for their trades, she saw the value in the skills they had both inherited, but deep down she knew they were destined for more. They deserved more than the secrets they had been forced to keep for twenty-six years.

"We moved to this stinking city from Penryth over ten years ago. Brigid gifted me for a reason, and I will fight with flame and steel for what is rightfully mine," she said.

Adarian's sapphire eyes, so different from her forest green ones, clouded with tiredness.

"Is it really worth wasting your life waiting for a birthright that might never come?" he asked.

Smothering her frustration, Aemyra elbowed her way past her brother and back out into the street. The smell of freshly baked bannocks was making her mouth water and her boots were sure-footed across the uneven streets as she headed for the baker's. Her thin cloak was barely enough to protect her from the winter chill gusting in through the city gate.

A few people called out to Adarian as they made their way south, thanking him for repairs, or inquiring about a horse to be shod.

The bitterness took root in Aemyra's heart again.

"Is this truly enough for you?" she muttered as her twin drew level with her.

He dropped his eyes to the dirty ground. "It is honest work."

She was thankful that her brother could not see her eye roll. Pàdraig had molded them both into skilled metalworkers, but Aemyra had no passion for it.

Instead of ridiculing her brother, she looked away from the south gate and over the battlements. Above the crumbling rooftops of the lower town, she could make out the crimson spires of Caisteal Lasair. The lofty turrets lurked just beyond the bridge across the loch that separated the rest of the city from the nobility who called the caisteal home.

Aemyra had never been on the other side of that bridge. She had remained confined by the high battlements to the lower town of Àird Lasair for ten long years. Yet she was still unwilling to leave her post.

Adarian, Orlagh, Pàdraig . . . they all had their parts to play.

Besides, Aemyra had no interest in exploring the rest of Tìr Teine on foot.

As if she had willed it with her thoughts, the ground under their feet trembled, the puddles of filth rippling. People turned their faces to the clouds in both anticipation and fear.

The overcast sky was suddenly brightened as the king's magnificent golden dragon rose from behind the caisteal and spread his wings with an almighty roar.

Kolreath. The oldest of the last three dragons in existence.

As the pewter gray sky opened and the rain clouds finally spilled over, Aemyra was the only one in the street who didn't shrink from the second screech the dragon loosed into the air. The rain droplets turned to steam on her cheeks as Aemyra gazed up at the beathach she had coveted for years.

"The king has to die eventually, Adarian," she muttered, Kolreath's enormous wing beats loud enough to cover their conversation as the mighty dragon flew overhead. "And when he does, I will be ready to take everything I was born to be."

CHAPTER TWO

WHISPERS ABOUT THE KING'S MADNESS HAD BEEN SWEEPING through Àird Lasair for years. Fantastical rumors about severe punishments and black moods that had him sending even his most trusted advisers to the dungeons.

Some even went so far as to say King Haedren's fractured mind was no longer capable of holding court and he was often seen wandering the hallways of Caisteal Lasair in nothing but his nightshirt, muttering to himself.

Aemyra highly doubted the last one, given that he had been spotted flying with Kolreath only two moons past.

"Surely it won't be long now."

"Queen Katherine will be beside herself when he goes."

"No female heir for a hundred years."

"All those boys . . ."

Aemyra heard each and every whisper and tucked them into the special pocket in her memory where she stored such things. Perhaps the moment she had been waiting ten years for would soon come to pass.

After successfully stuffing her stomach with three buttery bannocks, she was now perched in her favorite corner of the forge, as it was an excellent place to overhear gossip. Thanks to the city guards, farmers, and merchants all needing things repaired or made for them, Aemyra was well informed of the comings and goings of everyone who called Àird Lasair home.

As she sat on the stool with her favorite pliers in hand, she kept her eyes on the suit of chain mail draped over her knee. Her ears were on the guards clustered by the door as they sheltered from the rain, enjoying the heat from the forge.

The mail was badly damaged, some idiot knight had gotten too close to a spear while hunting. Either that or his friend had thrust the spear in his direction by accident, given his resemblance to a pig.

Based on the size of the suit of mail, Aemyra decided that the latter scenario was more probable.

Her stained fingers gripped and bent the metal with practiced magical ease, and she leaned back to casually observe the crowded forge. It was no match for the spacious rooms they had left behind in Penryth ten years ago, but their family had done well in the city.

When the former smith had conveniently died without an apprentice the same week they had arrived, Pàdraig had dutifully begun working the bellows. His talent for metalwork had spoken for itself and business had quickly grown.

Adarian was bent over the anvil, blue eyes illuminating with every strike of the hammer on the strip of metal in front of him. The sparks flying from the point of contact could just as easily have been from his own magic. Aemyra knew that sometimes they were.

As he was forever sweating through stained shirts, Adarian always preferred to work bare-chested and his skin glistened in the light from the fires. The buckets of water on the floor behind him sizzling as Pàdraig's apprentices shaped horseshoes.

"Oi!" Pàdraig bellowed. "Get over here, you wee rascal."

Aemyra glanced up at the sound of her adoptive father's voice and watched as a group of scruffy-haired children ran too close to the bellows, shinty sticks in hand.

Her little brother, Lachlann, skulked reluctantly over to his formidable father, dark eyes hidden under a scrunched frown.

The family of five from Penryth had initially raised eyebrows upon their arrival in Àird Lasair. Teenage twins as pale as the moon accompanying a couple with rich umber skin cradling their newborn son. When the town had found out they were all fire Dùileach, they attributed the abundant blessings to the family's roots in Penryth. After all, the Sunset Isle was well known as a breeding ground for all manner of magical creatures and was home to a large Dùileach population—it was rare for Penrythians to move away.

Despite their differences, the family had been warmly welcomed in the city. Even with their adoptive daughter's penchant for scowling.

A trait Lachlann seemed to have inherited.

"Put that stick down and make yourself useful," Pàdraig said without raising his voice.

"But we're in the middle of a game!" Lachlann whined, as the other children raced out of the warmth of the forge and into the sheeting rain.

Pàdraig pulled him back and deposited a bucket of nails into his hands in a way that had Aemyra stifling a laugh.

She knew Pàdraig's tricks. It would take Lachlann the rest of the day to heat and reshape the bent and broken nails with only his magic and pliers.

Dropping her gaze to her work, she heated each individual coil of metal and twisted delicately, magic and tools working in tandem to repair the mail.

Adarian hadn't looked up from his hammering once.

"It isn't fair," pouted Lachlann as he dumped his bucket beside her with a rattle and pulled another stool over.

"What isn't?" she asked lightly.

Lachlann pulled a bent nail out of the bucket and twisted it between his fingers. "Everyone else gets to play and I have to stay here and work."

Aemyra plucked the nail out of his grip and wrapped her hand around it, summoning fire into her palm. A split second later, she dropped a perfectly formed nail into Lachlann's hand and he flinched slightly at the temperature change.

"Think of it as magic practice," she said. "It will help with the finer aspects of temperature control."

Lachlann rolled his dark eyes at her and she stifled a laugh. They might not have been related by blood, but he had learned a few things from his big sister.

"Your father wants you to be careful around the forge because accidents can happen," she explained gently as a couple of guards at the door poked their heads out into the street.

Still focused on his punishment, Lachlann continued his complaining. "But we all control fire. Me, you, Mother and Father, and even Adarian. It's not dangerous."

Pulling her gaze away from the door, she fixed the ten-year-old with a serious look.

"We cannot be burned while we are channeling our magic, that is true, but fire is unpredictable, and greedy. It will not always stop just because we tell it to. Wildfire spreads great distances, consuming everything in its path. The fire in our forges has the power to melt even the toughest of metals."

Lachlann looked up to the glowing mouth of the forge behind Adarian.

"You see that shiny patch of skin on Adarian's shoulder?" she asked.

Lachlann nodded, enthralled.

"Where do you think he got it?"

Her little brother shrugged. Aemyra nodded toward the forge and his eyes turned large as dinner plates.

"Even fire Dùileach can get burned," she said, flipping the pliers in her hand.

Aemyra didn't see any harm in bending the truth if it made Lachlann more careful. It had been Aemyra's own magic that had caused her twin permanent disfigurement, not the forge.

As a child, she had struggled to control the immense well of power inside of her and it had often exploded with little warning. Adarian had been too slow to shield himself and now sported a burn scar that spread across his back.

Most of Aemyra's childhood incidents had been blamed on Orlagh's firebird, Solas. Likely the reason why the little beathach now held her in such contempt. With his flaming tail, and Orlagh's amplified magic as a Bonded Dùileach, they had avoided suspicion in both Penryth and Àird Lasair.

Nevertheless, when Aemyra had heard her twin screaming in pain, she had vowed never to lose control again.

And she hadn't.

But it was a fight, every single day, to keep it under control.

At the sound of laughter coming from the doorway, Aemyra lifted her head. Her expression hardened as she saw the captain of the guard stride into the sweltering space in full armor.

Sir Rolynd Nairn.

Nairn had a few more lines around his eyes and had grown his blond hair longer than the last time she had seen him, but she recognized the arrogance immediately.

Shifting the mail across her knee, she leaned forward and watched him swagger in, an iron pendant of the True Religion bouncing on his breastplate. His long red cloak was sweeping the ground. It would be only too easy for a stray spark to set it alight.

Aemyra's fingertips heated at the thought.

Twisting another link in the chain mail without looking at it, she kept her hands busy and one eye on the captain. Pàdraig's two apprentices were shooting covetous looks toward him.

Nairn smiled readily enough, but as he peered through the forge, he remained aloof. Like he was above them all.

Poncy prick.

One eager young guard clapped Nairn on the shoulder and Aemyra had to duck her head to hide her snigger as Nairn's nostrils flared in disgust at the familiarity.

"More than a year since the last royal wedding. We could use another Games—Calum barely got his caber off the ground last time."

"Suppose it might cheer the king?" another suggested.

Resting her head on the back of her hand so as not to get soot on her chin, Aemyra waited for the captain's response.

"Prince Fiorean will be here any minute. Resume your patrols before he orders you to be lashed for your laziness and insubordinate remarks," Nairn said.

Aemyra's chin slipped off her hand at the news and she watched the guards scramble for the exit, several of them getting stuck in a scrum at the door. Pàdraig winced as the wood creaked and he hastily approached the captain.

Prince Fiorean was a dragon rider, Bonded to the cobalt blue male, Aervor. What in Brigid's name was he doing visiting the forge himself? He had never condescended to do more than trot his horse down the cobblestones on his way out of the city in the ten years Aemyra had resided here.

Fighting the urge to pull her headscarf farther down her forehead, she dropped her gaze and twirled the pliers in a way she hoped demonstrated her skill with a weapon.

A loud hiss and a cloud of steam encompassed the room as Adarian plunged the strip of metal he had been working into water. She watched her brother attempt to wipe his slick, soot-stained skin on the filthy apron he was wearing and she frowned.

Hoisting the mail into the crook of her elbow with some difficulty, she stepped into his path.

"Did you know the prince was coming?" she asked, quietly enough that Lachlann wouldn't overhear.

Adarian wouldn't meet her gaze and her mouth dropped open.

"You *did* know," she whispered, suddenly furious with him for keeping a secret from her. "Whatever for?"

Before her twin got a chance to reply, Pàdraig called softly across the room, "Aemyra."

Adarian brushed past her, and the suit of mail almost slipped out of her grip. Dumping it on top of the stool in a huff, she skirted past the anvil to her father's side.

Refusing to look nervous, she focused on the large brooch fastening Nairn's cloak to his armor. "Good afternoon, Captain."

He nodded his head in lieu of a response. Many found him attractive, with his sunshine hair and light eyes, but he irritated Aemyra immensely.

Pàdraig cleared his throat, face taut. "I need you to retrieve the sword you forged for the prince. Sir Nairn tells me one was commissioned a week past?"

Having heard nothing about it, Aemyra wondered why Pàdraig hadn't known about such an important contract. Happy to throw Adarian into hot water over something that wasn't her fault, she opened her mouth.

Sir Nairn interrupted. "Forgive me, the sword was not commissioned to be made by this girl. The prince spoke with your ward."

Bristling at the way the captain spoke the words *this girl,* Aemyra crossed her arms over her chest. "*I* am his ward."

Before Nairn could lose his patience, an intoxicating voice sounded from the door.

"Apologies for the confusion. I spoke with a young man named Adarian last week."

The captain moved to the side as Prince Fiorean strode into the forge and out of the rain. A clattering noise behind her told Aemyra that one of the apprentices had just dropped a horseshoe. Likely her jaw as well.

If she hadn't been furious at her twin for sticking her with the chain mail while he forged a sword for a Daercathian prince, Aemyra might have been at a loss for words as she beheld Fiorean's face up close.

His hair was unbound, so it spilled across his shoulders, the damp strands framing his face sleekly. The deep auburn shade was a signature trait of the Daercathian royal line.

The black fitted tunic he wore was stark against his pale skin. His face was angular like a mountain cat with a cutting edge on his cheekbones that Aemyra was sure would rival her dagger.

Her attraction to him angered her instantly.

"Shame. If you had been in the market for a new plow, then I would have sent you to my brother. You should have come to me for a sword," Aemyra said, dropping her gaze to the flagstones.

Sir Nairn bristled, puffing up his chest so the Savior's pendant clattered against his breastplate. "You will address the prince properly, girl."

Pàdraig shifted uncomfortably, but Aemyra dipped into an ungainly curtsy.

"Your Highness," she added.

The prince inclined his head ever so slightly in her direction, and she noticed the color of his eyes for the first time. Green, like most of the Daercathian clan, but a hue of dark emerald that contrasted so perfectly with his hair that Aemyra became even more irritated by his good looks.

She watched Fiorean's eyes rove over her shirt, the thin fabric necessary when working the forge.

Her skin glistened with sweat and Aemyra was a little disappointed that he wasn't able to see the hard muscles that lurked beneath her sleeves. She couldn't even be satisfied when his gaze lingered on her breasts, as she knew with absolute certainty that it wasn't out of any flickering attraction, but to further prove his point that a woman would not be able to fashion a sword as well as a man could.

Even the fucking royals are turning their backs on the Goddess in favor of the True Religion . . .

How the "Chosen" priests had gotten their claws into the royal branch of the clan when they were so gifted with Goddess magic was a mystery.

As Aemyra thought it, she was relieved to see no Savior's pendant hanging around the prince's neck. Wisely keeping her mouth shut, she heard Adarian stride back into the room, his boots heavy on the stone floor.

"Apologies for the delay, Your Highness," Adarian panted, facing the prince and the captain.

The fire in the forge banked higher as Adarian laid the sword box on the anvil. Her twin had thrown on a clean shirt, which Aemyra thought looked ridiculous against his filthy skin. His face was smeared with soot, shaven hair stained even darker than Lachlann's.

Prince Fiorean waved away the apology, eyeing the long box. "No matter. You have fashioned it according to my mother's specifications? The queen is rather anxious to begin preparations for my breithday."

Aemyra leaned over as Adarian opened the box to reveal a long claymore sword. When she saw the hilt, she had trouble stifling her laugh.

The captain missed it, but the prince's eyes darted up to hers.

"Is there something amiss?" Fiorean asked, his tone cutting.

Aemyra could feel Adarian silently begging her to mind her manners, but she couldn't help herself upon the sight of the giant garnet embedded in the crossguard. The gem such a dark red it appeared black in the dim light.

"Like I said, you should have come to me for a sword."

The flames at her back danced in Fiorean's eyes as he contemplated her words. Reaching into the box, he pulled the sword free, holding the tip up to the low ceiling before testing the balance.

Just as Aemyra thought, the large gemstone made the sword top-heavy.

She couldn't hide her satisfied smirk as Fiorean realized the exact same thing.

Adarian shifted his feet uncomfortably.

Tearing his eyes from Aemyra, Fiorean studied the extravagant gold-inlaid hilt, brushing the pad of his thumb over the garnet and the flat steel.

The captain looked on approvingly.

"It will do nicely. The queen will approve of your craftsmanship," the prince said to Adarian, placing the sword back in the box and passing it to the captain.

Adarian and Pàdraig both bowed, but Aemyra had to bite the inside of her cheek to keep herself from laughing. The sword Adarian had made was indeed beautiful, but it was good for nothing more than personal decoration—how fitting.

The captain turned to leave, but the prince caught her expression.

"Do you not find it to be a weapon fit for my breithday, Miss . . . ?"

Failing to wipe the amusement off her face, she replied, "I think it will make an excellent addition to your attire, Your Highness."

Fiorean's features hardened when Aemyra both refused to tell him her given name and insulted him in the same breath. His eyes narrowed in rapid succession at her plain brown headscarf, the fitted breeches, and the dagger she wore sheathed on her belt. They lingered on the layered gold necklaces that were peeking out from the open top button of her shirt.

He smiled when he noticed the gold piercings in her ears to match.

"Well, we all have our little embellishments, now, don't we?" Fiorean drawled without warmth.

With a final, terse nod toward Adarian and Pàdraig, he swept from the forge and into the bleak weather.

Aemyra lifted one hand up to her necklaces, feeling the warm metal against her skin as the rain swallowed the two men.

"I made that sword *exactly* the way the queen detailed in her letter. The garnet was non-negotiable, family heirloom apparently," Adarian practically growled as he ripped the shirt off his back and handed it to Pàdraig. "Could you not have at least *pretended* to be polite for our sake?"

Aemyra glared at him. "Because they have done so much to earn our respect? Did you see the stupid pendant around—"

Adarian had his filthy hand clapped over her mouth before she could insult the True Religion, his eyes on the door.

"Not here. Not now," he whispered.

Aemyra considered biting him but thought better of it when she noticed Lachlann watching them closely.

"Go to the house, my little terror," Pàdraig muttered gently.

The two apprentices pretended to be hammering metal into shape even though Aemyra hadn't seen them dunk so much as a single shoe into the water since the captain had arrived.

Hauling the chain mail off the stool and throwing it over her shoulder, she left the forge.

The captain may have looked at her like she was beneath him, and the prince might not have seen the value in her skills, but as Aemyra stepped out into the rain and she let the freezing air cool her fiery temper, she reminded herself that the Goddess Brigid had.

CHAPTER THREE

THE RAIN WAS STILL PISSING DOWN COME NIGHTFALL AS THE twins trudged through the soaked streets.

"Fire Dùileach weren't built for the cold," Aemyra grumbled.

"You shouldn't begrudge any Dùileach their season of power. Winter solstice was only last week," Adarian replied.

Narrowly avoiding a young pickpocket, Aemyra made for the tavern. "I passed Brenna's temple to give my menstrual offering last week and the altar was practically buried underneath gifts for the Goddess."

Adarian flexed his fingers, no doubt stiff from clutching his tools all day. "The earth Dùileach who have sought refuge here are glad of the freedom to worship. Spare a thought for those who are stuck in Tìr Ùir, cowering in the Eternal Forest with their beathaichean."

Aemyra clutched her cloak more tightly around herself as the warm glow from the tavern windows illuminated the rain pattering down in front of them.

Tìr Ùir was reachable in just five days by ship, or two weeks via the Blackridge Mountains, and yet could not be more different from Tìr Teine. Magic had been outlawed there for decades, and with magical creatures confined to their territories by the treaty, Bonded Dùileach had nowhere else to go.

"Let's raise a glass to those poor sods tonight, then," Aemyra muttered, eagerly reaching for the chipped door as her brother turned back to the small pickpocket.

The child grinned as Adarian tossed him a copar, displaying several missing teeth as he snatched the coin and scampered off.

"I'm happy to wait another few months for Beltane, you're even more insufferable then," Adarian said, stamping his boots on the stoop to get some feeling back into his feet.

Her twin was right, Aemyra usually spent the summer feeling like she had an itch she couldn't scratch. Sweating through her sheets, and with a tendency to set chimneys alight, it took consistent effort for her to control her power during the three months of the year when the fire Goddess was the strongest.

"You're my twin, Adarian. You're stuck with my insufferable presence for life," Aemyra said as she pushed open the door to Sorcha's tavern. Inhaling the ale and grease smell of the place, she felt her stomach rumble.

"Should have eaten you in the womb, then," Adarian answered, letting the door swing closed behind them.

"Missed your chance there, I'm afraid. But if you're hungry . . ." she teased, weaving her way through the crowded tables toward the bar. "Sorcha said she made a fresh stew."

Adarian trailed her without complaint, no doubt starving after the long day.

The tavern was full of the regular patrons. A fisherman and his husband lounged comfortably by the fire after a day on the loch, and a group of women were engaged in a fierce card game. The fire was dancing merrily in the hearth, and the many candles perched on shelves and window ledges gave the whole place a rosy glow.

Flexing her fingers as they began to warm up, Aemyra spotted the priests from halfway across the room, her steps faltering.

Three men. Their black robes making them look like the very de-

mons they preached to purge from the hearts of Dùileach. Their iron
pendants looked heavy around their necks. She hoped someone would
strangle them with the chains one day.

Adarian followed her gaze and stiffened as he too noticed the
priests of the True Religion, the *Chosen,* as they called themselves.

Soggy pamphlets were strewn across their table, black books neatly
stacked against the wall. Judging by their soaked robes, they had been
preaching in the square again.

For men who campaigned about selflessness, they were about the
most self-obsessed people Aemyra had ever had the misfortune to
meet.

"How can men without magic have overthrown an entire territory? Tìr Ùir is bigger than Tìr Teine," Aemyra whispered to her
brother as they reached the bar.

"There are a lot more priests than there are Dùileach," Adarian
said quietly out of the corner of his mouth. "And the Ùir wulvern are
far easier to kill than dragons."

Tying her headscarf a little tighter, Aemyra let her hand rest on the
dagger belted at her hip and craned her neck to see where Sorcha had
gotten to.

Impatient, she reached behind the bar and pulled out a bottle of
Sorcha's best òmar. The amber liquid sloshed around as she poured
herself two fingers' worth into a cup and inhaled the intoxicating
scent.

"I'll charge you for that."

Lifting her eyes from the drink, Aemyra smiled as Sorcha appeared, carrying a barrel of ale on one shoulder. "I could always pay
you in other ways?"

With a snort, Sorcha dumped the barrel underneath the bar with
a thud that shook the stool Aemyra was sitting on.

Turning, the barkeep spooned generous measures of stew into two
bowls. Steam curled deliciously off of the gravy and Aemyra wasn't
sure if it was the sight of Sorcha's curves or the food that made her
mouth water.

Adarian could barely wait for Sorcha to tear off a hunk of hard bread before he was shoveling carrots, onions, and gravy into his mouth.

Aemyra took the bread from Sorcha, letting her fingertips gently brush the woman's wrist, her bottom lip snagging between her teeth.

She was rewarded as Sorcha's gaze darkened, but Aemyra busied herself with her lamb stew as the barkeep sped off to tend to her patrons.

"Be careful in front of those priests," Adarian said, surfacing from his supper. "Sorcha won't want you making a scene."

His words made Aemyra's temper spike as she dipped her bread into the gravy. "They can preach twisted morality from that boring book of theirs all they want, doesn't mean I'm going to listen."

A slurp and a glug of ale from her brother before he replied, "I'm serious. You need to pick your battles, it isn't only magic that is outlawed in Ùir—"

Before her brother could finish, Aemyra had spun her fork in her hand and plunged it down into the wood between his fingers.

Adarian's only outward response was the bobbing of his Adam's apple.

She leaned in close to her brother.

"They won't be outlawing *anything* here. Besides, have you heard of me lying with a man in years?" she whispered fiercely.

He shook his head.

She smiled, but it wasn't a pleasant sight. "It isn't because I don't like cock, Brother."

"Who likes cock?" came Sorcha's breezy voice from behind them as she clicked her fingers to draw a barmaid's attention to several dirty tables.

Aemyra popped the bread into her mouth and lounged back in the rickety stool, balancing it on one leg.

"One would think my brother does, given the number of marriage proposals he has rejected now," she taunted. "What's the latest count? Three?"

Adarian blushed again and she chuckled. Goddess, making her brother squirm was practically her favorite pastime.

"Four," he ground out, if only for politeness' sake, since Sorcha was clearly waiting for an answer.

To Aemyra's delight, Sorcha gasped. "Oh dear. It's a pity the Goddesses require women to propose, soon there won't be a woman in Àird Lasair who hasn't been heartbroken by our blacksmith."

He cleared his throat. "Apprentice blacksmith."

Aemyra removed the fork, the wood splintering slightly. "Apprentice, my left tit. You've been running the forge together with Pàdraig for years now. Keeping royal commissions from both of us, apparently."

Adarian began protesting as Sorcha sat another mug of watered-down ale in front of him.

Sorcha bent toward Aemyra, distracting her with those spectacular breasts. Before she could get the chance to take a closer look, the barkeep had a cheese knife underneath Aemyra's chin.

Sorcha tapped the splinters in the wood with a finger. "You damage my bar again and I don't care how good you are with your tongue. I'll throw you into the gutter with the rest of the rats."

Aemyra grinned savagely and pointed toward the three priests with her spoon.

"You mean those rats?" she asked, loudly enough for the whole tavern to hear.

A few muffled snickers met her ears, and she watched as the Chosen puffed up with indignation, their faces flushing.

Aemyra ignored them and leaned farther into the blunt point of the cheese knife with a grin. "So, you think I'm good with my tongue?"

Not bothering to blush, Sorcha leaned over the bar and pressed her lips to Aemyra's, making Adarian mutter a stream of curses and focus more intently on his dinner.

Unfortunately, Aemyra didn't get the chance to deepen the kiss as a male voice cut across the room.

"You have no respect for the ways of the Savior," a young priest exclaimed, his words clipped with outrage.

Aemyra broke away from Sorcha, relinquishing her full lips with reluctance.

The animated chatter that had filled the tavern a moment ago died to a nervous whisper as Aemyra picked up her glass.

"The Savior can cleanse your soul if you relinquish your heathen ways," the priest continued.

Aemyra froze with the drink she had been looking forward to all day against her bottom lip. Instantly furious as the priest's eyes darted between Sorcha and Aemyra.

The whispers turned into outraged muttering.

Trying to keep her temper, Aemyra laughed.

"You are aware of which city you are in? Perhaps you mistook the five temples for something else, but I would encourage you to give your preaching a rest—we have no need of the Savior here."

A few patrons banged their mugs on tables in support of Aemyra's words.

But the priest was evidently looking to prove himself in some way. His older companions were acting as if he were well within his rights to accost someone like this.

"You should focus on the duty you were born to as a wife and mother. A woman's true calling lies in her womb," he said, looking pointedly at Sorcha.

Aemyra heard several chairs scrape back as the tavern regulars stood, ready to defend Sorcha. His words stung, but the most terrifying thing was the way he said them—as though he believed them wholeheartedly. Not wanting this to descend into a brawl, Aemyra lifted one finger off her cup and the regulars halted.

Clearly this little priest had underestimated how strongly most in Tìr Teine still clung to the matriarchy. Even after a century waiting for a true queen to rule them.

Meeting the eyes of the young priest over the rim of her cup, Aemyra took a long, slow sip of òmar. She watched his eyes widen at her audacity as the liquid burned pleasantly. The fact that this boy thought she owed him even an ounce of respect was laughable.

No wonder so many like him, mostly men with no magic of their own, had eagerly converted to the True Religion. It was the only way they could exact control over others, and it was no secret they despised powerful women.

"Why should my womb be any concern of yours when that pendant around your neck has clearly replaced your cock?" Aemyra asked calmly.

A flush crept up the priest's neck as she pushed Sorcha back behind the safety of the bar and unsheathed her dagger. The Chosen were famously celibate, and they even encouraged people to wait until marriage to explore their own bodies. No doubt this boy had never even touched a woman.

After the way he had spoken to her, Aemyra sincerely hoped he never would.

"I would think *very* carefully about your next words," Aemyra said in a measured tone, eyeing the priest over her extended arm, which now ended in steel. "Insult me all you want, but insult the working women of this city—the ones made in the image of our Goddess—and I will gut you where you stand."

The young priest's mouth was flapping open and closed like he was a fish caught out of Loch Lorna. His gaze flickered to where Adarian was sitting.

"Don't look at him," she said, without turning around. "He isn't the one you should be worried about. Apologize to Sorcha. Now," Aemyra ordered, close enough to be pressing the point of the dagger against the priest's sternum. She felt the fabric give and knew that she had pricked his skin, but he didn't back away.

She cocked her head, letting him know that he would have one chance to apologize for his words.

But it wasn't the young acolyte who finally answered. It was the graying priest behind him who stood on his chair and addressed the room while waving one of his pamphlets.

"Embrace the ways of the Savior and set your souls free from the demonic magic possessing you. Look at how the evil flame has corrupted this young woman. Those without magic are already close to salvation. Cleanse yourselves and come into the light," he said emphatically, his rotund chest thrust forward.

Clearly the priest had been expecting a cheer, or at the very least lackluster applause, because he looked marginally disappointed when his words failed to rouse the patrons of the tavern.

Giving the three priests a smile, Aemyra allowed just enough of her magic to race out of her until the flames of every candle, torch, and brazier flared brighter.

"We *are* the light," she said, her voice carrying throughout the room.

It had been the encouragement everyone else had been waiting for. The fishermen suddenly held glinting orbs of water in their palms and the women threw down their cards with a whistle of conjured wind. Chairs scraped against the stone floor as everyone scrambled toward the priests.

Aemyra got there first.

She relished the way the young priest's eyes widened in fear as he attempted to flee, even more so when he tripped on his own robes and went sprawling to the floor.

Feeling the third priest attempt to restrain her, Aemyra thrust her head back and heard the satisfying crunch of his nose breaking. Thanking Brigid for her tightly tied headscarf, she swept the man's legs out from under him and bared her teeth.

If they saw her as a demon, then she would gladly become one.

Adarian drained the last of his ale and slammed his mug on the countertop in front of Sorcha. "She'll pay for mine," he said, jerking his thumb in Aemyra's direction before rolling up his sleeves and joining the fray.

As the young priest finally found his courage and swung for Aemyra, she gave a feral grin before she began to solve Sorcha's rodent problem for her.

CHAPTER FOUR

HISSING THROUGH HER TEETH AS HER SPLIT KNUCKLES STUNG, Aemyra followed her brother through the dilapidated streets. When the first chair had been broken and its leg wielded as a club, Sorcha had thrown them all out into the damp night with more force than was strictly necessary. Granted, Aemyra was responsible for most of the blood currently covering Sorcha's usually spotless floor.

Too wired to head home, the twins made their way into the heart of the city.

Men and women skilled in the art of pleasure beckoned from doorways into dimly lit rooms that lurked beyond. The satisfied moans coming from the open windows above were enough to have Aemyra gritting her teeth with frustration that Sorcha had kicked her out.

Rounding the corner and almost colliding with a man selling spiced apples from a steaming cart, Aemyra allowed the fragrant scent to fill her nostrils as they approached the center of the square. At least a hundred people had gathered as the playing company performed. Their crude stage had been erected with dirty strips of once vibrant fabric framing the wooden boards.

"Come, let's watch for a bit," Adarian said, pushing down the hood of his cloak now that the rain had stopped.

Aemyra groaned. "I don't really fancy being told how wonderful the royals are tonight."

But knowing Adarian enjoyed the theatrics, she followed her brother to a vacant spot against the wall. The wizened woman in the middle of the stage croaked through a story Aemyra had heard often enough that she could recite it from memory.

"Two hundred years ago Tìr Sgàile fell to the curse!" the woman shouted, the whites of her eyes shining. "The territory fell into ruin and the Spirit Dùileach of Clan Beaton, blessed by the Great Mother with the gift of foresight and healing magics, were lost."

The rest of the crowd was enraptured as the dancers threw out long strands of black silk before falling dramatically to the ground.

"I hope they have padding on their knees," Adarian whispered, making Aemyra snort as they leaned against the wall, half-concealed in shadows.

"The four remaining territories battled for dominance of the fallen land in the heart of Erisocia. For fifty years a brutal war raged until it almost cost us our Bonded beathaichean. A thunder of dragons a hundred strong flew to war—only three returned," the woman continued.

A stunning actress wearing a crown of paper flames and a poorly dyed red wig appeared from within the shadow silk. "Mighty Queen Lissandrea and her formidable beast, Kolgiath, proposed a peace treaty, signed in magic and blood, confining beathaichean to the borders of their respective territories. Ensuring their lives would never again be the cost of our greed."

A cheer rose from the crowd as the actress pretended to sign an extravagantly long piece of parchment that drooped off the stage.

The old crone grinned, showing yellowed teeth, as she leaned toward the enthralled audience.

"Tìr Uisge battled fiercely with their kelpies, as did those from Tìr Adhair, who took to the skies with their griffins and pegasi!"

Two young women danced across the stage and the one wearing blue robes threw a bucket of water over the front row. Uproarious laughter met this little stunt, and the narrator held her hands out for silence.

"I wonder if the Chosen have started preaching in Tìr Adhair too," Adarian mused.

"I doubt the griffin clans have paused their civil wars long enough to notice," Aemyra replied, attempting to clean the dried blood off her knuckles.

The crone waited as a dancer holding leafy branches pranced across the boards to represent Tìr Ùir.

"After the war, Queen Lissandrea heralded a new age for Tìr Teine, restoring our greatest power . . . the dragons!" the narrator said, striding for the front of the stage dramatically, sweeping her decrepit robes around her.

Gooseflesh prickled on Aemyra's arms. This was the one part of the performance she enjoyed.

A muscled actor was always painted gold to represent Lissandrea's ancient dragon, Kolgiath. The crimson Rhyian and the silver Sylthria were often depicted by stunning female dancers—it was how Aemyra had met Sorcha.

The former dancer had saved up every copar, sgillinn, and òr tossed her way until she had enough to buy her tavern and turn it into a thriving business. Stroking her bruised knuckles, Aemyra wished she had hit the priest harder for belittling Sorcha's hard work.

On the stage, the three dragon-dancers pranced to cheers and applause that seemed to shake the town square.

"The might of Clan Daercathian grew for a century after the war, and our territory flourished with prosperity. Until . . ."

Aemyra knew what was coming as silence descended upon the courtyard.

"Until Clan Daercathian stopped producing female heirs." The narrator clutched her throat as if distraught and two of the dancers acted out the birthing of many sons. Each puppet thrown above the crowd had an overly large appendage between its legs.

"For as long as no female was born to the clan, First King Vander ruled the crown would pass to his son, and his sons after him."

Aemyra stifled a yawn, knowing where this was going. After the way the priests had spoken, she didn't particularly want to listen to the playing company list the many attributes of male rulers. Echoing her sentiments, Adarian pushed himself off the wall and made ready to leave.

"Without the strength of our ancient queens, the dragons failed to thrive."

The twins whipped their heads up at the words.

Aemyra blinked in disbelief as one actress went from depicting childbirth to crawling across the stage toward three painted eggs. Before she could reach them, each one exploded in a small puff of smoke. Interest piqued, Aemyra had to give the playing company points for style.

Spines straightened in the crowd and a heavy silence stretched as tight as the black silks unfurled across the stage.

A sense of urgency had entered the crone's voice and Adarian stiffened.

"As the years passed without a female heir, the dragons weakened. The bronze Neamh perished before she had grown into her fire, the pale pink Rionnag was granted only ten years with Prince Cearon before she faltered underwing and they were both lost. Even the bright blue Seoghal, the most beautiful she-dragon who'd ever lived, barely survived her two years of maturing."

The old woman's voice cracked with grief and Aemyra followed Adarian's gaze to where two city guards were loitering on the corner. A third disappeared up the street.

"It's fine. She's just talking about the dragons," Aemyra whispered to her twin.

Adarian's answering look was one of warning. It was common knowledge that the dragons had begun to die when no female heir had been born to the Daercathian clan, but no one dared say it aloud.

"The ancient might of Tìr Teine remains," the narrator intoned, her arthritic fingers clasped in front of her as three actors in green, gold, and blue robes drifted across the stage.

Gealach, Kolreath, and Aervor. The last three dragons in Erisocia.

Then a fourth actor appeared. Dressed in onyx robes clearly meant to represent the legendary wild dragon—The Terror.

By all accounts, the ancient dragon had been formidable. Never having Bonded to a Dùileach, he had nested alone on the Sunset Isle and haunted Tìr Teine with his fire. Until Kolreath and the king had chased him from the mainland almost thirty years ago and black scales had never been seen again.

Pàdraig liked to say that The Terror had to have died before Aemyra was born because Penrythians could only endure so much. Hence his favorite nickname for her.

The painted actors were circling one another dramatically, and the crowd cheered as the actor portraying the king's dragon, Kolreath, spread his arms to riotous applause and The Terror faded into the shadows.

Aemyra caught the crone's quick glance toward the guards, and she strained her ears to hear what the next words would be. Adarian's hand came down on her arm as both a warning and security.

The crone took a deep breath and raised her voice from the middle of the stage.

"Our blessed matriarchy is crumbling. Chosen priests stood before us today, preaching lies and sowing discontent. On their journey into our city, they desecrated Goddess groves and I bring news that three Savior's towers have now been erected to the east of the Deàrr Mountains."

Frantic muttering broke out through the crowd and Adarian's grip on her arm tightened as the guards advanced.

"People of Àird Lasair, we must remain true to our Goddesses!" The crone's words were rapid as the dancers flanked her. "In two hundred years of peace, we have known but one conflict—the failed coup of Prince Draevan Daercathian."

Adarian made to pull Aemyra from the square, but she stood firm as the dancers smeared their hands with red paint. The crowd was enthralled, refusing to move as more guards materialized.

"The exiled prince Bonded to the dragon Gealach fought valiantly for the Goddesses. A crusade to rid Tìr Teine from the influence of a queen consort who worshipped the Savior."

The city guards were now pushing people out of the way to get to the stage. Singular cries rose up as those gathered in the square were shoved to one side or struck for refusing to make a path. Shouting had broken out in earnest. What the crone was talking about was treason.

Mentioning the might of ancient queens was bad enough given that the king had four sons, but to talk about Draevan Daercathian in a positive light was signing her own death warrant.

The crone's voice remained steady as the noise within the square grew. The guards were halfway to the stage and the sound of more footsteps was echoing from the northern streets.

They were visibly trembling, but the dancers stood courageously before the crowd as they smeared red paint across the puppets representing each royal prince.

Aemyra wasn't the only one whose mouth was agape.

"We need to get home," Adarian whispered, tugging her sleeve. "The city guards will burn them for this."

Ignoring him, Aemyra remained rooted to the spot as the dancers let blue ribbons fall from their hands like rivers of tears. Crackling fire erupted from behind the stage and the crone raised her hands above her head.

"Do not forsake the Goddesses! One day a true queen will rise and usher in a new age of prosperity for us and for the dragons."

Her voice rang out over the shouts and cries of the crowd as Sir Nairn arrived and began plowing through children and adults alike to get to the stage. The dancers finally scattered as the captain of the guard climbed onto the boards with his sword drawn.

"Time to go," Adarian growled in her ear.

Wishing she could intervene, the last thing Aemyra saw before

Adarian hauled her away was the faded velvet drapes being torn down as Sir Nairn backhanded the crone.

The blood from the old woman's split lip was as bright as the captain's cloak.

"Don't run," Adarian hissed as they turned a corner. "It will only make you look like you were involved."

Keeping her thoughts to herself, Aemyra hastened after her brother. They were more deeply involved in treason than anybody in this city knew about.

They walked quickly, being overtaken by others who had scarpered when the screams began to intensify. Daring a glance over her shoulder, Aemyra breathed a sigh of relief when she saw that the guards were not pursuing them.

The winding streets twisted, houses converging on one another lopsidedly in this part of town. Sneaking through the alley that was their familiar shortcut, the twins made it home without being spotted.

Adarian drew the heavy bolt across the door with finality and Aemyra tried to calm her racing heart.

"Something you both wish to share?"

Their mother's voice came from behind them and Aemyra swore her heart strained with fright.

Orlagh was standing in the middle of the room with a blazing look in her eyes and her slender arms crossed. "What have I told you both about getting into fights?"

Aemyra jerked her thumb over her shoulder to where distant cries seeped through the wooden door. "We had nothing to do with that."

Solas quirked his tiny head from his perch on Orlagh's shoulder, looking directly at Aemyra's split knuckles. She failed to hide them before her mother's eyes narrowed.

"Heather popped in for some more salve and regaled us—in great detail I might add—of how my children were brawling in the streets."

Adarian shifted uncomfortably under her gaze. "We weren't brawling in the streets."

"At least not until Sorcha kicked us out," Aemyra added helpfully.

When Orlagh's dark eyes narrowed, Adarian made a show of hanging his cloak properly on the peg by the door so it would dry.

Aemyra dumped hers in a heap on the kitchen bench. "The priests were in Sorcha's tavern. They insulted her, and every woman in this city. I couldn't let it stand."

Orlagh scoffed, "So you dragged your brother into it?"

The smoke-spice scent of the peat fire filled the room as Adarian slumped into the armchair with a groan. "She didn't have to. You should have heard the way they were talking. As though Aemyra and Sorcha were somehow beneath them because of their sex."

"Neither of you should be getting involved," Orlagh said firmly, using her magic to heat a bowl of water, a practiced eye on Aemyra's bruised knuckles. "The king should have driven those zealots out of the city the very day they entered."

Aemyra sat on the kitchen bench and studied Orlagh's face. The dark skin of her cheeks was illuminated by the firebird.

"Just be grateful Solas wasn't there," Aemyra said, looking at the beathach who was no bigger than a common starling. "Sorcha heard them preaching last week about how we steal their magic and bend the beathaichean to our will."

Orlagh looked up, genuine fear in her eyes at her daughter's words.

"That cannot be true," she whispered.

Solas's feathery head grazed Orlagh's lower jaw. The two of them had been Bonded since Orlagh's eighteenth breithday. The firebird had simply flown in through her window, set the curtains alight with his flaming tail, and never left.

"It's surprising how many lies people will believe if they are said with enough conviction," Pàdraig said, coming down the creaking stairs with a curious Lachlann clad in tartan nightclothes. Evidently the ruckus outside had woken him.

"But it's obviously not true," Orlagh said as Lachlann crawled sleepily into Aemyra's lap. "Anyone who knows any beathach will understand that we could never *force* a Bond they didn't also seek. It is a mutual partnership, a sharing of magic and souls—the Chosen taint it with their filthy words."

Solas clicked his beak as if in agreement and Aemyra stroked Lachlann's tight curls, one eye on the door.

Adarian looked up from the fire. "The True Religion is growing in popularity in other territories. If three towers have already been built here in Tìr Teine, how long will it be until more people convert?"

"The Chosen gained a strong foothold in Tìr Ùir after the Fifty Year War but I never thought we would allow them inside our territory. Much less replace temples with towers," Orlagh said.

Aemyra thought of the pendant that had been worn proudly on the captain's chest. If the royals were no longer loyal to the Goddesses, how long would it be before the common folk turned their backs as well? Especially after the violence they had just witnessed in the square.

Pàdraig cleared his throat. "There is no Dùileach alive who would willingly turn their backs on the Goddess who blessed them. The people of Tìr Teine still await a true queen, as do we."

Avoiding everyone's eye, Aemyra pulled the bowl of water toward her and dabbed at her knuckles.

A loud bang came from the street, followed by distant shouting.

"Perhaps this is a problem better discussed in the morning?" Pàdraig said, glancing at Lachlann.

Orlagh's keen eyes assessed the twins. "What happened after the tavern brawl?"

Aemyra hesitated. Lachlann was entirely too quiet for his own good as he pretended to be asleep on her knee.

"The playing company grew too bold," Adarian said.

Aemrya whipped her head up. "Is it too bold to speak of faithfulness? Of worshipping the Goddesses?"

Her twin's sapphire eyes were knowing. "It is when Draevan Daercathian and the true queen are mentioned in the same breath."

Orlagh and Pàdraig exchanged knowing looks, their silence weighted. Suddenly wide-awake, Lachlann asked, "Did they tell dragon stories too?"

Aemyra nodded.

"I wish I could have an egg ceremony," Lachlann said, sitting up.

Both Adarian and Aemyra smiled sadly as Orlagh stood from her chair and made to chivy her son back up to bed.

"Don't we all, wee man," Adarian said.

Lachlann looked up hopefully. "Maybe another dragon will lay some eggs and then when I'm sixteen and it's time for my ceremony I'll walk up to one of the pedestals, lay my hands on the biggest egg there, and I'll have a dragon of my own to name and ride."

Aemyra opened her mouth to explain that, since the only dragons still alive were male, more eggs hatching would be an impossibility. But as her little brother gave a jaw-cracking yawn, she decided to let him live in hope a little longer.

A clattering noise came from outside that made Orlagh flinch. Pàdraig checked that the door was bolted.

"What happens if the True Religion does take over here?" Lachlann asked, a hint of fear in his voice. "Will they stop me from Bonding?"

"Of course not, *mo luaidh*. If you wish to Bond and a beathach accepts it, then you will," Orlagh said.

The little boy reached out to stroke Solas's brown feathers. "And I'll get more fire too!" Lachlann said, letting a small flame gather on his palm.

Orlagh reached across and curled her son's fingers closed, extinguishing the fire.

"Yes. But that should never be the reason why you choose to Bond. Partnering with a beathach is as much a gift from the Goddess as your magic. It is a thing to be cherished, nurtured, not to be drained for its power."

Lachlann looked crestfallen, as if he had failed some sort of test, and Aemyra relinquished him into Pàdraig's strong arms.

"Think carefully on it," Adarian called after their little brother as he was carried upstairs. "Once you Bond, you can't ever leave Tìr Teine."

From the way Orlagh brushed her cheek against Solas's soft head, the restriction of the two-hundred-year-old treaty was a small price to pay.

"Clean those knuckles properly," Orlagh said softly, before following her husband and son upstairs.

Once alone with her twin, Aemyra threw the cloth back into the bowl.

"The playing company will have been thrown into a cell," Adarian said tersely. "Or worse."

"Worshipping the Goddesses is no crime," Aemyra said stubbornly.

Adarian's sapphire eyes were hard. "Yet."

Remembering the way Sir Nairn's cloak had draped across a crimson-painted puppet, Aemyra's stomach turned.

"Don't say that," Aemyra whispered.

Her brother leaned forward, elbows on his knees. "I'm sure it started this way in Tìr Ùir too. Non-Dùileach already believe half of the things those priests preach. Even if they haven't converted yet, it's only a matter of time."

Aemyra dropped her voice to a hushed whisper as the shouting echoed from the street. "You know our orders. We have to wait."

"Until our territory is overrun? *Three* towers in Clan Leuthanach lands, Aemyra. Less than a hundred miles from this city," Adarian continued, struggling to keep his voice low.

Her brother didn't often voice his frustrations and it put Aemyra on edge. Scratching underneath her headscarf, Aemyra suppressed the urge to tear it from her head. "Tìr Teine has dragons, Adarian. It will not fall to zealots."

"Three dragons. Two of which are Bonded to members of the royal family, whom we can suspect have sympathies with the Chosen."

There was no ignoring the fearful cries through the thin walls.

"One dragon loyal to the Goddesses won't be enough to protect us if it comes to a fight," Adarian warned.

As if echoing his words, a pained scream tore up the street and Aemyra plunged the room into darkness, extinguishing the candles with her magic.

"Pàdraig was right, now is not the time to talk of such things."

CHAPTER FIVE

THE GODDESS GROVE BY THE WEST WALL LAY IN RUINS.

Unable to sleep after what had happened in the square, Aemyra had crept from the house before dawn to see for herself. This grove had been nothing more than a small fountain draped with ivy, but the crone had not been lying. The priests were doing more than just preaching and the city guards were doing nothing to stop them.

"Cailleach forgive us," she whispered, fingering the broken fragments of what had once been a statue of the Great Mother.

It was quiet at this hour in the lower town, with the market stalls covered and shutters closed. Looking at the trampled snowdrops at her feet, Aemyra cursed the Chosen priests to Hela's realm.

This senseless destruction confirmed that the priests weren't here to worship their Savior in peace. They wanted to eradicate Goddess worship entirely and, in his madness, the king was allowing it to happen.

"I am ready to fight for you," Aemyra growled, clenching her fingers around the broken piece of slate until it bit into her skin. "Remove the king and I will burn the stain of the Chosen from this territory for good."

Tipping her head to the dark sky, she loosed a long breath and prayed to all of the Goddesses that they would help her find the right path.

Consumed with her thoughts, Aemyra didn't notice someone sneaking up on her until a strong hand clamped over her mouth.

Fear, swiftly followed by rage, stabbed through Aemyra's gut as her assailant hauled her away from the wall and into a dark alley.

Her first thought was that one of the priests from the tavern had somehow found her, but none of them possessed this level of strength. Aemyra managed to unsheathe her dagger, only for the tall man restraining her to disarm her with ease.

The weapon clattered to the cobblestones, the sound loud in the quiet night, as the shadows swallowed them both.

She bit down on the large hand until she tasted blood. Her attacker cursed from the depths of his hood, but kept his other hand fixed around her waist, dragging her farther into the deserted alley. Aemyra knew better than to scream. The city guards would only come running and she wanted to gut this lowlife herself.

She aimed a punch, but the man intercepted it with terrifying ease. Long fingers wrapped around her wrist and twisted until she felt her bones grind.

Weaponless, Aemyra did the only thing she could.

She summoned her fire.

"Burn in Hela's realm, scum," she ground out, power surging to her palms.

Releasing more magic than was sensible, Aemyra was beyond caring about her secrets. There was a blinding surge of fire, followed by the acrid stench of smoke as the man threw her against the wall.

Her head rattled sickeningly and her magic guttered out, but at least he had released her.

Blinking to clear her vision, Aemyra had expected to find her attacker hightailing it out of the alley with his cloak alight.

Instead, the man pushed his hood down to reveal a cunning smile.

"I thought I had taught you better than that," he said.

Aemyra backed up against the crumbling wall in case her knees gave out as she recognized the forest green eyes illuminated by the fire now snaking across his palms.

Draevan Daercathian was in Àird Lasair.

Aemyra felt a tug in her chest as she drank in the face she hadn't seen in ten years, but resembled her own more closely than that of her twin.

"Didn't you miss your father?" Draevan asked.

Wits returning to her, Aemyra shoved Draevan up against the opposite wall. With an indulgent quirk of his lips, her father relented to her aggression and extinguished his fire, plunging them both back into darkness.

"Are you completely mad?" Aemyra hissed. "As far as I'm aware, you are still outlawed from this city."

The sliver of moonlight spilling over the high rooftops was just enough to make out her father's amused expression.

"Come now, Aemyra. There can be only one reason why I have made the journey," he said.

Aemyra narrowed her eyes, hardly daring to believe the moment they had waited a decade for was upon them.

Draevan pulled the hood of his cloak up, concealing the deep auburn hair and forest green eyes that would identify him as a Daercathian to even the drunkest swine in the lower town. "Come. I need to get off the streets and you are needed at the temple."

Bending to pick up her dagger, Aemyra glanced toward the ruined grove and suppressed a shiver of fear that the Goddesses actually might have been listening.

Following her father up the street, they kept to the shadow of the battlements. Brigid's temple loomed ahead of them, a large square building constructed with the same crimson bricks as the caisteal across the bridge. The high windows were illuminated by the eternal fire within, making it the very beacon of light within the city.

Each Goddess had a temple in Àird Lasair, but as the capital of fire territory, Brigid's was the most impressive.

Aemyra hurried to keep up with her father's long stride. Leaving the filth of the streets behind, they climbed the marble steps, which gleamed thanks to the ministrations of the priestesses.

Turning her face to the starless sky, she wondered where her father's dragon was.

"Is Gealach——"

"Not until we're inside," Draevan interrupted, glancing over his shoulder as if he could feel the caisteal watching them from across the bridge as they ascended toward the golden doors.

Her father, walking behind her, ushered her into the temple, its serene warmth a balm to her soul.

The large altar was laden with offerings, and thousands of candles lined the walls with blessed light. They were completely alone at this hour as the eternal fire blazed in splendor against the back wall.

Painfully aware of her father's presence behind her, Aemyra subconsciously rubbed her headscarf.

She was every inch her father's daughter. Where Adarian had inherited blue eyes from the mother they had never known, Aemyra possessed the unmistakable Daercathian traits.

"You have done well to remain hidden under King Haedren's nose for so many years," Draevan said once the golden doors were closed.

Aemyra turned to face him. "I didn't have much of a choice."

Her words were laced with resentment, but her father did not rise to the bait. Orlagh and Pàdraig had sworn themselves to Draevan's cause long before the twins had been born. When the Prince of Penryth had bid them sail for Àird Lasair and put his plan in motion, they hadn't questioned it.

Until it became apparent that they had left a prosperous life on the Sunset Isle to wait in this festering shit hole of a city for Goddess knew how long.

"You haven't written in more than six months," Aemyra finally said.

A faint smile passed over her father's face, as though the idea of frequent correspondence with his only daughter amused him. Aemyra might now be a woman grown, but standing in her father's presence she felt sixteen again.

His auburn hair had fallen out of its braid, leaving long strands cascading across the lapels of his pristine black tunic.

Her vision was swimming with fire and she blinked to clear it. "Can I take your return as a sign that my true family finally wishes to claim me?"

The bitterness in her tone was not difficult to miss and she was lucky her father, famed for his quick temper, did not rise to the bait.

"It is not a question of want, Aemyra. I have no desire to watch you burn over your birthright," Draevan replied, his forest green eyes sincere.

"There's still time," Aemyra replied callously.

The corners of Draevan's mouth lifted. "You should not taunt the Great Mother in the temple."

She rolled her eyes. "This isn't Cailleach's temple. In case all the fire didn't already give that away?"

His gaze roved across his daughter's features as if memorizing her adult face, or finding fault in what he saw.

"My spies tell me that the king does indeed hover on the edge of the Otherworld."

Aemyra's stomach swooped.

Draevan's eyes narrowed as he stared down at her. "Are you ready to assume your rightful title?"

"I have been ready since I set sail from Penryth at age sixteen, Father," she replied, lifting her chin. "How many journeyed with you?"

"My ship arrived yesterday, General Maeve's the day before. Fifty Dùileach accompanied us and are sheltering in the catacombs beneath our feet."

Aemyra's face fell. "So few? The royal guard alone numbers a hundred men, how can you possibly hope—"

"Do not question me," Draevan said, his tone harsh enough to remind Aemyra which parent she was speaking to. "Each of our Dùileach fighters is worth ten of King Haedren's men. Too many would have attracted suspicion. This is not my first coup, Aemyra."

Privately, she hoped this one would be more successful but wisely curbed her tongue.

Her father read her expression well enough. "This plan has been in place since your infancy, do not insult the sacrifices we have all made to get us to this point."

They both turned as the high priestess emerged from a side room and locked the golden doors. Her ruby headdress gleamed in the fire-light, her crimson robes sweeping the floor.

She exchanged a knowing look with Draevan, who nodded in recognition.

"Kenna acts as our liaison and her priestesses will also take the oath tonight," he said.

Anxiety flooded Aemyra's system, and she suddenly wished she was wearing something finer than her oldest pair of breeches.

Hiding her singed sleeve behind her back as Kenna approached, Aemyra tried to smile through her sudden nerves. Kenna made the sign of Brigid's cross in official welcome and turned toward the statue of the Goddess, the rubies in her headdress clinking musically. "The time to fight in Brigid's name has come."

In response to her words, the eternal fire banked a little higher.

Kenna turned her enigmatic eyes toward Aemyra. "The oathing is but the first step. Make no mistake, even with the priestesses and the Penryth Dùileach sworn to you, it will be a fight."

A muscle twitched in Draevan's jaw as if in agreement. "Queen Katherine might possess no magic of her own, but do not underestimate her, or the other royals. The power she wields is her words, and they are just as dangerous as our magic."

Kenna's blue eyes narrowed as she excused herself to prepare for the ritual. The high priestess was well acquainted with the royal family and, despite Queen Katherine's faith, was often invited to the caisteal to dine. Her support would be instrumental in winning Aemyra her rightful throne.

"I vow to all five Goddesses that I will protect the people of Tìr Teine," Aemyra said quietly as priestesses began to file into the room.

"I don't doubt it," Draevan replied, shirking his cloak. "My grand-father might have been exiled by King Realor after the Battle of the Five Brothers, but *you* are the true heir. The first female born to Clan Daercathian in more than a century. They might be able to outlaw me to Penryth, but they cannot banish a Goddess-blessed female with royal blood in her veins, no matter how diluted."

Her father's words were like steel, and she eyed the black hilt of the sword sheathed at his side—Dorchadas. The blade was as legend-ary as her father. The stories of the bloody battles he had fought on his crusade for the Goddesses were still told in taverns across the territory.

Aemyra looked down at her hands, feeling the well of power that lurked within her. Depth of power that had only ever belonged to the Daercathian royal line.

No one knew that it wasn't coal, or wood, or peat that fueled the forges of Àird Lasair.

It was Aemyra herself.

"A hundred years is a long time without a rightful heir, Aemyra. But people have long memories no matter what they have become ac-customed to. They will rally behind their true queen," he said, his voice steady. "Especially when they see how the Goddess has blessed her."

Aemyra felt her fire prickle at the edges of her skin as if it were pressing to be let out. As a Bonded Dùileach, her father possessed considerable magic, but Aemyra's un-Bonded power had rivaled his from childhood.

"Kolreath has been forced to commit atrocities in the king's name for too long. Upon his death I will Bond to him and give the people a queen they deserve," she said.

Draevan observed her for a moment, as if he were seeing some-thing beneath the surface that he hadn't yet glimpsed.

Aemyra lifted her chin. "You trained me well, Father. I have not forgotten my sixteen years of education at your hand."

The scars on her body from his thorough tutoring with a blade wouldn't allow her to.

It seemed a lifetime ago now. Using the secret passageways in Caisteal Penryth to scurry unseen between Orlagh's apothecary and Draevan's study, Aemyra had been expected to arrive before dawn to study languages, history, and politics with the door barred and books open. While the caisteal servants witnessed Orlagh's daughter pounding herbs into fine powder during the day, Draevan had been raising a little queen in the wee hours.

"I hope you continued training with the sword," Draevan replied, scrutinizing her figure. "I was decidedly unimpressed in that alleyway."

Shouldering the disappointment, Aemyra replied, "My brother has not bested me in a sparring match since we were eighteen, Father. There is plenty of space behind the forge for me to practice footwork and combinations."

"Good. I have no intention of losing you," he replied stiffly.

Aemyra tried not to wonder who he would mourn more if the worst came to pass—his daughter, or his heir.

The priestesses began to chant as they ushered Draevan's soldiers into the room and Aemyra's blood stirred. This time, she did not pull away when her father reached for her.

"When the Goddess whose very temple we stand in blessed you with such power, I resolved to make you ready to restore our clan to the matriarchy," he said, tracing her palm where Kenna's blade would soon slice her skin.

Aemyra worked to stop her disappointment from showing on her face. She knew that her father loved her, but he loved power more. And she was his key to it.

Without her, he was just a prince born into the wrong branch of the clan. Draevan may have cemented himself as one of the last dragon riders, but he could never truly change the fate of Tìr Teine.

Until he had fathered a daughter. A Goddess-blessed babe with forest green eyes and auburn hair reminiscent of the ancient Queen Lissandrea herself.

When the twins' mother, a commoner Draevan had loved beyond reason, had died in childbirth, he had done the only thing he could. Trusted the twins with two of his most loyal servants who possessed enough power to hide the truth for as long as was necessary. Had he found out, King Haedren would have killed her to protect the succession of his own male heirs.

"You won't disappoint me, magpie," Draevan said in a gentler tone, touching one of the gold pendants on her neck. "Your time will come."

Her father smirked at the sight of her wearing almost every single piece of jewelry that he had gifted her over the years. The only things she had inherited from her father that she didn't have to hide.

With a deep breath, Aemyra prepared to take this first step toward giving him what he so desired.

Draevan craved power, and a way to finally exceed the shame his ancestor had brought on their line.

Aemyra desired to restore Tìr Teine to its former glory. To be Queen Lissandrea born again.

All she needed was a gold dragon of her own and the title that was rightfully hers.

Kenna cleared her throat beside them and they both turned. A genuine smile spread across Aemyra's face when she recognized the young priestess who was holding the chalice.

"You grant me the highest honor, Your Grace," Eilidh said, her hands shaking slightly.

Eilidh had been six years old when Aemyra had rescued her from the back of a cart bound for the caisteal dungeons. Thankfully Sir Nairn had been so distracted with his purge of the city's criminals upon his promotion to captain that he hadn't noticed Aemyra spiriting the orphaned thief away to the temple.

Kenna had immediately given Eilidh shelter, and the opportunity to work as a scullery maid. A few years later, Eilidh pledged herself to Brigid.

Surprised by the girl's nerves, Aemyra smiled warmly, hoping she could offset Draevan's intimidating presence. A gold headband, which signified Eilidh's ascension from attendant to priestess, now decorated her brow.

Kenna turned her inscrutable eyes on Eilidh as the temple grew crowded with priestesses and soldiers facing the altar. "Shouldn't you be contemplating your oath in quiet reflection?"

Blushing, Eilidh stumbled slightly on her robes as she backed away from Aemyra and bowed her head.

Aemyra could hear muffled coughs and people shuffling their feet. Several soldiers stifled yawns and she suppressed the urge to laugh. She wasn't the only one who had gotten a poor night's sleep.

All eyes were on the queen standing before the altar in her wrinkled shirt as the high priestess reached up to pull the headscarf from Aemyra's head.

She tensed instinctively, but Kenna's fingers were gentle as she revealed the auburn curls Aemyra was always so careful to keep hidden.

"I, Kenna, high priestess of the fire Goddess Brigid, do claim you, Aemyra Daercathian, as the true queen of Tìr Teine from this moment until your final moment."

If possible, the eternal fire surged higher behind the statue of the Goddess, and Kenna raised the knife. The blade glinted in the light of the fire, even as dawn lightened the sky through the high windows.

Aemyra held her right hand out willingly and allowed Kenna to make a deep cut across her palm. Bright red blood, the exact color of the jewels decorating the high priestess's headdress, welled in her palm and Eilidh hurried forward with the golden chalice.

Meeting her father's eye, Aemyra swallowed nervously as Draevan Daercathian sank to his knees. With her back to the altar, the eternal fire was roaring in her ears and she felt sweat drip between her shoulder blades.

Draevan's expression was devout as he unbuckled Dorchadas from around his narrow hips and laid it at her feet.

"Daercathian blood runs in her veins and I claim her as the true queen," Draevan said, his voice echoing through the cavernous temple.

Then more voices were raised across the temple as soldiers and priestesses followed suit.

"I claim her as the true queen."

Draevan remained kneeling, making the sign of Brigid's cross carefully with his hands, his expression one of utter devotion. When the chalice was half-full of Aemyra's blood, she removed her hand with a nod from Kenna and let the last few drops spill onto the altar in offering. Praying that she could remember the right words, she raised her face to the eternal fire.

"I ask Brigid to lend me her strength to protect my people. I beseech Beira to bless me with wisdom to lead them. I implore Cliodna to give me grace as queen and beg Brenna to bring balance to my rule. May the Great Mother Cailleach bless my reign."

The fire scalded Aemyra's face but she did not turn until she heard every person behind her sink to their knees.

Heart straining against her rib cage in a way that made her lightheaded, Aemyra pressed her thumb into the wound on her palm. Without words, she anointed her father's brow with her blood as Eilidh passed him the chalice, granting Draevan the honor of being the first to oath himself to the new queen.

Lips and teeth stained red from her blood, he wrapped Aemyra's hand reverently with his handkerchief as he stood. The colors of Clan Daecathian, crimson and gold, were patterned upon it.

"My daughter, and my queen," he said quietly.

As the light of dawn began to filter through the temple, the priestesses and soldiers formed an orderly line behind Kenna to make their oaths before the city awoke.

Aemyra's thumb brushed the rubies of Kenna's headdress as she anointed her with blood, going through the motions of a ceremony she had only ever read about in books.

When the next person knelt before her, Draevan leaned forward to whisper into her ear.

"You were born for this."

With a smile, Aemyra looked upon the people gathered within the temple. When those who worshipped the Goddesses found out that the priestesses had accepted Aemyra as queen, there would be no undoing it.

"The moment you unleash me upon this kingdom, Tìr Teine will know what it means to belong to fire," she replied.

CHAPTER SIX

ORLAGH HAD BEEN CASTING SURREPTITIOUS GLANCES AT Aemyra's bandaged palm all day.

After what had happened before dawn, Aemyra was finding it more difficult than usual to play the part of a blacksmith's daughter.

Pàdraig had scolded her for cracking his best pot, and Adarian had been singed twice when the fire had surged suddenly behind him. Both had left the forge at the earliest opportunity to avoid further injury.

"Are you sure you don't wish to accompany me to the herb garden?" Orlagh asked, Solas curled in the crook of her neck.

Aemyra glanced out of the forge to where the rain was bouncing off the ground. "Will there even be any herbs left?"

Picking up her basket, Orlagh clicked her tongue. "You're worse than Lachlann for complaining."

"Then go fetch him to squat in the rain and pluck leaves off weeds," Aemyra said. "I need to practice."

Aemyra had been itching to hold her sword all day. Draevan's comments had been niggling at her since the night before.

"You must never forget where you come from, Aemyra. Pride and unchecked power will only lead to unhappiness. Let yourself rest," Orlagh said.

Aemyra unwrapped the bandage from her hand, revealing the sharp slice underneath. "The moment I make my bid for the throne, you will be in danger."

With a knowing look, Orlagh pulled up her hood to cover her dark curls. "We have been in danger from the moment you were handed to us in singed swaddling clothes. Try not to cut yourself into ribbons. I'd rather the herbs I gather today be used on the needy people of this city and not on my headstrong daughter."

Bending so her mother could give her a swift kiss on the forehead, Aemyra let out a tired breath as Orlagh set out from the forge with Solas glowing in the folds of her cloak.

Draevan had an army of Dùileach and a dragon to protect him, but Aemyra worried for her family. The True Religion would not take kindly to a woman on the throne. Closing the door, she hoped that a few hours of swordplay would help relieve some of her tension.

Slipping into the back room where the walls were lined with chisels, tongs, pliers, and strips of steel, she crossed to the wooden chest eagerly. Her sword was nestled inside, covered by tattered old cloaks.

Gripping the leather scabbard with one hand, Aemyra pulled the sword free as she got to her feet.

The steel sang as it met the air and she admired the shine of the metal, backlit as it was from the fire in the other room.

She had spent hours painstakingly carving ancient runes into the crossguard, not only to improve her grip, but to ensure that she would have a weapon truly worthy to serve the Goddesses. It was the sword's only embellishment. No fancy jewels, nor gold nor silver, had been melted down and added to the hilt.

The sword was exactly the right length for her height, and the balance was impeccable.

Taking a deep breath to center herself, she swung it once in her wrist to loosen her joints and felt her knees bend automatically. With a smile, Aemyra let her bones melt to the point where the sword became an extension of herself.

With each movement, she reminded herself of who she was, of who she would become for her people.

As her muscles began to burn with exertion, she relished the pain and allowed it to stoke her anger for the Chosen priests. When she wore the crown, they would no longer be allowed to spread vicious lies about Dùileach, or incite violence against women.

Swinging the sword aggressively, Aemyra knew that Crown Prince Evander would never sit the throne after his father. Prince Fiorean could take his jewel-encrusted sword and shove it up his—

"Hello?"

Freezing with her blade midair, Aemyra peered through the gap in the door. The forge was obviously unoccupied, the late hour usually enough to have patrons waiting until the following day to make inquiries.

Wiping the sweat from her brow, Aemyra winced as the salt stung her wound. Knowing that Pàdraig hated to turn away business, she pushed the door open.

A tall man lurked in the shadows, facing away from her, and she instinctively raised her sword.

"What do you want?" she asked.

When he stepped out of the rain, Aemyra recognized the disdainful expression instantly.

"Prince Fiorean," she said, more of an address than a question.

When his eyes rested on her sword, Aemyra lowered it. "Apologies. I don't usually make a habit of pulling a weapon on someone unless I plan on following through with the threat."

His emerald eyes tracked the point of the blade, narrowing when she refused to curtsy.

"I saw the fire and thought someone was working," he said, his deep voice quietly confident. "My horse threw a shoe on the journey home and is now quite lame."

"Then you should seek out a groom, not a blacksmith," Aemyra retorted, placing her sword on the table.

Instead of responding, Fiorean held her gaze and she hated the way her pulse sparked. There was three feet of space between them and yet his eyes held her captive.

Breaking first, Aemyra straightened her headscarf before crossing the floor. "We might have several shoes that are suitable," she muttered, catching the scent of floral soap and horsehair as she passed the prince.

Knowing she reeked of peat, sweat, and iron ore, Aemyra refused to be ashamed of her ragged appearance. It hadn't stopped a hundred people oathing themselves to her the night before.

Nevertheless, the luxury of Fiorean's garb irritated her as she lifted the lid on two barrels.

"How are you enjoying your new accessory?" Aemyra asked as she scrutinized several varying sizes of horseshoes.

Fiorean bristled. The obscenely large garnet was clearly visible, the scabbard crafted specially so that it could be seen. The gemstone gleamed in the firelight.

There was a part of Aemyra that could admit she was a little jealous.

"My breithday is not for a number of weeks but my mother was so pleased with your brother's work she bid me wear it immediately," he replied, parting his cloak to reveal the sword belted on his narrow hips. "It is an exemplary weapon."

His tone suggested that he expected Aemyra to take offense, but her voice was quiet when, lifting her eyes, she replied, "My brother is better than me in every way that matters."

Those shapely brows peaked, his angular jaw tensing with surprise.

"Except when it comes to weapons," Aemyra added with a sly smile.

Fiorean glanced toward where her own sword lay.

"If you wish for a demonstration of my skill, I will gladly give you one," Aemyra said, holding up three shoes for him to choose from.

He hesitated.

"Afraid to get your hands dirty?" she asked.

The prince went still as he observed her. Then, with one careful step, Fiorean reached forward. His motions were sure as he selected the shoe in her left hand, calluses from years of swordplay rasping against her own. Without her noticing, his fingers reached beyond the curved metal to brush against her wound.

A jolt of electricity speared through Aemyra's gut and she fumbled the horseshoe. Before it could land on either of their toes, Fiorean expertly plucked it from the air.

"I assure you, I have no qualms about roughing it," Fiorean said in his assured, soft-spoken voice. "You might not appreciate the finer details of my weapon, but I assure you the blade will cut just as deeply."

The thought of picking up her sword and issuing a challenge right here in the forge was deeply appealing, but Aemyra knew better. She was so close to claiming her true place, she couldn't jeopardize it now.

Fiorean opened his mouth to say something but was interrupted by a pair of broad shoulders muscling in through the door behind him.

For the briefest of moments, Aemyra thought it was Adarian, until the mud-flecked face turned in her direction. Her heart stumbled in her chest.

Two princes now stood in the forge.

"What's taking you so long, Brother?" Prince Evander grumbled. "I'm getting soaked out there."

The fire behind her grew unstable, and she hid her hands behind her back, concealing the slice on her palm. It could easily have been a simple temple offering, or an accident while mending armor, but Aemyra suddenly felt as though all her secrets were too close to the surface.

"Nothing, I have what I came for," Fiorean said hastily, turning his back on Aemyra.

Unfortunately, Evander had already spotted her.

"Ah, is this the blacksmith's ward who insulted you?" Evander asked, slapping Fiorean on the shoulder. "I see why she's gotten under your skin. She's a pretty one."

Fiorean didn't reply, his expression unreadable.

Aemyra didn't dare speak. Not even as Evander pushed past his younger brother with the confidence of a man who had never been denied anything.

"She looks harmless enough," Evander continued.

With those words, he dared to reach out and cup Aemyra's chin like he was appraising a horse at auction.

The unwanted touch was an annoyance, but the way his green eyes, several shades lighter than his brother's, were roving hungrily across her curves was nothing short of a violation.

Aemyra couldn't wait to topple him off the throne.

"Don't sully yourself with commoner filth," Fiorean said, angling his body between them.

Aemyra kept her eyes on the ground and tried to stop the prickling of fire in her veins. Since when had men begun to think that they could treat women this way without consequences?

The five Goddesses might be wrathful, and temperamental, but with knowledge and the strongest magic passed down through the maternal line, they ensured that those responsible for bringing life into the world maintained its proper balance.

Evander's hand began to drift down from her chin, but Aemyra dared not release her magic. Draevan would cleave her in two with Dorchadas if she ruined his plans now.

"Unhand her, Evander. That's enough." Fiorean's hand closed around his brother's wrist, pulling it from the edge of Aemyra's shirt. "I long for a bath and a decent cup of wine after our day. Come."

Evidently the thought of the luxuries that awaited them across the bridge was enough for Evander to remember himself. Straightening his cloak, the fur trim tickled the russet stubble on his chin as he stared down at her. Aemyra longed to singe every hair on his head.

One day, she just might get the chance.

"Indeed. My lady wife will be waiting for me," Evander said, stressing the word *lady* in a way that was obviously meant to belittle Aemyra.

"Poor woman," Aemyra muttered under her breath.

Fiorean stiffened, but Evander hadn't heard her, as he clapped his brother on the back once more and strode through the door into the rain.

"Have you no sense of self-preservation?" Fiorean asked when they were alone, his tone somewhere between admiration and derision.

Standing her ground, Aemyra replied, "You should show your subjects the same respect you demand from them."

Fiorean's curtain of auburn hair had parted, giving Aemyra a glimpse of a well-hidden scar that traversed the left side of his face. Wondering how a prince had come by such an injury, she couldn't help but stare.

It was too small to have been caused by Aervor's talons. The cobalt male hatched to Abhainn and Kolreath had Bonded to Fiorean as an adult dragon.

The prince caught her staring and, with practiced ease, angled his head so that his hair concealed the scar.

"I must apologize on Evander's behalf. He should never have touched you without your permission," he said.

"Don't patronize me," Aemyra replied, bristling at his measured tone.

Fiorean glared at her. "Remember to whom you are speaking. Respect goes both ways."

"The forge is closed for the night. I must ask you to leave," she said.

Those emerald eyes glittered dangerously and flames sparked at his fingertips. Evidently Prince Fiorean also had a temper.

Aemyra longed to shove them down his rutting throat and let him choke on the flames.

"I was under the impression this was your warden's forge. My mistake, my family will take our business elsewhere in the future," Fiorean said, his tone scathing.

Without another word, he dropped the horseshoe at her feet, narrowly missing her toes, and threw himself out into the street.

Clenching her fists so hard that she reopened the cut on her palm, Aemyra resisted the urge to fling the shoe at the back of Fiorean's head and damn the consequences. Slamming the door closed to drown out the sound of hooves clattering up the street, Aemyra groaned. Pàdraig would be furious about the loss of business, not that it would matter for long.

Turning, Aemyra grabbed her sword from the table and resumed her practice. Raising her arms, she brought the blade down in a rush of steel that seemed to cleave the very air in front of her and her blood thrummed in response. Tongues of fire snaked from her fingertips and merged with the weapon until it glowed.

She had forged this sword with sweat, blood, and magic. It would not fail her when the time came.

CHAPTER SEVEN

T HE WIND WAS HOWLING, STRAY EMBERS FLICKERING AT THE edges of her vision as the gilded scales slipped farther away.

Feeling as though she was falling, Aemyra scrabbled for purchase as the wind tore tears from her eyes. This was nothing at all like she had imagined and yet she clung desperately to her destiny. The crown was uncomfortable on her head. Heavy enough that her neck ached and her muscles strained to keep her on the back of the golden dragon she had waited her whole life for.

A push from the enormous wings and suddenly she was falling, pulled from the back of the mighty beast by the weight of the very crown she coveted . . .

"Fuck . . ." Aemyra cursed as she hit the wooden floorboards with a thump. Clawing her way back to consciousness, she sighed in relief that it had only been a dream.

A split second later, she registered the tapping at the window.

Blinking blearily, she stumbled to her feet and opened the latch to allow the silver swyft inside. The little bird deposited the scroll on the rumpled sheets and soared back into the night.

Instantly awake, Aemyra snatched the parchment up with shaking fingers as she recognized her father's seal.

There were only three words written on it.

To the temple.

The hazy remnants of her dream came back to her. Aemyra was no Seer, and the ancient ones had all perished when the curse claimed Tìr Sgàile, but perhaps it had been a sign from Brigid.

The king was dead. Finally.

There were voices coming from downstairs, hushed whispers between Orlagh and Pàdraig.

Aemyra grabbed her headscarf from the floor. Dressing quickly, she pulled on her favorite breeches that molded to her thighs like a second skin. A crisp white shirt and tight navy tunic were followed by her dagger and belt.

Then, as if she had known the day was going to be upon her, she reached for the sword she had brought home from the forge. Slinging it across her back, leaving the hilt within reach behind her head, she buckled it on.

With one last tug on her headscarf, she stepped out of her tiny attic bedroom without a backward glance.

Slipping downstairs into the room her twin shared with Lachlann, Aemyra suddenly felt overwhelmed with what would come with the dawn.

Lachlann was already awake, dark eyes wide as he clutched a pillow to his chest. Adarian was sprawled across his too-small bed, one arm flung over his eyes.

"Adarian. Wake up."

Not wasting time being gentle, Aemyra shook him violently.

"W-wha?" he slurred with a sleepy snort.

Aemyra smacked his stubbly cheek. "We need to get to the temple. It is time."

Her words were enough to have his sapphire eyes flying wide. Adarian suddenly sat up, almost smacking her in the head.

"Temple, right . . ." he muttered, rubbing sleep from his eyes as he took stock of Aemyra wearing every weapon she owned.

Both of them glanced toward Lachlann, who looked as if he might start crying.

Aemyra reached for him as she got to her feet. "Come."

The little boy stood automatically, slipping his hand into his big sister's. Squaring her shoulders, she walked into Orlagh and Pàdraig's room with Lachlann in tow. His parents' hushed whispers had obviously woken him.

"Who told you?" Aemyra asked when she entered.

Orlagh didn't look surprised by her daughter's nighttime attire.

"Marilde needed herbs. The kitchens were abuzz with rumors," Orlagh replied.

Pàdraig's face fell and Aemyra straightened her spine. "We all knew this day would come," she said.

Orlagh looked as if she had something stuck in her throat, but Solas tweeted indignantly, his feathers ruffling.

They all knew how dangerous Draevan's plan was, and Aemyra gently pushed Lachlann toward his parents.

"Have you so little faith in me?" she asked with more bravado than she currently felt.

A small sob escaped Pàdraig's throat, but Solas clicked his beak angrily. Looking at the flush that crept up Orlagh's neck, staining her skin several shades darker, Aemyra allowed herself to soften slightly.

"You gave us both a life, a good life, when you did not have to. The three of you will always be our family."

Aemyra met Orlagh's soft brown eyes, remembering how those hands had cleaned her scraped knees, how she had rocked Aemyra back to sleep after nightmares, then patiently taught her how to control her magic. Orlagh was the only mother she had ever known.

Willing herself not to cry, Aemyra reached around her neck and unfastened the clasp that kept the three necklaces joined. Gathering them into her palm, she offered them to Orlagh.

"No, I couldn't possibly——" she began to protest, but Aemyra grabbed her mother by the wrist and closed her fingers over the jewelry.

"They were a reminder of my heritage while I could not have any other." She looked nostalgically around the small bedroom with the tartan quilt cover and Pàdraig's slippers beside the bed. "You got me this far, now I have no more need of them."

Orlagh evidently understood what was in Aemyra's heart and accepted the necklaces, holding them tightly. Orlagh did not cry, but Pàdraig's cheeks were wet as Adarian stepped into the room. A quiver of arrows was strung across his back, a hammer hanging from his belt. His mouth was set in a grim line, but he was not balking from the task that was ahead of them.

Lachlann was looking between his siblings like he was suddenly seeing them differently. Before he could cry, Aemyra knelt, the floorboards creaking.

"You know we do not share blood," Aemyra said softly. "But you will *always* be my baby brother, don't let anyone tell you otherwise."

His bottom lip started wobbling as she pressed a kiss to his brow.

"Will we have to go to Penryth now?" Lachlann asked, looking between his siblings, his voice quivering.

Aemyra mustered a smile. "Only if we fail. A ship waits in the harbor should things not go according to plan."

"We will start packing now, *a chuisle*. Just in case," Orlagh said, looking as though she couldn't wait to see the back of this city and return to the island where she had been born.

"I have a hankering to see the salamander lagoon again," Aemyra said with a forced smile. "Perhaps I can journey there as queen and take you for a swim. The waters are as warm as a bath."

The idea seemed to cheer Lachlann and she couldn't resist squeezing her baby brother one last time.

Rising to her feet, Aemyra looked toward their parents, as if waiting for their blessing.

Pàdraig didn't move, one strong hand on Lachlann's shoulder, but Orlagh lifted her chin, Solas's tail feathers flaring brightly.

"Go," she finally said. "Fulfill the destiny Brigid has bestowed upon you both."

With an ache in her heart that she hadn't expected, Aemyra watched as Adarian hugged Pàdraig, and then Orlagh, before mussing Lachlann's tight curls fondly.

Aemyra couldn't let herself embrace them. This wasn't goodbye after all.

With nothing more than a curt nod, Aemyra turned away from the only family she had ever known—in the hopes that her people would accept her.

THE DAMP STREETS WERE QUIET AND THE MOON WAS FULL AS THE twins slipped through the lower town. Their footfalls barely made a sound, thin cloaks whispering on the wind.

Avoiding the busiest streets where the forge and the market sat, Aemyra led her brother through the twisting alleys that she could navigate blindfolded.

"They haven't rung the bells yet," Adarian whispered as they paused behind a broken-down cart, propped up and rotting against the wall.

Aemyra fixed him with a glare. "I trust Father's note. We must get to the temple before the city guards begin preparing the streets." She looked pointedly at the array of weaponry they were carrying. "Anyone spots us sneaking around with these, questions will be asked. The last thing we need is to be hauled into a cell now."

Giving her brother a small shove ahead of her, they continued through the bowels of the city.

Hearing laughter and moans fall upon them from the half-open windows as they loped between pleasure dens, the late hour kept them from being hailed for custom as they hurriedly traversed the city. With a population of some twenty thousand, and most streets converging on one another with no logical sense, the twins didn't attract too much attention.

Lost in her thoughts of what might happen when she made it to the temple, Aemyra jumped when the bells began to ring.

"Fuck," Adarian swore.

Shutters banged open and startled residents began to shout as the ominous bells pealed into the night. Deep, rhythmic clangs that could only mean one thing.

King Haedren was dead and now the whole city knew it.

Thumping her fist against the nearest wall, Aemyra cursed every Goddess who was listening and Adarian immediately intoned prayers for forgiveness on her behalf.

"We're going to be spotted," she seethed, as several whores hung out of the windows above them, breasts bared in the moonlight.

"It might work in our favor," Adarian said, clutching her shoulder. "If the streets grow crowded, we can slip past the guards unnoticed. The gates will only close until the king's body has made its journey to the temple."

Cursing the full moon for illuminating them so well, Aemyra slunk out of the shadows and across the wide street into the next alley as people began to awaken with the bells. The city guards wouldn't raise the gates for anyone, lest Haedren's soul escape before the proper rituals were given.

Skirting around the square, Aemyra pushed Adarian ahead of her as they came level with Sorcha's tavern. The streetlamps illuminated the barkeep, who stood on the front stoop, drawn out by the commotion.

Aemyra hesitated. They had been involved on and off for years. Sorcha deserved to find out the truth from her lips. The time for keeping secrets was over.

Adarian hovered in the next alley, one hand nervously fiddling with the bow strung across his shoulders, a hiss of air through his teeth a command for Aemyra to return to his side.

When she ignored him, Aemyra heard Adarian's curse.

Sorcha wiped her hands on the cloth tucked into the thick belt around her waist. Her frown deepened as she spotted Aemyra emerging from the darkness like a shadow of death.

"Sweet Mother have mercy . . ." Sorcha said, clutching her heart. "Goddess, you *scared* me, Aemyra."

The woman reached for her, taking one automatic step forward, and as much as it hurt Aemyra to do it, she held up one hand.

Sorcha stopped, blinking rapidly. Her raven locks spilled across her shoulders, olive skin stained pale in the moonlight.

"I'm sorry," Aemyra whispered.

She watched as Sorcha's brow furrowed, the clanging of the bells putting her on edge as much as Aemyra's attire.

The barkeep was eyeing the sword warily. "Come upstairs and we can talk."

"I can't."

Knowing she would never touch Sorcha again, Aemyra was suddenly overcome with an urge to know that she was provided for. Reaching up, she pulled the gold studs from her ears and pressed them into Sorcha's calloused hands.

Those dark eyes widened in disbelief, suddenly realizing that this was a goodbye.

"I can't accept these," Sorcha said, her voice steadier.

Aemyra held up her hands, unwilling to let Sorcha give them back. Her tavern did well and was undoubtedly the only one in the city that didn't have actual vermin occupying it, but those gold studs were worth more than Sorcha might make in a year.

"These will help you get out of the city if things go poorly," Aemyra found herself saying.

"Why would I need to leave Àird Lasair?" Sorcha asked, an edge of panic in her voice.

Aemyra felt for her dagger and pulled it from her belt fluidly.

Sorcha bunched her free hand in her woolen dress, no doubt for the knife she wore strapped to her thigh. Knowing that Sorcha would be too slow even if she tried to use it, Aemyra hooked one finger underneath her headscarf and pulled a coil of hair free. Wrapping it around her finger, she severed the lock with one deft stroke and sheathed her dagger in the same movement.

"There is a skiff floating in the harbor bound for Penryth. If things go badly for me, get on it," Aemyra said firmly.

Sorcha dropped the folds of her dress and held out her hand, looking for answers. The barkeep's eyes widened as she jerked her gaze up to Aemyra's face. Then followed the sound of the bells to the spires of the caisteal.

"I thought you wrapped your hair to protect it from the forge," Sorcha said, her jaw hardening as she unraveled the lies. Suddenly registering the green eyes and auburn hair had only ever belonged to the Daercathian royal bloodline. "That you bedded me only when it was black as pitch because you were insecure about being seen naked."

"I'm sorry" was all Aemyra said, backing away from Sorcha before she could make her feel any guiltier.

The sound of the bells covered her footsteps as she took off at a sprint to join her twin in the alley.

"What in Brigid's name was that?" he hissed furiously.

It took all of Aemyra's self-control not to punch his teeth down his throat.

"She deserved to hear it from me," she ground out as they hurried up the street.

Sorcha had been warned and would journey to Penryth at the first sign of trouble. Now Aemyra had to make sure that wouldn't be necessary.

Nearing the north gate that led into the Deàrr Mountains where the dragons nested, Aemyra looked between the caisteal that would soon belong to her and the temple where she had so often sought refuge over the years.

The twins stopped when they saw the woman garbed in borrowed priestess robes guarding the bottom of the temple steps.

"Maeve," Aemyra said curtly, nodding to Draevan's general.

The general sniffed and tore her gaze away from Aemyra, focusing once more on the sprawling streets that led to the temple. Clearly they hadn't been the only ones caught out by the bells.

Without Maeve inside the caisteal walls, they would have to rely on Draevan's spies and informants already within. Not an ideal start to their coup, but far from a disaster.

"He's waiting for you inside," Maeve said without looking at the twins.

They hurried up the steps, stopping only when they reached the golden doors. As Aemyra stepped inside, her reflection was staring back at her from the giant glass globes. Adarian's sapphire eyes darted around nervously as Aemyra tugged the cloth free of her head at last and let it fall to their feet.

She let her locks of deep auburn hair tumble from their wrappings until they spilled over her shoulders and down her back. A strong gust blew in from the west to whip several strands across her face just as the faintest light of dawn began cresting the horizon.

"We're done hiding," she said, feeling freer already.

The streaks of burnt orange and gold highlighted the sky and Aemyra smiled, lifting one hand to caress the stubble on Adarian's chin that he was always so careful to shave each morning. The light caught the red strands, gilding them gold.

The sun burst into the sky in one great flush, illuminating the Daercathian twins on the cusp of fate.

Kenna smiled in welcome, pausing in the act of turning the glass globes to bow to Aemyra.

"Welcome, my queen."

CHAPTER EIGHT

"OUR SOLDIERS SURROUND THE TEMPLE," DRAEVAN SAID from his position by the singular window.

Kenna had given over her own attic chambers to hide Aemyra until they could reveal her during the presentation of King Haedren's body. With perilously few options, the quarters were decidedly cramped.

"Hidden in plain sight, I hope? Ow." Aemyra sucked in a breath as she was fastened into her jeweled dress by a graying priestess.

Draevan didn't so much as look up from the swyft scroll he held, and Aemyra exchanged a nervous glance with Adarian.

Kenna had left with the sunrise to help the royal family deal with the demise of the king. The other priestesses had begun preparing the altar as though nothing was amiss. With the city guards ferrying the common folk through the streets as they jostled for the best position to watch the procession, Aemyra was safest in the lofty rooms at the top of the temple.

"The bells have quieted," Eilidh said, hands fluttering around the golden skirts.

Aemyra held her tongue as she was laced into the elaborate dress.

Eilidh, hardly able to contain her excitement, had been about as help-ful as a fiddler on a deer hunt.

Feeling as though she might vomit with nerves, Aemyra stepped into a pair of heeled shoes that she knew were going to make her feet swell.

The noise from inside the temple three floors below was growing and Draevan kept a watchful eye on the caisteal bridge through the small window. All morning people had been journeying to the temple either to lay their offerings or attempt to secure a place inside for the cleansing ceremony. Little did they know they were about to bear wit-ness to something far more momentous.

The sheer number of mourners had buoyed Draevan's mood. The more witnesses they had to Aemyra's claim, the harder it would be for Katherine and Evander to contest.

But not impossible.

Footsteps sounded on the rickety staircase that led to Kenna's rooms and Aemyra turned, causing the priestess who was coiling her hair to click her tongue with impatience.

"I summoned you an hour ago," Draevan said, leaving his post by the window as the three newcomers entered the room.

The addition of more bodies made the space even more claustro-phobic. It didn't help that Aemyra's skirts had the circumference of a small carriage.

"Allow me to present your queen's guard," Draevan said, his clipped tone betraying his impatience as they sank to their knees.

Aemyra swallowed, trying to place their faces. Knowing they must have been present at the oathing ceremony, she struggled to identify them.

"Iona hails from Tìr Uisge and has fought by Maeve's side since our first coup," Draevan said, gesturing to a woman with ice blond hair. One side of her skull was shorn to the scalp. "She will be your water guard."

Aemyra nodded her head, but before she could formally greet Iona, her father had moved on.

"Nell escaped Tìr Ùir thanks to their expert skill in tracking and hunting and will be your earth guard." Without pausing for breath, Draevan pointed to the brunette. "Clea will fulfill the role of air guard."

Aemyra offered a small smile to them all in turn. "And what of my fire guard?"

Draevan touched the hilt of Dorchadas as he turned. "My cousin by marriage, Laoise, has been granted the honor. Until she arrives, your brother will bear the responsibility."

Adarian puffed up his chest with self-importance. Her twin looked magnificent in a tunic of dark blue that brought out his eyes, the tight breeches and fluted boots accentuating his muscular legs.

"You have your orders," Draevan barked at the three soldiers. "Your elements and your swords are sworn in service to your queen, and you relinquish your right to Bond. Should anyone protest the true succession today, you know what to do."

Aemyra wet her dry lips as the priestess coiling her hair finished her work and ducked out of the room.

"No going back now," Adarian whispered, appraising her queenly appearance.

"Are you sure gold is the right choice?" she asked nervously, hands fluttering over her dress. "Shouldn't we have gone with red?"

Draevan turned from where he was conversing with Nell, eyes roving over his daughter's elaborate gown.

"Absolutely not," he said firmly. "Red is what every Ùir woman wore when they came in droves to secure a marriage to one of the princes." Draevan sent Nell off with a message and strode over to Aemyra. Even with the heeled shoes, she had to look up into her father's eyes. "You are not asking permission to enter the clan today. You *are* the clan."

Gold was making a statement. No Daercathian had worn it since the last female monarch, Queen Earie, had died in 1793.

Steeling herself, Aemyra loosed a shaky breath, willing her nerves to dissipate.

You are descended from ancient queens. Fire runs through your veins. Embrace it.

Sparks stuttered in her palm and Draevan eyed them skeptically. "The dowager queen and crown prince will contest your claim in front of the crowd."

"I know," Aemyra said, blowing out a terse breath.

"They will have no choice but to respect the law of matriarchal succession. It matters not how diluted your royal blood is. When people see the depth of your power, and that you have the priestesses' support, they won't question it."

"I know."

Draevan began pacing. "The True Religion will sow seeds of dissent the moment the ceremony is over, but the damage will have been done. You must only be ready to—"

"I *know,*" Aemyra replied through gritted teeth.

Their position was precarious enough. She didn't need her father reminding her of every way this could go wrong.

Aemyra rubbed her bare arms, scrubbed free of any lingering dirt or soot from her past life by an overzealous Eilidh.

Her hair had been washed until it shone like Brigid's fire itself. It felt strange to wear it flowing down her back instead of bound tightly and covered with the headscarf.

A pretty appearance wasn't going to make this situation any less dangerous.

The king was dead, but the queen, the crown prince, the captain of the guard, and even the priests were all obstacles that blocked the path to Aemyra's throne.

But looking into Eilidh's eager face, they seemed insignificant. The priestesses were on her side, as were the Goddesses, and the people would recognize that. She had freed Eilidh from shackles a decade past, now Aemyra would ensure her right to worship Brigid for the rest of her days.

"I promise to uphold the ways of the Goddess, and to always do what is best for our people," Aemyra said fervently.

Eilidh's smile stumbled as Draevan snorted, arms crossed over his midnight black tunic. "An easy promise to make, a harder one to keep."

Her father's words fueling her nerves once again, Aemyra tried to get comfortable in the dress.

She had thought about becoming queen more times than she could count, but only now was she beginning to feel the true weight of the crown she would carry.

A deafening roar split the sky and Aemyra resisted the urge to clap her hands over her ears as the window rattled and Eilidh disappeared down the stairs.

Her father, far more used to dragons than either of his children, smirked. "Kolreath has left his nest. The procession has begun crossing the bridge."

Aemyra's heart started to race and she lurched toward the window. Her palms were sweaty as she gripped the sill, peering through the grime to the street far below.

Haedren's body lay upon a large litter draped in crimson and gold, borne toward the temple on the shoulders of his sons. The sun was blinding as it reflected off the waters of Loch Lorna, flowing between the caisteal and the rest of the city. Four heads of auburn hair crossed the wide bridge and, at Kenna's side, Dowager Queen Katherine wore a dramatic black veil. Ignoring the procession, Aemyra craned her neck to catch a glimpse of Kolreath high above.

Draevan pushed her away from the window. "Later. Focus on the announcement and steady your magic."

Biting her tongue, Aemyra forced herself not to shed the dress, grab her sword, and run outside to Bond to the golden dragon she so desired.

"One thing at a time," Adarian whispered, stepping a little closer to her. His shiny boots were dark enough to absorb light—obsidian next to her radiance.

Several queens had ruled without being Bonded, but Aemyra desired a dragon far more than she wanted the crown. Had thought of nothing else since witnessing her father take flight with Gealach as a child.

Deep down, she knew they were right. The only other person likely to want to claim Kolreath was Evander, and he was currently carrying his father's body across the bridge with his three younger brothers. Bonding could wait a little longer.

Nell popped their head back around the door. "We must get into position."

The balls of her feet throbbing in the shoes, Aemyra followed her father down through the private quarters at the back of the temple.

As the royal family prepared to lay the body of the king on the altar, they had no idea someone was readying themselves to take the inheritance they thought was owed to them.

Her queen's guard wore serious expressions and held their hands extended before them, as though poised to summon their elements at the first sign of trouble.

Priestesses lined the narrow corridors, bowing reverently as Aemyra and Adarian let their father lead them toward their destiny.

She had to admit that they looked every inch the royalty they were. Her brother stood with an almost kingly air, his immaculate posture born from years of horsemanship and intricate metalwork. Her golden dress was nothing short of queenly.

Reaching the lower level, the heat from the eternal fire seared Aemyra's cheeks as she halted in the small antechamber usually used for preparations. The enormous fire would conceal her entrance but it was making her thighs sweat under the thick skirts.

The bodhran and pipes stirred her blood as they called the king's soul to the Otherworld to be judged by Hela. The music swelled around them, rousing and emotional enough that Aemyra felt her throat thickening at the thought of the king she had never met. Her father had always said that Haedren would have killed her on sight if he found out about her, but she had often wondered if Draevan had been exaggerating.

Regardless, with the True Religion tightening its noose around the royal family, and the dragons almost extinct, Tìr Teine had never needed a queen more. Aemyra just hoped she could be the queen they needed.

The music faded and an expectant silence filled the cavernous room on the other side of the eternal fire. With some not-so-gentle pushing from Draevan, Aemyra made her way out from the antechamber into position behind the flames.

Thanks to her magic, the roaring fire did not harm her.

Kenna was intoning the cleansing ceremony, anointing the king's body with oils and herbs as those gathered repeated the words and implored Hela to release Haedren's soul to Brigid. It was but the first in five days and nights of mourning rituals.

Rituals Aemyra was about to seriously disrupt.

With her heartbeat thundering in her ears, Aemyra felt her feet growing slick inside the heeled shoes and she hoped she wouldn't fall.

Great Mother, guide me. Brigid, give me strength. Beira, keep me steady.

With a nervous glance to her right, chest heaving, Aemyra locked eyes with her father. He could not see beyond the fire, but he was listening carefully for Kenna's invitation.

Chest tight, Aemyra struggled to draw breath and wasn't sure if it was due to her nerves or the stiff corset. The eternal fire filled her swimming vision and she almost missed Draevan's sharp nod.

Giving up on the attempt to draw air into her lungs, Aemyra held her breath as she summoned more magic than she had ever been allowed to in her life.

Calling it forth from that sacred space in her chest, it raced out from her willingly. With shocking compliance, the eternal fire ripped in two.

Screams tore from throats as Aemyra walked unharmed through the flames.

Tendrils of flame snaked out from the roaring fire to cling to Aemrya as though they were reluctant to relinquish her. They attached to the gold dress, lighting her up like a living flame.

So illuminated as she emerged on the other side of the altar, Aemyra's golden gown sparkled blindingly enough that those gathered had to shield their eyes.

She was suddenly glad for the tightly laced corset. It was keeping her heart inside of her body.

With the Daercathian clan crest embroidered into the stitching of the sleeves and scooped neckline, the full skirts made her feel more regal than she had in her life. Despite her lack of weapons, she had never looked so powerful.

The gasps finally reached her ears and Aemyra refused to lower her viridian eyes as she strode confidently around the altar toward Kenna, heels clicking on the marble floor as her father, brother, and queen's guard followed her through the flames.

Some might have thought it disrespectful to seize power at such a moment, but they needed to strike the royal family while they were vulnerable. The truth might be on their side, but they were still at a disadvantage.

The Dowager Queen Katherine was standing at the front of the gathered crowd, Sir Nairn by her side. Her heavy gown of black was complete with a mourning veil, and a Savior's pendant glinted on her chest. Her four sons were gathered around her, easily identifiable by their dark red hair. The three women standing in the next row must be their wives. Prince Fergys, Evander's eldest son and heir, was the only royal child present.

Behind them, necks were craning as people tried to get a better glimpse of the woman bearing a striking resemblance to the queens of old.

Katherine's furious eyes were darting between the twins and Draevan. Evander, who clearly didn't recognize Aemyra, was swaying where he stood.

Fiorean, however, seemed ready to put a sword through her gut.

The muttered expletives and startled whispers ceased when Aemyra reached the high priestess and sank into the lowest curtsy she could manage. Her years of etiquette training finally paying off, it was a far cry from the purposefully inelegant bows she had given the prince.

Kenna smiled and spread her arms wide.

"People of Àird Lasair, esteemed lairds and noble families, we have waited a hundred years for a queen. For a century, Clan Daercathian has been ruled by the eldest male descendant in accordance with the declaration by the first king, Vander, in 1790. He set forth a precedent that the crown would pass to his sons, and their sons after them, only so long as no female of royal blood was born.

"King Haedren is dead and the Penryth branch of the clan has brought forth a female heir at last," Kenna called out, her voice echoing off the walls. "As such, the line of succession must now change in accordance with the will of the Goddesses."

The tension was so thick that Aemyra could have cut it with Sir Nairn's broadsword, and the crowd seemed to be holding its collective breath. As one, the priestesses lining the walls sank gracefully to their knees in obeisance, clearly demonstrating where their loyalty lay.

Kenna welcomed Draevan toward the altar, the reflection of the eternal fire dancing in his eyes as the exiled prince finally stepped into his power.

"I present to you now our rightful queen and heir to the throne of Tìr Teine. My daughter, Aemyra Daercathian."

She had expected gasps or outraged yelling, and a childish part of her had always fantasized about cheers, but she hadn't anticipated a silence so loud it hurt.

There was no time to wonder what it meant, as Kenna gripped Aemyra's wrist and pulled a ceremonial knife from her crimson robes.

Aemyra flinched as the high priestess slashed the blade across Aemyra's palm, reopening her wound. Then she heard the Dowager Queen Katherine's shrill voice echo through the temple.

"This is treason!"

Not one person took up the cry as the high priestess held Aemyra's hand over the king's body to give the ceremonial offering of the heir.

Time seemed suspended as the first drops of blood hit the wrappings. When Brigid's eternal fire flared in a dangerous crescendo behind the altar, swollen with Aemyra's offering, several people gasped.

Draevan's smile was all teeth.

"Brigid has accepted her. All hail Aemyra Daercathian, Queen of Tìr Teine!"

Chapter Nine

C HAOS ENSUED.

Sir Nairn called for the city guards, who were instantly prevented from advancing by the priestesses. Small scuffles broke out, and weapons clattered to the ground. Guards closed ranks around little Prince Fergys and his mother, Charlotte.

People were shouting questions and arguing with one another until the noise in the temple grew to a furious crescendo. Aemyra spotted several fingers pointed angrily in her direction, but she refused to cower before them. The weight of her true surname had settled on her shoulders, and she shed her old life like a second skin.

"Silence!" Katherine finally shouted above the clamoring crowd.

By some miracle, the temple quieted as the dowager queen gathered the skirts of her heavy black dress and climbed the steps to the dais, the captain and her sons not far behind.

When the Dùileach of the queen's guard armed themselves with elemental magic, Katherine halted. Aemyra's hair stirred in the wind of Clea's making and the familiar brush of Adarian's fire steadied her.

From behind his mother, Fiorean shot a look of pure venom in their direction.

"You befoul the body of my late husband with your inferior blood and dare to speak such treason publicly?" Katherine hissed, looking between Aemyra and Draevan.

Draevan didn't move a muscle, hands resting on the hilt of his sword. Instead he stared down his long nose at the dowager queen and sneered. "The Goddess and the priestesses have claimed my daughter as queen. Your priests have little influence in this territory and there are too many witnesses for Aemyra to conveniently disappear now."

Necks were craning among the gathered crowd, the situation balanced on a knife's edge.

Katherine's lip curled behind the black veil and Aemyra's stomach turned. She had always thought that Draevan's comments about Katherine poisoning the king had been in jest. But as she watched the fury pour out of the small woman clothed in mourning black without a shadow of grief behind her eyes, Aemyra wondered if her father had been speaking plainly after all.

"You should have come directly to the king upon her birth," Katherine hissed. "This matter should have been handled privately."

Sir Nairn shouldered his way past the four princes to whisper in Katherine's ear again, his crimson cloak dragging on the ground, and the dowager queen stiffened.

No doubt she had just been informed of the fifty Dùileach soldiers surrounding the temple.

The dowager queen removed her glare from the twins and turned toward Draevan. "The Penryth Daercathians have ever had treasonous inclinations. I am certain we will discover a bylaw that prevents your secret bastard child from ruling. Until then, Evander remains heir to the throne."

"Did you not witness Brigid's acceptance? Or the depth to which the Goddess has blessed Aemyra? I can bring out the ancient texts if you feel the need to remind yourself of our laws, Katherine," Draevan said loudly enough for those gathered in the temple to hear.

The whispering grew agitated, and Aemyra watched Fiorean drop his hand to his sword.

"I respected my late husband's wishes by having his body laid to rest in this temple," Katherine said spitefully. "That does not mean I believe in your heathen rituals."

The dowager queen lifted the veil from her face as she turned with dramatic slowness and said in a gravelly voice, "Lairds of the court, people of Àird Lasair, this news has shocked us in our time of mourning and must be put before the Great Council. For now there will be a temporary truce between the two branches of our clan. After the burning, we will vote on the succession."

Aemyra narrowed her eyes at the vague words, the sweeping phrases. Nothing Katherine had said had claimed Aemyra as part of the clan, nor as the true queen. From the sounds of the jeering coming from the crowd, the people of Àird Lasair did not like the idea of a vote.

"Lissandrea born again."

"Traitorous plan."

"Finally a true heir."

"Suspicious timing."

The presence of the priestesses was enough to deter outright violence, and with Draevan's Dùileach guarding the temple, they were safe enough inside.

But there was still a fight to be had.

For a moment, Aemyra thought the crowd would resist. That she had just caused too much of a commotion for people to leave without further inquiry, but as the priestesses pressed them forward, they went willingly enough.

They had witnessed a young woman display more powerful magic than had been seen in generations. By nightfall there wouldn't be anyone in the city who didn't know a true queen had declared herself. By tomorrow, every farmstead and hamlet north of the Forc would be abuzz with rumors.

Sparing a glance for Evander, Aemyra quietly thought that there was no person less suited to rule. His black clothes were wrinkled and his short hair was hanging unkempt around his ears. He looked like he had been dragged from a pleasure den and he reeked of stale wine. Only a mother's blindness could convince Katherine that he would make a better ruler than Aemyra.

Nevertheless, with the way Fiorean was looking at her, Aemyra would rather have been standing in her breeches and holding her dagger than in the golden ball gown.

Little Prince Fergys was watching her with wide eyes, his fingers summoning the smallest tongue of flame to his palm as though trying to emulate her trick with the eternal fire. It was something Lachlann would have done.

"Your timing is highly suspicious," Katherine spat at Draevan. "Am I supposed to believe you returned to this city the very same week the king dies yet played no part in his demise?"

From the way Draevan tilted his head back to the lofty ceiling, he looked to be praying to Brigid for strength. "News travels through Caisteal Lasair as quickly as swyfts fly to Penryth. I could accuse you of foul play just as easily."

It could have been Aemyra's imagination, but it looked as though Katherine's already pale face whitened further at the accusation.

"Watch your tongue," Fiorean threatened, displacing Sir Nairn to stand beside his mother.

Draevan smirked. "Come now, Katherine. You don't give yourself nearly enough credit for how much of a cunt you can be."

Fiorean reached for his sword at the insult, but Katherine simply held up a warning hand toward her second son and turned her gaze to Aemyra, who willed herself not to break eye contact as those gray eyes roved across her hair, her face, her body. Evidently finding the obvious similarities between Aemyra's features and Draevan's.

Then Katherine turned her gaze on Adarian.

"This one's eyes are blue, not green," she declared in a haughty tone. "And his hair might be too short to tell, but the hue of his beard is significantly lighter than that of the girl. Her hair must be dyed."

Draevan rolled his eyes. "My son takes after his mother, that is true, but where my daughter is concerned the resemblance is undeniable."

As her father's hand wrapped around the hilt of Dorchadas, whether as a comfort to him or as a threat, Aemyra hastily jumped in to avoid bloodshed.

"I can name a dozen members of our clan who have blue eyes, Evander's own son being one of them," she said, pointing to Prince Fergys.

Clasping her hands, Katherine moved carefully to angle herself in front of her grandson.

"It matters not. Bastard-born as you are, and by a traitor no less, you have no right to rule. Your mother was not royal," she said viciously.

Kenna swiftly stepped between them before Aemyra could forget herself or Draevan could draw his sword.

"The Goddesses dictate that inheritance and magic can be passed down from *either* parent to a child of *either* sex. In the eyes of the Great Mother, the concept of bastardy does not exist."

Katherine opened her mouth to interrupt, but Kenna held up a hand. To Aemyra's great surprise, the dowager queen held her tongue.

"Things may work differently in Tìr Ùir, but here in Tìr Teine we still live by the ways of the Goddesses," Kenna continued.

"But——" Katherine started in an attempt to interrupt.

"Is it not true that the True Religion will recognize a legitimate heir born out of wedlock if the father claims the child as his own?" Kenna asked, fixing Katherine with a look that told everyone gathered that the dowager queen was about to lose.

Sir Nairn was standing stiffly in his armor, and Fiorean's piercing green eyes were thrown into the shadow of his frown as Draevan smirked.

"I have ever respected your faith, now you must respect the faith of the territory Aemyra is set to rule," Kenna finished, her voice firm but gentle.

Katherine's gray gaze turned to ice and Evander looked as if he needed a drink.

"You will never sit the throne," Katherine hissed. "If you so much as try——"

Before Draevan could unsheathe Dorchadas in retaliation, Aemyra surged forward with her skirts rustling on the floor.

"Threaten me again and you will see exactly how much I resemble my father."

The high priestess sighed.

"How dare you? You are but a commoner dressed up in finery. Sir Nairn, remove her of her falsehoods," Katherine screeched in disbelief.

Aemyra stood her ground, but Draevan's eyes were on the captain.

"Lay a finger on my daughter, and you will lose your arm," Draevan growled.

Her queen's guard had closed ranks and Aemyra didn't need to turn to know they had summoned their elements. She would love to see Iona drench Fiorean's perfect hair with a well-aimed jet of water.

"This isn't helping," Kenna said stoically, turning to look upon the king's body still present on the altar. Katherine followed her gaze, her gray eyes hardening at the small drops of blood staining the wrappings.

"At ease, Sir Nairn," she simpered. "These Penryth ruffians are not worth the time it would take to gut them."

Fiorean's hand was still on the hilt of his sword, the large garnet glinting in the light from the eternal fire, and Aemyra didn't dare take her eyes off him.

Draevan spoke in a voice so low that it might have tricked everyone else present into thinking he was in control of his temper.

"Go back to your caisteal and tell your beloved priests their days in Tìr Teine are numbered. We will respect the burning rites for King Haedren and abide by this truce you have declared, but come sunrise on the sixth day, my daughter will sit the throne."

Katherine began to back away, Savior's pendant clutched in her white-knuckled hand. "We shall see."

Outnumbered, the royal family did the only thing they could do—retreat.

With a final withering look in Draevan's direction, Katherine stormed off. Her guard dog, Sir Nairn, was dispatched to retrieve Prince Evander from where he had slumped down in a recess behind one of the pillars. The wives hurried after Katherine, dragging Prince Fergys behind them.

Aemyra shared an incredulous look with Adarian. Had their father's plan actually worked?

With a withering look in the captain's direction, Draevan jogged down the steps to put the next phase of his plan in motion. Aemyra knew she would soon have to follow.

Instead of retreating with his family, Fiorean fixed his emerald gaze on Aemyra and waited expectantly for the queen's guard to part for him.

"Let him through," Aemyra said, surprising herself at how regal her voice sounded.

Hands clasped behind his back, Fiorean stepped onto the dais. The light from the eternal fire at her back danced across his angular face, his anger so clearly simmering beneath the surface.

Fiorean stood as though carved from marble, staring at Aemyra.

No longer forced to keep her magic secret, and with the temple well secured, Aemyra was not afraid.

"You look uncannily like your father. How odd that I never noticed before," he said.

Aemyra lifted her chin.

"So, you claim me as your true queen? I can summon Kenna for a chalice if you wish to make your oath."

Fiorean gave her a darting smile that was gone almost as soon as it had appeared. "You may not be a blacksmith, but you are no kin to me."

"Careful with your challenges, Prince, I no longer have to pretend to be helpless."

As if testing her words, Fiorean reached across his father's body toward the eternal fire. The flames latched on to his arm hungrily, embers dancing between his fingers.

Bonded to his dragon Aervor, Fiorean was more powerful than her.

For now.

Almost without conscious thought, Aemyra's own fire escaped her palms and snaked up her forearms. Fiorean let go of the flames, not a trace of fear present on his face. Instead, he clasped his hands behind his back and leaned toward her.

"Do be careful on the way up, Princess, it is an awfully long way back down."

Drawing his eyes off of her, his curtain of hair flowing down the back of his fitted black tunic, he strode from the temple, leaving her feeling decidedly unsettled.

Aemyra stood there, wearing a dress fit for a queen . . . and wondering why she still didn't feel like one.

CHAPTER TEN

SEQUESTERED IN AN ANTECHAMBER FULL OF RITUALISTIC PARA-phernalia, Aemyra was fighting with the ball gown.

"I'm sorry, Your Majesty, there are just so many *buttons*," Eilidh said in a despairing voice.

Breathing shallowly, Aemyra tried not to lose her patience as she watched Adarian raise a celebratory cup of wine with their father.

"A little premature, don't you think?" Aemyra growled, jerking her arms out of the beaded sleeves and scratching her skin.

Draevan ignored her, striding over to where Maeve, now clad in full armor, lingered in the doorway. Noting Aemyra's anxious expression, Adarian crossed the floorboards.

"Father was instrumental in getting us this far, it will take time for him to relinquish control to you," Adarian said quietly.

"He is not the king," Aemyra said a touch petulantly as Eilidh pulled her off balance.

Cursing, she kicked off the damnable heeled shoes and sighed in relief as her feet returned to the flat position the Goddess intended them to be in.

"There will be time enough for you to show your strength," Adarian warned. "Let the people grow accustomed to the idea of a queen before you shove your sparkling personality down their throats."

Finally, the dress loosened and the skirts fell like a cloud around her calves. Stepping out of them, she accepted her breeches from Nell and allowed Eilidh to begin unlacing the corset.

"As long as strength is what they perceived from their first glimpse of me," Aemyra said, breathing easier as the corset was loosened. "I worry for our family. Lachlann especially."

Adarian looked over to where Draevan and Maeve were conversing in low voices. "We have five days to put the next stage of the plan in motion and your soldiers are well equipped to deal with the guards and priests."

"Yes, because the True Religion have been known to *love* women in positions of power. I'm sure they will offer me the keys to the caisteal themselves," Aemyra scoffed as she fastened her breeches.

Nell passed her a clean shirt, which she tossed on over her head, eager to get on her way.

"Gealach flies from Clan Leuthanach lands as we speak, and soon he won't be the only dragon on our side," Adarian said quietly.

Eilidh stilled in the act of attempting to wrestle the golden dress into her arms and Aemyra escorted her brother away from keen ears. It wasn't that she didn't trust the priestesses, but they couldn't risk anyone thwarting the most crucial stage of the plan.

Hiking to the nests in the Deàrr Mountains and Bonding to Kolreath was Aemyra's task alone.

Pulling on her boots, Aemyra scanned the room for her weapons and noticed Kenna's approach.

"Your Grace, I seek permission to enter the caisteal and speak with the dowager queen," Kenna said.

Frowning, Aemyra shook her head. "It is too dangerous now that you have declared for me. You would be walking into the chimeras' den with nothing to protect you."

Kenna smiled warmly, eyes crinkling at the corners. "You forget that my relationship with Katherine has been forged over years of differences. It will not be so easily broken."

Aemyra exchanged a disbelieving look with Adarian, but as she laced her boots with finality, the high priestess spoke again. "Just this morning I wrapped the late king's body and provided counsel to his wife and children. I believe I can help smooth your transition to power."

Unconvinced, Aemyra glanced toward her father, wondering if he would sanction such a negotiation. She was grateful that he had already been placing spies and courtesans within the caisteal for years. She wondered exactly how many servants and kitchen boys had been tasked with ferreting out information over the last decade, and if they would look out for Kenna inside the walls.

Accepting her belt from Eilidh, Aemyra buckled it around her hips and reminded herself who was queen.

"Perhaps under our current flag of truce," she replied. "But you must take two soldiers with you."

The relief in Kenna's smile was palpable, the silver streaks in her dark hair illuminated by the sunlight streaming in through the windows.

"Your Majesty," she said, making the sign of Brigid's cross.

Aemyra returned the gesture before reaching for her sword. It was well past noon, and the sun would set by the time she reached the dragon nests.

Maeve had departed and Draevan had his goblet poised at his lips. Aemyra straightened her spine under his scrutiny. She would not give her father reason to find fault in his new queen. The look in Draevan's eyes was enough to remind Aemyra that her throne was not yet won.

Her father might have allowed himself a cup of wine, but Aemyra did not miss the way his eyes darted across the room, or how he appeared to drift away into thought. She recognized the look of a man hatching plans and analyzing every scenario.

He strode toward the twins, his expression hard.

"The temple gate is open, follow the sheep path through the hills and into the forest until it thins at the base of the mountain," he said, bending his head to Aemyra.

With the weight of her sword between her shoulder blades, Aemyra felt her stomach churn with excitement.

"Do not get caught," Draevan whispered.

With a curt nod, Aemyra backed away from her father and brother. For the queen to venture out alone after making such a public declaration was testament to how precarious their current position truly was.

"General Maeve requests more reinforcements by the exits, should the city guards see fit to lay siege to the temple," Draevan announced into the room.

It was more than enough to elicit shocked gasps and cries of "Sacrilege" from the priestesses as they flocked out of the antechamber and into the temple proper. The distraction was enough for Aemyra to sneak out through the back door unnoticed.

The frigid wind hit her in the face and reminded her that, despite the clear skies, it was still very much winter. Trusting in the long walk and her own magic to warm her blood, Aemyra set off for the city wall, her breath clouding in front of her.

Boots striking the hard ground with purpose, she knew that if Kolreath and Gealach flew together for her then no one could oppose them.

Aervor was the youngest of the last dragons, and the smallest. No matter how powerful a Dùileach Fiorean was, he would be no match for Aemyra once she was Bonded.

The pathetic bleating of sheep met her ears as she approached the temple gate. It swung open without a creak, the hinges well oiled, as the priestesses often used this path to select sacrifices.

She soon left the city behind, the scent of damp grass and animal dung filling her nostrils. The fresh air burned her lungs and soon her nose was streaming with the cold, but she fixed her gaze on the snow-capped peaks ahead of her.

Praying that Kolreath preferred to nest low on the mountain, all Aemyra could do was put one foot in front of the other and hope no one was following her.

Feeling as though she had lived three days in one, she should have been exhausted. Having woken in her attic bedroom before dawn, then declared herself queen at midday, she now sought a dragon as the flush of sunset pierced the bare tree boughs above her head. Instead, she felt exhilarated, energized by the idea of flying on dragonback under the light of the moon.

The path grew overgrown and several times she had to double back on herself to make sure she was traveling in the right direction. Finally, the trees thinned and she glimpsed the rocky mountain path just ahead.

Lost in thought about what she was going to do when she finally came face-to-face with Kolreath, she didn't hear the voices until the last moment.

"I have warned you about this before."

Pressing herself behind the nearest tree, Aemyra strained her ears.

"This territory is threatened, Evander."

Recognizing Fiorean's voice, Aemyra wondered if she should make a mad dash for the mountain path or remain hidden.

Fiorean seemed to be struggling with his brother. "The devils are now inside the walls. Think of your wife, of your *children.*"

Aemyra's eyes were wide as the two brothers came into view between the trees and fear stabbed through her gut. Was Evander on his way to claim Kolreath?

"We know nothing of the girl, but her father is as ruthless as he is coldhearted. You can be assured they will not stop at ripping your inheritance out from under you," Fiorean hissed.

"Let them. I don't care," Evander slurred.

The crown prince was drunk. Considerably, from the sound of it.

There came the noise of a small scuffle, followed by a muffled thump.

"You *must* care," Fiorean said.

Another thud reached Aemyra's ears, and she briefly wondered if one of them had punched a tree.

"I have turned a blind eye to your whoring and drunkenness for too long. Father is dead, you are the king. Start acting like one."

Evander made an incomprehensible noise, followed by a whine.

"I cannot. Not as long as you live," Fiorean muttered, voice low.

Evidently growing up with his brother had taught Fiorean to interpret Evander's petulant cries.

"Charlotte and the children need a husband and a father," Fiorean continued. "Tìr Teine needs a strong king to assume the throne, and by my leave you *will* be that king. Now get up the path."

Aemyra's eyes flew wide as she understood that Fiorean was attempting to lead Evander to Kolreath.

She could no longer wait and hide. Easing herself out from behind the tree, Aemyra cursed the glow of the setting sun.

Her boots were soft and sure as she skirted the tree line, spine rounded as if she could make herself smaller. The mountain path was feet away, and if she could just make it behind the large boulder . . .

"What was that?" Evander slurred.

Fuck.

Skidding to a stop, Aemyra froze as though it would prevent the princes from spotting her. She was still six feet away from the boulder.

"You."

Fiorean's voice was colder than the air around them. Knowing when she was caught, Aemyra straightened and fixed them both with a look full of disdain.

It was Fiorean who spoke first. "Running away from your duties already?"

His emerald eyes were scathing as he scanned her worn breeches and stained shirt.

"Have my soldiers already succeeded in removing you from the caisteal? I should increase their wages for their efficiency," Aemyra said loftily. "If you are looking for new accommodations, there are several lovely homes overlooking Loch Lorna." She pretended to appraise the forest. "Unless you would prefer something more . . . rustic?"

Evander sniggered from where he leaned against the nearest oak, his tunic hanging sloppily from his shoulder.

"I suppose a blacksmith's daughter would know. Your lodgings in the lower town had to have been far more modest," Fiorean said, taking several steps forward. "Granted, my brother has not relinquished the royal chambers to his usurper quite yet, but the temple must already exceed your expectations."

Aemyra glared up at him. "I do not care for expensive furnishings or feasts. My primary focus is saving the territory I rule."

Something ignited in Fiorean's eyes, and Aemyra sensed his intention a split second before he hauled Evander to his feet. Knowing she had to reach the dragon first, Aemyra broke into a run.

Unburdened by a drunk sibling, Aemyra scampered up the mountain path like a deer pursued by a wulvern.

Sweat beaded on her forehead with the exertion and she pushed herself harder, almost rolling her ankle on the uneven ground. Fiorean was cursing behind her, whether aimed at her or his brother, she didn't dare glance around to find out.

When a fork appeared in the path, she made the mistake of hesitating.

The prince barreled into her from behind, throwing her against the rocks.

"You wouldn't know the first thing about ruling," Fiorean spat, catching her wrist as she tried to claw at his face, long fingers encircling her pale limb.

She managed to turn herself to face him. "I was sneaking into my father's study from the age of five. I know more than you think," Aemyra said, allowing her fire to blossom underneath her skin.

Fiorean used his own magic to protect himself. His shields were strong, but the heat must have been blistering.

Even still, he didn't let go.

Evander slipped off the rock he seemed to be holding on to for support.

"A stable boy would make a better king than your brother. I knew more about the duties of the monarch before my first flowering than his wine-addled mind could remember now," Aemyra said.

An outraged protest sounded from behind Fiorean as Evander pushed himself up.

"I'll give you s'mthing to fill that loud mouth 'f yours," he slurred.

The insult was too much for Aemyra, who thrust her free hand toward Evander. Fiorean dropped Aemyra's wrist and whirled. There was a flash of fire, a streak of auburn hair, and suddenly Aemyra found herself against the rock with Fiorean's hand around her throat.

"Touch my brother and you die right here, Princess," Fiorean said, tightening his grip.

"Can't remember my proper title?" Aemyra asked, tone venomous.

Fiorean glared at her. "Daughter of Draevan Daercathian, the Prince of Penryth. You do have a birthright to claim, but it is the title of princess *only*."

"Keep telling yourself that," Aemyra said, her words slightly strained from how tightly Fiorean was pressing against her windpipe. "Did I offend your pride by insulting you? Or was it my pointing out the lack of redeeming qualities in your brother?"

Fiorean growled deep in his throat and Aemyra felt the ridges of the rock pressing into her back.

"I will not let you endanger my family," Fiorean said, his face so close to hers that his auburn hair draped across her shoulder.

"If you cannot see that I am trying to protect my own, then you are a fool," Aemyra hissed. "Do you really want to kill me during a truce your own mother declared?"

Her words must have hit a nerve, for Fiorean finally released her. The smell of lilacs lifted from his hair as he stumbled away from her, eyes wide.

Aemyra's smug satisfaction was short-lived when low growling came from farther up the path.

Whirling around, she felt her jaw slacken as she witnessed Kolreath approaching the three of them with a wicked gleam in his amber eyes.

Her mouth dried and she couldn't help but stumble backward. Everything in her body was telling her to run as far away from this creature as she could get.

Even Fiorean had paled.

Evander was blinking slowly, evidently trying to figure out if the dragon was a drunken apparition or really stalking down the mountain toward them.

The rocks under Aemyra's feet shook as the golden beathach advanced, his claws cracking the stone beneath him. Kolreath's right wing was scraping against the mountainside, leaving bloody streaks across the rock. The dragon didn't seem to care that he had ripped his scales open to the bone.

Was he grieving the loss of his Dùileach?

The enormous jaws parted to reveal yellowing, cracked teeth and Aemyra summoned her shields. It wouldn't be enough to protect her from dragonfire, but it made her feel better when she launched herself toward the dragon.

"No!" Fiorean cried out from behind her.

Kolreath balked, twisting his golden neck skyward, eyes rolling in his head as Aemyra advanced. She didn't register the danger until she felt Fiorean's arms clamp around her waist and he threw them bodily to the ground.

Just as a stream of amber fire rent the air around them.

"Brenna's tits, that was close!" Evander shouted from behind a gently smoking boulder.

Kolreath was still growling, his body weaving back and forth on the path as his wings flared in agitation.

Aemyra shoved Fiorean off of her and got to her knees. He fixed her with a glare so full of loathing, it might well have incinerated her before Kolreath's fire got the chance.

"You will never Bond to a dragon. Kolreath belongs to Evander by birth," Fiorean said, grabbing her ankle and dragging her away from the dragon she was still desperately pursuing.

"Dragons belong to no one," Aemyra growled right back. "Beathaichean choose their Bond."

"Oof."

Evander had stumbled out from behind the rock and was determinedly walking up the path toward Kolreath.

"Don't you fucking dare!" Aemyra screamed at Evander, desperately kicking out at Fiorean with her free leg.

Stones dug into her skin, the bones of her ankle grinding under Fiorean's tight grip. A scream of frustration tore its way up Aemyra's throat as Evander staggered closer to his father's former beathach. The whites of Kolreath's eyes were showing, and the dragon began snorting noxious puffs of smoke from both nostrils.

Aemyra's foot finally made contact with Fiorean, her toes catching him in the solar plexus, and he released her. Scraping her palms as she lurched to her feet, Aemyra had barely gotten herself upright before Kolreath let out a mournful screech and launched himself away from the two desperate Dùileach at the base of the mountain.

"No!" Aemyra cried, ducking as the six spikes on Kolreath's tail lashed above her head as he disappeared into the sunset.

Evander sank to his knees with a drunken giggle, as though this had all been a diverting game.

"Looks like Kolreath doesn't choose you," Fiorean said, slightly winded as he got to his feet and straightened his dirty tunic. "And *you* are the fool. For thinking that a true queen will change anything in this territory."

Utterly enraged, Aemyra unsheathed her dagger and pointed it at Fiorean, ready for the fight.

Surprising her, Fiorean sneered down at the sharp blade like Aemyra was far beneath his notice. As Kolreath was swallowed by the golden sky, Fiorean hauled a stocky Evander to his feet and let the forest swallow them.

With an ache in her chest, Aemyra wondered why his words reeked of regret. As though he was afraid to even hope.

Kolreath had looked tormented.

For the well-being of the beathach she coveted, she should allow the dragon a few days to mourn. He had rejected Evander's advances as much as hers. But could she take the risk?

Aemyra sank down onto a boulder as dusk gathered and her skin prickled in the cold air.

She had thought that after the priestesses had oathed themselves to her, and she had proclaimed her birthright, things would get easier.

Perhaps Fiorean was right.

She was a fool.

CHAPTER ELEVEN

AEMYRA HAD SLEPT FITFULLY AFTER RETURNING TO THE TEMple bearing the news of her failed Bonding attempt.

Draevan's disappointed silence had been worse than the argument she had expected.

Hugging her knees to her chest as she sat on the top step outside the temple, Aemyra gazed across the bridge to the caisteal above the loch. Lone candles flickered in high windows and she wondered if Fiorean was behind one of them, plotting her demise.

Even the birds were silent at this hour, the bitter cold enough to have them burrowing deep into their nests. Scanning the skies, Aemyra prayed that Kolreath would return to his nest before the dawn and sighed when she saw no sign of the golden beast.

The lower town was dark as pitch and Aemyra squeezed her legs to her chest as her thoughts turned to her family. She had no choice but to try and Bond Kolreath again at the earliest opportunity.

A distant thud from the direction of the caisteal caught Aemyra's attention and she squinted through the gloom. The temple provided an excellent vantage point, but it wasn't until Kenna was halfway across the bridge that Aemyra recognized her.

Her sigh of relief was short-lived when she saw that Kenna was running, the light of the moon reflected on the calm surface of the loch far below the bridge.

The high priestess fled the caisteal as though Hela's hounds were behind her.

Aemyra was on her feet in an instant. The guard on duty was dozing, slumped in his chair, and she shoved him forcefully in the breast-plate.

His eyes flew open, armor clanking as he straightened, blinking.

"Get my father and awaken the guard," Aemyra said urgently.

As he clanked into the temple, Aemyra sent up a fleeting prayer to Brigid to protect them all. Summoning fire to her palm, she saw that Kenna was across the bridge now, and Aemyra hastened down the steps.

"Get inside!" Kenna's voice rang out across the wide street as she sprinted for the temple and Aemyra stumbled to a stop, blood chilling at the fear lacing the high priestess's words.

Fire flickering in her palm, Aemyra peered through the darkness for any sign of a threat as Kenna drew closer to the temple.

She was level with the steps now, climbing the first few, stumbling on her crimson robes.

"What's happened? What's wrong?" Aemyra asked desperately, retreating back to the doors.

Out of breath, Kenna was unable to answer as she raced up the steps toward Aemyra. Extinguishing her fire, Aemyra reached for the high priestess, ready to drag her into the safety of the temple.

Kenna extended her hand, fingertips straining.

Aemyra heard the deadly whistle of the arrow a split second before Kenna fell.

"No!" she gasped, flinging herself to where the high priestess was now lying sprawled, arm outstretched toward the safety of the doors.

Knees smarting with the impact as Aemyra landed beside Kenna, she saw the arrow protruding from between Kenna's shoulder blades and knew the high priestess was gone.

Before she could do anything else, Draevan sprinted out of the temple, Dorchadas already drawn.

"Get inside," he barked, his keen eyes noting the arrow, the priestess, and Aemyra's shaking hands in seconds.

Unable to register that Kenna was dead, that she had witnessed her murder, Aemyra failed to move.

"Inside. Now!" Draevan repeated, hauling Aemyra up by the scruff of her shirt and throwing her through the doors ahead of him.

Fighting to get control of her breathing as her father dragged Kenna's body into the temple, she heard the golden doors close with a resonating thud.

The noise rising from the catacombs beneath her feet told Aemyra that Draevan had woken her soldiers.

"I need to find Eilidh," Aemyra choked out through the thickness in her throat as she looked down at the body of the high priestess, who had been like a mother to Eilidh. "This news should come from me."

Maeve clanked into the temple, heading directly toward Draevan. "We await your command."

Aemyra didn't bother to take offense that she was being overlooked in favor of her father, as she spotted a scroll clutched in Kenna's hand.

Unfurling her fingers, Aemyra smoothed the parchment and her blood chilled as she read the words.

The Covenanters are here. I failed—K

"Father," she said, her voice cutting clean across whatever Maeve had been saying as she extended the scroll.

Draevan's expression hardened as his eyes scanned the words. Lips thinning, he looked down at Aemyra.

"Get your brother and make for the harbor."

She was already shaking her head. "No. We must stay and fight."

Maeve looked inclined to agree with Aemyra until Draevan took one threatening step forward. "The Covenanters are in Tìr Teine. If Katherine has been sequestering battalions of the army of the True Religion inside the caisteal, then we are done for." He exchanged a glance with Maeve.

Still in shock, Aemyra worked to get her wits about her. "They are still just men! We have magic . . . you have a *dragon*—"

Draevan grabbed a fistful of Aemyra's shirt and shoved her away from the door as several more arrows thumped into the wood.

"I will not condemn the innocent people of this city to dragonfire, nor will I endanger the priestesses more than we already have," he said, a silent command dismissing Maeve immediately. "We leave and regroup."

Aemyra unsheathed her own sword, runes scraping against the slice on her palm as a second volley of arrows rained down as a final warning.

"Kenna might have just saved our lives," Draevan said, eyeing the scroll clutched in Aemyra's hand.

Two hundred innocent priestesses lived in this temple, fifty Dùileach were at her disposal. If they could only hold the city long enough for her to Bond . . .

"Where is Gealach? If we wait fo—"

Draevan's grim expression told her that she still had much to learn as priestesses poured into the temple to bar the doors and windows. Despite their closeness to the Goddess, few of them were Dùileach. Only half of them were trained fighters.

"Evander and Katherine will not harm the priestesses when they are no longer sheltering us," he said firmly. "Get to the harbor. I will lead the Covenanters away from the temple."

Without waiting to see if his daughter would follow his orders, Draevan melted away and Aemyra was left with no other option.

Sprinting back through the living quarters, Aemyra found that her brother was already awake and dressed for battle.

"For the love of Cailleach, Aems, what's going on?" Adarian asked, blue eyes wide and crusted with sleep.

Sword hanging uselessly by her side, she willed herself not to break down. "Kenna is dead."

Aemyra's heart was pounding. She had known that claiming her throne would be dangerous, but she had expected to face her enemies head-on, not flee from them in the night.

Aemyra touched the bruised skin of her throat and knew the time for clemency was over. Fiorean had spared her in order to strike when the rest of the city was asleep. Hoping to slaughter them all in their beds.

"We must get out of the temple before we condemn the priestesses."

Fear laced through her chest as she thought about what was happening. Fifty Dùileach were enough to stand against the city guards, but not the Covenanters. They weren't even supposed to *be* in Tìr Teine.

Grabbing her brother's hand, she hauled him down the corridor as he was still stringing his bow.

"Father?" Adarian asked.

"Already ahead of us," Aemyra replied breathlessly.

If only she had Bonded Kolreath when she had the chance. If Fiorean and Evander hadn't gotten in her way . . .

They ran down the staircase that led to the back door, the steps steep enough for her ankles to bark in protest.

As they emerged into the lightening dark, Aemyra skidded to a stop. Men wearing black armor with towers emblazoned on shields were advancing on the gate.

Flattening herself to the wall, she felt her own fear echo through her twin.

The temple was surrounded by Covenanters.

Adarian pulled the hood of Aemyra's cloak up over her head, concealing her auburn hair.

She fought against him. "I will not flee before the dawn as though I am not the true heir to the throne."

Suddenly, Adarian's face was illuminated by a blast of magical fire. A cry went up from the Covenanters as they spotted Draevan and a group of Dùileach fleeing through the forest, away from the temple and the city.

They gave chase.

Adarian held her hood in place. "We have no choice, Aems. Father is no stranger to war. If he says we must retreat and regroup, then we need to trust him."

Not giving her time to argue, Adarian launched into a headlong sprint down the steep sides of the hill, toward the gate, pulling her along with him. Flashes of magic and the clash of steel came from farther down the hill, but their way was clear.

"I will not cower like a fox before the hunt," Aemyra said, drifting toward the sounds of battle.

Adarian's hands clasped her face, pure fear in his eyes. "We will all die if we do not retreat. If there was any other way, Father would be here with us. Your Dùileach are only making a stand to give us a chance."

Pulling away from her brother, Aemyra listened to the sounds of death coming from down the hill.

"I can't do this, Adarian," she whispered. "I won't run from this."

Her brother looked toward the lightening sky. "Father won't wait. The ship will leave without us."

She grabbed his arm. "I am the heir to the throne. He won't leave without me."

"The same cannot be said for his son," Adarian muttered.

Aemyra narrowed her eyes. "Our father does not view us as expendable, and you know it." As she spoke the words, she realized from his expression how badly Adarian wanted to believe her. "Father loves us. Albeit in his own way, but I will not fail the first task he has set out for me. I cannot."

Adarian rubbed his face, his rough fingers rasping against the stubble on his jaw. "All right. Where do you think Kolreath is?"

Aemyra lifted her eyes toward the jagged mountain peaks. The dragon must have returned to his nest by now.

"Are you sure you can do this?" he asked.

Aemyra set her jaw. "Have I ever given you reason to doubt my skills before?"

"No. Just your common sense."

"Well, I don't think anyone who Bonds themselves to a dragon has much of that anyway."

Not wasting any more time, Aemyra broke into a sprint, Adarian behind her. She could fix this. With Kolreath on her side, the Covenanters would be forced to lay down their weapons long enough for Gealach to arrive.

They raced through the gate, past startled sheep, and into the heart of the forest. Several times, Aemyra stumbled across tangled roots and Adarian's strong grip was the only thing that kept her from falling.

The muscles of her thighs were straining with the steep ascent, breath steaming in the cool morning air like the mist that shrouded the surface of the loch bordering the city.

"All that planning for it to end like this?" Aemyra gasped as they ran.

Adarian shot her a pained look. "You still declared yourself in front of the people."

"What good did it do?"

"They will not forget it."

Aemyra cursed. She should have let Draevan run Katherine through with Dorchadas when he had the chance.

"Some welcome to the clan," Adarian said, arms pumping.

Aemyra huffed a laugh. "We've always been part of the clan. Too bad we never seem to get to enjoy any of the perks."

The forest was muddy underfoot and she had to focus on not slipping as they ran. She was soon gasping for breath as she tried to keep up with her long-legged brother.

"Not that way!" Aemyra called out as the dirt track the royals used for hunting came into view. "Careful!" she gasped, grabbing Adarian by the back of his shirt and pushing him down into the thicker foliage.

Just as they made it out of sight of the path, an arrow whizzed past her ear.

Fuck.

"Go! Faster!" she said, urging Adarian into a full-on sprint through the trees, barely avoiding a branch to the face.

Another arrow was shot, narrowly missing her shoulder. Adarian skidded to a stop as one buried itself in the mud beside his left foot. They were being herded.

"Turn back," Adarian ground out as Aemyra barreled into the back of him, his solid weight almost knocking the breath out of her.

No fewer than a dozen guards were on horseback, their hooves churning up the ground and flinging great clods of earth out behind them.

Knowing they were outnumbered, Aemyra allowed her brother to push her back the way they had come. Bowstrings twanged, and Aemyra's heart squeezed painfully every time she heard an arrow thud into a tree.

"There's too many to fight," Adarian panted, his eyes wide with fear even as he pulled his hammer from his belt mid-stride.

Aemyra reached out to grab her brother's arm. "Not like that anyway."

Understanding flashed in Adarian's eyes and he dropped out of his run.

Turning to face the galloping horses, the twins held out their hands as the leader of the group eagerly drew his sword.

Summoning her magic, Aemyra felt the familiar surge of power through her veins, sparks crackling in her blood. The act of using her magic was so exhilarating that she was forever fighting against letting it burst forth from her.

Now she could.

Without words, Adarian loosed a roar that twinned with her own as they cast out a storm of wildfire toward the Covenanters. The rush of flames was deafening, trees creaking with heat as the sap emitted loud pops.

She saw fear ignite in their eyes a split second before her fire consumed them.

When Adarian's magic drained, Aemyra kept her hands raised until the screams of dying men and horses ceased.

Letting go before she drained too much of her energy, Aemyra pushed her swaying brother downhill.

"There will be more Covenanters. Dragon later, boat now," she said firmly.

Her lungs were burning from the smoke, and they had just lit a beacon in the forest that would guide everyone to their position. As she ran down the slope toward the other side of the city, Aemyra sent up a desperate plea to Beira to keep their feet swift.

As the lochside harbor came into view, thundering hoofbeats closed in on them.

There was only one Dùileach powerful enough to have summoned a shield to avoid being burned by the twins' combined magic.

As they tore through the harbor, she looked over her shoulder and saw Fiorean astride a midnight black stallion, bowstring taut.

"To the left!" Aemyra shouted to Adarian just as the arrow flew past him. With the docks in sight, her brother began to slow.

"Don't you dare!" she yelled. "Get on that ship!"

After such extensive use of their magic, Adarian was nearly drained.

Draevan's face appeared over the side of the ship in response to her cry. His calculating eyes narrowed as he saw his children fleeing from Prince Fiorean.

The telltale whoosh of an arrow met Aemyra's ears and she swerved to the right not a moment too soon. A flash of pain in her upper arm told her that Fiorean's arrow had grazed her.

"Faster!" Draevan called, leaning over the rail to urge his children on.

The sound of hooves clattering on the cobblestones grew louder and Aemyra briefly wondered why the fuck Fiorean wasn't on his dragon.

Adarian was hurrying up the wooden dock toward Draevan's cries, his arms and legs pumping.

Knowing they couldn't both outrun Fiorean, she skidded to a stop.

Turning her back on the docks, Aemyra unsheathed her sword. After all of these years, she was finally going to get to use it.

Instead of peppering her with arrows, Fiorean reined his horse in and flung his bow and quiver of arrows to the ground with a clatter.

"You clearly don't understand how this works. When someone gives chase, you are supposed to run," Fiorean said.

Aemyra thumbed the grooves in the hilt of her sword and rolled her shoulders.

"I've never been known to run from a fight," she replied, flexing her wrist and swinging her sword. She didn't dare summon her fire. Her only chance of winning against a Bonded Dùileach was fighting without magic, and she kept one eye on the sky in case his dragon decided to make a late entrance.

Steeling herself as Fiorean slipped from the back of his horse and brandished his own sword, she planted her feet.

"Let's see how good you are without that fire of yours, shall we?" she taunted.

Glaring at her, Fiorean launched his attack, but she was ready for him. The first impact was always the worst, and it went through her right arm with a jolt that clacked her teeth together. Goddess, he was strong.

Parrying with all of her might, she managed to get beneath his thrust and pushed him back, their swords sliding across each other with a screech. Wrong-footing him, she swung for his nondominant side, managing to slice his tunic open just underneath his arm and he spun away from her, sword held defensively. He looked down at the small cut, eyebrows raised.

"Very good. You're already better than I expected. But it's going to take more than slicing me up like a piece of meat to best me."

He redoubled his attacks, swinging for her head, then her chest, then her legs, forcing her to circle him backward, making her dizzy.

"Did you really think you could steal my brother's throne from under his nose?" Fiorean asked.

Gasping for breath, she blocked another blow.

"I don't see him here fighting to get it back," she replied.

With a strikingly bold move, Fiorean swept his sword at her, and she was forced to duck into a rolling dive if she wanted to keep her head attached to her neck.

"Evander is a little busy at the moment," Fiorean said.

Aemyra rose to her feet in just enough time to block his next blow. "With what? Draining the caisteal stores of Truvo's best vintage?"

Fiorean bared his teeth as he swung for her again.

Fighting off his advances, she searched for any opening she could find, her mind scrambling to remember all of her lessons in swordplay. Finally, Aemyra was grateful for the years of bloodied noses and bruised ribs. Thanks to her father's ruthlessness, he might be about to save her life.

"Your ship is leaving, Princess," Fiorean taunted, spinning his sword in a lazy arc, in an attempt to make her turn around.

Aemyra didn't dare, knowing Fiorean was only trying to get under her skin. As the last handful of Dùileach fought desperately to keep the Covenanters out of the harbor, Aemyra shouldered the burden of their sacrifice. The Covenanters wanted her dead so the Chosen could keep a male heir on the throne, and her Dùileach were dying to cover her retreat.

Aemyra screamed her rage into Fiorean's face as she slashed with her sword, cutting clean through the leather buckles holding his tunic together. She didn't even draw blood.

Her shoulders were burning from the repeated lifting of the sword, but she couldn't give up. This wasn't sparring practice, this was the real thing.

Fiorean wouldn't stop until he had plunged that sword right into her heart.

And he looked like he would enjoy it.

The sound of wing beats reached her ears, and she almost dropped her sword in despair. Aervor was here.

Fiorean smirked and stepped back, pulling off the flapping tunic and dumping it at his feet beside the quiver of arrows. His black shirt billowed around his torso as he wiped the sweat from his brow with the sleeve.

Aemyra stumbled at the sudden distance, embarrassingly glad of the break. Until she risked a glance above them and saw the color of the dragon in the sky.

Glimmering golden scales reflected the sunrise.

"I told you my brother was otherwise occupied," Fiorean said.

No.

Evander couldn't have. An undeserving piece of shit like him could not possibly have claimed the last dragon. Because now . . .

Now her chances of Bonding were gone.

Furious at the injustice of it all, Aemyra decided that she was done playing fair. Rage pulsing through her veins like wildfire, she grew faster. Ducking under another swing of Fiorean's sword, she twisted and pulled the dagger free of her belt with her left hand. Slashing upward, the blade followed the hilt directly toward the scars Fiorean always tried to keep hidden.

He reeled away from the weapon, his instinctual fear giving her the opening she needed.

Aemyra kicked him in the crotch, and he fell on all fours, gasping.

Having seen the weakness in his blade from the moment the box had been opened, she trapped his hand under one boot and stomped her heel on the crossguard.

The gold metalwork buckled immediately, severing from the steel with a satisfying clank. She flung the blade across the cobblestones as the wind from Kolreath's wings whipped her hair around her head.

"Hate to say I told you so, but you should have come to me for a sword," she spat.

Out of the corner of her eye she could see her father's ship pulling farther away from the dock, the sails billowing toward safety. She prayed that Evander wouldn't have the sense to go after it with Kolreath and set it to the torch.

Before Fiorean could recover, Aemyra reeled her leg back and delivered a hard kick to his jaw.

As he sprawled defenseless on the ground, she raised the dagger to his neck and grabbed a fistful of the auburn hair that was so like her own. Wrenching his head around, she beheld the scarred side of his face that nobody ever saw uncovered.

Glancing between the ridiculously bejeweled sword and the monstrous scar, Aemyra laughed.

"You really are a self-centered shit, aren't you?" she hissed into his ear.

Before Fiorean could recover his strength, she slammed his head into the ground in front of her. She didn't hear a crack, but his eyes turned glassy.

"I will feed you to my dragon," he seethed, sounding like he was drunk.

She allowed herself a vicious smile as Kolreath landed, the ground beneath her feet shaking under the ancient creature's weight.

Aemyra let go of Fiorean. "You do that, pet. Maybe your dragon would actually be able to best me in a fight."

Looking at the giant garnet on the ground, Aemyra scooped it up and bounced it once in her palm. Fiorean cried aloud in sheer rage, rather than pain, as she held it up to the light. The wine-colored gem really was quite remarkable, but no substitute for the dragon she had just lost.

"It will remind me of how good your blood looks on my blade," she said.

At that moment, Kolreath loosed a roar so loud that several windows exploded. It must have been a signal, because the caisteal bells began pealing and shouts rang out from the battlements circling the city, on the opposite bank of the loch.

The truce was officially over.

"Time for me to go," Aemyra said, releasing him. With blood leaking from his head, Fiorean slumped against the cobblestones.

The sound of clanking armor reached her ears as Evander dismounted from his dragon. Obviously concern for his brother enough to stop him from asking Kolreath to incinerate her on the spot.

His first mistake.

Evander's green eyes were glittering madly as he advanced, his fire unstable and swollen from his recent Bonding. Aemyra knew she had to get out of there, sharpish.

The ship was already several hundred meters away from the dock, sails disappearing into the mist. The loch was so large that she couldn't see the other side.

Out of options, she sheathed her dagger and regrettably left her sword behind, before tearing for the water in a headlong sprint.

Tongues of fire followed her, but either Evander was a terrible shot, or the Goddess was still watching out for her, as they all went wide.

Nearing the end of the pier, Aemyra pumped her aching legs and pushed off the dock. Arching her back and throwing her arms above her head, she dove into the frigid waters of Loch Lorna.

CHAPTER TWELVE

"Where are they?" Aemyra yelled across the cabin of the creaking vessel.

Draevan had his palms pressed on the table that sat between them, his torso bent over the maps.

"I already told you, I don't know. Perhaps the harbormaster was mistaken, or maybe Orlagh was busy with a patient," her father said. "There could be any number of reasons why they didn't make it to the ship."

Aemyra pointed her index finger into his face, too far gone in her worry to think better of it.

"You better hope that they get out after us," she seethed.

They hadn't even arrived on the Sunset Isle yet and tensions were already growing. The passage through Loch Lorna, past the Deàrr Mountains, and out into the sea had been remarkably uneventful. Mostly thanks to Iona, who had plucked Aemyra from the loch and guarded them from dragonfire as they escaped the city.

But every moment they sailed farther away from the mainland, Aemyra felt as if cold hands were gripping her heart. With the knowledge that her family hadn't escaped Àird Lasair when they should have, she had no idea if Orlagh, Pàdraig, and Lachlann were alive or dead. She could only hope Sorcha had sequestered them in her tavern. Everyone who had been publicly involved with Aemyra was now in danger.

"Fucking Hela," Aemyra cursed, slamming her hand down on top of the table.

They had known to get out at the first sign of trouble. Berths had been purchased, supplies smuggled. If any of them were caught . . .

The image of the arrow buried in Kenna's back swam through her mind and Aemyra clapped a hand over her mouth as the ship swayed.

They were sailing through the waters of the Saiphir Sea, skirting the border of Tìr Uisge. Despite frequent raiding parties and skirmishes, the waters had been empty save for a gray kelpie Aemyra had spotted dancing across the surface of the water on the other side of the treaty line. While the kelpie had been beautiful, Aemyra mourned the loss of her desired beathach more than she cared to admit.

Kolreath was Bonded to Evander.

There was no undoing a Bond, save for killing one of them, and despite Draevan's bloodlust where the Àird Lasair faction of the clan was concerned, Aemyra wasn't sure that she shared his sentiments. She would have ended Fiorean's life to save her own, but she wasn't about to murder him in his bed in order to claim Aervor.

"Find me a way to get the throne back without further bloodshed," Aemyra ordered her father, plucking Kenna's scroll from the table.

Draevan looked up at her, his auburn hair tangled from the fierce sea winds.

"I can assure you that further bloodshed is necessary," he replied. "Thanks to you not killing Fiorean when you had the chance."

Aemyra scowled as she fingered the edges of the parchment. "I want to be a queen the people deserve. Not a monster who kills members of her own clan."

Draevan fixed her with a pitying look. "You are of the same clan, but not kin. Fiorean would not have hesitated to slit your throat, had he been given the opportunity. Knowing Katherine, those were her exact orders."

Feeling like she wanted to scream, Aemyra clenched her fists together as her father scanned the maps in front of him.

"The time for fairness is over," Draevan said, his words vengeful. "From now on, whoever takes up arms against us must die. Even our own clan."

Taking a breath, Aemyra stood a little straighter—hard to do when the ship was rocking from side to side in the waves.

"I would like to remain a queen that my people can support without fear of losing their lives," she said, smoothing the now crumpled scroll.

Draevan ignored her, gesturing to the western edge of a smaller map. "We will arrive on the Sunset Isle shortly." Her father closed his eyes for a moment to commune with his dragon, before opening them again. "Katherine was as prepared as we were for the king's death. She had the Covenanters hiding in the caisteal, waiting to strike. They likely snuck through the Blackridge Mountains before the weather turned during winter solstice."

Aemyra squinted at the map and pointed to Tìr Ùir. "Could more come through the Eternal Forest?"

Draevan was already shaking his head. "That would be a death sentence with the earth Dùileach sheltering there. Not to mention how treacherous the passes are in midwinter." His eyes glanced toward the Smàrag Sea. "But there is nothing stopping more of them from taking the ship instead."

The inside of the cabin suddenly felt airless. Katherine had never fully severed ties with Tìr Ùir, where her father was the admiral.

Biting her wind-chapped lips, Aemyra turned to gaze out of the window behind her. She couldn't even see mainland Tìr Teine anymore and she felt cast adrift in more ways than one, the scent of the sea enveloping her.

Kenna had been killed. Her family and Sorcha were missing.

Fighting the nausea that roiled through her gut, Aemyra swallowed.

"Kolreath and Aervor haven't come after us. Perhaps they have already flown to Eshader Port to ready it for the Ùir armada," she said.

Draevan was quiet as he pulled a smaller map in front of him, a more detailed drawing of fire territory.

"They won't dare attack the ship now that Gealach is overhead. Nor would they go so far as to seek help from Clan Iolairean. The phoenixes worship the ways of the Goddess even more loyally than we do. But perhaps Clan Leòmhann might be persuaded to support Evander. Their chimeras would be lethal fighting on the ground."

The small whitecaps beyond the salt-encrusted window rose and fell as Aemyra contemplated the enormity of the task before her.

Convince an entire territory to support her as queen when the rest of her clan didn't.

"My cousins will be waiting for us on the Sunset Isle. We are not alone in this," Draevan said, correctly interpreting the stiffness of her shoulders.

Aemyra sighed. "What if they won't support me either?" she asked, turning back to face her father.

He straightened. "They know better."

Dorchadas gleamed darkly at his hip, a permanent reminder of how far her father was willing to go to ensure her rule.

Draevan followed her gaze and placed his hands lazily on the hilt. "They would not dare betray me. I didn't marry the late Laird Fenella blindly. The woman was sickly, but she was powerful in both wit and title. Balnain will prove essential to our cause."

Tucking behind her ear a strand of hair that had escaped from her long braid, Aemyra wished there was something more she could do. Some alliance she could bring to the table.

Her thoughts drifted once more to wings and fire before she squashed them down.

"Balnain sits directly in the middle of Tìr Teine. You mean to cut off Katherine's allies before they can group together . . ." Aemyra said as her eyes darted across the map.

Draevan tapped the two coastal towns in the northwest corner of the map.

"We cut the territory in half at the Forc. No army will cross the river, for fear of ambush, and no caravan will take the road, for fear of the same," Draevan said, mouth tight.

Aemyra's eyes were still scanning the map, looking for potential allies.

"What of ships?" she asked. "If Katherine has time to rally the armada from Ùir, we are doomed. There is no naval force in Tìr Teine to match it," Aemyra said, looking toward the river that almost bisected her territory. If Katherine sent ships up the Forc, and had their forces converge on it . . . there would be no question of Evander winning this war.

Draevan took a large swig of wine and tore his eyes away from the map. "We have much to think over. Rest until we dock this evening. Gealach is keeping watch."

Fear bit at Aemyra's chest. She needed to be stronger if she had a hope of leading her clan, never mind ruling all of Tìr Teine.

Aemyra suddenly felt like she couldn't breathe in the stuffy cabin.

"I need to get some air," she ground out, her boots loud on the wooden floor as she passed her father and threw open the door. Her dark blue tartan dress was held up to mid-calf with a thick belt, since her breeches and shirt had been ruined during the fight with Fiorean.

Storming up the steps and banging her elbow as the ship rocked, Aemyra emerged blinking into the sunlight.

The deck was busy with sailors shouting orders. The few Dùileach who had also escaped were using their collective powers to help steer and protect the ship.

Aemyra crossed over to the rail and stuck her face into the wind, hoping it would calm her racing mind. Laughter caught her ears and she turned to see the ship's cat dancing around the deck, orange tail swishing in agitation, with his gaze fixed on the seagulls in the sky.

Iona was straddling the railing, throwing scraps of fish to the sharks as she altered currents and calmed the waves around them.

The queen's guard had made it out of Àird Lasair unscathed, and she spotted Clea across the deck. The air Dùileach's magic filled the snowy white sails that stretched into the cerulean sky.

"Aems!" Adarian called out, hopping down from the rigging like he had been born a sailor. "Any news?"

Hair blowing over her face, she grabbed the fly-aways and tucked them behind her ears.

"No," she said quietly, looking into the water. "We just have to pray to Cailleach that they are safe."

Adarian's face was downcast, but he nodded. "I am sure of it. Orlagh and Pàdraig knew the plan. They will get Lachlann out before anything happens."

Nausea roiled in her stomach at the thought of what might have happened to those who had pledged themselves to her. If the priestesses had been harmed because of their oaths . . .

Adarian looked concerned. "I thought you got over the seasickness yesterday?"

She accepted the waterskin he handed her. "I don't think I'll ever get used to this infernal swaying."

In comparison, Iona was quite literally in her element as she jumped overboard to swim with the sharks.

Aemyra summoned a small flame into her palm. "Fire isn't much use out here," she said miserably. "All those years we hid the extent of what we could do, trusting that it was the right thing. Now look at where keeping secrets has gotten us."

Like she had been doing for four days, Aemyra dipped her hand into the pocket of her dress and rubbed her thumb over the smooth garnet that was as large as a quail's egg.

"I had hoped we could avoid outright war," she whispered.

Her brother looked north, over the great expanse of ocean, toward where the conflict-ridden Tìr Uisge lay.

"I think war was coming for us whether we wanted it or not," Adarian said. "This is bigger than who sits the throne, Aemyra. We may be the last territory they have touched, but the Chosen will not stop until they have driven the ways of the Goddesses from the hearts and minds of every citizen of Erisocia. If Katherine and Evander plan to let that happen, you would have had to stop them eventually." He looked across the deck to where a sailor was securing a length of rope. "When they have torn down our temples, they will go after the beathaichean."

Adarian motioned for the sailor to join them at the rail. He was young, but with a generous smattering of gray in his dark hair.

"Martyn, would you share your story with my sister?" Adarian asked.

Aemyra turned to the air Dùileach, recognizing him as Clea's partner.

"Your Majesty," Martyn said, with a bow of his head. "The Chosen journeyed to Port Astra last year. They spent months convincing people that Dùileach were trying to oppress those with no magic." Martyn shifted his feet uncomfortably. "The priests spread rumors that Bonding granted individuals too much power and made them unstable. Non-Dùileach grew fearful, and our own people rioted against us."

Grief lined his face, and Aemyra remained silent. Tìr Adhair was no stranger to civil wars, but never before between Dùileach and non-Dùileach.

"Clea's Bonded simurgh was felled by an arrow," Martyn said, his voice trembling. "Mine clawed out the eyes of three priests before a club finally made contact with his skull."

Aemyra suddenly understood the haunted look in his eyes. Both Martyn and Clea had lost their beathaichean and would stop at nothing to overthrow the True Religion now. Her father hadn't only recruited talented Dùileach to their cause, he was already building her an army fueled by loyalty.

Martyn was called away by the quartermaster and Adarian stepped closer to her.

"Tìr Teine might only have three dragons left, but the Chosen have failed to overthrow this territory because of them," Adarian said.

"Two of those dragons are now fighting for the royals," Aemyra said dejectedly. "Who have clearly sided with the True Religion thanks to Katherine's influence. I wish Father had succeeded in his coup to prevent her from marrying King Haedren, our territory would be stronger for it."

Adarian shook his head. "It's well known that Haedren wanted the Ùir armada to strengthen our territory. His actions in marrying Katherine were misguided but well intentioned."

"You defend a mad king who allowed the Covenanters to infiltrate his own caisteal?"

"We all make mistakes, Aemyra," he said quietly.

Aemyra clutched the rail as she struggled to keep her magic contained as she thought of how she had let Kolreath slip through her fingers. "Why do the Chosen hate Dùileach so much? What have we ever done to them?"

Her brother continued searching the horizon and shrugged. "Because we were born with power and they were not. They saw their chance to take it for themselves in Tìr Ùir after the Fifty Year War." Adarian turned to her. "But we were gifted our power, while the Chosen *take* it. And those who grasp for power will never keep it."

Aemyra felt the truth in his words, but it didn't make her feel much better.

"I have grasped for power," she said dejectedly.

To her surprise, Adarian smiled. "No. Father grasps for power. He is the one down there poring over maps and charts and sending silver swyfts with messages to everyone who owes him a favor. You are up here worrying about the fate of those we left behind in Àird Lasair." He gave her a nudge. "You might want to be queen, but you want it for the right reasons."

A member of the crew called out to Adarian and with a quick clap on his sister's back, he went to lend his strength to unfurl the second sail.

Removing her hands from the rail, she left behind two charred handprints before sinking down onto the step. Running her fingers over the healing cut on her palm, she hated that the priestesses' oaths had come to nothing. The public declaration hadn't made any difference, and now she was returning to Penryth without a crown.

Checking the bandage around her right bicep, she comforted herself in knowing that she had at least escaped with her life. There had been a moment when she had heard Fiorean's arrow loose from his bow that she hadn't been so sure.

Given that Aemyra had dueled who she was sure was the best swordsman in Àird Lasair and lived to tell the tale, she should be grateful that she wasn't more wounded.

Remembering the way she had cracked Fiorean's head against the cobblestones, she refused to feel sorry for it. If she hadn't been completely ruthless, he would have killed her. Draevan had confirmed as much. At least Evander had been too concerned for his brother to set Kolreath after the ship. By the time they were behind Iona's shields, the dragon could not reach them.

Before she could think too much about the fear in Fiorean's eyes as she had thrust her dagger toward his face, a shout went up from the bow. Aemyra jumped to her feet, automatically scanning the skies.

Iona hopped up onto the deck, riding a wave of her own creation, her palms holding swirling torrents of water. Following her lead, Aemyra summoned her flame. Although, if Fiorean and Evander had finally found them and decided to attack with two dragons, Iona's shields might not be enough to protect them.

An earsplitting screech rent the air and Aemyra steeled herself, wishing that she still had her sword.

Striding for her twin, she met him in the middle of the deck, both automatically assuming fighting positions back-to-back. The clouds above them swirled and Aemyra held her breath, ready for whatever appeared.

Before she could summon more flame, Draevan strode from belowdecks, his auburn hair falling from its knot, a grin on his face.

"Stand down!" he commanded the crew, utterly at ease.

Gealach, her father's enormous emerald dragon, sailed out from the clouds with his wings spread wide.

When Gealach opened his massive jaws, Aemyra glimpsed rows of dagger-sharp teeth before he loosed a tongue of fire so hot that even she flinched from it.

The ship's cat sprinted belowdecks, but Draevan gazed lovingly up at his dragon, as if the mere presence of his beathach lifted his spirits.

As the viridescent scales glittered in the sunlight, Aemyra watched the wing membranes ripple as Gealach banked to circle overhead. At over a hundred years of age, the dragon was twice as long as the ship and immensely powerful.

Running across the deck, Aemyra hoisted herself up into the rigging, needing to get closer to the dragon. The rocking of the ship and her skirts made it difficult to get her footing in the ropes. With her shoulders protesting, she clambered into the crow's nest.

The air Dùileach funneled more wind into the sails and the ship juddered as it attempted to keep up with the dragon.

Gealach completed his circle around the ship and banked to fly overhead once more. Aemyra watched him approach, feeling smaller than she ever had before. She had never seen her father's dragon this close and was surprised when she could make out several scars on his underbelly and wings. Whether they were from long-ago fights with other dragons, or from battles fought with Draevan, she didn't know.

As the dragon passed directly overhead, Aemyra tilted her face back and felt tears prick at the corners of her eyes. Without conscious thought, she raised her hand above her head as if she might be able to brush her fingertips across those scales, just to know what they felt like.

Just once.

But Gealach didn't pause his flight, nor did he hesitate as he flew west to where Aemyra could just about see the outline of the Sunset Isle from her perch.

Tears flowing freely down her cheeks, she watched as Penryth came into view and its beauty hit her like a punch in the gut.

The sun was beginning its descent in a furious flush of oranges and dusky pinks behind a singular mountain that loomed so large, she felt as if Gealach himself would not be able to fly above it.

Beinn Deataiche, the Mountain of Smoke. The jagged peak was covered in snow, and the slopes were cast in its shadow. With the sunset staining the water in a spectacular array of color, and the mountain dominating the dense forest that sprawled across the rest of the isle, Aemyra knew why it had been named as such.

If she thought that she felt close to Brigid in the temple, it was nothing compared to this. This place was . . . ethereal.

Goddess, she had missed it.

As Gealach spread his wings and loosed a roar loud enough to shake the foundations of the great mountain, Aemyra felt tears wet her cheeks as she returned home.

She might not be Bonded, but she was still the queen.

Remaining in the crow's nest as the crew sailed them through the rocky shores that led to the deep inlet where her father's caisteal sat, Aemyra tried to envision the future that now lay ahead of her.

An exiled queen fighting Covenanters and clansmen without a dragon.

How could she ever hope to succeed?

CHAPTER THIRTEEN

Aemyra had forgotten how different the Sunset Isle was from Àird Lasair.

Not only was it cleaner, quieter, and significantly less populated—there was a general aura of contentment that hung over the harbor town that sat between the ocean and the base of Beinn Deataiche.

It had once been an active volcano, and the first dragon eggs were said to have formed out of the molten rock. Hatching upon the first fire Dùileach touch, dragons had been born into the world.

Upon arrival, Aemyra had considered climbing it on the off chance there was a forgotten dragon egg somewhere in the crags.

Many Daercathians had scoured the ancient nests in an attempt to find more eggs and had been chased away by The Terror when he had still nested in the mountain.

Aemyra's reality was that The Terror was gone, and so were the rest of the dragons.

Wrapping her arms around herself, Aemyra stared into the clear waters of the lagoon and wished Lachlann were here to see the wonders of the island. They had received no word of her family since arriving in Penryth three days ago.

The moss was damp under her cloak as she rolled the gemstone she had stolen from Fiorean between her palms. Steam lifted lazily off the surface of the lagoon, while jet black salamanders curled up in the crevasses that leaked heat from the heart of the mountain. Their vibrant orange stripes spilled across their backs like lava over ancient rock. One tiny beathach no bigger than the size of Aemyra's fist lifted his head, licking a bulbous eye with his tongue.

"You won't overhear anything from me," Aemyra said, pocketing the gemstone.

Salamanders were sleekit creatures. Prone to eavesdropping, they were the favored beathaichean of Dùileach nobles. Their ability to detect poison from an impressive distance of four feet was not to be sneered at either.

Aemyra liked their padded toes. The noise they made pattering across the damp rock combined with the thick heat of the lagoon soothed her turbulent thoughts. Until a chatter of firebirds burst over the tops of the trees, splitting the tranquility.

They flew in the direction of their breeding grounds on the southern peninsula. As she watched their flaming tails illuminate the overcast sky, Aemyra thought of Solas. She had always wanted to visit the firebird groves with Orlagh but had never made the time to make the journey across the island before they had moved away.

Cliodna, deliver them safely across your seas to us. Keep my family safe.

Aemyra dipped her fingers into the lagoon, certain the water Goddess would hear her.

Orlagh would come back to the Sunset Isle and resume her position as Healer on High, Aemyra told herself. Pàdraig would fashion armor and arrowheads for her army and Lachlann would frolic like she and Adarian had once done, surrounded by plentiful magic.

With a weight on her shoulders that had nothing to do with the golden cloak she wore, Aemyra rose reluctantly to her feet.

Despite the winter season the air was warm. Another blessing from the mountain.

Turning away from the lagoon, she walked the familiar path back to Caisteal Eilean. Tucking a stray curl behind her ear, Aemyra stopped upon the heather-strewn hill overlooking the town, enjoying the bite of the sea breeze.

Four large temples marked the borders of Penryth, but many homesteads dotted the hills that sat in the shadow of the mountain. Neat stone houses with thatched roofs hugged the coastline around the busy harbor, and Aemyra could hear fishermen hauling in their catch. Seagulls begged loudly for a mouthful, while ospreys perched observantly on the steep cliffs.

Caisteal Eilean was surrounded by the sea, nestled on a spit of land barely large enough to contain the structure. Less than half the size of Caisteal Lasair, it loomed on the other side of the bridge that connected it to Penryth.

Within those walls, Aemyra had been molded into a queen. From her father's study she had gazed out of the window at the peak of Beinn Deataiche and watched Gealach soar into the snow.

Skirting the edge of town, Aemyra hoped the walk would ease her troubled thoughts.

Even in midwinter, some of the brambles had begun to bloom thanks to the heat of the mountain. Aemyra skimmed her hands across the budding bushels, wiping her stained fingers on her skirts hastily when she realized they were bitterberry hedges.

A potent poison, and one Orlagh had ensured her children could identify from early childhood.

With a smile, Aemyra meandered down the path. Remembering how she and Adarian used to gallivant through these lush fields, chins sticky with blackberry juice. Solas clicking his beak furiously above them when they refused to return home until they had gorged themselves on the tart fruit.

Hopping over the fence and almost snagging her cloak, Aemyra took the familiar shortcut toward the caisteal. Oil lamps burned in every window she passed, a permanent offering to Brigid.

Spotting the tree where she had shared her first kiss with a shy stable boy, Aemyra had to fight an outright blush by the time she made it to the north of the village and heard the clacking of a loom. Wondering if Glennis the weaver still lived there, Aemyra hurried her footsteps before the woman who had taught her everything she knew in the bedroom spotted her.

As she left the wilds of the island behind, the flapping of kites and ribbons tied to posts assaulted her senses. The sea breeze had worked itself into a stiff wind and the residents' offerings to Beira were being readily accepted. After a decade in Àird Lasair, Aemyra had been forced to realize how far those on the mainland had slipped away from the Goddesses.

Here, groves were positioned in the four corners of every village and hamlet. Runes were etched into doorposts and window frames. Cloidna's blessed water was used every time someone entered or left a home, and temples had been occupied since the ship had docked with families mourning the loss of those who had perished in the escape from Àird Lasair.

Grief lay heavy on the town, smothering their hope until it choked Aemyra to hear the silence.

She had left this island as a girl with a headful of dreams and returned a woman who understood the cost.

The smell of salt filled her nose as she crossed the bridge into her father's caisteal.

As she strode up the drafty steps toward the great hall, torches illuminated the heavy tapestries and bookcases that concealed secret passageways she no longer had to use. The thick wool of her red tartan dress was finer than anything she had worn in these gloomy halls as a child.

The stone walls blocked what little sunlight there was, but Aemyra could hear Adarian's voice rising above the clamor coming from inside the hall.

"We cannot rule out stragglers making it ashore."

Summoning her strength, Aemyra pushed open the heavy wooden door and entered the hall where her father had been holding council for three days straight.

"Swyfts have been sent to Balnain. My brother is readying his fleet as we speak and soon we will have ships posted at the three tributaries of the Forc. Uisge invaders are unimportant now," Laoise, Draevan's cousin by marriage, reported.

The sound of chairs scraping back assaulted Aemyra's ears as everyone seated around the large wooden table rose to their feet and bowed.

"Your Majesty" chorused throughout the room.

Draevan looked up from where he was standing in front of the enormous fireplace but remained silent.

Aemyra resisted rolling her eyes. When only ten people viewed her as queen, it quite took the shine off of it.

"Please, be seated," she replied softly. "Are we discussing our allies? Have we received word on how quickly we might mobilize?"

She strode through the room to take her seat at the head of the table. Conveniently, it was also the closest chair to the platter of steaming pies.

"Not yet, Majesty. We expect to receive a reply within the week. Swyfts may fly quickly, but they cannot reach the mainland in a matter of hours," Maeve replied.

The tough woman had made it out of Àird Lasair with two cracked ribs, a broken finger, and a sizeable gash across her upper arm. Despite Maeve's frosty demeanor, Aemyra was glad to have her on the council. Maeve's insight into strategy was invaluable.

"I am pleased to hear that Laird Edouard is amenable to our plans," Aemyra said to Laoise. "If your brother succeeds in holding the river, he will be handsomely rewarded."

Laoise's tawny eyes gave nothing away. Possessing the gift of fire, Draevan's cousin completed the queen's guard. Nell, Clea, and Iona were also granted a council chair, both as queen's guards and representatives of the territories they hailed from.

"If we could recruit a few more water Dùileach for my brother's fleet . . ." Laoise began.

Iona was already shaking her head. "The Dùileach of Uisge are far north in Pavykan, behind shields of ice. Queen Siv and her family have not been seen in years. Even the un-Bonded are fleeing from persecution at the hands of the Chosen and I doubt whichever landing party made it to Ballan serves the Goddesses."

Maeve smirked in Iona's direction. "I spared *you* when you snuck onto this island without invitation. You don't wish to extend the same courtesy to your Uisge brothers and sisters who have so recently breached our borders?"

The two women began bickering and Aemyra exchanged a look with Adarian. War was indeed upon them on all fronts.

"We should not expect help from Tìr Adhair either—by all accounts another civil war has broken out among the griffin clans," Clea said, clearly worried for her home territory. "King Virean is more territorial than the chimeras of Clan Leòmhann. He will not send aid."

Suddenly the smell of the pies turned her stomach and Aemyra pushed the platter farther down the table.

"Fear not, Majesty," Laoise said, throwing her braids over one shoulder. "My people are fierce warriors, even shepherds will face down a pack of wolves to save one lamb."

Aemyra fixed her with a look. "We are not fighting wolves . . ."

Draevan looked up as if his daughter's words had jerked him out of deep thought. The shadows under his eyes were deep purple, his face pale. They were all exhausted from the five days' hard sail, and she was certain her father hadn't slept since they had arrived in Penryth.

"It has been over a week since Haedren's death," Draevan said from his position in front of the fire. "The mourning period for the late king will be over, and Katherine will no doubt crown Evander at the earliest opportunity."

Adarian shifted uncomfortably and Draevan took a swig of wine, draining the goblet he held.

"She needs to make a proclamation as queen," Maeve said, looking pointedly in Aemyra's direction.

Eyes widening, Aemyra glanced between the faces gathered. "We agreed it would be too presumptuous. Without the backing of the royal family and the security of the priestesses, anything I say will be too easy to dismiss."

Draevan leaned over the back of the nearest chair, knuckles straining against the wood. "If we do not challenge Evander's rule, everyone will assume that you have yielded the throne to him. We will send swyfts with a signed declaration this evening."

"Once you officially declare yourself queen, you can start making alliances," Maeve said, voice steady. "And we desperately need alliances."

Aemyra's stomach twisted, and she felt Adarian's eyes fall on her. She knew that one of the best ways to make alliances as a queen was to marry.

Maeve noticed her apprehension. "One step at a time, Your Majesty."

Draevan was still staring at the map, rolling the stem of his empty goblet between a thumb and forefinger. "We can assume that since Clan Leuthanach has already sided with the Chosen, they will support Evander. We need to secure our alliances with Clans Iolairean and Leòmhann quickly."

Aemyra let out a tense breath, at least her father hadn't mentioned marriage. Yet.

Plucking an apple from the basket in front of her, Aemyra picked up a knife and began peeling it. More for something to do with her hands than hunger. These council meetings made her unbearably anxious.

Greer's eyes followed her hands and Aemyra felt her stomach turn again. Kenna was supposed to be the high priestess serving on her council, not this stone-faced old woman. Discarding the peel, the priestess narrowed her eyes at it and Aemyra quickly swept it off the table before she could divine any meaning from the shape it had taken.

"I need you to ride to Ballan, Adarian," Draevan said, looking up from the maps. "The village has been put to the torch by the Uisge raiding party and I have reports of several dead and injured. I suspect Covenanters from Dagát were among them."

Aemyra fiddled with the knife. She might not have a dragon, but she wasn't useless.

"Of course, Father," Adarian said, standing. Then, almost as an afterthought, he remembered to bow to Aemyra. Laoise followed him from the room, already buttoning her wine-colored cloak under her chin.

Feeling as though everyone in this room had a purpose but her, Aemyra glared at her father and addressed the table.

"Leave us."

The wooden floorboards creaked as seven pairs of boots filed out of the room, the worn rugs thrown across the floors muffling their steps.

Left alone with her father, Aemyra fisted her hand around the gemstone in her pocket.

"You wish for me to make an official declaration to the Teine clans and yet you advise me to remain passive here in Penryth. I have made offerings in every temple and sat around this table planning a war that my people may never forgive."

Draevan's face shuttered. "Securing alliances farther afield is just as important as remaining in the Goddesses' favor. These things take time, and careful planning."

"I am a *queen,* not a priestess," Aemyra snapped. "My people are grieving because of a mistake *we* made. I need to show them that I am a queen worth following, that the cost of claiming the throne will be worth it for the future I can give Tìr Teine."

Her father gave her a piercing glare. "Forgive me if I wish to handle this delicately. Your ascension to the throne has not exactly gone as planned."

"And whose fault is that?" Aemyra asked through gritted teeth, refusing to let her father place the blame squarely on her shoulders.

His forest green eyes were fathomless. "Perhaps if you had claimed a dragon when you were supposed to, we wouldn't have been forced to flee."

If her father had run her through with his sword it would have hurt less.

"Your brother will handle Ballan. Now, the tailor is waiting in your chambers with some more appropriate dresses for you," Draevan said, dismissive.

Clenching her jaw, unable to summon the courage to remind him that she was the queen, Aemyra strode from the hall. Tears were burning at the back of her eyes, but she refused to let them fall.

She would be a strong leader, and a good queen to her people. She would not sit in this caisteal and let other people plan her war. The time for being passive was over.

Sprinting up the stairs, tartan skirts bunched in her hands, she headed for her chambers. Bursting through the door, she saw that the withered tailor was indeed perched on a stool, holding a fistful of pins.

"My sincerest apologies," Aemyra panted, completely winded from running up the stairs. "But I will not be needing your services today," she said, pulling at the laces of her corset. The dress came off over her head in a swift movement, followed by her shift, until she was completely naked save for her boots.

The old woman didn't bat an eye.

Aemyra cursed as she rifled through her wardrobe and found nothing save for dresses that grew progressively fuller and frillier. She was about to give up when the old woman coughed pointedly.

Peeking her head out from the wardrobe, Aemyra saw the tailor point a gnarled finger in the direction of the four-poster bed. Lying on top of the quilt cover was a pair of riding leathers.

Jaw dropping, Aemyra hurried to the bed and grabbed them. They were made from the supplest of dark brown leather, and thick enough to withstand dragon scales.

The tailor chuckled. "Your father asked for fighting leathers."

The woman gave her a sly smile, but Aemyra failed to return it.

Her childhood dream of Bonding to a dragon was over, but she was still queen. It was her responsibility to act like one. Aemyra would not stand idly by while her people were suffering. She fisted the leather breeches in her hands until the material creaked.

"I believe it is time for Tìr Teine to return to the matriarchy once more."

CHAPTER FOURTEEN

Wishing she hadn't been forced to relinquish her sword back in Àird Lasair, Aemyra turned the corner to the stables. Adarian was already saddling his horse when she tested the weight of several swords from the weapons rack.

"I'm going with you," she said firmly, voice echoing across the yard.

Her brother lifted his head from tightening the girth. "You heard what Father said, you've to—" Adarian's eyes widened when he noticed what she was wearing. "He certainly spared no expense."

Aemyra shrugged, selecting a one-handed sword. "Perks of being the queen, I guess."

Her new leathers fit perfectly. Better yet, they were tailored with convenient pockets for her to sheathe weapons and essential items.

Just like the dagger on her hip, her leathers bore no unnecessary embellishment, but held a distinct power in their simplicity.

"Would you listen if your humble brother asked his queen to stay here?" Adarian asked with a sarcastic smile.

Aemyra approached her twin. "My people need to see that the

queen is on their side. If a village has been attacked by a raiding party, then I will provide assistance. I'm a better healer than you anyway."

Knowing when he was beaten, Adarian called over his shoulder into the stables, "Give my sister the tamest nag you have. She isn't the best horsewoman."

Five muttered greetings of "Your Majesty" met her ears from the shadowy barn. The smell of horse was heavy in the air and a young woman with sunshine hair handed Aemyra the reins of an old chestnut gelding.

"He'll be gentle with you, my queen," Dianne said, swinging herself expertly into the saddle of a bay mare who was already dancing on the spot, hooves clacking on the hard ground.

Aemyra eyed the horse warily as she hauled herself up. Adarian hadn't been joking, she wasn't a good horsewoman.

"It will be a hard ride," Adarian warned, gathering the reins of his gray destrier. "I want to reach Ballan while there are still villagers left to save."

Aemyra steeled herself. "Then what are we waiting for?"

Digging her heels into the gelding's sides, Aemyra tried to rise and fall with the horse's rhythm as they clattered across the bridge, succeeding only in bruising her tailbone. They opened up into a canter as they left the town behind.

Soon the rolling fields converged into lush forest, and they were forced to ride single file up tightly winding dirt paths.

"Ease up as we climb," Adarian called out over his shoulder a while later.

Wincing as her aching muscles cramped, Aemyra nudged the horse toward her brother.

"What's your plan when we arrive?" she asked, reins rubbing against newly formed blisters.

Adarian peered ahead as though he could see around the mountain toward what awaited them. Dianne's curtain of sunshine hair cascaded down her back as she led the way, Laoise just behind her.

"Our party will split in half," Adarian said, ducking to avoid a low-hanging branch. "We ride into the village to find survivors and treat the wounded, the rest will circle the perimeter in case any Uisge invaders or Covenanters stayed ashore."

Aemyra's horse tensed underneath her as he sensed her anxiety.

Adarian frowned. "Uisge raids happen all the time and Covenanters have been using the islands as outposts for years. Don't you remember Pàdraig showing us some of the weapons he won from them?"

"Where are they, Adarian?" Aemyra asked, voice almost covered by the calling of starlings above them.

Her brother's face fell, his well-concealed worry for their family rising to the surface. "I don't know. But I keep faith that they are safe." His stallion bobbed his head, chomping at the bit. "Evander would have made it known if he had them in custody."

Aemyra silently agreed. Sending up a fleeting prayer to any Goddess listening, she clicked her tongue for her horse to follow Dianne through the forest.

An hour later, they stopped to fill their waterskins at a mountain spring. The crisp water soothed the dry tickle at the back of Aemyra's throat and she splashed some on her face, the frigid bite refocusing her wandering thoughts.

As they approached Ballan, the smell of smoke unsettled the horses. Three riders peeled away to circle the town, and Aemyra followed the others down the main path.

The trees ended abruptly, giving way to scrubby grass and sandy shingle that slowed the horses. Even from this distance, Aemyra could tell there wasn't much left to save.

"Great Mother have mercy . . ." Laoise muttered, making the sign of Brigid's cross.

Aemyra focused on the creak of the saddle to steady her nerves. Waves lapped hungrily at the shore, the sea stretching unbroken all the way north toward Tìr Uisge.

"Dismount here," Adarian said softly before the entrance to the small hamlet.

Eyes wide with shock, Aemyra followed her brother between the burned husks of cottages. Splinters of wood had once been thick fences, and half-sunken boats littered the beach like flotsam.

Their feet were soft on the ground, small puffs of ash drifting up around their ankles with every step through the gently smoking ruins.

"Uisge invaders don't usually burn everything. They steal grain and precious metals, or attempt to make camp in the foothills if they seek refuge," Dianne said quietly, blue eyes scanning what was left of the cottages.

Aemyra unsheathed her dagger, the stillness unsettling her. "Spread out, find any survivors."

Her twin took the main road with Dianne at his side, and Aemyra didn't miss the jealousy in Laoise's eyes. If Adarian wasn't careful, he would end up sparking a war of his own on the Sunset Isle.

Stopping to peer into a charred cottage, Aemyra immediately wished she hadn't when she saw the bodies. The door had been barred from the outside, the thatched roof now collapsed on top of the trapped occupants.

Cailleach, spare their souls . . .

"Aemyra!"

The shout had her sprinting across the uneven ground toward her brother. Adarian and Dianne stood shoulder to shoulder in the middle of the road, the body of a large man supine before them. He held a dirk in one badly burned hand, his rising chest defying the damage done to his body.

Dianne lifted a pale finger and pointed to something clutched in the man's hand. Crouching down, Aemyra eased the pennant away from the stiff and swollen fingers and unfurled it.

"Father was right," she muttered, recognizing the emblazoned tower on the white fabric. The survivor was a Covenanter.

Scanning the destruction with fresh eyes, Aemyra noticed the villagers' pitchforks littering the ground, the blackened cottages that had housed the vulnerable. Covenanters had come from Uisge to lay waste to her home and slaughtered any who stood in their way.

Had they given up on trying to break Queen Siv's shields of ice and set their sights south instead?

"Why would they do this?" Dianne asked. "The priests who came before left willingly enough when we turned them away."

The Covenanter gave a wheezing cough and Aemyra barely suppressed her grimace when some of his skin sloughed away. Dianne excused herself to be politely sick in a wheelbarrow.

Aemyra hardened her heart. This man had attacked her people. "This pain is nothing compared to what Hela will do with your soul."

The man had no eyelids left and his eyes bulged as Laoise ripped a tattered Daercathian flag bearing Draevan's crest from a crooked post.

"We are no strangers to the Chosen in Balnain. Their ships sail up the Forc to try and infiltrate the heart of Tìr Teine." Her gold-tipped braids clinked musically as she fisted the ripped banner. "When we barricaded the bridges and choked the mouth of the river, the Covenanters came next."

The three of them were silent as Laoise crouched in the dirt, her hand placed reverently over the golden dragon embroidered on the flag.

"The Balnain fleet was strong enough to send them south. These villagers were not so lucky."

Aemyra crumpled the white pennant in her fist, rage washing over her.

Covenanters, Chosen . . . Aemyra didn't care what they called themselves, only that they had snuffed out the lives of her people with malicious intent.

"How dare you," she seethed, pressing her boot against the burned Covenanter's thigh. His screams barely made it up his charred throat.

"S-stopped uuuh, u-us," he wheezed hoarsely.

Frowning, Aemyra bent closer.

"B-black s-scales."

With the final word, his chest sank and he breathed no more. Aemyra shared a concerned look with Adarian as she got slowly to her feet, thoughts whirring.

"What?" Dianne asked as Aemyra hopped over the broken fence and hurried to climb a small hillock, the others behind her. Cresting the rise, she staggered to a halt.

"Black scales," Aemyra said, hardly daring to believe it.

"It cannot be," Adarian said.

The white pennant in Aemyra's hand felt heavy as she twisted it through her fingers. The cottages behind them were badly burned, but still standing. The bodies still recognizable as human.

What lay before them was nothing more than a wasteland of ash and smoke.

There had only been one dragon in living memory with black scales.

"The Terror died decades ago," Laoise said confidently.

Regardless, hope hatched inside Aemyra.

"Pàdraig always said he was waiting for a queen that never came," Adarian said softly.

Their adoptive father had told them stories of The Terror since their infancy. The obsidian dragon had never Bonded. Because of his fearsome reputation, no Dùileach had ever been stupid enough to try.

"He defended the village?" Dianne asked. "How do we know this wasn't Aervor or Kolreath?"

Squatting close to the ground, Aemyra ran her fingers through the residual cinders and tried to get a feel for the magic that ran through The Terror's veins.

There was something there, but it was more like her own intuition rather than tangible magic. Lifting her head, she scanned the charred trees until she saw several that were broken in half, their tops hanging drunkenly off the trunks. As if they had been clipped by an enormous wing.

Her eyes followed the broken branches until they fell on a small patch of the mountain that wasn't covered in snow.

There.

She couldn't see him, but the feeling in her gut was confirmation enough.

"It's him," she said firmly.

Pocketing the pennant, Aemyra made her decision.

If he was truly still alive, then The Terror had remained unseen for decades for a good reason. He was wild and unpredictable, but he had destroyed an entire battalion of Covenanters after they had killed her people.

"Build pyres for the bodies you can find and finish the burning," Aemyra said, straightening.

Dianne and Laoise wore twin expressions of shock.

"You cannot be serious."

"He is a myth!"

It was a mark of how dire their current predicament was that Adarian didn't try to stop Aemyra when she waited for his blessing. Her twin checked that her sword was sheathed securely before stepping back as if to appraise her.

"Make sure you don't die. I have absolutely no interest in becoming king."

CHAPTER FIFTEEN

AEMYRA'S BREATHS FELT LIKE SHARDS OF BROKEN GLASS IN her lungs, and the higher she climbed into the frigid peaks, the more she contemplated the enormity of the task ahead of her.

She might have grown up watching her father take to the skies with Gealach, but as thorough as her father's education had been, Draevan had steadfastly refused to reveal how he had Bonded.

As a result, she was petrified.

Breaking her nail down to the quick while hauling herself over a ridge, Aemyra hissed in pain and begrudgingly thought that an egg ceremony would have been far easier.

Clan Daercathian had adapted the story of how the eggs had formed from within Beinn Deataiche into one of their most well-known traditions—holding egg ceremonies each year on the summer solstice. At the age of sixteen, every fire Dùileach had the opportunity to Bond to an egg, regardless of whether they were of noble or common birth.

Even though no ceremony had been held in generations, Aemyra had often daydreamed about walking through the circle of plinths that gleamed in the sunlight, wondering which egg might sense the power inside of her and hatch.

"Fucking *Hela,*" Aemyra cursed as the rock under her foot slipped away and she broke another two nails clawing at the mountainside to avoid tumbling over the edge.

Muscles straining, Aemyra hauled herself to her feet. Brushing her scraped and dirty palms across her thighs, she kept walking.

"You aren't the first Daercathian to Bond to an adult dragon," Aemyra said to herself. "If they can figure it out, so can you."

The sun was beginning its descent as the day passed into late afternoon and Aemyra's stomach grew hollow. Regretting not eating one of the pies that morning, she stopped to take a sip from her waterskin.

Refusing to give up, Aemyra kept the names of her fierce female ancestors close to her heart.

Warrior queen Lissandrea and the enormous golden Kolgiath, who had flown to war. Her daughter Aesandra, who had Bonded to Rhyian after the war was won—naming her after the living flame. Princess Isobeil had defied her parents and claimed the wild Sylthria before her first flowering.

Giving herself a shake, Aemyra fisted her hands by her sides. "If Isobeil can do it at half my age, I have no reason to be afraid now," she muttered, breath misting before her.

The men of their clan might have torn down their legacy, but Aemyra would build it back up. It mattered not that the beathaichean were tethered to their territories, she had no interest in traveling to Uisge, Ùir, or Adhair. Tìr Teine was where she was needed most, and a dragon would help her save her people.

The path had become steeper now, snow clinging to the slopes around her. Having to use her hands as well as her feet in order to climb, she barely noticed the frigid temperature, she was sweating so profusely.

As the air grew thin in her lungs, Aemyra wondered if she would find the damn dragon at all.

The thought of failing again was almost too much to bear and she climbed until the clouds were skimming her cheeks like a damp kiss. She would not leave her father to face two dragons alone.

Spotting a small path that looped around the side of the mountain, Aemyra took a chance and followed it. Her feet were aching in her boots, but she dared not rest. This high up, the clouds were thick, and she squinted through the gloom.

When something crunched underfoot, she immediately drew her dagger. The quick shriek of steel was loud in the silence. Glancing down, she saw the remnants of a sheep carcass, bones bleached white from exposure.

She was close.

Overcome with the sheer enormity of her task, Aemyra sent up a prayer to Cailleach to protect her. Trying to stop her knees from trembling, she reminded herself that she wanted a better future for Lachlann. As queen, she would ensure Sorcha and the other women of Tìr Teine would be safe from oppression.

Palming her dagger, Aemyra knew she would make a better ruler than Evander. The healing slice on her arm stung as if reminding her that she had an unsettled debt with Fiorean.

To avoid the True Religion planting roots in Tìr Teine, and to help keep the people she loved safe, she would Bond herself to the most dangerous dragon in living memory and become a queen to rival Lissandrea herself.

"You can do this for them," Aemyra muttered to herself.

Solas had chosen Orlagh, not the other way around. The eggs had hatched *after* the Dùileach touched them. So Aemyra would have to become just as terrifying as the dragon she hoped to claim.

She held her dagger ready as she walked through the swirling mist. Reaching a plateau, she squinted through the clouds, trying to find another path.

Until a low growl sounded and she froze.

The mist was so thick she could barely see three feet in front of her. But she could smell dragonfire, and the rotten meat on his breath.

He was close.

The small plateau she was standing on was empty save for bleached bones and some tufts of wool caught on sharp rocks.

Before Aemyra could think about getting her back to the wall, a dark shape lunged at her from above. She saw fire flickering through teeth a split second before she leaped to the side and landed among the skeletons as The Terror's jaws closed on empty air.

He was huge. Bigger than Aervor.

Bowels cramping, Aemyra forced herself to get a grip on her courage and scrambled to her feet as the dragon hauled itself around the mountainside.

The long neck was supple as it snaked around, the fluted crests on his face making the dragon infinitely more beautiful than she would have imagined. His back legs were packed with muscle and huge chunks of rock were breaking off from the mountainside as he angled himself to attack Aemyra again.

The front legs ended in horrifically sharp claws and she held her dagger up uselessly. With no idea what else to do, she decided to announce herself.

"I am Aemyra Daercathian," she yelled, even as his dark wings eclipsed what little light there was. "I am the first female heir born to my clan in a century, and the true queen of Tìr Teine."

It quickly became apparent that The Terror had no interest in who or what she was and he lunged again.

As Aemyra scrambled across the rock face, she didn't have time to wonder why he wasn't incinerating her. Perhaps he enjoyed playing with his food first. Legs trembling as she scurried across the plateau, she almost tripped over the rib cage of a goat.

Before she could get behind a rock, the dragon's tail whipped around and the mountain in front of her exploded. Covering her face at the last moment as she was flung backward, great chunks of rock rained down upon her. Blood trickled into her right eye, and she felt something crack as she landed on the ground.

With a growl that sounded like a thunderclap, The Terror advanced again.

"Fuck, fuck, fuck . . ." Aemyra cursed under her breath as she scrambled through the bones littering the ground. Those mighty wings flapped above her, and Aemyra had never felt so small.

Gritting her teeth, she pushed herself to her knees. Giving thanks that the steep mountainside made it difficult for the large dragon to maneuver, Aemyra ran for her life.

The Terror roared into the sky and suddenly white-hot flame was pouring over the top of the rock Aemyra had ducked behind, narrowly avoiding the singeing of her hair.

Furious, she got to her feet as the dragon reeled his face back to strike again.

"I am Aemyra Daercathian," she repeated, wiping blood out of her eye. "I am the true queen."

The dragon snaked his long neck forward, and Aemyra threw herself behind the rock to avoid being snapped in two by his teeth. The Terror loosed another jet of warning flame, the stream passing over her head, her skin prickling with the warmth.

A sick smile spread across Aemyra's face. If this was how it was to end for her, then she would make it an end worth remembering. Summoning her own fire, she coated her left arm in flame and stepped out to face the mighty beathach across the plateau.

The dragon parted his lips as if getting ready to taste her, and Aemyra loosed a ferocious cry of her own before launching herself at him.

The Terror snaked down with his massive jaws spread open, but she managed to duck to the side, knees straining with the movement. Arms and legs pumping, she made it to his foreleg, where she gave a desperate running jump and tried to snag her fingers on the wing joint.

The Terror gave an enraged cry and launched himself into the sky, Aemyra's fingers closed around thin air as she went tumbling to the ground, landing hard on her side.

Completely winded, she managed to roll away just as his barbed tail slammed down into the ground where her body had been moments before.

"Brigid protect me," Aemyra gasped, desperately trying to avoid the tail attempting to sweep her off the side of the mountain. "Beira bless me."

Her muttered prayers having no effect, she managed to scramble to her feet and face the dragon once more, split eyebrow bleeding and body aching.

This was it. She was never going to be queen. She was never going to be a dragon rider.

As The Terror advanced, she noticed that his scales weren't black at all. Instead, they were the dark purple of a deep bruise. Where the sunlight caught them, close to his eyes and wings, they were almost amethyst in color.

For some reason this little thing that nobody else knew was a comfort. If only she could die knowing what those scales felt like . . .

The dragon gave a roar loud enough to shake the mountain, and Aemyra finally dropped her dagger. Not in fear but in acceptance.

When the weapon clattered to the ground, The Terror narrowed his eyes.

"You are my last hope to save Tìr Teine," she said.

Pulling the white pennant out of her pocket, Aemyra let it flutter to the ground, where she stomped it underneath her boot.

The dragon took two mighty steps forward, those front claws gouging out chunks of rock like a knife through butter, and Aemyra hoped he would make it quick.

The dragon's mouth opened to display rows of sharp teeth as long as her body.

With his face so close, something registered in Aemyra's mind. Recognition from a drawing in one of Draevan's old texts that she had pored over as a child. The illustrations had faded from where she had traced the ink with her fingers.

"Impossible," Aemyra breathed, the dragon mere inches away from her face.

The Terror's tail whipped onto the ground, cleaving four long gouges in the rock.

Four. Not six.

The double-fluted crests above those amethyst eyes were the only confirmation Aemyra needed.

"You're female," Aemyra said.

The dragon's nostrils widened as if scenting the air where she had dropped the pennant.

It wasn't possible. There were no female dragons left, everybody knew that.

But The Terror had hatched long before Queen Earie had died. Some speculated that he, *she,* was older than Kolreath himself.

Could it be possible?

Aemyra felt her heart give a lurch of hope as the dragon stared at her instead of advancing with teeth and claws.

Blinking away the blood trickling into her eye, Aemyra risked a step forward. The Terror let out one low growl but didn't move as she stretched her hand toward the snout.

The scales overlapped in a shimmering kaleidoscope of jet blacks, deep mauves, and glittering violets. Pressing her lips together in concentration, she reached out her fingers, desperate to touch the hide of a dragon for the first time.

It was the moment she had desired more than becoming queen.

After a lifetime of dreaming, Aemyra finally made contact with the warm scales. Her skin registered the heat of the dragon, the unforgiving solid hide, and she suddenly felt complete.

Then Aemyra burst into flame.

CHAPTER SIXTEEN

T HEIR BOND FORMED WITH A RUSH OF ANCIENT MAGIC AE-
myra could never have prepared herself for.

Fire skittered through her veins, the deep well of power Brigid had blessed her with expanding tenfold. The dragon's magic rushed in, pressing against Aemyra's skin until her heart tried to escape her rib cage.

Dragon and Dùileach loosed primal cries that echoed between the mountain peaks, never breaking their point of contact despite the pain.

Aemyra's body began to shake, and the obsidian dragon pressed her against the mountain as if determined to maintain their connection. The dragon's consciousness swept in behind the wildfire consuming her body and Aemyra briefly forgot who she was.

Such was the ancient beathach's power, her very soul quaked to feel the merging of their magic. For the first time understanding the enormity of what was happening.

Lost within the roaring inferno, she barely registered her lips growing chapped as she weathered the firestorm wracking her body. Pain split her skull as the pressure crested inside her, doubled thanks to the newly forged connection with another consciousness.

Aemyra clutched the obsidian scales like they were the only thing tethering her to this world, feeling the vibrations of the dragon's pain-filled growls. Panting, Aemyra tried to regain control of her body despite feeling as though the blood in her veins was being razed to cinders.

Steadily, the magic grew easier to bear and Aemyra gritted her teeth as the Bond settled. Stretched tight as a bowstring, her magic swollen and eager to be let loose, Aemyra trembled as sparks crackled at her fingertips unbidden.

The dragon's pupils were blown wide.

Now Aemyra could feel something else alongside the magic. Emotions, feelings, *memories* that didn't belong to her were surging in and overwhelming her senses. A Tìr Teine she didn't recognize, cities that had long since crumbled passing beneath her. Blood, fire, and smoke accompanied memories of such intense rage that Aemyra had to steady herself when it felt as though a pair of wings were flexing across her own back.

As the last of the fire dulled to embers within her, Aemyra finally let her hand slip from the dragon's face and she fell to her knees, weeping.

She was Bonded.

It was done.

Surprising her, the dragon let out a small whine and nudged Aemyra's cheek with her snout.

This was too much.

This was *everything*.

Aemyra gasped, pressing a hand to her chest as if she could keep it all from spilling out.

A dragon had chosen her. Had chosen *her*.

With a laugh that sounded more like a sob, Aemyra let the tears fall and wondered why Orlagh or Draevan had never told her how wonderful being Bonded was. She might never have believed them had she not experienced it herself.

Looking up at the enormous creature, she felt more insignificant than she ever had before. What did queens or kings matter in a world where dragons existed?

After a few moments, Aemyra rose unsteadily to her feet and drew level with the amethyst eye that already seemed familiar to her.

"Thank you for choosing me." The words seemed trivial, but there was nothing else to say.

The dragon let out a low rumble from deep in her throat, and Aemyra reached up to press both hands to her dragon's face. A face that was three times the size of her own body.

If it was possible to actually *hug* a dragon, she supposed that it was what she was doing as they adjusted to each other's consciousness.

"As intimidating as 'The Terror' is, I think you're going to need a new name," Aemyra eventually said with a smile, and the dragon seemed to be waiting for a suggestion.

Looking up at the magnificent creature that had somehow deemed Aemyra worthy to share her life, she took in the dark hide, the glistening scales, the elegantly fluted crest of her head and deadly spikes that littered her spine and tail.

Deciding that her dragon was quite terrifying after all, Aemyra grinned.

"Are you ready to change the world, Terrea?"

The dragon lifted her head to the sky and loosed a torrent of fire so hot that Aemyra cringed from it. Before she could blink the white spots out of her vision, Terrea bent her head and began pushing her toward the edge of the cliff.

"Uh, only one of us has wings, remember," she said hastily, tripping over a rock.

The dragon seemed incensed about something, and Aemyra tried not to panic. Swiping her dagger up off the ground and tucking it into her belt, she searched within her for the answer. The Bond was so new that their fledgling connection was overwhelming, but there was only one tangible thought coming from Terrea.

Fly.

A grin spread across Aemyra's face, and she launched herself at the dragon. Surging past the serpentine neck, Aemyra choked on a delighted sob as the dragon stretched her foreleg out. Hesitating for less than a heartbeat, she stepped onto the scaly limb lightly, using the knee and shoulder joint to rappel upward.

"This is incredible . . ." Aemyra laughed as her hands found easy purchase among the ridged scales.

Hardly daring to believe this was real, that she was Bonded to a dragon and about to experience their first flight, Aemyra settled herself into the space between Terrea's neck and back.

Tucking her feet behind the wing joint to make herself feel a little more secure, Aemyra clutched the spikes in front of her and prayed to Beira that she was going to make a better dragon rider than horsewoman.

Bonding to a dragon was one thing, riding one was another.

Terrea didn't give her a moment to consider the drop before launching herself off the edge of the mountain and into the clouds.

Aemyra's shriek was swallowed by the rush of air as she left her stomach behind. Terrea tucked her wings tightly and dove into the clouds, Aemyra's riding leathers squeaking against the hard scales underneath her.

Pressure built in her head as the dragon banked across the sky, strong updrafts stretching the thin wing membranes on either side of her. Risking a glance behind them, Aemyra watched as Terrea used her barbed tail to counteract the currents of air and keep herself balanced.

I had no idea the air moved so much . . .

Something that could only be described as a snort came through the Bond and Aemyra almost slipped from Terrea's back. She had watched Orlagh and Draevan communicate with their beathaichean but had never expected it to feel as though their minds had merged.

Terrea began climbing, wings pumping strongly, and it was a challenge for Aemyra not to be impaled by the spikes either in front of her face or at her back.

No wonder Evander had been in full armor . . .

The sky was far more unstable than Aemyra could ever have guessed, and she was suddenly grateful for all the offerings she had given to Beira over the years. But as Terrea leveled out and her wings spread wide on either side of her body, Aemyra risked a glance down.

The view of the world from above took her breath away. She could see clear across the Saiphir Sea toward the outline of Tìr Uisge. Below them, the tall pine trees of the Sunset Isle looked like blades of grass. The boats on the water nothing more than drowned ants.

"This is unbelievable," Aemyra breathed, flames she was struggling to control licking across her skin.

She had no idea she would be able to see for miles from up here. Terrea banked, turning them back toward the mountain, and Aemyra whooped aloud for the sheer joy of being alive. Happiness soaring through the Bond, Terrea loosed her own blissful roar into the sky as sparks cascaded from Aemyra onto her scales.

This was better than anything she could have imagined.

The sun was beginning to set, casting them both into shadow, and she felt tears spring to her eyes once more.

There was no undoing what had just happened between them, save death itself. Neither of them would ever be alone again. The last female dragon and Daercathian in existence. Aemyra spread her palm over the black scales of Terrea's neck, pale against the dragon's dark radiance.

"I was right. People will look to us and see hope," she whispered.

When they reached the clouds, Aemyra trailed her fingers through the swirling mist, wondering why she had always thought they were solid.

"I could stay up here forever," she said wistfully as Terrea hummed, the vibration passing through Aemyra's fingers and warming her very heart.

They flew steadily, learning each other, settling into this new partnership. There were no more battles of will, no death-defying drops to the surface of the ocean that lay a mile beneath them. They had already tested each other on the mountainside. From the moment they had embraced the Bond, there was only quiet acceptance, and an unspoken agreement to respect each other.

It was the easiest and most uncomplicated relationship Aemyra had ever experienced.

"Where are we going?" she asked, leaning forward as if Terrea might hear her better as the dragon flew higher. The air around them was growing thin, but Aemyra's magic was keeping her warm as Terrea emerged into the world above the clouds.

"Blessed Brigid . . ." Aemyra whispered.

In that moment, she decided that she would be happy to remain up here with her dragon, lost among the watercolor clouds, just a girl and a beathach who had finally found each other after years of searching for something more.

HAVING SPENT THE FIRST TWENTY-SIX YEARS OF HER LIFE WITH her feet planted firmly on the ground, watching her father take to the skies without her, Aemyra never wanted this first flight to end.

She had no idea how Evander had managed to descend from the skies above Àird Lasair so soon after bonding to Kolreath. Aemyra hadn't stopped trembling for hours, and Terrea wouldn't have allowed their separation until the Bond was solidified.

But after flying through the night, Aemyra was stiff, and the overwhelming magic had finally settled enough to land. Even if her mind did feel decidedly squashed from the new presence making room within her.

The sun was just cresting the horizon when Penryth came into view, and as the great black dragon descended toward the ground, the bells began to toll.

Seconds later, screams sounded from the village.

Terrea growled deep in her throat, but the dragon kept her jaws firmly closed in spite of the soldiers running out of their barracks, arrows nocked in their bows.

Terrea splayed her wings to slow their descent, and before the soldiers could shoot, Aemyra fashioned a flaming crown atop her head.

With how much her magic had grown, Aemyra came dangerously

close to burning her scalp, but the strands of living flame were enough to give the soldiers pause.

As Terrea lowered herself gracefully to the ground, Aemyra had to marvel at how well they were already communicating through the Bond. There were no words, no language of their own, just a simple sharing of thoughts and desires.

The gathered crowd threw their hands up in front of their faces to protect themselves from the gusts of wind that Terrea's wings were creating. When she landed, Adarian sprinted out of the caisteal with a look of utter disbelief on his face.

The stone bridge cracked under the dragon's claws, but thankfully it didn't collapse beneath her weight. Eyeing the narrow space, Aemyra realized that she now had to find a way to dismount. In front of her entire court.

Fantastic.

She sensed something from Terrea, almost like the dragon was amused by her predicament, despite being surrounded by soldiers who still clutched their weapons tightly.

With a groan as her muscles protested, Aemyra swung her right leg in front of her and had no choice but to skid down Terrea's left side. The hard scales bumped against her back as she shot down the dragon's shoulder joint and, for a moment, Aemyra thought she was going to miss the bridge entirely and go careening over the side to hit the water below. Until her boots struck the ground with an excruciatingly painful jolt.

Biting back her shout of pain, she kept the burning crown atop her head as she strode away from her dragon on aching legs.

Terrea lowered her face, lips peeling back from her teeth. The beathach made it abundantly clear that if anyone loosed an arrow, they would be incinerated.

Aemyra held her chin high as everyone in front of the caisteal bowed to her.

Trying to hide the limp Terrea had given her with the tail thrashing back on the mountain, Aemyra felt the weight of the true crown settle

on her shoulders. Claiming a dragon was about to look easy compared
to the task ahead of her.

Adarian was approaching with a look of relief on his face.

"You idiotic, arrogant *fool*," her brother said, face as red as his
growing crop of hair. "When you didn't return last night, I thought
you had died."

Exhausted and aching all over, Aemyra rolled her eyes. "How
quickly did you expect me to climb a bloody mountain?"

Spotting her split eyebrow, Adarian lifted his face, prompting Terrea to snarl warningly. "I've got a few choice words I'll use for you later,
Beastie. But right now my sister deserves a clip around the ear, queen
or not."

Aemyra felt Terrea immediately take a liking to her twin and she
pulled Adarian in for a hug.

Her brother remained rigid in her arms. "I can't lose you too."

"Has there been news of our family?" she asked, instantly on edge.

"Nothing yet, but I made an offering this morning that they are
safe." His arms crushed her against his solid chest in a fierce hug.

"Ow, careful," Aemyra gasped, her crown of flames extinguishing
in a puff of smoke. "I think Terrea broke one of my ribs."

Adarian's eyes narrowed in the dragon's direction. "*Extremely* choice
words," he threatened.

Aemyra felt Terrea practically purring down the Bond and she
whirled to face her beathach.

"When you first met me, you tried to club me to death with your
tail, but you like *him* instantly?" she asked aloud.

Terrea snorted a puff of smoke before bunching her powerful legs
underneath her body and launching herself into the sky.

Coughing and eyes watering, everyone gathered turned their faces
skyward to watch the ancient dragon take flight.

Adarian nudged her. "Right. Let's get you inside and fed."

"And into a bath," Aemyra groaned, stretching her stiff legs. The
ride on horseback had been nothing compared to her subsequent
flight through clouds and stars.

Falling into step with her, Adarian made sure no one in the crowd approached as they bowed to their queen. Aemyra disguised her limp as best she could, smiling at the sudden acceptance. Bonding herself to a dragon had won more loyalty than any temple visit would have ever done.

When the twins crossed under the portcullis, Aemyra stopped walking and huffed a laugh as her eyes fell on her father leaning against the caisteal gates, a satisfied smirk on his face.

"I should have known," she said ruefully.

Adarian looked between them. "What?"

"You knew The Terror was still alive and nesting in Beinn Deataiche this whole time?"

Making a show of examining his fingernails, Draevan was slow to respond. "I suspected. Gealach has displayed an aversion to the north side of the mountain for as long as we have been Bonded. It was the only reasonable explanation."

Adarian bristled with outrage. "Evander wants her dead for attempting a coup, the True Religion surely see her ability to resurrect the royal matriline as a threat, and yet you hoped she would go after the most bloodthirsty dragon in living memory?" Adarian asked, bristling with outrage.

Draevan shrugged. "She seems to have survived."

"There was nothing left of that village but *ash,*" Adarian ground out.

Aemyra winced as she recalled the heat of Terrea's fire.

"They are dragons," Draevan said calmly. "We cannot control the instincts of our beathaichean, but it seems The Terror did us a favor by ridding the stain of the Covenanters from these shores." Draevan pushed himself off the wall. "You should be glad that your sister's dragon has such a formidable reputation. It will make our enemies think twice before attacking."

Wishing to be rid of them both and sink into a warm bath, Aemyra swayed where she stood.

Noticing, Draevan turned on his heel. "Come with me," he said.

Urging her brother to stay put, Aemyra followed their father to his chambers.

Once through the door, he gestured to one of the leather arm-chairs before the fire. She sank into it gratefully and reached for the goblet of wine and a fresh meat pie that had evidently come straight up from the kitchens.

Too hungry to mind her manners, Aemyra took a bite that was certainly unbecoming of a queen.

"Is your Bond cemented?" Draevan asked, taking the other chair in front of the fire after the servants were dismissed and the door closed.

Aemyra slowed her chewing. "I think so. You never really explained to me what it would feel like."

Draevan leaned forward, his elbows resting on his knees. "You had to figure it out for yourself. A dragon searches within your soul before deeming you worthy of a Bond. If I had given you a plan to follow, if you hadn't been acting completely on your own instincts and emotions, the outcome could have been vastly different."

"Your arrogance almost cost me my life," she replied.

Draevan's eyes glittered. "Then may I express how glad I am that you let go of your own in time for your dragon to see beneath your swaggering insolence."

She was too tired to argue with him.

"Can you feel your dragon now?"

Closing her eyes mid-bite, Aemyra searched within her. It took a moment, but she could feel Terrea, somewhere high above. "Yes. About four miles away, flying southeast."

A triumphant grin from her father. "Good. Good. And your magic?"

Aemyra wiped her greasy lips with her sleeve. "I wouldn't recommend giving a demonstration in here if you're fond of the upholstery."

By the Goddess, her father actually laughed in response. A sound that she had never, not in twenty-six years, heard pass through his lips. Aemyra was ashamed at how proud it made her feel.

"I'm leaving tomorrow with your brother," Draevan said.

"Where to?" she managed to ask, sipping the wine. It was good. A rich, full-bodied red from Truvo, if she wasn't mistaken.

Draevan stretched. "Adarian will journey to Atholl, Maeve will take the bulk of our army to Strathaven. It shouldn't take more than two days by ship. You will remain here while the army makes camp. I journey to Àird Caolas, as I believe the chimeras need more convincing to join our cause."

"But—"

"I will not risk sending you alone to the mainland until we are certain of our allies. Laird Riya Iolairean will rally her host of phoenix warriors in the south. They will join the Balnain fleet at the mouth of the Forc within the month."

Despite her exhaustion, Aemyra bristled. "I am the queen, I will not linger here and hide while I let others risk their lives for me. I want to fight."

Draevan smiled. "There will be time enough for fighting. Conserve your strength for when it matters and use this time to get to know your dragon. How is your proficiency in the Seann?"

Aemyra rolled her eyes and replied in that language. "As fluent as ever, as you should know. You taught me yourself."

The corner of her father's mouth lifted in a smile. "Ah yes. I specifically remember the time you refused to sit down to your lessons until I had taught you how to flip your dagger."

Aemyra nestled back into the chair. "So you made me conjugate every noun three times over, if I recall. I've never been so bored."

Even as the words slipped easily from her tongue, Aemyra held back how often she had wished Draevan had acted more like a father and less like a tutor while she had been growing up. Adarian had always viewed Draevan as a secondary parent, content with the love Orlagh and Pàdraig showered on them.

While Aemyra loved her brother fiercely, she understood their father in a way most people never would. Especially his flaws.

"I suggest we keep the surprising information about your dragon between us for now. We don't need anyone attempting to use you like a broodmare."

Aemyra dropped her eyes to the worn rug. Of course her father had spotted Terrea's telltale characteristics.

The Bonding of the last female dragon and the first female Daer-cathian in a century could be interpreted as a sign from the Goddess that all was not lost.

Perhaps Lachlann's boyhood dream of having an egg to call his own was more than just a foolish hope after all. But Aemyra would be damned if she allowed someone else to make that choice for her.

An awkward silence descended on the room and Aemyra knew when she was being dismissed.

"Thank you, Father," she said, setting her goblet down and getting stiffly to her feet.

Draevan cleared his throat. "I leave at first light. We will see each other in Strathaven before the week is out."

Aemyra refused to let her limp show until she closed the door behind her.

Wincing by the time she made it to her chambers, she finally peeled off her leathers and hesitated when her eyes fell on the garnet she had discarded by the bed.

Plucking it from the bedside table as she stepped into the welcome heat of the bath, Aemyra connected to the fledgling Bond with her dragon. The ancient magic thrummed through her veins, and she knew instinctively she was now the most powerful Dùileach in Tìr Teine.

Sinking into the bath, heating it instantaneously with her new depth of power, Aemyra turned the gemstone over in her hand. Its weight steadied her.

The gem had been stolen from Fiorean in a moment of anger, but it had become a reminder that she would do whatever it took to protect her family and her people.

With those words in her mind, she sank under the water, auburn hair pooling around her like dragonfire.

CHAPTER SEVENTEEN

"AGAIN," AEMYRA PANTED, LIFTING THE SWORD SHE HAD borrowed from the Strathaven armory.

Facing off with Maeve, she watched the general wipe the sweat from her brow.

"I yield, my queen."

The camp was waking up, horses snorting and stamping their feet.

"You still need to teach me how you shot that flaming arrow," Aemyra said, crossing to the bench where they had discarded their waterskins.

Maeve grinned. "Gladly, Your Grace, although with your aim I highly doubt you will hit the target regardless of whether the arrow is flaming or not."

Allowing the insult, Aemyra drank deeply from her flask. Flying for four days around the Sunset Isle before crossing to Strathaven had solidified her Bond with Terrea. When they had rejoined her army, Aemyra felt ready to step into her role as queen.

Summoning fire to her palm, Aemyra turned back toward Maeve. "Shall we continue?"

The general looked longingly toward the breakfast tent. "Might we have some porridge first? I don't think you will see battle for a few weeks at least."

Suddenly a roar sounded above them, horses whinnying shrilly as they tried to flee the emerald dragon that had emerged from the mist.

"Famous last words," Aemyra muttered, dropping her flask back onto the bench as Draevan guided Gealach to land on the beach far below.

The dragon made a tight turn, his left wing almost clipping the cliff face as he descended to the sand.

"He's in a hurry," Maeve mused.

No sooner had a concerned look passed between them than they rushed out of camp. People were popping their heads out of their tents at the commotion and Aemyra's boots thudded on the hard ground as she raced to her father. There could be any number of reasons why he had returned with such urgency.

"If Clan Leòmhann will not support me . . ."

Maeve was shaking her head. "We'll worry about that if your father confirms it."

Aemyra jumped over tent ropes and dodged smoldering campfires with her thoughts racing. What if the chimeras had already sided with Evander? Fiorean could have been sent there as an envoy with Aervor before Draevan had arrived. Or what if Draevan had received news from Balnain—had her small fleet of ships been burned before they had even set sail?

She didn't let herself finish the thought as she hurried down the cliff path toward the beach, the heavy garnet bouncing in her pocket. Maeve was right, better to let Draevan bring her the news and then she could act accordingly.

Slipping slightly on the crumbling path, Aemyra held on to the heather sprouting out of the side of the rock to make sure she didn't tumble right over the edge.

As soon as her boots hit the sand, she was running again.

Draevan dismounted heavily from Gealach, the dragon's sides heaving as he drew in lungfuls of air through his fluted nostrils. Evidently Draevan had pushed him hard on their flight back.

Aemyra's anxieties grew.

"Father!" she called out, not caring if it was undignified for a queen to be seen racing across a beach toward a relative.

Draevan lifted his head, already pulling off his leather gloves, his auburn hair escaping its knot.

"What is it? What's happened?" Aemyra asked, skidding to a stop. He had been gone for just over a week, what could possibly have gone wrong in that time?

Draevan approached her carefully, like she was a horse that might spook, before nodding a greeting to his most trusted general.

Aemyra knew the look of grief that was etched onto her father's face. Something was very wrong.

"What happened?" she repeated. "Did Clan Leòmhann not agree to support my claim? Will the west fight for Evander?"

Wanting to strangle the news out of her father, Aemyra waited with her heart in her mouth as Gealach yawned, his massive jaw parting to reveal the fire that lurked at the back of his throat.

Maeve spoke when the silence stretched. "Laird Camryn has been cooperating nicely. Strathaven has an excellent armory, *and* a well-stocked granary—"

"My news concerns your younger brother, Lachlann," Draevan interrupted, as if he had finally found the strength to say it. "And your adoptive parents."

White-hot fear stabbed through Aemyra's gut.

"I received a messenger swyft this morning with the news that they have been killed."

Aemyra couldn't breathe. Her lungs closed up, and she made a choking sound that caused Maeve to hurry to her side. Shaking her head as if she could banish the words from her ears, Aemyra pushed the woman away.

No. Not Lachlann. He couldn't be gone. They couldn't be.

A world without her baby brother was unthinkable. Aemyra had wanted to change the world for him, had even begun hoping he might one day Bond to a dragon of his own.

"No. No, it can't be true."

Her path forward suddenly grew hazy, the weight of grief on her soul shaking the very foundation of her beliefs. Lachlann had been delivered into her arms, she had cut the cord tying him to Orlagh and . . .

Orlagh.

A keening sound made its way up her throat before she could stop it. This grief was too much. Losing one of them would have been impossible to bear, but losing all three?

Aemyra staggered as the beach spun and she blinked to clear her vision. She growled at Draevan.

"Who?"

Her father's eyes were haunted. Straightening himself, he drew a deep breath in through his nose.

"Evander ordered a sweep of the city to find anyone with ties to you. Athair Alfred, the leader of the Chosen and Katherine's closest companion, sent fifty Covenanters out to assist the city guards. They found your family as they tried to escape. The three of them were taken into custody and when they refused to give information, Prince Fiorean gave the order for his dragon to execute them in the caisteal courtyard."

Aemyra became aware that someone was screaming. Screaming so loudly that Gealach roared in protest and took flight.

It wasn't until she felt Maeve's arms restraining her that Aemyra became aware the noise was coming from her.

"Let me go!" she yelled, trying to claw her way out of the general's grip.

Maeve, while strong, was no match for Aemyra's magic as it exploded out of her. Maeve leaped backward to avoid being burned as the rage and grief poured out of Aemyra in great tongues of flame. The few longboats that had been hauled up onto the beach were incinerated, the crimson and gold banners staked into the ground turned to ash within seconds. The golden dragons of the Daercathian clan's crest melted like they didn't matter anymore.

Because they didn't. Her baby brother was dead. Pàdraig and Or—

Terrea's roar could be heard above the camp as the beathach felt her pain. Aemyra wasn't sure if it was a human scream coming from her mouth or a dragon's roar as she felt embers choking in her throat.

"You *promised* me," she roared at her father.

Shaking with the effort of bringing her magic back under control, she launched herself toward the cliff path. She didn't make it two steps before Draevan pulled her back, trapping her arms to her sides in a viselike grip. Her father's own magic shielding him from hers.

"Let go of me! I will kill him. I will make Fiorean pay for this!" Aemyra screamed, struggling against her father's grip as stinging tears flooded her eyes. "I have Terrea. I have the biggest chance of killing him. Let me go!"

Draevan said nothing and continued to hold her until she had struggled herself into exhaustion, cinders drifting across the beach like dark snow.

Her flames finally winking out, the air thick with smoke, Aemyra collapsed against her father.

"It's my fault. I should have killed Fiorean when I had the chance. If I hadn't shown him mercy when we escaped, they would still be alive."

The words came out between wracking sobs, and her father held her in his embrace without contradicting her.

Because Draevan agreed.

The weight of the garnet she carried in her pocket felt unbearable.

"I will avenge my family. You cannot stop me," Aemyra swore, her voice thick with tears.

Draevan finally released her and sat back heavily on the ground as if he didn't have the energy to stand.

"We will get revenge by reclaiming your throne," Draevan said, his words low and threatening.

Maeve was staring down at Draevan, waiting for his next order.

"We move our forces south at first light the day after tomorrow,"

Draevan said, his voice dripping with poison and his eyes far away. "We join with Adarian at Atholl and march onward to the northern Forc, where the Balnain fleet lies in wait."

Aemyra blinked away her tears and remembered that she was supposed to be the queen. She needed to be stronger than this. She had to learn how to bear this grief before she broke the news to her twin.

Blessed Brigid, how could she tell Adarian?

"The river lords stand with the queen the Goddess chose. As you can see from our camp, Strathaven is mobilizing as we speak," Maeve reported.

Screwing up her eyes, Aemyra stood.

Praying to all of the Goddesses that Adarian would not blame her for the death of their loved ones, she could see only one way to absolve herself.

Draevan was already lost in his plans. "I will leave you alone this evening. There is much I must discuss with Laird Camryn before we depart."

Her fury giving way to an exhaustion so complete, it was an effort for Aemyra to even make it to the top of the cliff path, never mind into the lavishly furnished rooms that Laird Camryn had provided for her in Caisteal Stratha.

Finally reaching them, she collapsed on top of her bedcovers. She lay there smothered in grief, her leathers still on, pillow growing damp beneath her face as the day wore on. As the soldiers outside the caisteal walls prepared for war, Aemyra hardened her heart for vengeance.

CREEPING SILENTLY OUT OF HER ROOM, AEMYRA WOUND THROUGH the airy corridors, the smell of the sea blowing in through the open windows.

Aemyra cursed the poorly oiled hinges of the door that led to the room her council had commandeered.

Igniting a small flame at her fingertip, Aemyra slipped inside. Scanning the disordered spread of maps, several chairs, and candle stubs, her eyes fell on the desk beside the window. Aemyra rifled through every swyft correspondence that had reached them here in Strathaven until she found what she was looking for.

Reading by the light of her own flame, Aemyra hardened her heart when she realized how much her father had kept from her.

He knew exactly where Fiorean was.

None of the guards stopped Aemyra as she left, heading for the cliffs where Terrea and Gealach had made their nests. Her father's dragon was snoring softly, resting after his long flight from Àird Caolas. The she-dragon was awake and waiting for her Dùileach.

Her crested head resting on dark claws, Terrea sent a multitude of thoughts and feelings down the Bond. There was sadness of course, a touch of confusion, and an overwhelming amount of empathy. Enough to make Aemyra wonder what her dragon had endured throughout her long life.

Aemyra reached up to stroke the softer scales between Terrea's jaw and neck, marveling at the fact that she was able to get so close to such a mighty creature. Her heart gave a painful thump as she realized Lachlann would never get to meet her beathach.

Squeezing her eyes shut before the tears could overwhelm her, Aemyra pressed her forehead to Terrea's cheek.

"I have to do this," she whispered. "I have to be the kind of queen who won't let senseless violence stand."

Terrea agreed with a low growl, getting to her feet. No sooner was the dragon up than Aemyra was hoisting herself onto her broad back.

Gealach didn't stir as Terrea drifted from the cliff top on whisper-soft wings, the two of them soaring east, in search of the person who had dared harm those dear to a queen.

Chapter Eighteen

THE FLIGHT HAD TAKEN THE REST OF THE NIGHT, AND THE EN-
tirety of the next day.

The Blackridge Mountains, marking the border between Tìr Teine
and the cursed Tìr Sgàile, loomed miles ahead. As Terrea's night-dark
scales rippled in the moonlight, Aemyra considered the fact that she
would never see what lay beyond the mountains now that she was
Bonded.

It did not matter. Her priority was Tìr Teine, and the safety of her
people. For that reason, Fiorean and Evander had to be stopped.

As Terrea's dark wings bore them silently through the sky toward
Fiorean's last known location, Aemyra hoped they wouldn't run into
Aervor. Despite the cobalt dragon being younger than Terrea, with a
good fifty years of growing to do before he caught up with the other
male dragons, he had been Bonded to Fiorean for more than a decade.

Terrea was ferocious, that much was without doubt, but Aemyra
wasn't ready to do battle on her back. A fight between dragons was
deadly to all who participated. The Battle of the Five Brothers in 1833
had proven as much.

With a nervous swallow, Aemyra sincerely hoped it wouldn't come to that. She had inherited her father's ability to scheme and had grown up with a commoner's knack for observation.

Aemyra had an entirely different plan.

Several hours later, the moon filtered down through bare tree branches to dapple the forest floor. Having bid Terrea remain airborne, Aemyra had resigned herself to a long walk.

With no idea how to track a person through the tangle of trees, nor the ability to hunt for her supper, she pricked up her ears and gathered her wits. Hiking deeper into the forest, she decided to use the skills she did possess to find the inn Fiorean had been sighted at.

Aemyra headed out of the tangle of trees toward the dirt path that snaked through the Silent Forest, deciding to lurk in the shadows and see what she could overhear from travelers passing through.

Fiorean wasn't exactly an inconspicuous character, with his tall frame and auburn hair. If he was nearby, someone would have seen him.

Realizing the same could be said about herself, Aemyra turned her cloak inside out so that the plainer side was visible and scooped up some mud from the ground, smearing it on her cheeks and around her hairline. Then she pulled up her hood.

Hearing the creaking of wheels on the road, Aemyra slipped behind a tree and fell silent. There were men talking in loud voices, clearly not afraid of being overheard. Chancing a glance around the thick trunk, she saw a wagon driven by a portly man, three others lounging in the cart behind him. They all seemed mildly inebriated.

"Just up ahead, lads," the driver said with a sigh.

The inn.

Pulling her cloak around her, she followed the wagon from the tree line until a pleasant-looking building with clean windows emerged in a clearing. The inside seemed cozy and inviting and Aemyra's stomach growled. What she wouldn't give for a mug of ale and one of Sorcha's hot pies.

None of Draevan's correspondence had said a word about her former lover, and Aemyra prayed that Sorcha was still alive.

As the men disappeared through the open door, Aemyra resigned herself to a long wait.

After an hour spent freezing her toes off, she hadn't heard anything of note and was cursing every Daercathian who called Àird Lasair home.

"That great bloody dragon . . ."

The words washed over Aemyra, jolting her out of a stupor, and she snapped her head up in the direction of the voice. It was a young man. Slim, but tall. She couldn't make out what clan tartan he was wearing.

"Aye, saw it yesterday when we came back from hunting. Damn near gave us a heart attack. Then that prince was trying to encourage us to give up the boar we'd caught to feed his dragon. Not like we ain't starving or nothing." He belched softly. "Bloody royals think because they have magic, they're entitled to everything. The more I hear those priests talk, the more sense they make."

Aemyra's eyes narrowed. A prince and a dragon deep within the Silent Forest made no sense.

Unless . . .

The Covenanters.

The main trade route through the Blackridge Mountains toward Tìr Ùir passed directly through the Silent Forest. Fiorean was either trying to control trade to other territories, or swell the ranks of Evander's army with the militia of the True Religion.

Borrowed sword heavy across her back, Aemyra prayed Fiorean was indeed inside. He would pay for his affront to the Goddesses, and for what he had done to her family, with his life.

She waited until the hunter had wandered off to take a piss in the trees before she made her move.

"Who the fuck is——" he started to say, one hand clutching his limp dick. But he fell silent when he saw her face under the hood.

"Well, it's a bit small right now, love, but give it a minute in your warm hands and it'll soon do the job," he said, licking his lips.

Aemyra felt her gorge rise. No wonder this man loved the Chosen if this was how he viewed women. She looked at his face. "I heard you talking about the Daercathian prince. Is he inside?"

Finished pissing, he began working his cock in one hand and pursing his lips at her. "I'll tell you if you give me a kiss."

Aemyra's lip curled in revulsion.

As he stumbled toward her, she grasped her dagger and moved it so swiftly that the man didn't notice until the cold steel was touching his stiffening penis.

"You have one more chance to answer me before your favorite appendage becomes a snack for the wolves. Where is Prince Fiorean?" she asked firmly.

The man began shaking, cock rapidly shriveling in his hand.

"He's inside!" the hunter whispered hoarsely. "He pulled us from the mud when our horses threw us off and brought us up to the inn. He has a room at the top of the stairs."

Aemyra's chest contracted painfully. Fiorean had been here the whole time.

"Thank you. You have been most helpful," she muttered, letting her dagger drop from what was now just his fist, his cock having retreated in fear. Not wanting him to run off and warn anyone of her presence, Aemyra struck him once on the temple with the pommel of her dagger, and he sank to the hard ground with a muffled thump.

Hoping that anyone who stumbled across him would assume he was just drunk, Aemyra moved into the shadows.

Her heart was pounding, and she tried not to think about her baby brother lest she lose control of her magic. She was so close to her vengeance.

She crouched down behind a fallen tree trunk and tried to glimpse Fiorean through the candlelit windows. The inn seemed crowded at this late hour, but she'd easily spot his auburn hair. Her father's words rattled against her skull.

Prince Fiorean gave the order for his dragon to execute them in the caisteal courtyard.

Had her little brother known that death awaited him? Had Fiorean taunted her parents before commanding his dragon to burn them alive?

Fire Dùileach were no strangers to burns, but even the strongest magical shields could not protect them from dragonfire. Aemyra screwed her eyes shut against the grief and knew this was where her war would truly begin.

The door of the inn opened.

A hooded figure strode from the entrance, his silhouette illuminated by the roaring fire inside. She couldn't make out any of his features, but she recognized his walk from when he had visited the forge.

It was Fiorean.

Adrenaline surging in her veins, she made to follow him at a distance, doing everything she could not to accidentally step on a twig or bramble.

This was better than she could have hoped for. She had him alone and without Aervor.

He was walking swiftly into the forest with the stride of a man who had nothing to fear.

Tonight, she would make sure he feared her before he died.

Aemyra lurked behind the trees, the forest around them peppered with shards of moonlight as she watched his cloak billow with his momentum.

"Stop skulking in the woods, Princess. It is unseemly," he drawled.

Fucking Hela.

Heart pounding against her rib cage, she stepped out onto the soggy path. Fiorean did not turn.

She could try throwing her dagger and hope that it embedded itself in the meaty part of his back. It was unlikely, her throwing arm frequently went wide.

Fiorean turned slowly, his face moon-pale beneath his hood.

Dropping the pretenses, Aemyra pulled her own hood off and unbuttoned her cloak. She didn't want it getting in the way of her sword.

Fiorean had the gall to smirk. "You can keep your clothes on, Princess. Unlike my brother, I am a gentleman."

Her temper sparked. There was nothing gentlemanly about this prince who had taken her family from her.

"Last time I took your jewel, but tonight I will take your tongue," she seethed, holding up the garnet between her thumb and forefinger.

Fiorean cocked his head. "I see that you have been loath to part with me."

"It has been serving as a reminder," she spat.

"Of what? My good looks?"

"Of your murderous inclinations. Of the fact that I failed my family when I showed you mercy."

Fiorean stepped toward her lazily, hands still clasped behind his back. Each stride full of purposeful intent. Aemyra held her ground.

"How is dear Draevan? I do hope that he isn't too fragile after the unraveling of all his carefully laid plans. I am sure your father is despairing at having sired such a pathetic daughter who couldn't even hold on to her crown for a day."

Aemyra drew her sword, wishing it was the magic-forged weapon she had been forced to part with the day she had fled Àird Lasair.

Fiorean continued advancing, his left hand caressing a dagger strapped around his narrow hips.

"Does your twin blame you? I would, if it were me. Forced to play prince because his big sister didn't know her place in the world. Perhaps you will lose him next."

Having heard enough, Aemyra swung first. Fiorean ducked as she parried and then ducked again. He dodged her blade no matter where she swung it, his hands still empty.

"Fight me, you coward," she spat at him, bristling with anger.

"Are you sure you are ready for that, Princess?" he taunted, opening his cloak and palming the scabbard of a new sword.

Aemyra rocked on the balls of her feet. "No embellishments on this one. You're learning," she said, eyeing the plain hilt. "I beat you once. And this time I won't show you mercy."

Fiorean's eyes gleamed. "No magic?"

Aemyra shook her head, despite the flames crackling in her throat. "I want to see the light leave your eyes."

Fiorean drew his sword so quickly that she barely had time to brace for the attack. With the darkness still thick around them, Aemyra had hoped he would be at more of a disadvantage. To her surprise, he seemed to prefer the shadows.

Bracing for each ruthless assault, her muscles screamed as she circled him to get her breath back, his sword pointed toward her chest.

"You should have finished it when you had the chance. I won't let you get that close again," Fiorean promised.

Bending her knees, Aemyra aimed low, but Fiorean was ready, blocking the blow and aiming a punch with his other hand that landed on her cheek. Reeling, she stumbled backward, barely getting her sword up in time to block his next swing.

He was unyielding, and even though she knew he was tiring her out, she was powerless to do anything but defend against his every move. Her legs began to tremble and she unsheathed her dagger, attempting to use her sword to swing and her dagger to thrust. But each time he danced out of the way like he had endless reserves of energy, auburn hair flying around him like a curtain of blood.

Aemyra's breath was coming in great gasps and her arms felt like lead, but still she fought.

"You are the reason people have begun dying. This territory was at peace, and now you have started a war," he said venomously.

The words hit Aemyra like a punch in the gut as he struck her forearm with the pommel of his sword, her fingers releasing the dagger unwillingly.

Forgetting her earlier promise, Aemyra threw tongues of fire toward him, planting her feet in the dirt and letting them snake around his body. She had hoped that her fire would trap him, leaving him open to attack, but she hesitated when Fiorean simply extended his hands and stepped through it.

His shields were powerful enough to withstand even her amplified magic.

Gritting her teeth, she pulled more fire from that great well of power that lurked inside of her, careful not to take any from Terrea and give away her best advantage. Aemyra was forced to duck and then roll across the dirt again to avoid Fiorean's whip of fire that almost lashed around her ankle.

"You might have considerable power," Fiorean drawled, "but you do not yet understand how to use it."

His words made Aemyra furious. Orlagh and Pàdraig had taught her everything she needed to know about her magic. She might have been forced to keep the extent of it a secret, but using her fire felt as natural to her as breathing.

Throwing a cascade of golden flames from her palms, she cursed when Fiorean dodged them. Before she could react, thick smoke began billowing toward her. His long fingers guided the inky darkness, emerald eyes shadowed.

Sending forth bursts of flame did no good. The smoke parted but did not slow its advance, and Aemyra took several steps backward, heart racing. She could no longer see Fiorean.

Terrea's frightened roar echoed in her mind and Aemyra mentally slammed their connection closed. If Aervor was close by, Aemyra wanted Terrea out of harm's way.

Tightening her grip on the sword, flames crackling between the fingers of her other hand, she braced herself.

Smoke engulfed her, setting her eyes streaming and her throat tightening until white spots burst in front of her eyes. Aemyra's fire died out completely as she fought for breath, automatically crouching lower, seeking out any clear air she could find.

The smoke parted, moonlight gilding the trees around them and illuminating the black armor of the men who now surrounded her.

Covenanters.

Fiorean's smile did not reach his eyes as he stared down at her. "For one who proclaims to be queen, you are rather naïve."

Clawing at the dirt as the smoke choked down her throat, Aemyra cursed her own stupidity. Her father hadn't been keeping vital information about Fiorean's location from her. He had known it was a trap all along.

Smoke licked across Fiorean's shoulders as he crouched before her.

"I thought we might trap a general, or even a prince. Lucky me to have snared the false queen so easily."

Suddenly Aemyra's sword was kicked out of her grip, and she found herself flat on the ground. Eyes burning, she blinked furiously as Fiorean flipped her onto her back.

"Murderer," she hissed through her teeth as she thrust her hands upward to wrap around his neck. Without flinching, he grasped both of her wrists in one hand.

"There's no one to help you now," Fiorean whispered against her skin, his lips grazing her cheek. "I wonder how the pariah prince will react when he hears of his daughter's demise. Perhaps he will finally give up on his quest for control of this territory and concede defeat before more blood has to be spilled."

"Never," Aemyra managed to choke out.

Fiorean loomed over her, dark smoke casting the angles of his face into sharp relief.

"It seems I will have to find another way to torment him, then."

Fiorean slammed Aemyra's head back into the ground and the world went black.

CHAPTER NINETEEN

WHEN AEMYRA WOKE, SHE WAS IN A FEATHER BED AND THE pale light shining through the window told her it was sunrise.

Her head was pounding, and there was an odd taste in her mouth. Someone had bathed her and she was lying under the sheets in nothing more than a white slip. Pulling back the covers, she padded across the cold floor and stood in front of the window.

An azure sky stretched over Loch Lorna to the horizon, and although Aemyra gripped the windowpane for support, she didn't feel dizzy. Àird Lasair sprawled in front of her, chipped roof tiles bathed in the weak winter sunlight. She had never seen the city from this angle before.

Everything came flooding back.

Terrea, Lachlann, Orlagh, Pàdraig, Kenna . . .

Aemyra felt like she couldn't breathe.

Fiorean had kidnapped her and brought her back to Caisteal Lasair—for what? She had a vague memory of a dark cell, and the dungeons made more sense for a prisoner than the feather bed she had just vacated.

How long had she been unconscious for? Where was her dragon? Why couldn't she feel the Bond between them? Did her father even know she had been captured?

Aemyra spun from the window to look around the room. She was an idiot. What had she been thinking, running off to seek vengeance alone? She was supposed to be leading her army to overthrow this very city and now she was on the wrong side of the walls.

She hurriedly sought out a chamber pot, her bladder confirming she had been unconscious for far too long.

Running her fingers over her wrists, Aemyra gave thanks to Brigid that she wasn't in chains—although she vaguely remembered that she had been.

Why hadn't they killed her yet? Were they waiting to make her execution a public spectacle?

She wrapped one hand around her throat, anticipating how it would feel when an axe sliced through her flesh, separating her head from her shoulders. Perhaps Fiorean would burn her with his dragon too. Surely Evander would see it as justice for her treason.

She had to escape before that happened.

Draevan still had spies within these walls. If Aemyra could find one, they would surely help her.

Fiorean's location had been a trap. Her family had been executed and she had delivered herself to the enemy as a result of her own recklessness.

Before she could dress herself and make her escape, the doors to her chamber opened and Katherine strode in.

Aemyra froze, her head giving a painful throb.

"Don't worry. I am with Athair Alfred," the dowager queen said.

Aemyra refrained from commenting that the presence of the man responsible for polluting Tìr Teine with the word of the Savior only made her more uncomfortable.

Katherine gestured to the tray of food a servant had evidently brought earlier. "You must regain your strength. Please eat."

Aemyra didn't move.

"It isn't poisoned." Katherine sighed, heels clicking delicately on the floor.

Still, Aemyra refused to move, keeping one eye on the priest, who hovered in the corner of the room. His graying beard made his bald pate more severe as he surveyed Aemyra with extreme distaste.

The feeling was mutual.

Katherine sat in the delicate chair beside the table and pulled a stem of grapes toward her.

"How long have I been unconscious?" Aemyra asked, her voice dry from lack of use.

"Almost three days," Katherine commented. "That was quite a nasty blow to the head my son inflicted upon you. Combined with your night spent in the cells—well, I suppose we can all be glad that you survived it."

Aemyra frowned. "Why would you be glad that I survived anything?"

Katherine regarded her with those unsettling eyes. Like a doe. Aemyra knew what lurked behind them was as dark as Alfred's robes.

"Sir Nairn had you escorted to the dungeons on King Evander's orders, not mine. It is I who have seen you settled into rooms more appropriate to your station," Katherine said.

"You are a good deal too merciful, Your Grace," Athair Alfred interrupted, a disconcerting edge to his voice. "We had already come to an agreement about the princess's lodgings."

Aemyra remembered waking briefly in a cold, dank cell. Nausea roiled in her gut as she looked toward the priest who had wanted to leave her there.

"A few weeks ago, you tried to have me murdered in the temple. Why have you brought me back here?" Aemyra eyed the tray. "To fatten me up like a pig for slaughter? I am the *queen.*"

Katherine's eyes narrowed. "Are you?"

Between the pain in her head and Katherine's simpering, Aemyra's temper snapped. She summoned her magic and thrust her hand out toward the dowager queen.

Nothing happened.

Panic clawed its way through Aemyra's chest as Alfred smiled.

Reflecting inward, searching for the magic that had been part of her since birth, Aemyra felt nothing but a hollowness in her chest. No matter how she searched, she could not summon even one stray ember. It was why the Bond to her dragon was gone. Muted in a way that had nothing to do with distance.

A choked sound left her throat as she clawed at her own chest.

"What did you do?" Aemyra cried, looking between Alfred and Katherine.

Without a single hair out of place, the collar of her mourning gown buttoned up to her neck, Katherine slipped an empty vial out of her pocket.

"Ensured the safety of those residing within these walls. Quite the tonic the Chosen have managed to brew after their experiments in Tìr Uisge. I have Athair Alfred to thank for suggesting we administer it to you," Katherine said.

Aemyra had to hold on to the bedpost in order to stop herself from falling over. They had slipped something into her while she had been asleep, and it had taken away her magic.

"And you preach purity and honor," Aemyra spat.

Katherine shrugged, slipping the vial back into the folds of her dress. "You tried to usurp my son. I did what was necessary."

Aemyra felt suffocated in her own body. She had never before felt so weak, so vulnerable. She had always known that should one of her weapons fail, her fire would save her. She had defined herself by her gifts for her whole life.

She was powerful, she was blessed, she was . . .

Nothing.

Without her magic she was completely ordinary. Without her dragon . . .

Thoughts of Terrea interrupted everything else, and Aemyra hastily tried to discern if Katherine or Alfred knew she was Bonded. Sitting down heavily on the end of the bed before her knees gave out,

Aemyra endured the panic rushing through her bloodstream and willed herself to *think*.

She hadn't used the full extent of her fire to fight Fiorean, nor had she been able to summon any before they had slipped this magic-binding agent down her throat.

The sole thought that Terrea was safe was enough to keep her silent. It was a minor miracle her dragon hadn't burned the city down to find her.

Katherine smiled smugly, and Aemyra was content to let the dowager queen believe she had the upper hand. So she stared down at her flameless palms, avoiding eye contact.

If she hoped to make it out of Àird Lasair alive, and as queen, then she would have to beat Katherine and the leader of the Chosen at whatever game they were playing.

But first she needed to know where the pieces were.

Katherine lifted her eyes from the grapes she was plucking. "How did *you* come to be in Leuthanach lands? Last reports placed you somewhere along the northern coast."

Lying smoothly, Aemyra replied, "I accompanied my father and Gealach on a scouting mission. I slipped away from him in search of Prince Fiorean after the news of what he had done to my family reached us."

Alfred glared at her like he could sense the lie and strode closer to where Katherine sat, looming over her slight frame like a malevolent shadow. Alfred had been as much a part of Haedren's marriage negotiations as Katherine had been. No doubt the king had thought one Chosen priest in Tìr Teine a small price to pay for the support of the Ùir armada.

Aemyra wondered how deep-rooted their loyalty to each other was. From the look of things, Katherine was about as devoted to Alfred as Maeve was to Draevan.

Reverently, Katherine touched her Savior's pendant, where it rested against her lace-covered clavicle. "I desire to end this war before it even begins. You are your father's daughter and are a rightful

Princess of Penryth. No one will deny that. However, my son has been crowned king and all who reside in Àird Lasair have sworn fealty to him. Accept this and no more blood need be shed."

Katherine's eyes flickered toward Athair Alfred, some unreadable expression lurking in the depths of those eyes.

Aemyra knew that her father would be furious. Waking up to find her gone, and then Terrea returning without her? If Evander didn't order her execution, her father and brother would likely be lining up to do the honors themselves.

"Your sons seem to enjoy spilling the blood of innocents," Aemyra spat.

Nails digging into her palms, Aemyra willed herself not to fall to pieces in front of these two savages and wished she had access to her magic. She had been captured, and had failed to avenge her family. Failed to bring her baby brother's killer to justice.

As if reading Aemyra's thoughts, Katherine smoothed her dark dress.

"I suggest you eat. You will need your strength for what is to come."

Aemyra couldn't tell if Katherine's words sounded like a warning or a threat. The priest was looking at her like she needed to be punished, and yet Aemyra couldn't bring herself to cower before him.

"Why? So I can walk myself to the executioner's block?" she asked.

Katherine turned, one hand on the doorknob. "There will be no need to slaughter you. You are much more valuable to us alive."

Chapter Twenty

"Cleanse her soul. Withdraw the demons that possess her."

Aemyra struggled against the three men who were holding her down while Athair Alfred prayed over her.

After starving herself all day, Aemyra had discovered that the binding agent required regular administration to remain effective. Alfred had turned up at her door with Sir Nairn in tow before she could feel the first sparking ember return to her.

The captain had snapped his fingers at two Covenanters twice Aemyra's size and had them wrestle her to the floor. They had forced the binding agent between her lips until she choked, and held her down while Alfred read increasingly sanctimonious passages from the Tùr, the Savior's book.

"Grant protection against the wickedness and snares of evil. May the Savior intervene, we humbly pray, and thrust beyond the veil all evil spirits that possess the Dùileach and wander this world to the ruin of souls."

Aemyra bucked against the Covenanters' hold. She writhed as if the demons Alfred preached about really were possessing her.

"I drank the damned potion, will you stop your incessant chanting?" Aemyra cried.

Alfred glared down at her.

It was Sir Nairn who spoke. "Perhaps she would benefit from a few more days without food, Athair. She seems altogether too spirited."

Aemyra turned her attention to the captain, his light eyes narrowed with disgust from where he lurked near the door.

"Says the man charged with the protection of this city," Aemyra drawled. "You should see me with my magic, you'd really hate me then."

Struggling anew, Aemyra managed to wrench her arm out of the grip of one Covenanter and she reached up to try and strangle him with his pendant.

As her fingers wrapped around the metal, she hissed between her teeth and dropped it, her skin scalded by the metal.

She had thought it a rumor after Pàdraig had dismissed it as nonsense. But apparently the Savior's pendants could indeed repel magical touch.

The Covenanter looked like he wanted to spit in her eye for touching it, but the door opened, interrupting Alfred's droning prayers.

"Thank Brigid, I thought Big Al would never shut up," Aemyra said before she saw who had entered the room.

Katherine's calculating gaze fell on the Covenanters restraining Aemyra and she straightened the rigid set of her shoulders.

"The king requests the presence of the princess," Katherine said.

Aemyra stilled. "On second thought, I think Al was just getting to the good part."

Ignoring her quip, Katherine nodded to Athair Alfred, remaining where she stood with her hands clasped calmly atop her full skirts until Aemyra was released.

Glaring at them all, she got unsteadily to her feet, her empty stomach protesting even this small effort.

The dowager queen sighed. "Someone get the princess some water. I need her capable of walking on her own two feet."

The Covenanter looked to Alfred for permission, and she watched him nod stiffly. Narrowing her eyes as a cup was pressed into her hand, Aemyra wondered why they refused to take orders from Katherine directly.

No doubt it was due to her lack of male genitalia.

Her mouth dry, Aemyra hesitated before raising the cup of water to her parched lips as Katherine turned on her heel and strode off down the corridor.

Alfred snapped the Tùr closed and tucked the heavy book against his potbelly.

"It isn't poisoned," he said, clearly put out that he hadn't had time to finish his purification of Aemyra's soul.

"Shame," she replied, draining the stale water in one long draft. "A couple more passages and I would have drunk nightshade willingly."

Alfred gestured to Sir Nairn, silently giving him instructions, and Aemyra found herself pushed roughly from the room. She had to work to stop herself from falling flat on her face.

After days with no food and minimal water, Aemyra was struggling. But she would be damned if she would show weakness to these people. She had gotten herself into this situation, she owed it to her father, and those fighting in her army, to get herself out.

Pulling her arm away before Sir Nairn could grab on to her, she walked down the corridors with a heavy heart.

Closing her eyes and offering up a quick prayer to Brigid that she could find a way out of this mess, she smoothed the dark blue dress she was wearing and squared her shoulders.

The moment she got her hands on a weapon she would slaughter them all. Starting with Fiorean, and then Athair Alfred. She hadn't missed the triumphant gleam in his eyes when she had been restrained before him.

Meanwhile, Aemyra walked as meekly as she could through the caisteal, eyes darting left and right for clues or information she might be able to use. Three servants passed her, all of them avoiding eye contact.

That was a blow. She wouldn't be able to get a message to Draevan's spies without help. Aemyra tried to sharpen her wits as she deftly braided her messy curls to get them out of her face, her head throbbing. The sudden assault of the priests had shaken her more than she was willing to admit.

No matter what Evander had summoned her for, she needed to be thinking clearly. She wouldn't be able to fight her way out of whatever was awaiting her. No, she needed to wage war with her words and hope she made it out alive.

Sir Nairn herded her to a small receiving room, and Aemyra had to give thanks to Cailleach that she had not been forced to see Evander sitting atop her throne.

Nairn pushed the door open. "The Princess Aemyra, Your Grace," he announced, stepping to the side.

Evander was glaring at her from where he sat on a raised dais. Fiorean was on his right, Katherine beside him. Evander's wife, Charlotte, sat to his left. Even in his private chambers, Evander was wearing King Vander's crown, and she could see the hilt of the first king's sword resting against his leg.

But it was what was lying on a litter between Aemyra and the royal family that threatened to make her knees give out.

Evander's wife, Charlotte, was sitting rigidly, looking like she didn't even realize what room she was in.

Stomach roiling, Aemyra's eyes flicked traitorously downward to look again upon the small body of Prince Fergys. It hadn't been wrapped, and she could see the sores around his mouth were weeping pus.

Aemyra clapped one hand over her mouth lest she actually be sick.

Fiorean's eyes rose to meet hers as she did so, his expression unreadable.

"Look at my son," Evander commanded, his voice sounding years older than it had only weeks ago when she had last seen him, a touch of hysteria lacing the words.

Aemyra did what she was told, her whole body beginning to shake.

Fergys looked so small atop the litter in the middle of the room, and Aemyra suddenly wondered if Lachlann had too. Or if her brother's corpse had been unrecognizable after the burning.

The thought hardened Aemyra and her tears dried before they could fall.

Fergys must still be wearing the clothes he had died in. They were stained red with more blood than Aemyra could have imagined a small body held. His chin was smeared with it, the skin of his hands marked with pustules that had begun to fester.

Narrowing her eyes, she took a half step forward to examine the body.

Evander stood from his throne, sword in his left hand. "This is what you did to my son," he said, his voice laced with venom.

Completely wrong-footed, Aemyra's jaw dropped.

"What?"

Evander's features hardened. "The night you declared yourself queen, my eldest son began to sicken with this disgusting ailment. When my brother brought you into this caisteal three days ago, Fergys succumbed to it."

Raising her eyes carefully from the small body, Aemyra replied, "And what, may I ask, do you think my role was in this?"

Fiorean's emerald eyes darted between her and his brother.

Evander took one step toward her, but she held her ground.

"Waiting until we were distracted by our father's death, you snuck into this caisteal and poisoned our children before seeking refuge in the temple," he said. "Hamysh and Edwyn still hover on the brink of death."

The outlandishly far-fetched claim had Aemyra's eyes narrowing, and she glanced toward Katherine. Perhaps it wasn't only the dowager queen's words that dripped poison.

If someone was trying to frame her, she would need to tread carefully.

"At what point between revealing myself in the temple and you sending the city guards to slaughter us in our beds was I supposed to have gained access to the royal nursery?" she asked.

Evander's green eyes flashed, but Aemyra did not balk.

"If you want to know what a murderer looks like, turn to your right," Aemyra hissed.

Fiorean's knuckles whitened against the arms of his chair, but he sat as if frozen, his eyes trained on Evander's back.

"You lived in this city under our noses for *years*. Who knows what secrets you keep," Evander spat.

"I lived in this city as a *healer*. Together with my mother, we *helped* people." Aemyra lowered her voice when Charlotte cringed away from the noise.

Evander seemed not to care and sneered down at her. "Athair Alfred tried to purge you of your demons and has told me that your soul is beyond saving."

The priest wasn't in this room, but symbols of the True Religion were everywhere. White banners decorated the walls, and both Katherine and Charlotte were wearing Savior's pendants. Would Katherine really kill her own grandson just to frame Aemyra?

Aemyra folded her arms over her chest. "You are falsely accusing me of your son's murder as a way to sully my name and steal my crown."

Evander's face was contorting in fury, his skin slowly turning puce with rage. "*My* crown!" he yelled, spittle flying from his mouth.

Aemyra flinched. Gone was the sullen drunkenness, replaced instead by this violent rage. Evander had lost his father and his eldest son in the space of a few weeks, all while Bonding and becoming king. The terrifying glimmer in his eyes almost made Aemyra feel sorry for him. Almost.

"If you hadn't executed the most skilled healer in this territory, then perhaps my mother could have saved your son before he died," Aemyra ground out, her fury washing away her common sense. "I am not the one who started this war."

"You dare try to tell me, the king, what I should and should not do?" Evander roared, unsheathing his sword. "You stand there in your fine dress, staring down at my son's body and pretend you knew nothing about this? You think yourself innocent?"

Evander descended the steps and Aemyra willed him to come closer; she had been scrapping without magic in this cesspit of a city for years.

Before Aemyra could lose all sense completely, Fiorean rose to his feet. "You are far from innocent. Balnain has just launched an attack from the river. There are more than five hundred dead on the eastern Forc."

Aemyra stayed her hand. If her father wasn't coming to rescue her, at least he was still fighting on her behalf.

Aemyra reminded herself what kind of queen she aspired to be and tried for diplomacy.

"I am truly sorry for the loss of your son," she said, looking over Evander's shoulder toward Charlotte, who seemed scarily detached. "But I did not kill Fergys. He looks as though he has ingested some kind of toxic substance."

Evander seethed. "If you know the symptoms, you must also know the poison. You say that you have no desire to shed blood. Then how do you explain the six thousand soldiers marching from Atholl toward the northern Forc?" Evander asked, his voice shaking.

Knowing that her army would follow Draevan's command until she could escape, Aemyra met Evander's eyes with a steely glare. Fuck diplomacy.

"I did not draw first blood. You did. Their names were Orlagh, Pàdraig, and Lachlann," she shouted at her usurper. "You murdered them simply for having a connection to me. A boy the same age as your son who lies rotting on this very floor. *You killed them.*"

Evander lifted his sword. "My heir for Draevan's, then."

Aemyra instinctively ducked as he swung for her head, but the path of Evander's blade was stopped by another.

The weapons shuddered where they met, suspended in front of Aemyra's face. Shock and rage were painted on Evander's features as he glared into the face of her rescuer.

It was Fiorean who had saved her. Both hands were gripping the hilt of his sword, blocking his brother's blade from cleaving Aemyra's head from her shoulders.

She took a healthy step away from them both.

"You dare defy my orders?" Evander roared, looking like he was ready to duel over his son's corpse.

"Put the sword down, Ev. This won't bring him back," Fiorean said, surprisingly gently.

Aemyra watched the shadow of grief flicker across Evander's features until he sagged where he stood. Breaking out of her withdrawn state, Charlotte rose from her chair and crossed the floor to her husband. The woman did not speak, but the moment her hand alighted upon the king's arm, he dropped his sword.

"Enough," Katherine called down from her seat. "This has already been discussed."

The dowager queen was looking faintly sick, obviously ready to vacate this room as soon as possible. Aemyra found herself inclined to agree.

Evander's eyes were flitting back and forth in a panicked manner, as if he had forgotten something. Fiorean's face was unreadable as he slunk away from his brother to stand behind Aemyra.

Drawing himself up to his full height, Evander said, "Kneel and swear allegiance to me as the rightful king of Tìr Teine and I shall give you your life."

After being restrained, assaulted, and very nearly beheaded, Aemyra summoned whatever courage she had left. "I am the only female born of Clan Daercathian in the last hundred years, blessed by Brigid herself, and my claim to the throne supersedes yours."

Evander's lips curled back from his teeth and Charlotte clutched him tightly against her.

Before Aemyra knew what was happening, Fiorean had grabbed her arm, twisting it painfully. His knee knocked into the back of her own and pushed her to the floor. Feeling as if he were about to dislocate her shoulder, she couldn't struggle.

"She swears it," Fiorean said, sounding vaguely bored.

"See that you keep her obedient," Evander said to his brother as Charlotte led him to his chair.

The moment she was back on her feet, Aemyra shook Fiorean off, glowering when she saw Evander sneer.

It was the dowager queen who supplied the missing information. "You will both appear before the Athair at sunset on the morrow and swear your vows within the tower," Katherine said, the ghost of a vindictive smile on her face.

Aemyra's heart stuttered violently, and she rounded on Fiorean, who stood completely still, not facing her.

"Vows?" Aemyra asked, her voice trembling.

"Your marriage vows. You will marry Fiorean. He has been too long unwed, and this union will secure your rightful place within the clan as a Daercathian princess," Katherine said, heavily stressing the title.

No. No, this couldn't be happening.

"And you agree with this?" Aemyra turned to Fiorean.

He did not move or look at her, but the stiffness in his voice told her that he loathed the idea just as much as she did.

"It will keep a leash on your father's dragon," Fiorean said, his tone icy.

For the first time, Aemyra sincerely wished they had just killed her.

CHAPTER TWENTY-ONE

A EMYRA WATCHED THE SUN TRACK ITS PATH THROUGH THE SKY as if it were marking her final hours.

In a way, it was.

She was about to be dragged in front of Athair Alfred and forced to speak the words under metaphorical sword-point. Aemyra knew that keeping her as a hostage within the caisteal would stop Draevan from launching a full-scale attack on the city, but why betroth her to Fiorean?

She thought it unlikely that the Chosen wanted more Dùileach heirs from the royals. By all accounts, the young princes could barely summon a flame between them—but they had all been Goddess blessed.

Thoughts of the priestesses swam into Aemyra's mind. She could not see the temple from her window, but she prayed to Brigid that they were safe. Once she was married to Fiorean, she would be close enough to kill him while he slept and then she could avenge her family and Kenna.

It would be a moment worth enduring a sham wedding for.

She hoped her father would understand that she was doing this only to get close enough to kill Fiorean. If she could make alliances with Draevan's spies, perhaps they could help her escape the caisteal afterward.

Fisting the layered fabric of her skirt, she resisted the urge to tear the dress apart. The satin was smooth against her calluses and she had never felt less like herself.

With a resigned sigh, Aemyra finally stepped away from the window to where Sir Gavin was waiting for her in the wide corridor. The priest who had been standing outside her door all day stood rigidly beside him.

"Best get it over with then," she said dismissively, following Sir Gavin to the tower.

Today there would be no familiar faces, nor any priestesses. By all accounts they were confined to the temple until the succession was more settled. Aemyra feared for Eilidh, but all she could do was pray.

Her palms were sweating, and she tried to remind herself that even if she spoke the vows today, she would not have a husband come nightfall.

She would find a way to get out of the caisteal and, when her magic returned, she would call her dragon.

Then she would take to the sky with Terrea and burn them all to ashes.

The tower was located on the opposite side of Caisteal Lasair from Aemyra's rooms, the imposing black stone abutting the red brick of the caisteal like an unsightly growth. Beyond the hill the caisteal sat upon, the snow-covered peaks of the Deàrr Mountains were flushed with the sunset. Today she saw no beauty in the sight.

"Princess?" Sir Gavin cleared his throat.

Squaring her shoulders and trying not to scratch at the pins holding her hair in place, Aemyra walked through the doors.

To her surprise, the circular room had been lavishly decorated. Abundant petals littered the dark floor, vines and lush flowers draped in a carousel of color spiraling upward to the high ceiling—no doubt thanks to Katherine's contacts in Ùir. The lairds gathered were bedecked in all their finery and a cold sweat traveled from Aemyra's palms to the base of her spine, like the faint strains of the clarsach were plucking her nerves.

The people would believe this marriage to be legitimate.

Her skirts brushed the smooth floor as she advanced, light permeating the gloomy tower through the one window at the very top of the lofty ceiling. Athair Alfred and Fiorean were waiting in the middle of that beam of light, the curved pews all facing the illuminated spot in the center of the room.

Brigid, where are you?

As Aemyra walked between the pews, her father's lectures about queenly behavior rang in her ears. If she screamed and cried, if the priests were forced to drag her in front of Alfred, if she begged to be spared this indignity, the people would forever see her as weak.

She would rather shackle herself to a murderer than have them see her as anything less than infallible.

So Aemyra held her chin high, her expression carefully masked. She walked past Fiorean's younger brothers, who were clad in crimson clan tartan, their wives dutifully silent beside them. Exactly like they wanted Aemyra to be.

In her fine dress with her hair perfectly coiffed and shining like copper, she saw the appreciation in people's eyes as she passed.

She hadn't expected to see it reflected in Fiorean's gaze as well.

The dress was white, some symbolic reflection of the Chosen's particular views on purity. Like they could strip Aemyra of everything she was with the lack of color. Despite the plain hue, the bodice was well fitted, the satin skirts trailing heavily behind her.

Gone was the glittering gold of a queen.

As much as she hated him, Aemyra blinked in surprise as the sunlight gilded Fiorean's hair, bathing him in a golden glow as he watched her approach. The traditional fèileadh he wore, with their clan tartan draped over his hips and across one shoulder, struck an impressive figure.

A gold dragon brooch was holding the material together, and his auburn hair gleamed as it spilled across his shoulders.

The fact that he was handsome would not make him any easier to kill, and Aemyra let her eyes dart to the front pew, where Evander was watching her closely. The crown and sword of the first king was firmly in place upon his person.

It wouldn't surprise Aemyra if he wore them to bed.

When she finally reached the center of the tower after what felt like an age, Fiorean's expression was once again cold. Like none of this was affecting him in the slightest.

He wore no weapon, save for a small sgian-dubh, and Aemyra wondered if he had already commissioned the garnet he had stolen back from her to be set into a new sword.

She supposed that in a few hours, she might find out.

In a few hours, though, he might be dead.

With that thought, she turned her gaze away from Fiorean and listened as Alfred began his sermon. The priest's bald head glinted with sweat, his beady eyes lingering a little too long on Aemyra. As if remembering how she had looked restrained on the ground before him.

She shivered at the memory but was determined not to give him the satisfaction of her fear. Weak men would rather guilt strong women than become strong themselves, and Aemyra was content to show him what strength truly looked like.

"Please be seated," Alfred began in his gravelly voice, bidding all those who had gotten to their feet upon Aemyra's arrival to sit.

Having never been inside a Savior's tower before, Aemyra didn't know what to expect from the service. But she hadn't anticipated being bored to tears within the first few minutes.

"Savior, we pray you remind us to remain pure in your image, to carry your faith in our hearts each day of our lives and foster this gift of life you have given us," Alfred droned.

Forcing herself not to yawn after her sleepless night, Aemyra kept her eyes firmly on the golden brooch Fiorean wore.

As a Dùileach, she could not feel the presence of any Goddess within this dark tower. Since she would not be speaking her vows in front of the eternal fire or holding the burning branch, Aemyra felt slightly better about the whole affair.

Still, she did not look up at Fiorean.

When the long sermon finally ended and Aemyra's feet began to protest, Alfred gestured for Fiorean to take her hands.

The gentle scent of lilac and orange blossom met her nostrils before he reached for her, and suddenly their fingers were entwined.

Resisting the urge to pull away from his grasp, she endured it.

Aemyra had never touched Fiorean before, save in violence.

His hands were warm but calloused, with long fingers and a strong grip. She could feel the undercurrent of heat he allowed to pass beneath his skin. The hands of a Dùileach, of a dragon rider. Aemyra was powerless to watch as Alfred twined a white ribbon around their wrists, binding them together.

She didn't know why, but her heart was racing.

Finally daring to look up at Fiorean's face, Aemyra stifled a gasp when she noticed the intensity with which he was staring at her. There was hatred there still, no doubt reflected in her own eyes, but it concealed something else. Something more primal perhaps.

"We commit your souls to the Savior, bound together now so shall you find your way back to each other in this life—and every life."

Fiorean's green eyes were fixed on her as Athair Alfred bid them repeat the words. She watched Fiorean's lips move as he spoke the vows that would make her his wife in the eyes of the True Religion.

Then it was her turn.

She felt herself speak the words, her hands growing sweaty, and yet Fiorean's grip never faltered.

"Savior save us, bind us, and mold us. I am his wife in this life . . . and in all to come."

It wasn't until Aemyra had spoken the last word that she understood the look in her new husband's eyes.

Possessiveness.

The hall was riotously noisy.

Aemyra sat in the place of honor just to the left of Evander, with Fiorean on her other side. To everyone else it was probably the most coveted seat in all of Tìr Teine, but to her it felt like a trap.

Evander was already indecently drunk, having spilled his wine repeatedly over his plate of food until Katherine reached over and moved his goblet farther away.

Aemyra sat as stiffly as her new husband did.

"Come, now. Do you know how hard it was to get roast beef on such short notice?" Evander grinned wildly, gesturing to their untouched plates. "With the Balnain fleet blockading the Forc, we were lucky to have anything come in at all."

Aemyra spun to face him, momentarily forgetting that he had attempted to behead her the day before. "Blockading?"

Evander made an offensive gesture toward her and swigged directly from the jug of wine, to the obvious horror of his mother.

Aemyra pursed her lips in distaste but committed the information to memory. This was a very good sign. If the Balnain fleet held the Forc, and her army was pressing northeast . . .

Her eyes flicked nervously to her new husband. Fiorean's hands were flat on the table, and his posture stiff. If she could kill him tonight and slip from the caisteal using the servants' passageways, she could be at the northern Forc in four days, even without her dragon.

Aemyra fiddled with the serving knife.

Feeling Fiorean's eyes on her, she picked up her fork to sample some of the food.

It was truly a shame she had no appetite. The feast was immaculate.

The guests could be forgiven for forgetting that a war had broken out, as the minstrels played a lively tune that many a fair couple danced to. But Aemyra recognized the heavy cloud of grief that permeated even this supposedly happy event. The Covenanters lurking behind the tables did little to dispel the feeling of doom, and Charlotte was notably absent.

Athair Alfred whispered into Evander's ear almost continuously and Katherine was trying to listen so subtly that it became glaringly obvious. Elear and his wife, Elizabeth, were stoic at the far end of the table and Aemyra thought of their children, briefly wondering if what had killed young Fergys was infectious. If so, they would have a much bigger problem on their hands.

Seated closest to Aemyra, Nael and his wife seemed happy in each other's company. The telltale bunching of Margaret's dress spoke of the growing bump underneath. Fiorean's youngest brother was evidently about to father another child.

Platters of food groaned and ale flowed, but through it all Fiorean and Aemyra avoided looking at each other. The only words they had spoken that day were their marriage vows.

At the thought of what might await her in the next hours, Aemyra gulped her wine and choked slightly.

While it may have been the choice of most brides to get drunk in anticipation of their wedding night, Aemyra knew she needed to be clearheaded when the time came.

Fiorean himself had barely drunk more than a few sips of the vintage and had yet to touch his food.

"I don't think th—"

Turning at the sound of the dowager queen's voice, Aemyra saw Katherine reach across Alfred to place a gentle hand on Evander's arm. The king brushed off his mother's touch, and Sir Nairn loomed protectively behind her.

"It is time," Evander said with a grin as Alfred folded his hands over his stomach contentedly.

Startling Aemyra, Evander stood from the table, his chair scraping loudly enough that the musicians stopped playing. As the fiddles died out, the dancing pairs and dining lairds turned expectantly to their pretender king.

"My honored guests. I raise a toast to the bride and groom— Prince Fiorean and Princess Aemyra Daercathian!"

A thunderous roar went through the crowd and Aemyra grew even more still. She swore that Fiorean was barely breathing beside her.

Evander drained his goblet and looked down at her, his expression wicked.

"We have had our wedding, now we must ensure that the couple consummate the marriage."

The thunderous cheering grew louder as the guests began banging on tables and stomping their feet, calling for her to be carried to the royal bedchamber. Most disturbingly, the priests began to pray.

"What?" Aemyra asked, whirling to face Fiorean.

A flush was creeping up his pale skin, but he did not look at her.

Evander was grinning, but even Katherine had a distasteful look on her face as Sir Nairn whispered in her ear. Was this some tradition of the True Religion? Aemyra had heard priests preach chastity until marriage as one of the rules dictated by the Savior in order to save one's soul, but were they about to *examine* her?

Aemyra wished she hadn't attempted to eat anything, as the thought of what was about to happen threatened to make her sick.

"The ladies should take her to undress," Margaret said in a small voice.

With a feral grin, Evander reached down and hauled Aemyra up to her feet, her chair clattering to the ground.

"Why wait?" he asked, waving Margaret's protests away dismissively. "Shall we get started, then?" Before she could free herself, Evander dragged Aemyra out from behind the table and she heard Fiorean's muttered curse.

Evander laughed. "You'll get your chance soon enough, Brother."

Her arm smarted, bruises already flowering under his tight grip.

"You're drunk and not thinking clearly. Let her go," Fiorean said carefully, knuckles straining white on the back of the chair he had vacated.

"Sober as a judge, Fi," Evander replied. "And believe me, I wish I wasn't."

The hard edge had returned to his voice and Aemyra promised death with a glare.

"Let's get you bedded," Evander said in her ear.

They were soon engulfed by the riotous crowd, and Aemyra struggled to see where she was going, only the faces of leering men who dared a grope or a squeeze were visible as she passed.

As soon as Fiorean was dead, she would put this right.

No woman in her territory would ever have to suffer such indignation. She might not be able to travel to Tìr Ùir or Uisge to right the wrongs done by the Chosen there, but she would purge the ways of the Savior from this land with fire and fury.

Aemyra tried to walk faster, hoping she would find some sanctuary in the corridors.

But some of the crowd followed.

As Evander led them toward Fiorean's rooms, the jeering and laughing continued in a more restrained way.

Heartbeat loud in her ears, Aemyra failed to hear what was being said, or perhaps she was subconsciously blocking it out, but somehow Evander ripped the ivory dress from her body, leaving her standing before the group of men in nothing but her corset and shift.

"This is barbaric!" Aemyra shouted, refusing to cover herself.

She had never been ashamed of her body, but she would never have wanted to publicly expose herself in such a way. The leering eyes of the men who had followed from the hall looked over the thin fabric as Evander's grip grew fiercer. Aemyra suddenly understood why the women of Tìr Ùir were so shy and quiet. They had been disrespected and abused by men their whole lives.

"Brother."

Fiorean may have only uttered one word, but it held such deadly promise that Evander's hold slackened. He threw Aemyra's wedding dress to his friends, several of the men fighting over the scraps of satin like dogs. Then he drew his dagger.

Evander sliced the laces of her corset, ripping it from her until she stood in only her thin shift.

Afraid for what he might do next, Aemyra twisted in his grip and Fiorean seized his opportunity. Thrown off balance by her movement, Evander stumbled and Fiorean pulled Aemyra against him.

"I believe you entrusted me to keep her in check?" Fiorean asked, the words clipped.

Despite her rage, Aemyra stood stiffly, feeling Fiorean's heart beating against her spine.

"Oho! My brother knows his duty." Evander laughed.

Flushing a deeper shade of red, Aemyra was forced to remain in
Fiorean's hold as Evander ushered them up the stairs. Even after mul-
tiple protests and outright threats from his younger brother, he did
not leave.

Ten lairds accompanied them to Fiorean's chambers, joking and
laughing among themselves. Some were reminiscing about their own
wedding night, others offering unhelpful advice to Fiorean.

Aemyra committed every face to memory for the day she once
again held a weapon in her hand.

Evander opened the doors to Fiorean's bedchamber with a sadistic
smile before backing away.

"From a blacksmith whore to a prince's bride. You better be worth
it."

Aemyra strode into the room like she wasn't afraid. Two of the lairds
whistled appreciatively as her curves snagged against the thin shift.

"Fiorean's a lucky one."

"Sure you don't want to share?"

"She's got a temper, maybe your little cock can't handle her."

The lairds continued their jeering as Fiorean followed her into the
room, boots loud on the flagstones. A few hasty jokes slipped in before
he slammed the door closed.

Shivering in the cold, and more rattled than she cared to admit,
Aemyra eyed the room for something she could use to cover herself.
The only place that made the most sense was the bed.

As if issuing a challenge of her own, Aemyra lifted the sheets and
climbed in.

Fiorean cleared his throat, his eyes downcast as he strode slowly
toward the small settee in front of the fireplace. She watched him in
silence, noting the way his fèileadh hugged his hips.

Her heart stuttered despite herself.

But he only pulled the fur blanket off the settee and threw it onto
the bed.

"You seem cold," he said curtly.

Aemyra frowned, pulling the fur around her shoulders to cover her bare arms, which were indeed prickled with gooseflesh. Unarmed and vulnerable as she was, it comforted her to be covered and she looked around the room.

It was bigger than the one she had been staying in. Far larger than her rooms in Caisteal Penryth. Anything was an improvement on her tiny attic bedroom in the lower town.

But as she sat in what was to become her marriage bed with the man she hated most in the world, she realized that she would have traded this luxury for that lumpy cot in a heartbeat.

Fiorean sat down on the ottoman at the end of the bed and began removing his boots.

She knew what came next. Knew what he would expect. She also knew when he would be the most vulnerable.

"I am not going to touch you," Fiorean said, so quietly that she swore she had heard him wrong.

"What?"

He finally looked at her, his hair parting to reveal a conflicted expression.

"You do not need to fear me tonight. I take no pleasure in forcing a woman to bed and I certainly would not relish killing you while you are without weapon or magic."

Aemyra lifted her chin. "How gracious of you. As repulsed as I am by the idea of sharing your bed, I'll remind you that there are ten lairds and a false king waiting outside of this door for proof that you *have* bedded me."

As if to prove her point, a fist began pounding at the door, followed by sniggering laughs.

Fiorean suddenly stood.

She watched as he undressed himself by the light of the fire. He unclipped his belt and unfastened the brooch at his shoulder, letting his fèileadh unravel to the ground in one long bolt of wool until he stood in nothing but his long white shirt and socks.

He was lithe like a mountain cat. Muscular, but without the bulk. She found that his legs were shapely.

He caught her looking.

"Appraising me like I'm a bull at auction?"

Aemyra glared at him. "I think I got rather the worst of it, being dragged through the revels like a prize sow."

"Mm."

But as she looked, she could admit that Fiorean was a handsome man. Handsomer even than his elder brother, she supposed. Were it not for the scar.

Odd, that he had removed almost all of his clothes and yet his hair was still carefully placed to cover it. Bending down, he pulled off his thick socks, placing the sgian-dubh carefully on the bedside table.

Anger hardening her heart, she braced herself as he ripped the cover off the bed, rumpling the sheets.

She bit her lip in apprehension. Men frequently lost themselves in the throes of passion. At least the few Aemyra had taken to bed had proven to be so lost in their own pleasure that they had seemed to forget she even existed.

When Fiorean was sufficiently distracted, she would stab him through the eye with his own knife. All she needed was an opening.

Knowing this was the price she had to pay to save her territory, Aemyra let the furs drop from around her shoulders.

Then she lifted her shift over her head in one defiant motion.

Fiorean's gaze finally left her face, lingering on her breasts, where each nipple was taut in the cold air. He drew in a deep breath and jerked his head back up, eyes on the ceiling.

Climbing onto the bed, he knelt beside her, his hands gripping the post behind her head.

Aemyra pressed her lips firmly together and reminded herself why she was doing this.

But instead of touching her, Fiorean began to rock back and forth so the wooden post banged rhythmically against the wall.

Aemyra's eyes shot open in surprise as she heard riotous laughter and cheering coming from outside the room.

He wasn't even looking at her.

She lay there, immobile, as Fiorean rocked the bed. As the seconds slipped by without him touching her, she relaxed slightly.

Fiorean must have noticed because he finally dropped his gaze to her face. He held her stare as his arm moved rhythmically back and forth, hitting the bedframe against the wall just an increment faster each time. Even as her full breasts undulated with the motion, his gaze did not wander.

His emerald eyes held such depth of emotion, each one fighting for dominance, that she found herself wanting to ask what he was thinking.

Before she could chastise herself for taking an interest in any of Fiorean's inner thoughts, she tensed again as he reached for his sgian-dubh.

"If you cut me with that, you'll not live to regret it," she said.

He lifted one finger to his lips before slashing the meaty part of his palm until bright beads of blood pooled onto the sheets.

Aemyra's mouth dropped open as Fiorean wiped the small cut to stop the bleeding, pulling his shirtsleeve down to cover his hand.

Then he stepped off the bed and crossed to the door.

"The marriage is consummated," Fiorean announced into the corridor and his expression sparked to anger as his brother shouldered his way into the room.

Taking one look at Aemyra lying naked on the bed beside a small pool of fresh blood, Evander clapped Fiorean on the shoulder.

"Bit quiet for my liking, Brother. Next time try to liven things up a bit, eh?" He chuckled madly to himself.

Fiorean stiffened. "Your behavior is unbecoming of a king. Grieve how you see fit, but at least bathe before appearing before the court tomorrow?"

Before Evander could reply, Fiorean threw him bodily out of the door, slamming it closed.

Sitting up, Aemyra gathered the sheets to her chest.

"Why?" she asked.

Remaining silent, Fiorean draped the fur blanket around his own shoulders and made himself comfortable on the settee. As the fire in the brazier burned low and the room grew dark, Aemyra heard his breathing from across the room as loudly as if he were lying sleeping beside her.

It wasn't until she was dozing off that she realized she hadn't even tried to grab the knife.

CHAPTER TWENTY-TWO

AEMYRA WOKE FROM A FITFUL SLEEP WHEN THE MATTRESS dimpled.

She had tossed and turned until the candle burned out, contemplating how she would kill Fiorean but never quite deciding on a plan of action. With her magic still blocked, she was no match for a Bonded Dùileach even if she had a weapon.

Eyelids flying open as the bed creaked, she lifted her cheek from the pillow to see Fiorean climbing in beside her.

"What are you doing?" she whispered.

Cursing herself for falling asleep in the first place, she clutched the sheets up to her chin.

"It is considered bad luck for a groom to sleep apart from his bride on the night of their wedding," Fiorean said gruffly, his hair unkempt.

Aemyra looked up at the golden light of dawn that was already streaming through the windows. "But it's already daybreak."

Fiorean stopped trying to get comfortable and stared at her. "Are you always this dim-witted in the mornings?"

Aemyra tried to wriggle away from him as he plumped up the numerous pillows and leaned back on them.

"If the servants arrive and find us sleeping apart, then they will take that news to my brother. I wouldn't like to imagine what would be in store for either of us then."

The way he was so casually burrowing into the bed disturbed her and she shifted to the far edge of the mattress. Fiorean reached over his head and pulled his shirt off, throwing it into a crumpled heap on the floor.

"Clearly you are committed to making this as realistic as possible," Aemyra said, still clutching the sheets to her bare chest.

"Purely self-interest, I assure you," Fiorean replied, tucking one arm behind his head, looking the picture of ease.

Aemyra allowed herself a glance at his torso. It was just as lean and muscular as his legs, but there were numerous scars that littered his body. Some were nothing more than long-healed silver lines, others angrily pink and swollen, and there was one large shiny burn reminiscent of Adarian's.

Inclining her head, she asked, "Is that from Aervor?"

Fiorean followed her gaze and huffed a laugh. "If Aervor had shot his fire at me, I wouldn't be lying here beside you."

"Pity," Aemyra said.

Fiorean tilted his head. His facial scars were already covered by his unbound hair, but Aemyra had the feeling that the movement was habitual. Aside from the burn, the largest scar on his body traversed several ribs.

"Where did you get that?" Aemyra asked, not caring if it was too personal, since he had just muscled into bed with her.

"My father," Fiorean said stiffly.

Unwilling to feel pity for the man in the bed beside her, Aemyra replied, "You must have deserved it. My father only struck me when it was necessary. He wouldn't do harm without good cause."

Fiorean smirked. "Draevan? The man who tried to kill my mother and her entire court when she traveled here from Ùir? Clearly you don't know your father as well as you think you do."

"I know him better than anyone."

Fiorean peaked an eyebrow. "Really? You two were so close when he stayed in Penryth and you were forced to hide in the slums of Àird Lasair with the rabble? I don't know how you don't hate him for making you endure that."

Aemyra glared, fisting her hands into the sheets to stop herself from strangling him.

"My father had perilously few options, thanks to *your* father's madness over male succession. And I don't resent my years spent in the forge. I learned a lot about respect and humility. Lessons you clearly could have benefited from."

Fiorean was smirking.

"I know plenty about respect, and duty, and honor. But a prince does not have much need of being humble. Certainly not when he is the most powerful Dùileach in Tìr Teine."

He allowed his fire to snake around his forearm, like Aemyra needed another reminder of how vulnerable she was, lying in bed with him.

She leaned forward, eyeing the flames. "Tell your mother to give me back my magic and I'll soon prove you wrong."

Fiorean's green eyes were dancing in the flames, and he took his time studying Aemyra's face.

"Your little display at the temple was impressive, I admit. But no un-Bonded Dùileach has outstripped a Bonded Dùileach. Ever."

Swallowing the truth with difficulty, Aemyra replied, "You don't deserve your gift, or your dragon. You turned your back on the Goddess who blessed you when you began worshipping those hate-filled zealots. You might not be able to wear the pendant, but I hope Brigid curses the lot of you."

Fiorean let his flames wink out, his expression darkening.

"Don't pretend to understand this family after spending a few nights in the caisteal, Princess. You'll only embarrass yourself," he drawled.

Aemyra's temper spiked. "I understand enough. You have all forsaken the Goddesses to follow the Chosen. You disrespect the women made in her image and you slaughter innocent *children.*"

Her voice broke on the last word and Fiorean leaned toward her threateningly.

"Did I disrespect you last night?" he growled, his eyes dropping down to her bare collarbone. "Or did I spare you more indignity?"

"I will not sit here and *thank* you for not raping me. I don't care what scrap of conscience you possess that stayed your hand—but I will never forgive what you did to my family," Aemyra said, throat thick with unshed tears.

She would not cry in front of him. She wouldn't give him the satisfaction.

He glared right back at her. "You are *lucky* that your father forced you to grow up away from this court. You would never have survived it."

Aemyra glanced down at the scars littering Fiorean's body and found herself disappointed that no one had finished the job.

"Just like Fergys and Lachlann failed to survive it?" she spat. "Tell me, who is poisoning the children? Because you and I both know it wasn't me."

Fiorean refused to answer, fisting his hands in the sheets until they began to smoke.

"When I have my magic back, you will not survive me," Aemyra finished.

Fiorean pushed himself up to a sitting position, his face inches from Aemyra's. "Is that a threat?"

"It's a promise," Aemyra replied, refusing to cower under his glare.

She could feel his breath against her cheek, and she pushed herself up to her elbows, not liking the advantage he had by towering over her. The sheet slipped slightly, revealing the top of her breasts, and Fiorean's eyes followed it.

A soft knock sounded at the door and his eyes dragged slowly back up to her face.

"Enter," he barked, his emerald gaze penetrating.

The door opened and the first of the servants hurried in with breakfast and water for washing, eyes downcast.

It was a good thing too, because Aemyra was about to throttle him with her bare hands and damn the consequences.

After a moment's hesitation, Fiorean pulled away from her, ripping the sheets off of himself. Aemyra averted her eyes as he strode purposefully out of the bedroom and into the antechamber.

Now that a servant had seen them abed, he seemed eager to put as much distance between them as possible.

Aemyra was still seething with rage. She had to get out of this room and find one of Draevan's spies. Orlagh had often gotten information from the kitchens—perhaps she could start there.

Before she could dress, Margaret entered the room and Aemyra paused. There was something arresting about the young woman's face—a quiet power that still lay dormant perhaps.

"Princess?" Margaret asked quietly, bobbing a curtsy.

Aemyra gritted her teeth at the incorrect title but refrained from snapping when dimples appeared in the other woman's brown cheeks, dark freckles betraying her youth.

Clearing her throat, Aemyra got out of bed. "Margaret, I don't believe we had time to be formally introduced yesterday."

Another shy smile. "Please, call me Maggie. Mother Katherine has appointed me your chaperone."

Eyes narrowing, Aemyra swept her gaze over Maggie. Registering the tight curls already escaping their pins, the sage green dress stained at the hem.

"I'm no fool. I know when I am being managed," Aemyra said.

Maggie blushed as the servants stripped the bed and she spotted the ruined sheets.

Fiorean chose that moment to reenter the room.

"She will be no match for your delightful charm, dear sister," he said, in possibly the kindest tone Aemyra had ever heard him use. Unfortunately, he reserved none of it for her. "You are expected to accompany me on a public walk later."

"I would rather you fed me to your dragon," Aemyra snapped back.

Fiorean's eyes glittered. "Don't put ideas into my head."

His boots thundered heavily on the floorboards as he left, having exchanged the traditional crimson fèileadh for his usual black tunic and breeches. His hair was left unbound and shining down his back.

As Aemyra yielded herself to the ministrations of the servants, she wondered how he could possibly seem so calm. She had been humiliated, abused, and ridiculed. Her internal thoughts were a complete mess.

"You should eat, my lady," Maggie said, inclining her head to the tray of fruits and pastries that had been brought up with the bathwater.

Aemyra's stomach growled, but she turned away from the table. "I find I have no appetite this morning."

The servants exchanged a pitying look and chivied her in a motherly way toward the tub. Shivering in the chill air, she noticed the way Maggie was absentmindedly stroking the curve of her belly and glancing at the tray.

"By all means, help yourself," Aemyra said.

Stepping into the deliciously warm bath, she pondered Fiorean's code of honor. Why would it stop him from violating her when he clearly hadn't a single shred of remorse after killing her family?

Sighing, she rested her still tender head on the back of the tub, feeling exhausted.

"I know it must be painful, my lady. The salts will help," one of the servants muttered, her eyes on the dark bruises that circled her upper arm from Evander's grip.

Aemyra let them come to their own conclusions, pretending she needed the milk and salts they were adding to her bathwater. There was no ache between her legs, no pain deep inside of her. Just sheer confusion and irritation that while his fèileadh still lay discarded on the floor, Fiorean had taken the knife with him.

CHAPTER TWENTY-THREE

An hour later, Maggie was helping to button the back of her dress when Fiorean returned.

Given its high neck and long sleeves, Aemyra had a feeling the gown had come from Katherine herself and she scratched uncomfortably at the lace.

Fiorean's gaze swept over the empty breakfast tray. Maggie smiled warmly and departed with a musical "Good day."

When they were alone, he stood between the settee and the bed, hands clasped behind his back, observing Aemyra critically.

"This won't do," he said quietly. "Change."

Aemyra's temper flared. While the cream dress was modest, it was clearly expensive, with heavy skirts and lace filigree.

"Am I not to your tastes, Prince?" she seethed.

Fiorean picked some imaginary dirt from under his fingernails. "I have no intention of dressing my bride like my mother. You are a Daercathian and I desire you to appear as such. Now change."

His tone left no room for argument and Aemyra sighed. "Then I will need help with the infernal number of buttons."

Against her better judgment, she turned her back to Fiorean and waited for him to assist her. After a moment of hesitation, she heard him approach. When his fingers made contact with the nape of her neck, she shivered even though the room was warm.

His fingers were swift, methodically popping the buttons that trailed down her spine until Aemyra was holding the bodice of the dress against her chest.

He cleared his throat.

"I believe that should be——"

"Yes."

Fighting a nonsensical blush, Aemyra ducked behind the dressing screen to select another dress. Preferably one she could get into without assistance.

There were no gold dresses to choose from, and Aemyra knew it was no simple oversight. Brushing the smooth velvet and scratchy lace, she selected a deep red gown. She struggled a little with the laces but managed to secure it only a little lopsidedly.

With an impatient sigh, Aemyra swept back into the bedroom.

Fiorean looked like he hadn't moved a muscle.

"Well?" Aemyra asked, holding her arms out.

His eyes skimmed over the straight cut across her shoulders and the sleeves that dropped to the floor. It snagged on the corset that cinched in her waist, but having expected a snappy retort or scathing comment, Aemyra was almost disappointed when he said nothing and strode from the room.

With an eye roll, she followed.

"Where are we expected to go?" Aemyra asked as they reached the large, open corridors where parties of the nobility were milling about.

Heads turned as they passed, some bowing, others smirking at Fiorean.

She felt his hand on her elbow, and she automatically tried to jerk it back. His grip held fast.

"Come now, Wife," Fiorean said in a low voice, "surely you are pleased to share a leisurely walk with your husband?"

Aemyra understood his meaning and even though her stomach

rolled when he said the word *wife,* she allowed him to tuck her hand into the crook of his elbow and slow their pace.

"Perhaps you could show me the kitchens," Aemyra mused, craning her neck around corners.

Fiorean pulled her more tightly against him. "Looking for a rat hole to scurry out of ? You cannot possibly be hungry after such a large breakfast."

Aemyra tried to school her face into an expression of neutrality.

Maggie had polished off the breakfast tray with little prompting and Aemyra couldn't help but think Katherine had assigned her the worst guard imaginable. More than eight hours had passed since Aemyra had last eaten. The binding agent would wear off soon and then she had to find one of Draevan's spies who would help her escape.

Wracking her brain, Aemyra marked every corridor and window as they meandered through the spacious passages. All the while ignoring how her shoulder kept brushing against Fiorean's arm.

"Brothers!" Fiorean called out.

Dappled sunlight was streaming in through high windows as Elear and Nael strolled toward them with their wives. One was outfitted in an elegant dove gray doublet, the other in mud-splattered breeches and boots.

"Good morning," Elear said stiffly, his hazel eyes darting to Aemyra's face.

Elizabeth's scowl marred her beautiful face, and Aemyra gave her a feral smile that showed all of her teeth. To her delight, the woman shrank behind her husband.

Pitiful. These women have no strength.

"How are the children?" Fiorean asked with genuine concern.

Elizabeth placed one hand on her Savior's pendant. "Little Alistair has shown small improvement, but Edwyn is still gravely ill."

The instincts Orlagh had instilled in her had Aemyra speaking up.

"Did the healers administer charcoal?"

Elizabeth glared as if the very suggestion offended her and Elear's jaw was ticking.

"I swear to Brigid I did not poison your children. My mother was the best healer in Àird Lasair, and while I possess but a fraction of her skill, I might be able to help you," Aemyra said, crossing her arms over her chest. "If you would give me access to the gardens, I could find some herbs——"

Elear looked down his nose at her. "The royal healers have been with our sons night and day."

"And yet you say they are still sick," Aemyra replied.

Elear took one threatening step toward her; Aemyra held her ground. He was just as tall as Fiorean.

"You might be able to cure pustules and pox in the lower town, but you know nothing of complex medicine," Elear said.

Aemyra smirked. "Disease does not differentiate between princes and peasants. Royal children die just as quickly as poor orphans."

Elizabeth stiffened and Elear held out an arm protectively toward his wife. "Sheathe your forked tongue behind your teeth."

Aemyra curled her upper lip and caught the tip of her tongue between her teeth, delighting in the shocked expression on Elear's face.

"Give me a reason, Prince," Aemyra said, curling her hands into fists. "If I had access to my gifts, you would not be so careless with your threats."

Aemyra inclined her head toward Elizabeth. "I'm surprised your wife even conceived a child if this is how serious you are in bed. Perhaps I should show her what real pleasure feels like? There have been more than a few women in this city screaming my name into the darkness."

Elizabeth's cheeks flamed crimson and Elear seemed beyond speech.

Her eyes darting between the two brothers, Aemyra tried to get a sense of where their faith lay. Neither of them was able to wear the pendant, thanks to its magic-repelling properties, but their wives did.

Elizabeth finally spoke, her voice high and melodical. "A woman's purpose is to have children. That is what our bodies were made for."

The smile slipped from Aemyra's face at the sincerity with which those words were spoken.

Indeed, the royals were prolific, between the three brothers, they had produced twelve little Dùileach princes.

Surely Nael and Elear had granted their wives more freedom in the years they had been living at the Teine court? Had it not broadened their minds at all?

Fiorean tilted his head to the side as if waiting for Aemyra's answer.

She took a deep breath. "A woman's purpose *can* be found in having children. However, a woman is so much more than just a mother. She is an individual with her own passions and desires far beyond those of her husband. Just because we possess a womb doesn't mean that we don't also have a brain."

Elear looked one step away from summoning a priest, but it was the interest in Elizabeth's eyes that had Aemyra continuing.

"Women have the power to create *life*. To sustain it, nurture it. Regardless of magical affinity, the Chosen have forgotten that a woman's base power lies in her womb. Therefore the choice to use that power lies with them. And them alone."

Maggie stroked her bump reverently, and Elizabeth's beautiful face was creased in a frown.

Aemyra looked pointedly at Fiorean. "I would like to make an offering at the temple for Fergys and speak with the priestesses. If you could escort me from the cai—"

Elear interrupted. "We have no need of your offerings. The Savior cleanses all sins."

Before their argument could escalate, Fiorean's strong hand clapped around her upper arm.

"That's quite enough, Wife," he muttered. "We are running late."

"For what?" Aemyra spat.

With guards and Covenanters walking the halls, Aemyra had no choice but to remain with the group.

"Where are we go—"

Aemyra's question died on her lips as they emerged on the western side of the caisteal. The portcullis was open and a line of exhausted-looking people stood patiently waiting before a cauldron brimming with stew. Priests were stationed around the walls, some conversing with the commoners.

The breath caught in Aemyra's lungs as she looked upon her people. They were thin, with deep circles under their eyes.

"The Balnain fleet has cut off a large portion of our trade from Tìr Ùir, and your father has set fire to Uisge ships with his dragon. We must make do with what little we can grow ourselves or what we have in our stores," Fiorean said quietly.

Elizabeth and Maggie were already rolling up their sleeves, holding their skirts out of the puddles of rainwater that had collected on the uneven ground.

"This is the cost of your war, Princess," Fiorean said.

The words were whispered spitefully into her ear, the quiet syllables hitting Aemyra hard as a physical blow. Steeling herself, she rounded on Fiorean, thinking of the lavish breakfast tray.

"Perhaps you should ration your own meals. One of us managed well enough on a diet of porridge, bannocks, and mutton for years."

Without giving him time to answer, she filled the space next to Maggie.

Hoping Fiorean would think she was just doing her charitable duty, Aemyra ladled stew into wooden bowls and tried not to shrink away from the looks her people were giving her.

Like she had betrayed them.

"They're accepting food from the enemy too."

The low voice made Aemrya jump, and she narrowly avoided sloshing stew all down the front of her dress. Looking up into the familiar face of Marilde the cook, a good friend of Orlagh's, Aemrya felt herself breathe a little easier.

"They are starving and have no other choice," Aemyra muttered back.

Marilde threw a few sprigs of rosemary into the stew. "Should we have expected you to choose death?"

Woodenly handing another bowl to the next pair of grasping

hands, Aemyra frowned. When Maggie stepped away to coo over a toddler with skinned knees, she faced the cook.

Aemyra had frequently been drunk under the table by Marilde in Sorcha's tavern but would have never suspected her to be a spy. The woman was the very opposite of inconspicuous.

"The kitchens. I'll send for you when it's time," Marilde said quietly.

Aemyra's heart leaped. Had one of Draevan's spies really been known to her all along? When Marilde's eyes crinkled at the corners and she was afforded a glimpse of the slice across the cook's palm, Aemyra knew for certain.

The scar was too deliberate-looking to be from a cooking incident, and Aemyra felt her heart swell at the small rebellion of an offering made to the Goddess on her behalf.

With so many eyes upon her, Aemyra was unable to give the cook more than a subtle nod. Despite her own rumbling stomach, she ladled out food until steaming bowls were cradled between chilled hands.

Task finished, she rounded the table, not bothering that the hem of her dress dragged through the mud. Fiorean was right, this was the cost of war, but it wouldn't last forever. When she sat the throne, her people would prosper.

"Trudging through mud is unbecoming of a princess," Athair Alfred said piously, stepping into her path.

Aemyra peered over his shoulder, noticing the way her people were observing them.

She smirked defiantly when she saw Alfred's hand twitch. "By all means, hit me. Show my people how the Chosen treat women. I was not particularly keen on the way I was dragged from the hall last night."

Her voice carried, and a few hushed whispers began spreading around the courtyard. Alfred's eyes narrowed, but he dropped his hand.

"Come away, Aemyra," Fiorean said, stepping in.

Before he could grab her again, she took a healthy step back. The skirts of her dress were heavy, and she almost unbalanced herself.

People were beginning to stare, and Aemyra wondered how long it would take to get them on her side. Elear, Nael, and Fiorean were all Dùileach, and there were at least twenty priests present, but there had to be over a hundred common folk crammed into the square.

Athair Alfred seemed to realize this and held up his hands for quiet.

"We shall raise our voices in prayer to give thanks for the food we have been given by His Grace, the king," he said virtuously.

Aemyra's last hope of a sudden rebellion died when she heard heavy footfalls on the steps behind her. Evander had made a late appearance.

The whispering quieted as the people bowed, and Aemyra felt Fiorean step closer to her.

"May the Savior keep and bless you," Evander shouted, his voice ringing through the courtyard before Alfred began a droning prayer.

Aemyra narrowed her eyes at the people slurping from bowls, suddenly understanding what this was. They had been promised a meal in return for their devotion to the Savior.

"How many were forced to convert before being allowed to fill their bellies?" Aemyra asked, rounding on Fiorean.

It was Evander who answered.

"All of them. It was the Athair's idea, and rather a good one, don't you think?" he asked, slurring his words slightly.

Aemyra wrinkled her nose at the sour smell lifting from his clothes.

"That is despicable. Forcing starving people to worship a God they do not believe in so you can feel more secure in your rule?"

Evander's lip curled and he leaned toward her. "How do you know they don't believe in the Savior already, eh? I am the king, what truly matters is that these people obey my command."

His voice had taken on a nasty edge, the whites of his eyes bloodshot.

Fiorean placed a firm hand on Evander's dirty tunic. "When was the last time you slept?" he asked.

Evander pushed Fiorean away, stumbling into Aemyra in the process.

"Do not speak to me like I am a child. I may be your brother, but I am also the king. Am I not allowed to numb this grief how I see fit?" Evander asked, lips thinning.

Lowering his voice so only his brother could hear him, Fiorean whispered, "You would be better served by setting your mind to stabilizing your rule. We have already suffered under the rulings of one mad king, do not make us suffer another."

With a petulant scowl, Evander shoved him away again. "I'm not mad."

"Then prove it," Fiorean growled.

Pushing Evander toward Elear, Fiorean looked pointedly at his younger brother. "See to it he has a bath?"

Elear nodded and ushered Evander away willingly enough, Elizabeth gathering her skirts and following closely behind.

Every commoner assembled in the courtyard had their eyes closed in prayer. Only Marilde remained rebelliously alert. The cook gave the barest nod and Aemyra felt her fingers begin to tingle with returning magic.

Athair Alfred continued his chanting as Fiorean's emerald eyes roved over Aemyra's face, his brow furrowed.

She averted her gaze and resolved to endure Alfred's self-righteous preaching for as long as it took. Her magic would return and she had found her way out.

All was not lost.

CHAPTER TWENTY-FOUR

Aemyra's stomach was painfully hollow by the time Alfred had finished his sanctimonious speech. So focused on reaching for her magic, Aemyra hadn't noticed Fiorean leading her into the private royal gardens. The scent of comfrey, rose, and wild garlic clashed in the most wondrous of ways.

"Do you really know the cure for my nephews?" Fiorean asked, crossing his arms stiffly.

Realizing he was serious, Aemyra hitched her skirts and squatted in the dirt. Despite her own agenda, she scanned the leaves for something she could use to save Edwyn and Alastair.

A shadow passed over her and she squinted into the sky, seeing the outline of Kolreath soaring high above.

"If I could examine the boys, I might gain a better idea of how to treat them," she said, tingling fingers skimming mint leaves without igniting them.

Just a little longer . . .

"Out of the question." Fiorean sniffed.

Temper breaking, Aemyra rose to her feet. "If you want me to keep playing into this little marriage charade, then you will let me help your nephews." Her eyes snagged on the dagger at his belt and her lips curved. "Begin atoning for your transgressions now and perhaps Hela will take pity on you when I send you to the Otherworld."

"I could make your imprisonment a lot more difficult," he replied, hands clasped maddeningly calmly behind his back.

"Try it, Fiorean. Find out how far you can really push me before I snap."

He quirked an eyebrow. "I'm surprised you didn't try last night, actually. You're smarter than I gave you credit for."

Aemyra crossed her arms. "What do you mean?"

"Well, I had been expecting you to try and seduce me, or get me drunk, and then try to kill me." Fiorean gazed down at her almost thoughtfully. "It's what I would have done."

Aemyra felt her chest contract as her magic flourished within her. She had to keep him talking.

Staring at the scarred side of his face pointedly, she asked, "How did you get them?"

Fiorean stiffened and rose to his full height.

"Is your ego so fragile that you can't get over your pretty face being ruined?"

Fiorean's eyebrow peaked. "You think I have a pretty face?"

"I think you're compensating for how your scars ruin it by commissioning dysfunctional swords and inspiring fear with your dragon," Aemyra said, stepping toward him. "So insecure you won't let anyone see the monster that lurks beneath your skin. Tell me, did my family put up a fight before you burned them? Did you enjoy chasing after a terrified little boy because it made you feel powerful?"

Fury ignited in Fiorean's eyes, and Aemyra took a chance.

Pulling out the two long hairpins that Maggie had thoughtlessly used to secure Aemyra's thick curls, she aimed for his eyes.

The sharp pins almost made contact before Fiorean's hands shot out and wrapped tightly around her wrists. He dug his thumbs into the groove of her joints, causing her left hand to spasm and she dropped the pin. But her right hand held fast as she gritted her teeth against the pain.

"I promised not to touch you last night. Kindly do your husband the same courtesy," Fiorean spat, his nostrils flaring.

He shoved her away with such force that she almost stumbled into the pansies.

"Oh, the next time I touch you, it won't be with my hands," Aemyra promised, straightening her skirts and trying desperately to connect to her magic.

Fiorean looked almost thrilled by her response.

"And where would you get your hands on a weapon? Why aren't you bothering to pretend?"

"You're too clever to fall for my feminine charms," Aemyra said, walking over to where he stood, pocketing the second hairpin before he could take it from her.

Fiorean crossed his arms over his muscular chest. "Do you possess any?"

Her chest spasmed and she swore that she felt an ember return to her.

"Plenty," she replied, looking up at him from underneath her eyelashes. "But pretending not to hate you would have gotten me nowhere. Better to give you the honest truth and wait for you to let your guard down all on your own."

Fiorean's lip curled.

"Careful. I could have you thrown in a cell for that."

Aemyra risked another step closer, her heart pounding against the surging power in her blood.

"But you won't. You care far too much about what people think of you, how they view you. It's why you made me change my dress. It's why you spared me last night. Because even though I despise you with every bone in my body, you need the world to believe that I don't. You need leverage."

Aemyra was so close to him that their chests were practically touching. Fiorean's eyes dipped to her lips, looking like he was fighting dropping his gaze farther.

"I told you I can be charming," she simpered.

Fiorean sneered. "I think I preferred you with a little more fire."

A wild grin spread across her face. "I couldn't agree more."

Without waiting to hear his reply, she threw every scrap of flame that had returned to her at him.

The prince reeled backward, and she wasted no time in sprinting for the gate. Her velvet slippers sliding on the grass, she picked up her skirts to avoid falling over as Fiorean's roars of anger met her ears.

But her fire had returned. If he pursued her, he would not live long enough to regret it.

Terrea, I'm here. Come to me.

Aemyra felt for the flickering Bond in her chest as she ran between the manicured rosebushes. The kitchens weren't far from the gardens; she could incapacitate Fiorean and escape through the servants' entrance.

The sound of Fiorean's boots striking the ground grew louder in her ears, and she dared to throw a fireball behind her.

It went wide, a rosebush igniting as Fiorean ducked around it.

"You will not escape this city on foot, Princess," Fiorean shouted after her. "There are guards at every gate and temple. We will find you."

Aemyra stopped running. Facing Fiorean as he skidded to a stop, she smiled at him.

"I don't plan on escaping on foot," she said savagely.

Summoning a great blaze, she coated herself in flame that originated not only from her core, but from that of her dragon. She threw them toward Fiorean, and the prince barely managed to shield himself, the blast knocking him into the burning bush.

That one effort drained what little energy Aemyra possessed after a day without food or water. She drew her flames back to her palms as Fiorean blinked through the smoke. Every bush around them burned;

as he got to his feet the expensive fabric of his tunic ripped on the thorns.

"You're Bonded," Fiorean said. "To wha—"

Aemyra smiled. "Now you will all burn."

Keeping one flame-wrapped hand out in front of her lest Fiorean get any ideas, she hoisted the skirts of her dress up with her other hand and made to back away slowly.

But, reveling in the sensation of her magic, Aemyra had forgotten the first rule her father had ever taught her.

Watch your back.

She heard the clink of armor just in time and thrust her hand out toward the advancing Sir Nairn. His silver gauntlets shone in the light of her fire, and she desired nothing more than to see his blond hair go up in smoke.

Repelling her magic as well as it had her touch, the Savior's pendant around his neck flashed silver, deflecting her magic from his body entirely.

Aemyra's mouth dropped open as she watched her flame simply disappear.

Sir Nairn looked down at the iron pendant smugly. "The Savior protects us from the evils of magic. I was rescued as a child from the ruins of the home where my parents perished. The priest who saved me gave me this pendant so I would never feel the burning of Dùileach fire again."

Hatred flared in the captain's eyes and Aemyra felt the sting of injustice in his words.

"You cannot discriminate against every Dùileach because of one experience," she said, harnessing a flame in her palm. "Magical fires spread out of control just as easily as natural ones."

"Oh, it was no accident," Sir Nairn replied, venom lacing every word as he upended a black velvet pouch full of powder that went up her nose.

But it wasn't Aemyra who protested this time.

"You fool," Fiorean growled. "Did you not think to warn me first?"

Aemyra made to summon a desperate tongue of fire, but she felt the magic slip through her grasp.

"No."

Sir Nairn smiled smugly, tucking the pouch into his belt. "Forgive me, my prince. But I was under strict instructions from Athair Alfred to incapacitate the princess by any means necessary."

"You answer to my brother, not the Athair," Fiorean said through gritted teeth, uncomfortable with his magic muted.

The captain straightened. "The king has granted Athair Alfred autonomy over these decisions. He may act as he sees fit where traitors are concerned."

Before Aemyra could smack the smug smile from Sir Nairn's face, Fiorean fisted a hand in her hair and wrenched her head back. He thrust his other hand into her dress pocket and flung the long hair pin across the scorched grass.

"So. You cost me my own magic with your failed escape and revealed that you have Bonded. Smart plan, Princess."

His nose was almost brushing the skin of her cheek as his hand tugged at her hair.

"I am not Bonded, Evander claimed Kolreath," she said desperately.

Fiorean was panting hard as she struggled against him.

"You possessed a deep well of power even un-Bonded, but only one fire beathach amplifies magic like this." His emerald eyes flashed. "You found an egg."

CHAPTER TWENTY-FIVE

TERREA WAS COMING FOR HER. AEMYRA HAD FELT IT THROUGH the Bond before it had gone silent again and she couldn't let Aervor and Kolreath be ready when her dragon arrived. No matter how fierce her beathach was, the two male dragons would kill Terrea before she had the chance to rescue Aemyra.

"Fiorean, let me go," she begged as she was hauled through the corridors.

But her new husband had gone temporarily deaf as he dragged her up the stairs, her knees knocking painfully against the stone when she stumbled. Sir Nairn clanked along behind.

Trying to calm herself, she mentally prepared for what might await her when Evander discovered she had a dragon. What he might order done to her if they found out Terrea was female.

Aemyra's future children could spell the rise of the dragons. She had to escape before they could use her body against her will, or blackmail her into protecting the very people who sought to oppress Dùileach.

They entered the throne room to find Evander standing before the dais, evidently having escaped Elear's clutches. He was deep in conversation with Athair Alfred, and Fiorean hesitated.

Despite her predicament, Aemyra turned to look upon the throne that she had never seen with her own eyes. A monstrosity of molten gold, it sat like an inert flame before the enormous stained-glass wall. The painted window cast streaks of crimson, amber, and copper across the room, as if anyone needed reminding of which clan ruled here.

Momentarily dazed by the refracting light, Aemyra landed heavily on her hands and knees when Fiorean flung her from him.

"My prince?" Athair Alfred asked, eyeing Aemyra like she was something dragged up from the gutters of the lower town.

Evander laughed.

"Bored of her already, Brother? I'll turn a blind eye if you visit the pleasure dens now and again, but Mother says you must stay married to her."

Fiorean clasped his hands behind his back, a muscle straining in his jaw.

"She has a dragon," Sir Nairn clarified.

Threads of tension pulled taut within the room and Aemyra clambered to her feet, refusing to bow and scrape before her usurper.

"That cannot be true," Athair Alfred said.

"She starved herself until the binding agent wore off," Fiorean reported, his voice tense. "Her magic has grown significantly."

"Are there unhatched eggs on the Sunset Isle?" Alfred asked.

Aemyra quickly moved Athair Alfred up the list of people she was going to kill, nestling his name in between Fiorean's and Nairn's. Her stomach gurgled and she swayed where she stood.

Evander marched up to her, his jade eyes lecherous. "How could someone as worthless as you find an egg when all other attempts have failed?"

Before Aemyra could open her mouth, Evander struck her with a stinging slap that whipped her head back.

Tears of fury sprang to her eyes and she resisted the urge to spit in his face.

Fiorean's hand went to his sword.

"It will be a hatchling, nothing more. Easily captured," Evander said, spittle flying from his lips.

At that moment, a quick pair of heels sounded on the tiles and Katherine hurried into the room, black skirts flying.

"What is the meaning of this?" she asked, her eyes fixing on Aemyra's reddened cheek.

"It appears as though the princess discovered a dragon egg and Bonded to it," Alfred stated.

Katherine's eyes widened in fear, and she looked up to the vaulted ceiling as if expecting to see fire pouring down from above. "Where is it?"

The Athair lifted his chin. "We do not yet know. The young princess was just in the process of telling us."

"Queen," Aemyra hissed.

Before the word was out of her mouth, Evander hit her again. There was a glint of madness in his eyes and the sharp bite of his ring split Aemyra's lip.

"You have already killed one of my children. Was this the final step in your plan?" he cried, launching himself at her, wrapping his hands around her neck.

The unhinged look in his eyes suddenly made Aemyra believe what they said about his father.

"I am the king and you will tell me!"

Evander's thumbs pressed down on her larynx and, weak with hunger, Aemyra scrabbled in vain against his grip.

A strong pair of arms wrapped around Evander and wrenched him off of her.

She stumbled away, choking and gasping for air.

"Boys," Katherine warned.

Fiorean shoved Evander toward the throne and stood in front of Aemyra, his chest heaving.

"You might be the king, Brother, but she is my wife. If she needs to be disciplined, then I shall see her punishment carried out. But I will not tolerate your hands, or the hands of anyone else, being laid upon her."

With these words, he looked pointedly at Evander but also Sir Nairn and Athair Alfred.

Aemyra shot daggers toward her husband in response to his little speech. When Fiorean had the audacity to reach down and offer her his hand, she smacked it away.

"You steal my crown, and my magic, and still expect me to cooperate?" she hissed, wiping her bloody lip with the back of her hand.

Katherine's gray eyes were uncertain, but Alfred had a dangerous expression on his face as Sir Nairn whispered in the priest's ear. Perhaps she would cut off Nairn's pouty lips instead of scalping him.

"Enough of this mess. I know how to make her talk," Athair Alfred said, linking his fingers piously over his stomach. "Take the princess to the banks of the loch. She will summon her little dragon while the princes summon theirs. Either the beast will join our ranks, or he will die."

So it was to be blackmail.

If Aemyra's heart was still in her chest she could no longer feel it. She had no way to warn Terrea without access to the Bond. No way to tell her dragon to turn back from the city before Aervor and Kolreath launched their attack with claws and fangs and fire.

Alfred slipped from the room as if he couldn't bear another moment in Aemyra's presence, and she bitterly regretted that she couldn't send a tongue of flame to set his black robes alight.

Several guards were summoned by Sir Nairn as Aemyra was dragged out of the throne room by Fiorean.

"Do not make me put you in chains," he growled into her ear as she fought him with what little strength she still possessed.

"You will pay for every crime you have committed against me and my people," Aemyra snarled right back.

The walk through the caisteal and down to the banks of the loch took longer than it should have thanks to Aemyra's struggling. She had been struck twice more by an impatient Evander, each time resulting in a brotherly spat that Katherine had to break up.

The entire time, Aemyra was dreading whatever torture awaited her when they reached the water's edge. She could see Cliodna's half-drowned temple shrouded in mist on the opposite bank.

Knowing that the water Goddess had no affinity for her, Aemyra didn't hold out hope for divine intervention.

Digging her heels into the small stones, she lost one of the velvet slippers and hissed in a breath as something sharp poked the sole of her foot.

"I will dunk you into the loch if you keep this up," Fiorean growled into her ear.

Aemyra gave him a feral smile. "Fancy a dip, Prince?" she asked, aiming a swift kick at his shin.

Fiorean doubled over in pain as she made contact with enough force to nearly break it. Still, he held fast.

Aemyra felt the skin on the bottom of her foot rip open as they turned the corner. When she saw what awaited her, the pain in her heart completely eclipsed that of her body.

"No."

The cry escaped her lips without conscious thought, and her knees gave out when she saw who was kneeling, hands bound and mouths gagged, in front of the leader of the Chosen.

Sorcha and Orlagh.

"*This cannot be,*" Aemyra whispered.

Orlagh was still alive.

Despite the danger, her chest suddenly felt less hollow. The profound relief of seeing her mother alive brought instant comfort. Aemyra had spent years dreaming of the day she could openly call Draevan Daercathian *Father,* but it was only after believing Orlagh dead that Aemyra understood which parent had truly been her protector.

Feeling Orlagh's presence once more made Aemyra realize just how empty life had been without it, how utterly lonely.

Hope surged in Aemyra's chest. She could have her mother back.

Her fingers tracked through the pebbles as if trying to inch closer despite her limbs trembling with shock. Her mother would help her fix this; Orlagh always knew what to do.

"Get up," Fiorean said, strong hands pulling Aemyra to her feet.

"Peasants? This is the Athair's plan?" Evander hissed, rounding on his mother.

Katherine ignored him as Alfred spoke, flanked by two guards and a cage that looked to have been used for one of Nael's hounds.

"You care for these women, do you not? They will ensure the co-operation of both you and your dragon."

Sorcha looked like she wished she was holding her meat cleaver, but Orlagh's eyes were glassy.

"This is all my fault," Aemyra whispered.

Her words were so quiet that she thought no one had heard her, but Fiorean dipped his head until she felt his breath tickle the back of her neck.

"Do as Alfred says. We won't hurt your dragon, I promise you," he said, voice whisper soft.

Aemyra couldn't find the energy to be ashamed that she was quaking with fear. She couldn't let them die.

Katherine and Alfred wouldn't stop their scheming here. They would continue blackmailing Aemyra until she had leashed Terrea to Evander's cause and accepted her shackles of marriage. Then the last hope for Tìr Teine returning to the ways of the Goddess would truly be lost, along with the biggest advantage her army had.

Alfred gave an exaggerated sigh and nodded to Sir Nairn.

The captain stepped forward, his boots drawing level with Orlagh's knees as he ripped the gag out of her mouth.

Orlagh fell forward, gasping in lungfuls of air, a trio of golden necklaces peeking from beneath her filthy shirt.

"No, stop! Tell me what to do," Aemyra asked, her voice breaking.

Orlagh's dark eyes were lined with exhaustion, the face of a mother who had endured too much. Seen too much.

"It's okay, baby," Orlagh said quietly. "This is bigger than my life."

Aemyra began to struggle in Fiorean's grip again. "No. Don't you dare give up," she shouted. "You taught me better than this."

Orlagh raised her face to the gray sky and began to pray.

"Brigid, bringer of light, I command myself into your embrace. May your fire cleanse my soul, may your cross protect those I leave behind."

Fiorean was struggling to restrain Aemyra as she fought with all of her might to get to her mother.

"No!" Aemyra screamed loudly enough that she felt something rip in her throat. "Think of Adarian, he needs you too. We both need you."

Orlagh continued praying as Fiorean's fingers dug into Aemyra's skin.

Katherine cleared her throat. "Now is the time to swear your loyalty, and that of your hatchling, into our service if you wish for her to live."

Furious tears streaked down Aemyra's cheeks as she speared the dowager queen with a look of pure hatred. She couldn't be responsible for Orlagh's death.

"I swear it," Aemyra finally said, sagging in Fiorean's hold. She would find another way to win her throne.

Katherine exchanged a delighted smile with Evander and suddenly Fiorean's grip was no longer restraining her but holding her up.

Aemyra called out through her tears, "Mama?"

Orlagh stopped praying and met her daughter's eyes.

"You are the light," she said.

Fiorean loosened his hold, but before Aemyra could reach her mother, Sir Nairn unsheathed a knife and cut through Orlagh's throat in one horrific swipe.

"No!" Aemyra's scream rent the air as blood sprayed across the shingle.

Surging forward, she lunged for her mother.

But it was too late.

The scream that tore through Aemyra's throat was loud enough to send birds scattering from the trees as Orlagh's body slumped to the ground. Sorcha was scrambling to get away, sobbing through the gag.

This couldn't be happening. She couldn't have learned that her mother was alive only to lose her all over again . . .

"I still do not see a dragon," Alfred mused aloud, fingering his pendant and scanning the skies. "Although perhaps his small wings are struggling with the distance?"

Aemyra pulled her gaze from Orlagh's corpse to see Sorcha fling her head backward. The satisfying sound of Sir Nairn's nose breaking reached her.

In a blind rage, Aemyra sprinted for Sir Nairn, aiming for the knife in his hand before he could hurt Sorcha too.

A feral scream tore from Aemyra's throat, and she barreled into the captain, sending them both flying. Sorcha dove out of the way just in time, trying to work the gag loose with her teeth.

Aemyra scrabbled for the knife but Sir Nairn was fast.

She barely saw the blade before he slashed up and sliced through the skin of her exposed chest. So far gone in her grief, the sting of the cut only enraged her further. Aemyra grappled with the captain, both turning over the other on the ground until she ended up straddling his breastplate and fielding off his left hand as he swung at her with the knife in his right.

Crimson blood was streaming from her chest, staining the front of her dress a deeper red.

Evander was giggling as Fiorean held him in a chokehold while Katherine hovered anxiously behind them, her pale gray eyes fixed on Orlagh's body.

"You murdering coward!" Aemyra screamed down at the captain.

An enraged roar sounded. For a moment Aemyra thought it had come from her lips, until the surface of the loch began to ripple.

Everyone on the shingly beach froze, and Aemyra didn't know whether to laugh or cry that her dragon had finally come.

And she was no hatchling.

The enormous black dragon speared through the thick clouds, her serpentine neck outstretched and wings clamped to her sides as she dove.

"Take cover!" Sir Nairn shouted, flinging himself away from Aemyra.

Terrea landed on the banks of the loch with a thunderous crash that sprayed everyone with frigid water. Before anyone could react, the dragon clamped her jaws down on the guard standing beside Alfred, cracking him in two with a sickening crunch.

Evander was gaping at the massive dragon and Katherine looked ready to faint.

"The Terror," Fiorean said in awe as he stared up at the dark creature, lowering his sword.

Terrea sent a warning blast of fire streaming across the beach, the heat searing Aemyra's cheeks and melting the cage until it was nothing but an oozing lump of metal.

Alfred was mouthing prayers of his own as he held out his pendant toward the dragon like it would protect him.

If the Bond had still been open, Aemyra would have asked Terrea to eat him next.

Terrea's nostrils flared, scenting Aemyra's blood, and she opened her mouth, letting forth a bone-shaking roar that had flecks of spittle flying from her razor-sharp teeth.

Getting unsteadily to her feet, Aemyra staggered toward her dragon, who was poised with her black wings held aloft, her amethyst eyes scanning the air above them.

Terrea knew two male dragons lingered close by.

Aemyra all but collapsed against her warm scales, her head swimming. All she had to do was climb onto her back and fly to her father. Draevan would know what to do.

"Leaving so soon?"

Turning at the sound of Alfred's voice, Aemyra sagged beside her dragon's violet Starfire eyes at the sight of Evander holding his sword up to Sorcha's neck, Alfred looking on smugly.

No.

"Tether your dragon to our cause, and Sorcha will live," he said.

Orlagh had seemed ready to die for Aemyra's reign, but Sorcha's olive complexion was drained of color, terror marking every line of her face.

Orlagh's body was lying between them, blood seeping out of her neck in a final offering, and Aemyra had to fight to keep her legs from buckling at the sight.

Draevan had tutored her in politics from a young age, but she was now playing a game that she didn't understand. This was no petty grievance between minor lairds. She was gambling with people's lives.

Lifting her chin, Aemyra resolved that the only life she would gamble with was her own.

"*Sgiath,*" Aemyra said to Terrea in the Seann.

The dragon bristled, letting forth another roar, but Aemyra put both of her hands on her dragon's face, willing her to understand what was in her heart.

Aemyra would find another way to get out of Àird Lasair. If she had to bring them all down from the inside, then that was what she would do, even if it meant weeks or months of having to live alongside these monsters. But she would not let any more innocent lives be lost because of her.

Warm dragon-breath skimmed her face.

"Fly," Aemyra repeated softly.

After a hesitation that felt much longer than it was, the enormous dragon took one step forward and wrapped her claws around Orlagh's body. Aemyra's vision swam as Terrea spread her wings and launched herself into the air, her mother finally freed from the clutches of the Chosen.

Aemyra swayed where she stood, praying that her dragon would give Orlagh the final burning she deserved.

"My dragon will come when called," Aemyra said, utterly exhausted.

Alfred pointed at Sorcha.

"Escort this woman back to her cell. We may yet have need of her."

Evander snapped his fingers at Sir Nairn. As Sorcha was dragged to her feet, she stood a few inches taller than the captain and met Aemyra's eyes. There was nothing but hatred lingering in Sorcha's eyes.

Feeling strange, Aemyra put one hand to her chest and looked down.

The front of her dress was completely soaked with blood, the red satin ruined, and she swayed on her feet.

The last thing she felt before she lost consciousness was a strong pair of arms catching her and the sweet scent of orange blossom.

CHAPTER TWENTY-SIX

WHEN AEMYRA REGAINED CONSCIOUSNESS, SHE WAS LYING on the settee in Fiorean's chambers and her chest was stinging painfully.

With a groan, she tried to sit up.

"I wouldn't do that if I were you, Princess," Fiorean drawled from where he was kneeling on the floor beside her.

His right hand was dabbing at the wound on her chest with a damp cloth and his other holding a bowl of bloodstained water. A healer was hovering behind him, looking like he wanted to intervene.

"What are you doing?" Aemyra whispered nervously.

Fiorean's eyes were fixed on her wound. "I would have thought that was obvious," he said tersely.

Squeezing out the cloth once more, Fiorean carefully cleaned the blood off her chest, his fingers gentle with the edges of the wound.

"You were lucky. A few inches higher and Sir Nairn might have severed something important," he muttered.

"Maybe he should have thought twice about swinging a knife at my throat."

"Maybe you shouldn't have thrown yourself at someone holding a knife while unarmed."

"Perhaps I wouldn't have had to, if the person holding the knife hadn't just killed my *mother*," Aemyra growled, throat burning with unshed tears.

Fiorean's green eyes were glittering dangerously.

The healer stepped forward. "Your Highness, I think this arguing is unhelpful for the princess's recovery. She has lost rather a lot of blood and needs to regain her strength."

"I need to murder Sir Nairn," Aemyra spat, whipping her head around. "Can you assist me with that?"

The healer's face paled and he backed hastily out of the door.

"Sir Nairn has lost more than most at the hands of the Dùileach," Fiorean said quietly. "His early life in Àird Caolas was not an easy one."

Aemyra felt her face flush with anger.

"I don't care if Laird Lonan himself threw Sir Nairn into a cave full of chimeras, I will *kill* him for what he just did."

Fiorean placed the bowl of water on the floor, and Aemyra dared to look at the wound on her chest. It was deep but not dangerously so. A twinge on her forearm spoke of a second injury she hadn't felt while grappling with the captain.

"Well, at least the blade was clean and sharp," she said, trying to muster her courage.

Until she remembered that the same blade had cut through the flesh of Orlagh's neck.

"I'm going to vomit," Aemyra managed to choke out before Fiorean quickly held a different bowl up to her mouth.

Bile burned up her throat from her empty stomach, her split lip throbbing painfully. Tears stinging the corners of her eyes, she panted as she lay back onto the cushions, the room spinning.

"Here," Fiorean said quietly, offering her a goblet of watered-down wine.

She eyed it hatefully, knowing that it was probably laced with the potion that bound her magic.

Fiorean read her expression correctly. "It is from my personal store. This wine has not been tampered with."

She shouldn't trust him, but the blood loss had made her desperately thirsty. Grasping the goblet with both hands, she sipped it carefully.

"What an absolute mess," she muttered.

Fiorean did her the kindness of not responding as Aemyra screwed her eyes shut against the pain. Having her mother returned to her for a brief moment and then ripped away again was something she would never forgive Athair Alfred for. Sir Nairn was dead for carrying out the order.

Aemyra suddenly lost her taste for the wine when she thought of the look in Sorcha's eyes as she had been dragged back to the dungeons.

Before she could try to reach for the table, Fiorean plucked the goblet from her fingers.

"Why are you helping me?" she asked.

"Because this is my fault," Fiorean finally muttered.

Aemyra's brow furrowed as she once again glimpsed the man who lurked underneath the hateful exterior. The crackling fire behind the settee was a mocking imitation of the power she could no longer summon.

"I thought you would be finishing the job Sir Nairn started by now," Aemyra said, a slight tremor in her voice.

He didn't meet her eyes. "You're more useful to us alive. If you die now, your dragon—and likely your father as well—will burn this city to the ground."

Despite his words, Aemyra knew that her freshly Bonded, magical womb was now their greatest asset. Was it possible they wanted strong Dùileach children Bonded to hatchlings and blackmailed into the service of the Chosen? The thought made Aemrya even more nauseous than she already was.

"Wouldn't you have preferred to marry a woman from Ùir? You have all turned your backs on the Goddess anywa—"

"Have we?" he interrupted, lifting his eyes to hers.

Holding her gaze for a long moment, Fiorean uncorked a small vial from the bag the healer had left beside the settee.

Aemyra looked more intently around the room for any sign of Brigid. There was the large fire, obviously, but no burning oil or woven crosses.

Fiorean tilted a small vial over her skin and she jerked out of her thoughts.

He rolled his eyes. "Are you so obstinate that you can't tell when I'm trying to save your life instead of end it?"

Narrowing her eyes, Aemyra replied, "This is hardly a mortal wound, but now that you mention it, no. You are the one who brought me to Evander and told him about my dragon. Saving my life doesn't count if you were the one putting it in danger in the first place."

This time, Fiorean held her gaze. "I didn't know the Athair was with my brother. For what happened because of my actions you have my deepest sympathies. And apologies."

Before she could tell him to shove his sincerity up his arse, Fiorean spoke again. "Sir Nairn also witnessed your magic use. If I hadn't brought you to my brother, we both would have been questioned. Under duress."

Aemyra sighed. "You were right. I understand nothing about this court."

Fiorean held the vial up to her nose and she gave it a gentle sniff.

"It's mostly honey, I think. There's a faint trace of anise, which will do nothing more than give it an impressive color. Elear's favorite healers are certainly no Beatons." With a brisk nod of permission, Aemyra removed her grip from Fiorean's skin.

His fingers were gentle and efficient, but Aemyra remained rigid under his ministrations.

"Did your mother teach you all of this?" he asked gently.

Grief enveloped her again and Aemyra turned her gaze to the fire. Neither of them had access to their magic, but the flames were high in the hearth, like Brigid knew two of her children were in this room.

"Orlagh taught me how to heal with both plants and magic. Many believe fire to be the most destructive of the blessed elements, but they forget that fires cleanse just as much as they destroy," Aemyra said quietly, a tear leaking out as she gazed into the flames. They reminded her of Solas's tail.

Aemyra turned her gaze back to Fiorean.

"Where is my mother's firebird?" she asked in a quiet voice.

Fiorean stilled and his face adopted an unreadable expression. "He was consumed by Aervor's flames, alongside . . ."

Aemyra didn't need him to finish the words. The emptiness in Orlagh's eyes hadn't only been from losing her husband and child, she had lost her beathach. Part of her soul had already been in the Otherworld. Aemyra supposed it should have been some comfort to her that Orlagh was now at peace, reunited with her family and Solas—but it made her feel worse.

By reaching for the throne, she had condemned the very people who had raised her.

Brigid, hold them in your embrace until I see them again.

Aemyra sent up a silent prayer to the Goddess and begged to never have to endure a grief this heavy again. An ache began in her soul as she thought of her twin. She had to get back to Adarian.

With a determined sniff, she stemmed the flow of tears while Fiorean rubbed some of the healing salve onto the small wound on her forearm. Three stitches had been sewn in while she had been unconscious.

"You need to drink this," Fiorean said, rising to his knees so that his face was above hers, holding another vial in his hands.

Instinctively, Aemyra smacked his hand away, wincing when the movement jostled her wounds.

"We have already established that I'm not going to poison you," Fiorean ground out.

Aemyra glared at him. "No, you just want my magic stifled so you can keep me here and ensure my father doesn't burn this caisteal to the ground. Don't worry, I already feel a prize fool for falling into your trap outside that inn."

She didn't dare speak aloud her deepest fear, the true reason why she was being kept in this prison, married to a prince she hated.

"This doesn't contain the binding agent," Fiorean explained like she was testing his patience. "It is oil of henbane, for the pain. Your chest wound needs to be closed or it will fester, and the needle will hurt."

Still, Aemyra glared up at him.

"I don't want to be unconscious around you people any longer than I have to. And don't explain the finer arts of healing to me—I know far more about them than you do. Orlagh's third great-grandmother *was* a Beaton."

Something she said gave him pause, the shadows from the fire casting his scars into sharp relief. After a moment, he dipped his hands into the clean water bowl, before picking up the needle and thread.

"What are you doing?" Aemyra asked, nervously eyeing his hands.

"Tending to my wife's wounds," Fiorean muttered, testing the strength of the knot around the eye of the needle.

"But the healer . . ."

"I didn't need him to sew up your other wound, and I certainly won't need him for this one. If you want to look as scarred as I do, then I can call him back in, but if you want this to heal properly, you should let me continue," Fiorean said, his eyes meeting hers.

For the first time, Aemyra realized that he might have endured more pain than she knew about. As he tied his hair into a knot and revealed his facial scars, she wondered what else he was hiding behind his cool exterior.

Fiorean paused, both hands above her chest, the needle held between the index finger and thumb of his right hand.

Aemyra blew out a tense breath and nodded her permission.

His left hand probed gently at the edge of her wound, the lowest corner just above her right breast. His touch was gentle as he pressed the edges together.

"Last chance to change your mind," he muttered, his eyes glancing quickly to the oil of henbane.

"You've never had a problem hurting me before," Aemyra said, gritting her teeth. "Why develop a conscience now?"

The first bite of the needle was worse than she had been expecting. It drew cleanly through her flesh, and she pressed her lips together.

"Try not to move," Fiorean whispered.

She fisted her hands into the cushions underneath her as Fiorean worked.

He had completed fewer than four stitches before she spoke.

"Tell me something to take my mind off this," she almost begged.

Fiorean dragged the needle upward, the translucent thread pulled taut.

"What would you like me to tell you?"

Aemyra rolled her eyes.

"Fucking anything, Fiorean. Right now you could tell me about your first time with a woman or your morning shit and I would be grateful."

The corners of his lips twitched, but his eyes were fixed on his work.

"How did you come to claim The Terror?" he finally asked.

"You're supposed to be the one doing the talking. I'm in need of distraction," Aemyra complained as his fingers pulled her skin together.

"I am trying to concentrate as well, you know," Fiorean replied, his voice barely above a whisper.

Struggling not to audibly groan as the needle went through her skin once more, Aemyra risked giving him some of the truth.

"I had always wanted a dragon. I just never imagined what that Bond would be like until it was forged."

Fiorean looked pensive.

"I understand what you mean. My magic has always been greater than my siblings', but my father enjoyed pitting us against one another. Evander continually reminded me that, as the eldest, he would claim Aervor and become the most powerful." Fiorean's mouth opened slightly as he pulled the needle. "When I was eight, Evander rode with me into the Deàrr Mountains under the pretense of finding the dragon nests. He left me on a ledge and told me that if I wanted to know what it was like to fly, I should jump."

Aemyra witnessed the hurt of a small child pass over his face, the pain of humiliation that lingered all these years later.

Wishing that she didn't feel sorry for the man responsible for so much of her grief, Aemyra sighed as the thread pulled through her skin.

"That wasn't right," she replied.

Fiorean's hand stilled, and his eyes drifted up to her face as if he hadn't expected her compassion.

"Children can be unnecessarily cruel. I know Adarian didn't deserve half of the stunts I pulled on him when we were young," Aemyra said.

Fiorean's expression softened, and he returned to his ministrations. "You Bonded to a dragon who was supposed to be both untamable and dead."

Aemyra sighed, her chest rising, and Fiorean had to lift his hands away.

"Scared of me yet?" she asked.

Fiorean narrowed his eyes, yet the glare held less venom than usual. "Hardly. Although I don't know how I never realized you were of this clan. I used to pride myself in knowing everything that went on in this city."

Aemyra rolled her eyes. "Forgive me, but you don't seem the type to take notice of anyone below the rank of knight. Why would you have noticed a family moving into the city ten years ago when we looked just as dirty and tired as all the others?"

Fiorean lifted his eyes again, this time the expression on his face was a little too easy to read. "How did you do it?" he asked.

Aemyra didn't know what made her answer truthfully, but she felt compelled to pass on the knowledge Orlagh had left her with.

"The idea that we control our beathaichean and steal their magic is an absurd narrative pushed by the Chosen. Beathaichean are intelligent, sentient beings who make their own choices. But doesn't that make it even more exhilarating when they choose you?" Aemyra asked as Fiorean snipped the last stitch.

He cleared his throat and reached for a clean sponge. "You seem to control The Terror well enough."

Aemyra frowned.

"You have been Aervor's rider for years. You know that one could never hope to truly *control* a dragon, but we do respect each other enough to listen."

Aemyra couldn't touch the spot on her own chest because of her wound, so she reached forward before she could think better of it.

"It's here. The space somewhere between your heart and your soul that speaks to your beathach. Without the binding agent I would be able to feel Te—The Terror even now if I closed my eyes and concentrated. I don't need to tell my dragon what to do, although it's certainly faster."

Fiorean was leaning toward her, his emerald gaze fathomless as her fingers pressed against his skin through his shirt.

Then Aemyra understood.

She gasped quietly. "You don't feel it, do you?"

Fiorean sat back up and her hand dropped from his chest. He wrung the cloth out between his hands, the now clear water dripping back into the bowl with a tinkling plop.

"No. I don't feel that with Aervor," he replied stiffly, a flush creeping up his neck.

"Fiorean, look at me," she ordered, her heart pounding strongly enough that she thought her wound might open up again.

He lifted his face to her slowly and she was surprised to see that his emerald eyes were limned with tears.

"You didn't kill Lachlann, did you?" she asked, hardly daring to believe it.

Her heart near stopped when he shook his head and replied, "No. Aervor did."

CHAPTER TWENTY-SEVEN

FIOREAN'S REVELATION HAD BEEN TOO MUCH FOR BOTH OF them.

Three days had passed since Orlagh's death, and they had barely exchanged two words with each other. Instead, a silent sort of alliance had struck up between them. Aemyra hadn't actively tried to kill him, and Fiorean had left her largely alone.

Sleep had not come easily since the events at the lochside, and her days were spent under Maggie's watchful eye. With her food and water still laced with the binding agent, Aemyra clung to the hope of being summoned to the kitchens to escape the caisteal.

Her wounds were painful, but they were far easier to bear than the weight of her grief and guilt. It was only the thought of rescuing Sorcha from the dungeons and getting back to her army that kept her going.

Slumping huffily onto a stone bench, Aemyra ignored the book she had been trying to read for the last hour. "Surely you've finished the thistle by now?"

Maggie looked up from her needlepoint.

Aemyra groaned. "Some conversation wouldn't go amiss. This book is frightfully dull."

"Quiet contemplation is good for the soul," Maggie said, deftly swiping her needle upward.

Aemyra rolled her eyes. "Or a good way to go as mad as the late king."

The needle stilled.

Noticing the stiff way Maggie was sitting, the skirts of her dark green dress hiding her small bump, Aemyra softened her tone.

"I would very much like to find a friend at this court," she said, biting her lip and hoping that the younger woman wouldn't snub her.

After a moment, Maggie set her embroidery on her lap.

"Then you shall have one," she replied with a quiet determination. "I remember what it was like to arrive at this court knowing no one. It was a daunting prospect."

Maggie and the other royal wives had been shipped to Tìr Teine by their fathers. High-ranking nobles from Tìr Ùir, hoping to make an auspicious match with a prince. Aemyra wondered what Maggie might have chosen to do with her life had her father not decided for her.

There was nothing wrong with embroidering thistles onto cushions, as long as it wasn't only because embroidery was deemed an "appropriate" pursuit for a woman of Tìr Ùir.

"Will none of your family travel to see the babe?" Aemyra asked, eyeing the small bump.

Maggie shook her head. "It is quite the journey from Ramburgh, and my mother is frail. My father would not deem the trip necessary when he has four sons of his own."

The King of Ramburgh was a holy man, and a tyrant. Aemyra wondered if he had even blinked before selling his youngest daughter into marriage to a Teine prince.

Aemyra noted the bitterness with which Maggie spoke of her parents. "Do you miss your home?"

Even before the words were out of Aemyra's mouth, Maggie was shaking her head, her fingers pulling at a loose thread.

"No. I have found my home here," Maggie said. "Although I do miss my dearest friend, Florence." Aemyra stayed quiet, leaving an opening for the woman to elaborate should she wish to.

"Our mothers were close, and we grew up together. Her father is the Viscount Sevred, quite the formidable man, and we often hid ourselves away in the kitchens while our fathers spoke of business and our mothers held court," Maggie said, a wistfulness in her voice. "Florence married three months before I sailed for Tìr Teine, to the Duke of Rodover, if you would believe it. She's a duchess now."

Aemyra felt guilty for bringing on such melancholy. "And you are a Teine princess."

"Sometimes I wish we were just little girls kneading dough and helping decorate cakes in the kitchens again. No titles, no lands. Just us."

Something in Maggie's tone struck a chord with Aemyra and she felt tears prick at the corner of her eyes. Thinking of evenings spent drying herbs with Orlagh and the simple comfort of proximity and companionable silence.

Maggie was right, that was worth more than any title.

Perhaps even that of queen.

"I know what you must think of us," Maggie began, brown eyes downcast. "But Fiorean is unfailingly kind. He ensured I felt welcome in this territory."

"Then you must be acquainted with a different Fiorean than I am."

The words were barely out of Aemyra's mouth before she was remembering the gentle way he had stitched her wounds. She watched the way Maggie caressed her stomach between pulls with the needle.

"How do you stand it?" she asked.

When Maggie frowned in confusion, Aemyra elaborated. "Being married to a Dùileach, bearing children blessed by the Goddess, when it goes against your beliefs?"

Maggie's features softened at the mention of Nael. "The Savior believes every soul can be saved. Nael is a good person and he possesses only a drop of fire compared to Fiorean, or you."

Aemyra was certain that wasn't intended as a compliment.

"Were you not afraid to marry a Dùileach prince?" Aemyra asked.

Maggie straightened. "I am not as fragile as some may think."

Appraising the princess, Aemyra cocked an eyebrow. "No, I don't suppose you are." Aemyra took a deep breath and leaned against the back of the stone bench.

A pretty blush was darkening Maggie's brown cheeks, and Aemyra found herself smiling in response.

Until a scream sounded from the corridor.

One hand pressed to her bosom, Maggie strode in the direction of the noise.

"Since you have not been trained with a weapon and are currently with child, I would not advise rushing *toward* the sound of screaming," Aemyra drawled, fanning out her skirts as she stood.

With a quick swipe, Aemyra shoved Maggie's discarded needle into the pocket of her dress and looked through the open archway to where the raised voices were growing louder.

"She killed my son!"

Elizabeth rounded the corner, followed by Katherine and two priests. Elizabeth's cream dress was stained and her golden hair unkempt as she cast her wild eyes around the shadowy garden. Spotting Aemyra in front of a large potted fern, Elizabeth screamed ferally as she advanced with her long nails brandished like claws.

With a bored expression, Aemyra expertly intercepted the attack, wrapping her hands around Elizabeth's narrow wrists and trapping her arms down by her sides.

"Let me go!" Elizabeth shrieked.

Flexing her jaw as her ears popped at the shrill sound, Aemyra looked up to find Fiorean, Nael, and Elear advancing from the opposite direction and almost barreling into the priests.

"Well, now that we have established you can communicate with the caisteal hounds, perhaps Nael should take you out on his next hunt?" Aemyra asked, catching a glancing blow on her cheek from Elizabeth's thrashing head.

Elear looked ready to duel Aemyra in the garden, but Fiorean quickly stepped in.

"What is the meaning of this?" he demanded.

Elizabeth's wails of grief were hard to misinterpret, and Aemyra held her as gently as she could without her skin being scratched to ribbons by those perfectly manicured nails.

"Hamysh is dead!" Elear shouted, causing his wife's screams to turn into hysterical sobs.

The shadows of Aemyra's nightmares washed through her mind with a jolt of grief, news of another dead child triggering some greater despair. Elizabeth went limp in her hold, and Aemyra thrust the woman toward the dowager queen, who she noticed had red-rimmed eyes.

The priests looked to be eagerly awaiting Katherine's order to restrain Aemyra for more cleansing prayers.

She wondered briefly if Fiorean, the most powerful Dùileach in the royal family, had ever been restrained and prayed over by Athair Alfred. Aemyra wouldn't put it past the priest.

"My wife has been recently wounded. The past three days she has either been recovering in our chambers or Maggie has been accompanying her," Fiorean said firmly.

Maggie nodded her head as Nael's arms came protectively around her. "It is true. We have shared quiet company for the past several hours."

Elear did not look convinced. "Hamysh is *dead,* Brother. I will have the culprit executed."

Aemyra refused to shrink away from Elear's hateful glare, her hand dipping into her pocket and curling around the needle.

"If your son is dead, then it is by someone else's hand," Aemyra said. "I am a good deal less violent than you all seem to think I am."

Fiorean shot her a look that screamed "doubtful."

Elizabeth was shaking and Katherine was stroking her blond hair like she actually cared.

"Take her to the dungeons," Elizabeth sobbed. "Mother, speak on behalf of the king, command it."

Katherine hesitated and Elear threw his weight into Fiorean. "Since that woman has been within these walls, our boys have only grown weaker. Restrain her!"

As the two brothers grappled with each other, Aemyra kept the needle held tightly in her fist as the two priests hovered eagerly beside the archway.

"It seems as though your anger should be directed more toward the healers you mistakenly trusted than me," Aemyra said.

Her tone enraging him further, Elear scrabbled against Fiorean's hold, and for a brief moment she thought he might overpower his elder brother. Fiorean gained the upper hand by landing a spectacular right hook to Elear's jaw and emerged victorious.

His tunic rumpled and his usually smooth hair tousled, Fiorean pointed a finger at each of his relatives.

"You will do as I say and remain calm until the true murderer is brought to justice," he spat through gritted teeth at Elear. "Comfort your grieving wife and stop bullying mine."

The smirk was wiped off Aemyra's face when Fiorean rounded on her. His boots were loud on the damp stones underfoot, and he only stopped when his nose was an inch from her own.

"That includes you. If I find out you had anything to do with this, I will swing the axe myself."

She could feel his warm breath on her lips, his heaving chest pressed up against her corset.

Not waiting for his mother to order Aemyra's arrest, Fiorean hauled her bodily from the walled garden.

When they had rounded the corner, he gripped her right wrist and pried her fingers apart.

"I'll be sure to tell Maggie not to embroider in your presence next time," he grunted, flinging the needle aside.

Aemyra glowered but refrained from tormenting him further as Fiorean shoved her into the tightly winding staircase that led to their chambers. He had lost two nephews in the space of a fortnight.

Aemyra clicked her tongue. "They should have listened to me."

"They did."

Whirling around, Fiorean walked straight into her heavy woolen skirts and extracted himself with some difficulty.

"What?" she asked.

Fiorean glared up at her. "I administered the charcoal myself. All of the children who became ill upon your arrival recovered."

Aemyra's blood ran cold. "Then they were poisoned on two separate instances."

Sharing a grim look with her, Fiorean replied, "Someone within these walls is killing my nephews."

Climbing the stairs, her feet moved woodenly and for the briefest moment, her traitorous heart thought of her father. If Draevan's spies were attempting to break the royal family from within . . .

Aemyra recoiled in horror, placing one hand to the boning of her corset, suddenly feeling light-headed. That was not how she wanted to win her throne. She never would have wished such grief on anyone—even her enemies.

Evidently, Fiorean was already on the same page. "If I find out that your father had a hand in this . . ."

His spiteful tone irked her instantly.

Whirling to face him as they crested the stairs, Aemyra shoved him bodily away. She was allowed to think the worst of Draevan Daercathian, no one else.

"My father would never do such a thing," she hissed. "But your mother has made no secret of her hate for Goddess magic."

Fire sparked behind Fiorean's eyes, and he advanced toward her, backing her against the stone wall until she was forced to look up at him.

She attempted to drive her knee into his crotch, but her skirts got in the way and Fiorean shoved his thigh between her legs.

"Really, Princess? Do I need to take my shirt off again to remind you which of my parents was the violent one?"

Aemyra's chest was heaving with his proximity, and she squashed down the very small part of her that wanted to see him shirtless again.

"That won't be necessary," she replied with as much disdain as she could manage. "I would rather keep my breakfast down, as there is no privy on this floor."

Fiorean's lip curled. "You jump to Draevan's defense and yet are so quick to condemn me."

"My father has not killed anyone I care about," Aemyra sneered.

"Nor have I!" Fiorean shouted.

His voice rang through the empty corridor, and Aemyra fought to collect her thoughts.

"I am certain my father had nothing to do with it. We need to focus on who has access to the royal children and I must be allowed to inspect the body."

"Elear would never allow it," Fiorean snarled.

"Then you do it."

She pressed her palms flat against his sculpted chest and pushed. She hadn't put her full force behind it, but Fiorean backed away nevertheless.

Straightening her skirts, Aemyra tried to withstand the swirling grief within her.

Three little boys dead in as many weeks. The anguish on Elizabeth's face had been enough to crack Aemyra's already broken heart further.

Fiorean was quiet, his eyes far away as he regained his composure.

She had to get to the kitchens. Marilde would know someone connected to Draevan's network of allies in the capital. They would help her find out who was behind this.

On the opposite wall sat a large painting of Princess Isobeil and her shining silver dragon, Sylthria. The artist had been given a gift from the Great Mother, the brushstrokes seemed to imbue life into the painting. Isobeil's unruly curls were so like Aemyra's own.

Aemyra's fingertips stretched toward Sylthria's silver face. The dragon had been deemed untamable until Isobeil had proven her clan wrong, naming her beathach after the mist that clung to the mountains she loved so dearly.

"You miss your dragon," Fiorean said softly.

Aemyra snatched her hand away, her emotions uncomfortably close to the surface. "I miss a lot of things."

As Fiorean held the door to their chambers open, Aemyra's thoughts turned to Lachlann. If there was any way to bring him back, she would do it. She would barter with Hela herself to give her brother a second chance at life.

Elear's pride was preventing him from granting his sons the same. Aemyra set her own aside as she rounded on Fiorean.

"You will need wild garlic and willow bark," she said, thoughts whirring. "Honey for the open sores, and warm compresses—be sure to boil the fabric first."

Fiorean frowned, struggling to follow her rapid instructions.

"Do you even know what the herbs look like?" Aemyra asked despairingly.

"We do have a royal apothecary. I'm fully capable of reading labels," Fiorean quipped.

Ignoring him, Aemyra crossed to the small desk and flipped open the inkwell. Nearly breaking the quill in her haste to write the list, she pressed the parchment into Fiorean's hands, fingers now smudged with ink.

"And here I thought both of us were literate," he said, struggling to decipher her scrawl.

She threw the quill at him, point-first, as he tucked the list into the pocket of his tunic.

"I will retrieve the necessary items and take them to the nursery, although I will need to be quick about it," he said.

"Somewhere to be, Prince?" she asked.

Fiorean scratched his nose with one finger, something he did only when he was nervous. "Today is my breithday. There is to be a cèilidh dance held this evening. Or there was."

Aemyra arched one brow. "A cèilidh?"

"Indeed."

"I assume this was planned before Hamysh's death?"

Fiorean nodded solemnly.

"Isn't Evander aware that there is a war going on?" she asked drolly. "My father has marched my army from Atholl, and the Balnain fleet is burning Leuthanach fields of wheat as they advance up the river."

Fiorean cracked a slight smile. "I see you have been reading my correspondence."

Aemyra refused to look ashamed.

"I would agree that now is not the time for celebration; however, my mother did not want my breithday to pass without event, and people have traveled for it."

"Why didn't you tell me?" she asked.

Fiorean looked confused.

"That today is your breithday," Aemyra clarified.

"I have been a little preoccupied with the war we have going on," Fiorean replied sardonically.

Aemyra bit the inside of her cheek to stop herself from smiling.

"Do not leave this room," he said, departing swiftly, the list in his hand, and closed the door with a gentle thud.

With him gone, Aemyra felt like she could finally breathe again.

As she unlaced the back of her dress with deft fingers, she let the smothering grief wrap around her like a mourning veil.

She could only hope that when she finally won her throne, some of this unbearable weight would leave her. Wondering if Fiorean felt as guilty as she did, Aemyra stepped out of her dress and began thinking of how she might use tonight's cèilidh to her advantage.

The shadow of Kolreath was visible from the window, haunting the city as if to keep Terrea at bay.

Aemyra huffed a bitter laugh that the royals would be forced to pretend all was well in front of the attending lairds.

The more time she spent in this court, the less she liked it.

CHAPTER TWENTY-EIGHT

THE SOUND OF A FIDDLE HAD WOUND UP THE STAIRS AN HOUR ago, and Aemyra was sitting on the settee tapping her foot on the rug in time to the lively beat.

The music was helping to alleviate some of her grief and she closed her eyes, allowing the chaotic slide of notes to wash through her, lifting her spirits.

"Mhm."

Her eyes flew open to find Fiorean standing beside the open door, watching her.

Annoyed at being caught enjoying the faint strains of music, she stood and smoothed the skirts of her dress more self-consciously than she had intended.

"You're already dressed," she commented, noticing Fiorean's perfectly fitted fèileadh. It was tartan, but the pattern was in his habitual black.

His gaze was roving over the dark green dress she had chosen for the occasion. The fabric was the exact shade of her eyes, with long sleeves and a high neck to cover both of her recent wounds. It was modest enough, if one didn't notice the low back.

"Well, happy breithday," Aemyra said, trying for civility.

Fiorean simply stood there, his eyes unblinking.

"Is something wrong?" Aemyra asked, feeling suddenly too exposed with her hair pinned up and her back bare.

When no answer was forthcoming, she sighed in irritation and turned toward the wardrobe. It would be a nightmare getting out of this dress without Maggie's help, and she had already gone downstairs.

"Honestly, I have never met someone so uptight. If I hadn't already seen you without your breeches, I would be half-convinced you actually had a stick up your arse," Aemyra huffed, struggling with the dress. "Forcing me to change simply because I don't meet your idea of perfection, truthfully it's ridicu—"

"No."

Fiorean had come up behind her, speaking the word into her ear like it pained him to say it. His fingers brushed the bare skin of her back.

Her skin prickled despite the heat of the room, and she turned to face him.

Fiorean cleared his throat. "I mean, no," he repeated, his body language unsettled, "you look lovely."

Aemyra tried not to notice how his proximity unnerved her.

"Blacksmiths can scrub up well."

Fiorean gave her a brief attempt at a smile. "I thought you would never get the grime out from under your nails. It's a minor miracle."

She bit back her retort as he fiddled with the small box he carried. She looked down at it, and then back up to him.

"What is this?" she asked.

"Open it," Fiorean said as she took the box from his hands.

"This is your breithday, shouldn't I be giving you a gift?" she asked.

Fiorean arched one eyebrow. "What, pray tell, would you have given me?"

"A black eye ..." she muttered instinctively, but at the sight of his face she acquiesced. Biting back her smile, she looked down at the box. "Give me one afternoon in the forge and I'll make you a proper weapon."

More than a little apprehensive, Aemyra opened the box's lid, and almost dropped the whole thing. Nestled on a bed of black velvet was a garnet necklace. She fingered the large gemstone, now enclosed within a circle of black diamonds.

"I can't accept this," Aemyra said, looking into his face.

Not letting her say anything else, Fiorean took the box and plucked the necklace out with his long fingers.

Heart in her mouth, Aemyra turned around, wondering if there was some ulterior motive in giving her back the gemstone.

Fiorean looped his arms around her neck and carefully lowered the garnet onto her chest, clearly worried about it touching her wound.

Fastening the clasp, he remained standing behind her, so close that she could smell the lilac and orange blossom from the soap he used.

Looking down, Aemyra touched the garnet.

This stupid jewel meant many things to her. A broken promise, failed revenge, suffering. But all the while it had reminded her that she was meant to be queen.

There was no way Fiorean could have known that, but the fact that he was returning it to her at all spoke volumes.

She turned around to face him, blinking slightly as her nose almost brushed his chin.

"My father calls me 'magpie,'" she blurted out.

An amused look crossed Fiorean's face. "So, you have a penchant for bright, shiny things?"

Fighting to recover her composure, she took a healthy step back from him. "Yes. Like crowns. I believe the one that belongs to me is within this very caisteal somewhere. Shall we go fetch it?"

Fiorean smirked. "Careful, Princess, we might have called a truce, but you are still on the losing side."

"Queen."

"Mm."

With that, Fiorean turned on his heel and strode from the room. The sound of the fiddle and pipes floating in through the open door had Aemyra following.

The halls were empty as they made their way down the spiral staircase, but she could hear the buzzing of hundreds of voices drifting over the music.

Fiorean didn't seem particularly enthused about attending his own cèilidh, but Aemyra couldn't help but become swept up in the lively atmosphere. To her immense relief, there were no priests or Covenanters present at the celebration, save for Athair Alfred, who was seated next to the dowager queen. Katherine's omnipresent shadow, Sir Nairn, stood behind her chair.

Aemyra's chest wound throbbed under the necklace. The captain's breaths were numbered.

Lairds and nobles surrounded them on all sides, offering congratulations for Fiorean's breithday and requesting information on how the fighting was going north of the Forc. Aemyra pricked up her ears.

Before she could seek out even one friendly face in the crowd, Fiorean had slipped away with some minor laird and she was adrift.

Swept into the crowd with wit as her only weapon, she plastered a smile on her face and pretended to play the part of princess instead of queen.

Despite her circumstances, the whoops and cheers from the musicians were infectious, and Aemyra allowed herself to be pulled into a ring of dancers. The thumping beat of the bodhran and the drunken fiddle helped ease her grief.

While her green skirts were flying around her ankles, and curls fell out of her pinned hair, Aemyra was listening.

Tongues were loosening as the cèilidh swelled to a riotous rhythm and Aemyra was learning more about the war than she had in a week. Evidently the Balnain fleet had joined forces with the Iolairean phoenixes, but they dared not make a move until Clan Leòmhann declared for either side.

Judging by the presence of both Evander and Fiorean within the capital, they were waiting for the same news before marching.

But even as she danced with the people who should have been her subjects, Evander and Katherine glared at her from the head of the room. Neither of them had joined in with the dancing, and Katherine looked pale as Athair Alfred whispered in her ear.

Excusing herself from the sweltering crush of dancers, Aemyra made her way to the side of the hall where Maggie sipped from a goblet.

Ignoring the wine, Aemyra looked for something a little stronger as she wiped the sweat from her brow. Finding a bottle of òmar hidden behind a flagon of ale, Aemyra uncorked it with her teeth, grabbed a cup, and poured herself a generous measure.

Maggie's eyebrows rose as Aemyra groaned when the amber liquid slid across her tongue. The heat spread through her chest, dulling the pain from her wounds almost instantly. It would have been too easy to drain the bottle and forget the rest of her pain for a while.

The heavy expression on Maggie's face spoke of the grief she was trying valiantly to hide.

"I am sorry for the loss of your nephew. I do hope you don't share Elizabeth and Elear's sentiments?" Aemyra asked, having to raise her voice over the clamor of the room.

Maggie replied, "I understand the need to find someone to blame."

Aemyra smiled. "Spoken like a true diplomat. You're wasted here at court, they should be sending you out as an envoy."

Something akin to pride flushed across Maggie's face as Aemyra took another long draft.

"We have been forced to spend our days together, but it need not be entirely tedious," Aemyra mused. When Maggie frowned, she leaned closer. "I know the cook. I'm sure we would be welcome in the kitchens if you wish to bake again."

Her brown eyes softened and Aemyra left the bait dangling. As Nael danced exuberantly, fèileadh flying to uproarious laughter, Maggie stroked her belly.

"Could you have saved Hamysh?" she blurted out, her face pale.

Setting down her cup, Aemyra took a deep breath. "There are never any guarantees, but I do believe had I been allowed to examine him, I could have helped."

Their shared sad smile was interrupted by the appearance of an oblivious laird.

"Your Highness, may I have the pleasure?"

Both women turned as a vaguely handsome man with dark hair wearing Drummand clan tartan extended his hand.

Finding her cup drained, Aemyra decided to indulge him. It was a group dance and if others from his clan were with them, perhaps she might overhear something of use.

Leaving Maggie, Aemyra soon lost herself to the music once more. A light sweat breaking out on the back of her neck, she was suddenly glad of the low-backed dress and upswept hair. Not wanting to stop dancing for fear that the minute her feet ceased to twirl she would be forced to remember her pain, she spun under the man's arm and linked hands with the other dancers. Skirts and fèileadh were swirling in a horrible clash of clan tartan.

As the dark-haired man turned her about the room, Aemyra's gaze snagged on the brooch he was wearing. From a distance it could be mistaken for some sort of bird, but Aemyra stumbled when she saw the Penryth motto stamped across the dragon's wings.

Onair, chrùin, beus.

"Honor, crown, virtue," the man whispered into her ear in the common Cainnt.

The only outward sign Aemyra gave that one of Draevan's spies had found her was a tightening of fingers where they held hands.

Eyes flickering to the top table, Aemyra saw Evander conversing with Fiorean, and Charlotte looked like a shell of a person as Katherine tried to encourage her to eat.

"Do you have a message for me?" Aemyra dared to whisper.

The dark-haired man smiled, revealing crooked bottom teeth. "The kitchens at dawn."

With that, the man spun her into the next ring of dancers, and he was gone in a flash of green fèileadh. As another man filled his place, Aemyra tried to extract herself from his arms.

"Thank you, my laird, I do believe I would benefit from some re-freshment," she said with a wan smile.

"The dance isn't finished," he said gruffly, pulling her roughly into his embrace.

Aemyra reeled back, the garnet on her chest bouncing against her wound. "Take your hands off me."

"I am Laird Byrne of Kilmuir, and I will not be spoken to in such a manner," he declared pompously.

Throwing caution to the wind, Aemyra bent her knee and stomped on his foot. Hard. With the heel of her silk-covered slipper.

The laird let out a garbled cry and grabbed her arm.

Her injured forearm.

His thumb was pressing right on top of her stitches, and she cried out in pain.

The sharp sound cut through the music and several pairs of danc-ers turned to see what was going on.

"You little bitch, how dare you!" Byrne was saying, clutching his foot with one hand and her arm with the other. "Broke my bloody foot."

Aemyra was gasping in pain and could feel her forehead beading with sweat as his thumb dug in harder, right into the groove of her wound.

The sound of a chair clattering to the ground came from the top table as Katherine got to her feet, outrage clear on her face. Aemyra brought her other hand down and tried to claw Laird Byrne off of her quietly, before she could be accused of making a scene. Unfortunately his grip was strong.

"Release me," she demanded, her voice weak with pain.

Goddess, she needed to get her hands on a weapon if she was going to stay at this court without access to her magic for much longer.

No sooner had she thought the words than she heard the slide of steel behind her.

"Unhand my wife, or lose it," Fiorean threatened.

Aemyra sagged as Byrne finally let go.

"Apologies, my prince. But it seems that you need to take better control of your wife if she cannot show common courtesy at—"

Fiorean advanced until he was standing directly by Aemyra's side, sword held at chest height. "I believe you are mistaken regarding who lacks courtesy, Laird Byrne. My wife asked for refreshments and yet you believed you were entitled to more of her time."

Aemyra shivered, recognizing the dangerous tone in his voice.

"I beg pardon, my prince, I was only . . ."

Laird Byrne lifted his hands as if to plead his case and noticed his mistake at the same time everyone else did. His thumb was smeared red with Aemyra's blood.

Fiorean's eyes widened, and he immediately lowered his sword. His torso pressed against Aemyra's shoulder as he cradled her forearm like it was made of glass. The fresh bloodstain was now spreading across the green satin, obvious to those around them.

His face a mask of cold anger, Fiorean threw his sword down to the floor with a clatter and Laird Byrne looked relieved.

Until Fiorean drew his dagger with one fluid movement, grasped Byrne's hand with his own, and brought his blade down in a ferocious slice that severed the bone.

The gathered crowd gasped and scurried backward to avoid the spray of blood that poured from the stump. The hand fell to the ground at Aemyra's feet with a wet smack as the Laird of Kilmuir collapsed to his knees, cradling his arm and screaming in pain.

Katherine was suddenly at Aemyra's other shoulder, hands fluttering as if trying to pull her away from the blood. Maggie fainted, Nael barely catching her before she hit the floor, and Aemyra leaned more heavily into Fiorean to get away from his mother.

Fiorean wiped his dagger on the side of his boot and sheathed it before slipping one arm protectively around Aemyra's waist, cradling her bleeding arm in his other hand. Alfred's eyes narrowed in their direction.

"If anyone else here dares to lay even a finger on my wife, you will also lose your hand," Fiorean threatened.

Hushed whispers flew around the room until Evander began applauding. "Well said, Brother. If you wish to have a hand for your breithday, then you shall have it!"

The pretender king looked at his subjects, who immediately began clapping and cheering, lest they be chosen to lose a limb next. In the confusion, Sir Nairn pulled the dowager queen away in pursuit of Athair Alfred, who had stormed from the hall in a flurry of black robes.

Fiorean bent his head to Aemyra as Byrne was surrounded by his men, his lips almost brushing the delicate skin of her ear.

"Are you all right?"

"I'm fine," she replied, her eyes on the bloodstain spreading toward her skirts.

She heard Fiorean breathe a small sigh of relief.

Aemyra inclined her head to where the dismembered hand still lay on the floor, one finger twitching.

"I thought you said no fighting?"

"Have you suddenly developed a conscience?" he asked quietly. "Never had you pegged as a pacifist."

Aemyra watched as Byrne was dragged from the hall, the bleeding stump clutched in his other hand.

"You should have taken both of them," Aemyra replied.

Fiorean had one eyebrow raised in appreciation, the ghost of a vindictive smile on his lips. "Next time I'll let you do the honors."

As Evander began pouring wine onto the floor to mix with the blood and demanding that everyone resume dancing on top of it, Fiorean escorted her from the hall.

CHAPTER TWENTY-NINE

FIOREAN ACCOMPANIED HER BACK TO THEIR QUARTERS AND softly closed the door behind them.

"Let me see your wound," he said, gesturing toward her arm.

Aemyra turned so that her back was to him. "I'll need your help to get out of this dress first."

Fiorean hesitated before she felt his deft fingers loosening the buttons. She pulled the green satin sleeves down and extracted her right arm easily, the limb bare in the candlelight, and eased the fabric off her shoulders.

"Why is it wherever I go in this bloody caisteal, I end up injured?" Aemyra hissed through her teeth as the sleeve finally came away and she sat down on the bed, the bones of her corset digging into her hips.

"Probably something to do with your pigheadedness," Fiorean muttered.

Taking her forearm between his hands, he brushed his thumb over the smear of dried blood from the split skin. "It will take longer to heal now, and the scar might be larger, but it just needs to be cleaned."

"I can do tha—"

But before Aemyra could rise from the bed, Fiorean had crossed to the ewer and poured water into the basin. Bringing it back over, he knelt beside the bed and Aemyra snatched the cloth away.

"I said I can do it myself," she snapped, dabbing at the tender skin.

Gritting her teeth, she tried to ignore the throbbing pain shooting up her forearm. Fiorean's fists clenched in the sheets on either side of her thighs.

"When my *wife* is wounded, I will care for her," he said, voice dangerously low, emerald eyes thrown into shadow with the fire at his back.

Aemyra glared at him, holding the cloth out of reach with her good arm. "I am wife in title only, and I assure you I am perfectly capable."

"You've made that abundantly clear," Fiorean retorted, making a swipe for the cloth and succeeding in taking it from her. "But I am not so heartless that I enjoy seeing you in pain."

He held her arm firmly, but his touch was gentle. Watching as his capable hands cleaned the blood from her skin, Aemyra fought the urge to snatch her arm away.

"Is that why you smashed my head into the ground outside the inn?" she asked, taking savage pleasure in the way his jaw tightened. "Am I expected to believe you never wanted to cause me pain when you almost cracked my skull open?"

Fiorean withdrew his hands from her skin. "I repaid in kind the blow you dealt me in the harbor." His eyes lifted to where the garnet was resting against the injury on her bare chest, just above her corset.

"You were trying to kill me."

"No, I was attempting to incapacitate you."

Aemyra tried to pull her arm away, but he held fast. "By shooting arrows at me?"

"My aim is not so poor as yours. If killing you had been the objective, you never would have reached the docks," Fiorean replied, his face shadowed.

"So the plan was always to capture me," Aemyra said, her tone clipped. "No doubt you believe your treatment of me outside the inn was a mercy."

"Weren't you there with the sole intention of killing me?" Fiorean asked, his voice scarily calm.

Aemyra stiffened. "I should have let you finish the job, being married to you is an infinitely worse fate than death."

When Fiorean's face shuttered, Aemyra couldn't help the way her pulse stuttered. She prayed he couldn't feel it under his capable fingers.

He rose to his feet, throwing the cloth back into the basin with a splash. "I don't think we'll need to put another stitch in."

Aemyra moved her arm experimentally, feeling it throb dully.

"No, it will heal on its own," Aemyra agreed, wondering why her words sounded so stiff.

Fiorean turned to wash his hands in the basin and Aemyra refused to feel sorry for what she had said. She *wanted* to hurt him. She needed him broken and begging for her to spare his life after what he had done.

She fixed her gaze on Fiorean's back. His auburn hair hung straight past his shoulders, and he was draped in shadows from the fireplace.

Reaching up to clutch the pendant around her neck, she felt the small ridges of the black diamonds that now encircled the large garnet and frowned.

She had guessed that his guilt over the death of her family was prompting him to care for her. Now Aemyra pondered if she might be able to use that to her advantage.

Holding the dress to her chest, she padded across the thick rug toward him.

"Fiorean. I am more than capable of protecting myself," she said, fiddling with the necklace. "I, you see, I do——"

Her words halted as Fiorean turned to face her. Silhouetted against the flames in the fireplace, he looked unsettlingly godlike with his tall frame. His eyes were fixed on her face as he waited for her to continue.

"I might be a hostage here, but I am not powerless," she stated stubbornly.

Her words hung in the air between them.

Fiorean unclipped his dagger from around his fèileadh and extended it toward her.

"Here."

Not understanding, Aemyra's mouth dropped open as the prince willingly offered her a weapon.

"Take it."

Aemyra hardly dared to reach for the hilt of the blade. Aervor might have been responsible for Lachlann's and Pàdraig's deaths, but Fiorean had been responsible for his dragon.

He read the mistrust on her face well enough.

"This isn't a trick. I want you to be able to protect yourself. Seeing you like that tonight . . ." Fiorean's eyes closed briefly. "Let's just say the damsel in distress look doesn't suit you."

Brow furrowed, Aemyra reached between them and gently grasped the hilt of the dagger, curling her fingers around the worn leather. Leaving the scabbard in his hands, she unsheathed it. The blade glinted in the light of the fire, a faint smear of blood still lingering on the steel. Straightening, she twirled it with a flick of her wrist.

"It is a good blade," she said with a shrug. "But mine is better."

Fiorean seemed to be containing his smirk, knowing that she was too proud to admit that any other blacksmith's work could ever be better than her own.

Her arm felt complete again with a weapon in it, and Fiorean was looking at her like he approved.

Suddenly, she realized that she had everything she wanted. A weapon, and an unarmed prince standing in front of her with no witnesses.

Fiorean seemed to come to that conclusion in the same moment Aemyra did.

Her grief rushed to the surface, so intensely that it threatened to choke her. She would never see Lachlann's sweet face again, Orlagh's soft hands could no longer heal, and Pàdraig's deep singing voice would never again hum through the forge.

She tightened her grip on the dagger so hard that her hand began to shake.

Fiorean took one step toward her.

"Do it," he breathed, his expression one of pure despair.

She wanted to. She wanted to close the distance between them and plunge this blade into his neck. Wanted to watch as he bled onto the carpet and the life left his eyes.

"What are you waiting for?" Fiorean asked quietly, taking another step until he was standing directly in front of her.

With a swift movement, Aemyra had the blade pressed against his throat and Fiorean made no move to defend himself, his arms held loosely at his sides.

"You killed my family," she hissed.

He made no reply, so she removed the dagger and shoved him, the bodice of her dress falling around her hips. The hard thrust to his shoulders had him staggering backward, the thick wool of his fèileadh swaying. As his knees hit the settee behind him and he fell, Aemyra leaped upon him, pushing him back into the cushions.

She pressed the blade once again to his throat, so that he dared not swallow.

"You killed my baby brother. I helped bring him into this world, changed him as an infant, rocked him to sleep," Aemyra choked out as the tears began to fall. "Tell me why you let it happen. Tell me exactly what you did so I can decide whether you live or die."

She loosened the pressure of the dagger just barely, her arm shaking, and Fiorean began to speak, his emerald eyes trained on her face.

"Sir Nairn found your family as they were escaping through the city gate. Evander ordered their execution if they refused to disclose your whereabouts," Fiorean said carefully. "Kolreath and Aervor were on the battlements and a hundred score guards were crammed into the space."

A dangerous expression crossed Aemyra's face, and she felt Fiorean bring his hands up to rest against her corset. As if he wanted to steady her.

"They gathered to watch the execution of a *child*," Aemyra hissed, gripping the dagger so tightly her fingers were numb.

"I tried to negotiate with my brother. I tried to convince him that they would be better as hostages, but Pàdraig . . ." Fiorean paused, as if rethinking the wisdom of what he was about to say. "He tried to fight his way to the boy."

A low whimper left Aemyra's lips, and she added a hand to Fiorean's throat underneath the dagger, willing to strangle the life out of him before slitting it.

"He was tortured in the square by Sir Nairn to make your mother talk. She did not break."

Aemyra closed her eyes and swore a new vow to Brigid. Sir Nairn had altogether too much blood on his hands.

When Fiorean hesitated, she nodded for him to continue.

"When Pàdraig took down three guards by himself, Evander gave the order to the executioner to behead him," Fiorean said. "Evander was . . . unstable, and Kolreath was clawing at the battlements. Aervor felt the tension in the air and loosed his fire toward the body as the axe fell. I didn't intervene, thinking it would spare your mother and brother the horrific sight of the beheading. I never saw the boy, or the firebird, until it was too late."

"You allowed your dragon to fire into a small courtyard where a *child* was present. What possessed you to be so reckless? Dragonfire burns hotter than anything else in this world, even our magic cannot protect us from it."

Aemyra's voice had raised to a yell and Fiorean lifted his hands from her hips, pressing them across her mouth to get her to stop, clearly worried about someone overhearing and sending a guard up to their rooms.

"We didn't know that the boy was a Dùileach and none of us saw him burn through his bindings," Fiorean said. "I did what I could afterward to save your mother, to have her taken to the dungeons."

Raising her eyes to the ceiling, Aemyra focused on the wooden beams as her eyes welled with tears.

She had further endangered Sorcha and caused Orlagh's death over her desire to kill the wrong man.

Furious at herself, she fisted one hand in Fiorean's hair, exposing the scars that ran from his temple to his jaw. When she pointed the dagger directly at his eye, he dropped his hands from her mouth.

"You tried to kill me and Adarian when we fled the temple," Aemyra spat.

Fiorean's eyes narrowed. "And yet I did not. I wanted you away from this caisteal, no matter what my mother counseled. I still believed that my brother could be shaped into a fair and decent ruler."

"And now?" Aemyra growled, wondering if he still thought Evander could ever be redeemed.

He didn't answer, and somehow that small cowardice was worse.

"You are a selfish, arrogant prick of a prince. You do not deserve your dragon, you do not deserve your title, and you sure as shit don't deserve your life," Aemyra hissed, the dagger a hairbreadth from his eye.

Fiorean was visibly sweating, his pupils trained on the point of the blade. "It might surprise you to learn that I agree with you."

Curling her lip in distaste, Aemyra snarled in his face. "I hate it when men say whatever they think you want to hear the minute they lose their power. You might not have deliberately killed my family, but you stood by while three Dùileach lost their lives. Your whole family has turned their back on the Goddess and as a result Brigid has cursed you."

Fiorean went still underneath her.

"Aemyra. Please. Calm down."

She pressed the flat of her dagger against his cheek. "I assure you that no woman has ever calmed down after being told those words."

Beads of blood were appearing on Fiorean's alabaster skin, and Aemyra found that she rather liked the sight of it.

"Alfred stripped me of my powers, Katherine stripped me of my rightful title, and Evander stripped me of my dignity. Give me one good reason why I should spare any of you," she asked.

"Because you don't know the whole truth."

Fiorean flicked his gaze down to the blade once and she begrudgingly withdrew it, keeping it level with his straight nose instead of his eye. Fiorean loosed a tense breath as she released her hold on his hair.

"My mother was raised in Tìr Ùir, and if you think the Chosen are bad here, it is nothing compared to their tyranny there."

"Then why did Katherine willingly journey here with Alfred? Why was he allowed to preach within this caisteal and spread such poison?" Aemyra seethed.

"My mother has been a devout believer since her infancy." A dark look entered Fiorean's eyes, but it was gone a moment later. "She is a product of the treatment she endured while she lived in Ùir. When she married my father, she traded one life of suffering for another. She has many faults, but she will stop at nothing to protect this family."

Gritting her teeth, Aemyra thought better of insulting Katherine and remained silent.

"When my brothers came of age, did you ever wonder why they chose to marry women from Tìr Ùir?" Fiorean asked.

Aemyra shrugged. "We all assumed Katherine was trying to establish the True Religion here in Tìr Teine while raising the station of her friends and family."

Fiorean shook his head, a risky move given that the blade was inches from his nose. "We were trying to get as many women out of that territory as possible."

Shocked enough that she lowered the dagger slightly, Aemyra blinked as she tried to process this information.

"With each bride came her court. Ten ladies-in-waiting, five ladies' maids, twenty servants, not to mention the seamstresses and cooks who traveled with them. Three marriages saved hundreds of women."

Aemyra was shaking her head.

"Why not throw Alfred out of the caisteal, or go to Ùir yourself and stop their tyranny, the—"

Because of Aervor, she realized. As a Bonded Dùileach, Fiorean was unable to leave Tìr Teine. As was she.

He was staring up at her with an unsettling expression and she steeled herself again. Fiorean was working his way past her defenses, and she would be damned if he gained the upper hand in this conversation. Katherine might love her family, but she still hated magic, and Alfred was never far from the dowager queen.

Aemyra's hands were shaking, and she dropped the knife back to Fiorean's throat.

"How do I know this is the truth? My father kept me hidden because he knew the king would kill me to keep Evander on the throne."

Fiorean tilted his chin up away from the dagger as a bitter edge entered Aemyra's words.

"Careful, Princess," he said in a clipped tone. "You want to leave my vocal cords intact if you wish to get your answers."

Aemyra pressed harder with the dagger. "Stop calling me that."

That damnable smirk appeared on his face, and she hated that her gaze lingered on his lips.

"Kolreath is unstable," Fiorean finally said. "He has been Bonded to more Dùileach than any other dragon in history and the threads of his mind are unraveling. We suspected that their Bond drove my father mad, and now I fear Evander is proving it true."

Kolreath is mad?

It would explain why the Chosen had gained such power over the royal family. Three of the last five rulers had all been Bonded to the ancient beathach. Aemyra herself had been desperate to claim the golden dragon, Draevan had encouraged it . . .

Fiorean interpreted her shock correctly. "Being queen is about far more than riding a dragon and ruling your subjects. You still have a lot to learn."

Aemyra hated his arrogance. She hated even more that he was right.

"Keep talking. I still think your blood would improve the look of these cushions."

A small challenge entered Fiorean's gaze, but it was gone with his next blink.

"Growing up in this caisteal, watching my father descend into madness . . ." Fiorean paused as if searching for the right words. "I told myself that Evander would be a better king. That all I had to do was wait until he could assume the throne. I was a coward."

His hands were warm on either side of her face, and she loosened her grip on the dagger.

Fiorean was leaning into the blade. "I watched a blacksmith's daughter light up the temple like a sign from Brigid herself and feared she would be the end of us. But after Aervor . . ."

Aemyra felt the calluses on his palms as they gripped her face. His hands had done terrible things, but so had her father's.

So had her own.

Fiorean was gazing at her with such intensity that she dropped the dagger onto the cushions of the settee and did the only thing that made sense to her in that moment.

She yielded to him completely.

Not because she was trying to win his trust. Not because she saw it as a way in. But because she wanted to.

Fiorean saw the change in her eyes the split second before she moved, and he thrust his lips upward to meet hers in a devastating kiss.

His hands were already on her face, one wrapped around the back of her head to crush her lips closer to his own, the thumb of his other hand tracing the corner of her mouth.

Aemyra forgot everything other than the feel of him against her skin. With a guttural moan, his tongue snaked in hungrily.

Fiorean claimed her with the intensity of the fire he possessed, and Aemyra pressed herself against his chest, the top of her breasts spilling over her corset.

His touch was intoxicating, and he met every stroke of lust, each rage-filled kiss, with utter abandon. His tongue laved over hers, and desire pooled low in her belly as his arm snaked around her waist and pressed her more firmly against him, teeth grazing her split bottom lip.

She lifted her face to the ceiling, drawing a much-needed breath, and Fiorean redoubled his efforts, running his teeth along her jawline and trailing kisses down her neck. The golden brooch clipping his fèi-leadh over his shoulder scraped against the top of her breast and she gasped.

Fiorean approached kissing like he did sword fighting. A well-matched partner, attentive and focused, with a dangerous advantage over his opponent.

As his teeth sank down on her clavicle, she arched into him and ran her own fingers through his curtain of auburn hair.

She began to rock herself back and forth on his lap, the bunched satin of her dress rasping against his wool fèileadh. Fiorean moaned deep in his throat, his hands tightening on her hips, encouraging her. His tongue claimed her mouth again, and she felt the length of him begin to grow through the woolen tartan.

"Aemyra." He moaned her name like it was a prayer and she swallowed the sweet benediction with her own mouth.

Suddenly, the door to their chambers burst open with a crash and Evander stumbled in.

"Brother, you're missing your own—" Evander stopped short, swaying on the spot, his goblet of wine still held in his hand.

Aemyra broke away from Fiorean with an embarrassing sucking noise. Both of their chests were heaving, neither quite able to meet the other's eye.

Fiorean swiftly hid the dagger underneath the cushions before his brother could see it.

Evander was grinning.

"I was going to say come downstairs and have fun but clearly you are having enough up here!"

Evander winked exaggeratedly at Aemyra, his crown lopsided, and she stifled the urge to wrap her hand around the dagger's hilt and throw it directly at his face.

As if Fiorean sensed her thoughts, he wrapped his hand gently around her wrist.

"Would you take the hand of your king too?" Evander tilted his head drunkenly as Aemyra extracted herself from Fiorean's grip. She pulled the dress up to cover her chest as if to stop Evander's lecherous gaze landing upon her skin.

"They wouldn't let me keep it," Evander pouted. "I need you to bully a sense of humor into Athair Alfred. He's such a sourpuss, Fiorean. He really is. Come back downstairs."

Fiorean stood stiffly, tucking his shirt into his belt. With one last heated look toward Aemyra, Fiorean went with his brother.

Leaving Aemyra retrieving the dagger and wondering what in Hela's shadowy realm she was doing.

Chapter Thirty

A HANDSOME PRINCE WITH A TALENTED TONGUE HAD ALMOST been enough to make Aemyra forget what the spy had whispered to her during the cèilidh.

But not quite.

Aemyra had pretended to be asleep when Fiorean had returned and slipped out of the room before dawn.

Padding toward the kitchen on quiet feet, wearing a simple gray dress, she blended in with the weak light permeating the halls. Aemyra employed the same skills she had used to explore the secret passageways in Penryth and followed her nose to the lower levels undetected.

Warmth reached her skin through the thin cotton of her dress as she approached the kitchen door. The room beyond was already bustling with activity, kitchen maids and cooks scurrying to ready breakfast for those still sleeping.

"Take out that pail before I throw you to the pigs with it, you wee chit!"

Leaning against the doorframe, Aemyra watched the kitchen boy tremble as he retrieved the slops from the corner before Marilde could brandish her rolling pin.

"Glad to see some things never change," Aemyra drawled.

Three kitchen maids gasped and dropped into hasty curtsies. Marilde barely turned her head from the pastry she was rolling. The last time Aemyra had properly conversed with the cook it had been at Pàdraig's breithday gathering, when everyone had gotten uproariously drunk and Adarian had woken up in the cowshed.

"Couldn't wait for your breakfast this morning?" Marilde asked in her deep voice.

Smiling, Aemyra strolled into the kitchens like she belonged there.

The kitchen maids exchanged a look as Marilde wiped her hands on her apron. "Kincaid sliced his thumb off with a knife last week. You'd have been useful then."

Allowing the cook to steer her into the pantry, Aemyra replied, "My needlework has ever been more suited to stitching flesh than embroidery."

Scrutinizing a turnip, Aemyra lowered her voice. "Have you news for me?"

Marilde leaned against the crates of produce, utterly at ease in her domain. "Your father is aware of your predicament and pushes toward the Forc with your army."

Aemyra nodded. She had already figured out that much.

"You would be best served working from within these walls."

At this, Aemyra frowned. "My father doesn't want me to escape?" she asked, placing the turnip back atop the precarious pile.

"A queen must think about how best to secure her reign, and how best to achieve that end. Your first escape attempt was a failure, they will be more vigilant now."

Glancing at the mark of offering on Marilde's palm, Aemyra was sure there were more who resided within the caisteal who supported her. Together with the servants, they could create an uprising from within.

"There you are!"

Maggie's exclamation had Aemyra whirling around, heart in her mouth.

"What are you doing here?"

Two bemused dimples appeared in Maggie's cheeks. "Shouldn't I be asking you that?"

"She heard I was making pork pies this morning and wanted first pick," Marilde easily supplied the lie and sauntered back into the bustling kitchen.

Maggie crossed her arms over her bump. "I thought you were perhaps avoiding your husband?"

Memories of the night before flooded in.

The way Fiorean's tongue had expertly met her own, a challenge she wanted eagerly to meet in another kiss at the earliest opportunity.

Flushing, she pushed the thought aside.

"I am always avoiding Fiorean," Aemyra said, striding back into the kitchen with Maggie trailing her.

This court was driving her to distraction. Why else would she have kissed the man who was keeping her prisoner and whose dragon had killed Pàdraig and Lachlann? No matter how confusing his revelation had been, Aemyra was sure that Fiorean still wanted Evander's backside firmly on the golden throne instead of her own.

She was feeling lonely and isolated and not at all like herself. That was why she had kissed him. A momentary lapse in judgment was what last night had been. Her focus needed to be on escaping the confines of this caisteal, reuniting with her dragon, and making life better for the very servants who worked around her.

Her husband was definitely not her priority.

But, Goddess, the things Fiorean did with his tongue . . .

Flustered, Aemyra said the first thing that came into her head. "I thought about what you said at the cèilidh last night, about baking."

The princess's full lips plopped open in surprise and her brown eyes landed on the dough resting on the counter.

"Don't even think about it," Marilde warned, gesturing with her rolling pin.

"You would deny a princess and an old friend? How is your granddaughter?" Aemyra asked, eyebrows raised.

Everyone in the kitchen held their collective breath as Aemyra challenged the formidable cook.

A sly smile spread across Marilde's face. Aemyra had delivered the underweight newborn that looked more rat than human. Thanks to her grandmother's talent in the kitchen, the toddler now resembled a suckling pig.

And happened to be Marilde's pride and joy.

Thankfully, the cook's quick mind understood that it would give Aemyra the perfect excuse to return to the kitchens.

Perhaps she could also find a meal down here before the binding agent had been added to it.

Hope surged in her chest. If she had contact with her army and her magic restored, she might actually be able to topple Evander's reign from within.

"I promise I wouldn't be a bother. I could knead the dough if you like," Maggie said politely, cheeks flushing with happiness.

Marilde's head was bent to her work, looking so at home with her vocation that it reminded Aemyra of Orlagh.

"The rabbits need skinning, if you think your stomach can handle it," Marilde finally said, without looking up from her kneading.

Maggie paled noticeably at this and Aemyra grinned. "If you don't do it, she'll never let you back in here."

A queen could issue a challenge, but so could a cook.

With a laugh, Aemyra unhooked the brace of rabbits from the peg where they had been hung and handed a skinning knife to Maggie. "Rather you than me."

Surprising her, Maggie wrinkled her nose and pinched the foot of one rabbit between her thumb and forefinger.

"What is the meaning of this?"

The rabbit dropped onto the wooden board with a thump as Athair Alfred appeared in the open doorway, flanked by two acolytes.

"Why are you unaccompanied?" he asked, beady eyes looking through the room for someone to blame.

Aemyra placed herself in front of Maggie.

"I am chaperoned by the princess, as Katherine ordered," Aemyra replied.

"There is no authority figure present here. This is an inappropriate place for royal ladies to gather," the Athair continued.

Looking pointedly at Marilde, Aemyra replied, "I believe the only authority figure you need in a kitchen is the cook."

The servants kept their eyes averted as Alfred's lips thinned and the two acolytes beside him moved, their black robes skimming the floor.

"It is time for prayers. We shall accompany you upstairs," Alfred said.

Maggie made to follow the priests, but Aemyra held back. "I think I'll stay here. Marilde promised me a pork pie."

"Breakfast is usually served after prayers, but I believe we shall fast today," Alfred said, his eyes lingering on the flour that had stained Maggie's skirts.

Aemyra clenched her teeth. If the delicious smells coming from the ovens were making her mouth water, Maggie had to be starving. "You cannot stop a pregnant woman from eating."

Alfred lifted his eyebrows at Maggie. "It is always her choice."

Aemyra waited for Maggie to protest. Instead, the younger woman shot her a pleading glance and Aemyra didn't resist when the priests restrained her. The whole way up the spiral staircase she imagined how it would feel to sink her dagger between Alfred's shoulder blades.

"I can walk unassisted," Aemyra drawled to the priests flanking her.

Their only answer was to tighten their grips. Knowing she was about to have to endure Goddess knew how many hours of droning prayers in the tower, she dragged her feet.

"Oi!"

The deep voice rang out through the corridor and their small party froze as Fiorean hurried toward them. Groaning inwardly, Aemyra's stomach twisted as she remembered what had passed between them the night before.

"My prince, we located your wayward wife and are bringing her to prayers," the Athair said.

"Yes. I am positively rejoicing," Aemyra drawled.

Fiorean's eyes lingered on the two acolytes and his features hardened.

"Oh, my husband doesn't take kindly to other people touching me. I don't think he learned how to share as a child," Aemyra said, enjoying the muscle that was spasming in Fiorean's jaw.

Fiorean prowled toward the acolytes with predatory intent.

"Leave us," he commanded.

With a glare, the leader of the Chosen called off his dogs and marched up the corridor with Maggie in tow. Aemyra turned her attention to Fiorean, willing her façade of bravado not to crack as she met his emerald gaze.

"Don't expect me to say thank you, I would have freed myself before prayers, I assure you," she said, ignoring how her heart began to race as he advanced toward her.

Her voice was too quiet, the last word slipping out as barely more than a whisper as Fiorean shoved her into a broom cupboard. Without a moment to get her bearings in the tiny space, Fiorean slammed her up against the door.

"What are you playing at?" he growled. "I woke up to find you missing, none of the servants had seen you, and when I ventured out to ask Nael, his wife was also gone."

Glaring up at him, Aemyra replied, "And we were having such a lovely morning without you."

Fiorean looked ready to spit fire. With the heat pouring from his chest, he just might.

"What?" Aemyra asked. "Were you worried about me?"

Her tone was purposefully light, but the smirk on her face died as Fiorean tried to blink the truth out of his eyes before she read it there.

"You *were* worried about me," she breathed.

Fiorean looked down his nose at her, doing his best to bring some loathing into his expression.

"Haven't I proven to you by now that I can handle myself?" she asked, only half joking.

Again, Fiorean didn't answer. Instead, he lifted the back of his hand to trail his knuckles down her cheek. Her body prickled with goose-bumps at the touch, her stomach fluttering in a way it had no business doing.

Unable to deny it any longer, Aemyra admitted to herself that she was attracted to him. It was almost impossible not to be, she reasoned. He was a prince in possession of a tall frame, a pleasing face, and un-settlingly high cheekbones. Not to mention if his kisses were any indi-cation of how he would be as a lover . . .

"What were you doing in the kitchens?" Fiorean asked, his voice low as he fingered one of her auburn curls.

"Maggie mentioned baking was a favorite pastime of hers in Tìr Ùir," Aemyra replied, sticking to the most believable story.

Fiorean dropped his gaze to her lips and a light sweat that had nothing to do with his magic broke out on her skin, making her breath hitch.

Hearing the sound, he grasped her chin with his forefinger and tilted her face up toward him.

She hated herself for letting him do it.

"Aemyra . . ."

Her eyes finally met his at the sound of her name and before she could think better of it, she let him brush his lips against hers. Unlike the crushing anger of the night before, this kiss was tentative, ques-tioning. As if Fiorean were asking permission.

That was what made Aemyra hesitate.

Her hands were straining toward him, longing to fist in his hair. Heat was pooling at her core, and she needed to explore the danger-ous fantasies she had been entertaining during her sleepless night.

But it was hope from Marilde that stopped her.

"I can't do this," she whispered.

Fiorean backed away, eyes on the floor.

Before she could talk herself out of it, she threw herself out of the door and hurried to their chambers, knowing that if she spent one more moment in Fiorean's presence her resolve would break. Not wanting to be caught by Alfred and dragged to prayers, she dared not wander the corridors either.

When she was safely ensconced in her lavish prison, Aemyra found something poking out from underneath her pillow.

A token in the shape of Brigid's cross.

Thumbing the crudely made design, she allowed hope to flourish in her chest.

There were acts of defiance all around her. A sliced palm, a network of whispers, a Goddess-token. Aemyra could not let lust cloud her judgment when her people were relying on her.

A blacksmith could take a tumble in the sheets with a rival, but a queen could never take her enemy to bed.

CHAPTER THIRTY-ONE

THE PRESENCE OF A STONE-FACED PRIEST IN THE CORRIDOR, no doubt stationed there at Alfred's behest, was the only thing that kept Aemyra confined to her chambers. As the hours dragged on, she considered letting him march her to tower prayers simply for a bit of entertainment.

As the sun reached its peak behind heavy clouds, Aemyra sat up from her nest of cushions on the settee when the door finally opened.

"Thank Brigid, escort me out of these chambers before I go mad." She sighed.

Fiorean went still and Aemyra had the good sense to regret her choice of words.

He cleared his throat. "I believe you are the one who fled my presence earlier. Forgive me if my day was taken up with rather more important matters."

For the first time, Aemyra wondered if she had hurt his feelings by rejecting him.

"Is your ego so bruised that I am to be spared your infallible arrogance this afternoon?" she asked, plucking the dagger he had given her from the table.

His eyes followed the path of the blade as he unbelted his sporran and threw it onto the bed.

"If you're planning on using that on me, make it quick. I'd hate to suffer some drawn-out death because of your shoddy knife-wielding skills," Fiorean said.

"Not into knife play. Noted," Aemyra quipped.

Fiorean froze where he stood and Aemyra immediately regretted the flirtatious remark. Perhaps it wasn't advisable to make her changing feelings so plain. Not unless she could use it to her advantage.

Slipping the dagger into the pocket of her dress alongside the Goddess-token, Aemyra thumbed the corner of Brigid's cross. It was time to bring down this family from within the walls. When her father and brother led her army to the city, she would open the gates for them.

"Edwyn is getting worse," Fiorean said. "I'm taking you to examine him."

With that, he gave her no time to prepare before ushering her out of their chambers and up three floors.

The corridor was narrow, with painted doors lining the walls. The one at the far end had been left ajar and it creaked softly as Fiorean slipped in

The smell hit her first.

"Great Mother have mercy," Aemyra said, pressing the back of her hand to her mouth.

Edwyn was lying on a small cot, the only furniture in what seemed to be a quarantine room. At least the healers had enough sense to keep him away from the other children. Berating them internally, Aemyra threw the window wide, letting in the fresh air.

"Light a fire," Aemyra spat through gritted teeth, irritated that she could have done it with a flick of her wrist had the binding agent not still been in her system.

The hearth flared to life and Aemyra relaxed at having Brigid's presence among them as she pulled clean blankets from the top of the wardrobe.

Fiorean was staring at his hand, his posture stiff before the flames. "Athair Alfred abhors Goddess magic to be used in the nursery," he said quietly, almost to himself.

"Fuck Athair Alfred," Aemrya said, watching the way Fiorean eyed the room. As though remembering something he would rather forget.

Drawing herself up to her full height, Aemyra addressed a graying nursemaid wearing a pinched expression. "Bring fresh linens, clean water, and soap."

The fire was already burning the chill from the room with the strength of Fiorean's magic, and Aemyra knelt beside the cot.

The boy was breathing, but it was shallow. His small chest fluttered under her hands and his pallor was gray. When she peeled back an eyelid, his pupils were blown wide.

"Poisoning. Undoubtedly," Aemyra said.

Fiorean cursed behind her as she gently pried Edwyn's lips open. The boy barely stirred. Her heart near stopped when she saw the stains around his gums.

"Bitterberries," she whispered.

"What?" Fiorean asked.

Aemyra rested on her heels, automatically wiping her fingers on the sheets. Rising to her feet, she met Fiorean's emerald eyes.

"It explains why the royal physicians were unable to identify it. Bitterberries are the cause of many poisonings among the children of farmers, especially in the spring. The brambles are easily mistaken for blackberries, but their poison is so potent it can kill within hours."

"But Edwyn has been sick for a week. Even Fergys . . ." Fiorean trailed off, unable to finish his sentence.

But Aemyra wasn't listening. "Look at his gums."

Frowning, Fiorean carefully pulled Edwyn's bottom lip down. The little boy stirred but soon fell still again. Before Fiorean had even finished looking at the dark red stain left on his fingers, Aemyra was wiping them with the sheet.

"Someone has been poisoning them regularly," she whispered, the knowledge settling heavily on her heart. "Keeping them hovering on the edge of the Otherworld until they wished to send a message."

Fiorean's hand automatically went to his sword, and Aemyra could not ignore how much he cared for his nephews.

"Who has access to the nursery?" Aemyra asked.

Looking over his shoulder to the open door, Fiorean ran a tired hand across his face. "The nannies and nursemaids obviously, a wet nurse for Nael's boy, five governesses, the kitchen maids bring up trays . . ."

Aemyra froze.

Did it all come back to the kitchens? It would have been only too easy for Marilde to slip a few drops of bitterberry juice into pies or puddings. Enough for the children to sicken but not die until she strengthened the dose. Wringing her hands together, Aemyra eyed the newly roaring fire.

She had dismissed Katherine as a suspect, but Alfred's priests and Covenanters were everywhere. She already knew they were slipping the binding agent into her food and drink.

But why would Alfred poison the children of the family that were his key to converting Tìr Teine to the True Religion? Poison didn't exactly seem like Marilde's choice of weapon either. The cook was as subtle as a brick. Unless Draevan had sent the order . . .

Aemyra turned away from Fiorean, unable to look him in the eye. Not wasting any more time, she began stripping the bed herself. Edwyn's small frame was so thin it took barely any effort to lift him. Determined that this little boy would live, Aemyra barely registered the nanny bringing what she had asked for, or Fiorean's stern voice drifting up the corridor. Hours passed as she focused on washing the sores that had formed on the child's body.

By the time she was content with his conditions, the room was dark.

"You must turn him at intervals," Aemyra instructed the three nannies Fiorean had deemed trustworthy. "Wet his lips with sugared water four times an hour but do not let him eat."

Fiorean slipped back into the room, his expression indecipherable.

"He's always awful hungry when he wakes," the gray-haired nanny replied.

Aemyra crossed her arms. "The poison is likely in whatever food he has been ingesting. If he wakes, send for me. Charcoal mixed with honeyed porridge is all he is allowed."

The nannies curtsied obediently, and Aemyra turned her gaze to the sleeping boy as Fiorean approached her.

"You care about him," he said softly.

Aemyra bristled. "I care for all of my people. Too many children have lost their lives and I desire Edwyn not to be one of them."

Suddenly it wasn't a little red-haired boy lying on the cot, it was a dark-skinned child with unruly curls and Aemyra let out a shuddering breath. "I miss Lachlann," she said.

Surprising her, Fiorean's hand rested gently on her shoulder. Realizing how much her determination to save his nephew had moved him, she didn't brush him off.

"I could save them all, you know," she whispered into the quiet room, and Fiorean's grip tensed. "I could save you."

His hand dropped from her shoulder, and after a moment's hesitation he twined his fingers with hers.

"Follow me," he said.

AEMYRA HAD KNOWN SHE WAS SUCCESSFULLY BREAKING DOWN Fiorean's defenses, but she hadn't expected him to lead her straight out of the caisteal via a back passageway.

Determined not to let her guard down, Aemyra pulled her hand away when they reached the forest. She might be lusting after him, but he was still her enemy in this clan war over her succession. A war that was poised to rip her territory in half.

Unless she could convince him to support her claim to the throne instead of Evander's.

Even now that she knew the truth about her family's death, Aemyra still didn't trust him. Not fully.

Draevan would never accept an alliance with Fiorean unless he proved himself beyond all doubt. Aemyra couldn't admit how badly she wanted him to change his allegiance and she shivered.

Fiorean misinterpreted her thoughts.

"Disposing of you in the forest would rather counteract my having married you to use you as leverage, now, wouldn't it?" Fiorean drawled, his face ghostly pale in the moonlight.

Fiorean's strides grew lengthier as they walked. Night had fallen, and the woods were silent save for the rustlings of the nocturnal animals in search of a meal.

Aemyra had to squint in the darkness to look out for fallen branches and keep her ankles from rolling on the damp ground. Several times, Fiorean turned as if to help her over a large root or stump.

She took care not to look at him when he did, but she felt the tension even without his touch.

Finally they made it into a wide clearing, the mountain peaks towering above them.

"Why have you brought me here?" she asked.

Fiorean was staring at her in quiet contemplation, and she tried not to scratch the wound on her chest, which had become itchy underneath the necklace.

Shivering in the chill air now that they had stopped walking, Aemyra hoped it wouldn't rain.

"Since I have met your dragon, I figured that you should meet mine," Fiorean said quietly.

Then she heard the wings.

Craning her neck, she watched a blue dragon descend through the clouds that blanketed the stars.

Terrea was a creature of the night, but there was no question that

Fiorean's dragon belonged in a sun-streaked sky. Aervor's cobalt scales rippled as he landed heavily, claws digging deep grooves into the grassy meadow.

Aervor tucked his wings in tightly to his sides and shook his thick neck. Aemyra took one step backward, drawing level with Fiorean as the blue dragon settled himself. He was smaller than Terrea, but the six huge barbs on his tail and enormous claws looked dangerous enough.

Aemyra stared up at Aervor. "How on earth did you claim him when you were only thirteen years old?"

Fiorean gave her a shrewd smile. "My infamous arrogance, I suppose."

Aemyra rolled her eyes.

Where Terrea's facial crests were fluted elegantly, Aervor's appearance was . . . stockier. His head was broad, his neck less shapely than Terrea's. The cerulean scales on his neck stuck up slightly; it gave him the appearance of a ruff.

The dragon was staring at both of them quietly, his mouth slightly open to reveal rows of razor-sharp teeth.

The realization that those teeth were the last things Lachlann had seen before his death hit Aemyra like a kick to the chest.

"You decided to bring me face-to-face with the dragon that killed my baby brother?" she asked, reeling backward.

Fiorean tried to reach for her, but she held up a hand in warning. It was only the knowledge that she would never be able to completely control Terrea either that stayed Aemyra's hand.

As it was, Fiorean was standing between Aemyra and Aervor like he was a mediator at a joust.

"Do you really think I'm egotistical enough to pick a fight with a dragon?" Aemyra asked when she had recovered her senses.

"You're certainly stupid enough to keep picking them with me," he replied.

Annoyed that her defenses were crumbling, she spat back, "You're barely a challenge."

His eyebrows rose. "Says the woman who lost the last two."

"Third time's the charm?" she asked, feeling the dagger in her pocket.

Fiorean crossed his arms over his chest.

Aemyra relented. "Did you bring me here to threaten me? If I don't heal Edwyn you'll take Sorcha from the dungeons and burn her too?"

Fiorean had the audacity to look offended.

"The way you spoke about your Bond with The Terror . . . I, uh . . . mm." He seemed to be at a loss for words and he scratched his nose. "There will be battles to come. Evander has already begun talking about using our dragons in the fight against your father."

Aemyra's chest contracted painfully.

"You mean the fight against me," she said, mouth dry.

The image of Gealach locked in battle with Kolreath and Aervor while Aemyra remained a prisoner was abhorrent.

She needed Fiorean on her side and Sorcha out of this caisteal. Three dragons on her side would turn the tide of this war.

His expression was sincere when he said, "I hope that if you can teach me how to connect to Aervor in the same way that you are in tune with your dragon, then I will be able to control him better."

Aemyra let Fiorean's words sink in. He was asking for her help.

For the first time, Aemyra understood that they both wanted the same thing. Neither of them wanted the people of Tìr Teine to suffer. She just had to make him understand that the best way to ensure their safety was to place the crown on her head.

"That must have been one interesting council meeting today," Aemyra mused, observing Aervor from a distance.

Fiorean was already using her as leverage, it was time she began negotiating for her throne.

"All right, tell me about him," Aemyra said.

The dragon had curled up on the ground, dew clinging to his face from the wet grass.

"What?" Fiorean asked.

Trying to put her resentment toward the blue beast out of her mind, she focused on getting under Fiorean's skin.

Aemyra inclined her head. "Tell me about him. How does he fly? What does he most like to eat? Which wing does he favor?"

Fiorean stared at her blankly.

Aemyra tried not to sigh. This was going to be harder than she thought.

"You really don't know? How in Hela's realm has he been letting you on his back this whole time?"

Fiorean glared at her. "We have managed well enough."

"The fact that Lachlann died on your watch is proof that you haven't," Aemyra shot back. "Your pride is getting in the way. Perhaps you were less of a conceited swine when you initially Bonded at thirteen, but if you can't humble yourself, then the Bond will never establish properly."

"I was not a conceited swine—"

"Our beathaichean are not magical amplifiers for us to use at will!" Aemyra shouted.

They stood there breathing heavily, scowling at each other.

"I have been Bonded to Aervor for half my life. How can you claim to know better after only being Bonded a few weeks?" Fiorean asked bitterly.

Aemyra sighed. "Do you want me to share what I know or not?"

Eventually, Fiorean spoke through gritted teeth. "I am not blessed with the ability to expose my inner thoughts or feelings easily."

Aemyra bit back her snappy retort when she realized how much pride it had cost Fiorean to admit even that much.

"Well, it's never too late to learn," she replied mulishly. "What wing is he strongest on? Just like you or I favor one hand, so too will your dragon."

Fiorean shifted uncomfortably, and Aemyra bit back an impatient sigh.

"Does he always land on one side first? Or perhaps he pulls more strongly with one wing?" Aemyra prompted.

Fiorean's eyes roved over his dragon as if sorting through the memories of every flight they had ever shared.

"The left," he said firmly.

"Good. How can you use that knowledge to help him when he flies or lands?"

Fiorean shrugged. "I could turn him from the right so that he can have more space on the left? I usually just aim for anywhere that's open, since he's difficult to maneuver. Stubborn beast."

"What about old injuries? Aches, pains, that sort of thing?"

Fiorean looked blank.

"You are his Dùileach. You have a duty to take care of him. By all accounts, my beathach is centuries old. Perhaps older even than Kolreath. Aervor has a lifetime of memories and experiences before you that will have left their mark on his body and mind."

Fiorean tilted his head before pointing to a scar just below Aervor's right shoulder.

"He survived the Battle of the Five Brothers with King Realor in 1833; he limps when it rains. I think his front leg pains him sometimes," Fiorean said quietly, clearly embarrassed that he hadn't thought about it before.

"Good. Now you have to open yourself up," Aemyra said briskly.

Fiorean turned to her like she had asked him to strip naked and walk through the lower town.

She smiled. "It isn't so terrifying, you know."

Fiorean looked like he begged to differ.

"Close your eyes," she whispered, taking his hands. "Now think about Aervor. Not about controlling him or commanding him. I want you to think about his heart, his identity, even as it is separate from yours. Then remember all the moments you have shared together. Moments when you ceased to feel like a separate entity and were one with your dragon. Moments where you were so angry that if you opened your mouth, you felt like Aervor's fire would spill forth. Feel for that place behind your heart where he rests within you."

Aemyra knew it had worked when Aervor turned his head toward them both and mewed, his cerulean eyes alert.

Fiorean's mouth plopped open, and she saw tears slide down his cheeks from beneath his closed lids.

He gripped Aemyra's hands like they were his lifeline.

Aervor made a low, contented rumbling sound deep in his chest as Fiorean turned to his dragon.

"Now you know," she said, even as envy laced her heart, her own Bond still muted by the binding agent.

Here she was, helping her captor with his dragon, and still a prisoner in her own caisteal. If her father could see her now, he would disown her.

"Thank you," Fiorean breathed, not bothering to wipe away his tears.

This moment couldn't be for nothing, and Aemyra knew she had to ask. Fiorean would never be more vulnerable than now, would never owe her more than he currently did.

"Accept the truth," she said, gripping his hands when he tensed. "Tìr Teine will never know peace while a mad king sits the throne with a priest whispering in his ear. We have a chance to make this territory better—together."

There was a brief flash of hope in his emerald eyes before he ripped his hands away. Wiping his cheeks angrily, he looked between Aervor and Aemyra, torn.

"Listen to me," Aemyra said, the first droplet of rain catching her cheek. "This is my territory, my clan, and I have no desire to see my people burn. Evander might not be well versed in the histories, but you are. You know my claim is true even if you won't admit it."

Fiorean's jaw clenched. "You would ask me to go against my family? Would you have me kill my own brother to make you queen? Evander has already been crowned!"

Aemyra gritted her teeth and pushed back against him, their noses almost touching. "I would have you honor the Goddesses and do what is right!"

Aervor loosed a bone-shaking roar, stretching his thick neck toward Aemyra, displaying his long teeth and the gullet full of fire that lurked beyond. With the newly deepened Bond, Aervor leaped to the defense of his Dùileach.

Shit.

Fiorean threw himself toward her, tackling her to the ground. Before Aervor could take a step closer, an enormous black dragon landed in the meadow with an almighty crash to defend her Dùileach.

CHAPTER THIRTY-TWO

FIOREAN'S BODY PROTECTED AEMYRA FROM THE FLYING DEBRIS that was now raining down around them.

They hit the ground with a hard thump and Aemyra hissed in pain as it jostled both of her wounds. Fiorean threw his arms over her head just as a torrent of white-hot fire was loosed above them.

"What in Brigid's name—"

They both sat up to see Terrea facing off with Aervor in the clearing as thunder rumbled overhead.

Fiorean uttered the filthiest curse in the Seann that Aemyra had ever heard as they both scrambled to their feet.

The two dragons advanced on each other, mouths open with the threat of more flames hovering in the back of their throats. Aervor stretched his neck out toward Terrea in challenge.

Her dragon must have been remaining close to Caisteal Lasair in case Aemyra managed to escape.

The ground shook as Terrea stamped her front legs and her talons gouged great chunks of earth out from underneath her. With one more furious roar, she sent a second volley of fire shooting just to the left of Aervor's face.

A warning.

Aemyra held her breath as Aervor growled and Fiorean was frozen beside her, no doubt feeling the same rippling power emanating from Terrea.

The black dragon's ancient magic was undeniable as she took one confident step toward Aervor, growling menacingly with her amethyst eyes narrowed.

"We need to get out of here," Fiorean said, tugging on Aemyra's sleeve.

Wrenching her arm from his grip, she made to sprint for her enraged dragon, ducking when Terrea's barbed tail shot over her head.

"Are you utterly stupid?" Fiorean called out, grabbing the back of her dress.

Aemyra cursed as the dragons illuminated the meadow with their fire once more. As if the Goddess Beira agreed with Fiorean, another thunderclap sounded and the heavens opened.

The two sprinted for the trees as the dragons met in a fury of fire and teeth.

The ground shook, steam filling the air from where dragonfire met the pouring rain. Aemyra stopped under the boughs of an old oak tree, her hair already plastered to her skull.

Aervor's wing bent as Terrea pushed him to the ground. Fiorean winced and took one step forward as if he could help his beathach. Terrea's sharp claws were poised against Aervor's softer underbelly and Aemyra could feel the fear emanating from Fiorean. Thankfully, Aervor's smaller size worked to his advantage, and he freed his trapped wing.

But the black dragon wasn't finished. Terrea took another step forward and raked those dagger-sharp claws through the dirt, right in front of Aervor's face, as if to let him know how well they would tear through his scales.

Then something shifted as Aervor lowered himself completely to the ground, wings clenched against his sides, completely submitting to Terrea's dominance.

Aemyra smirked at Fiorean as he stood dumbstruck. "At least your dragon has better sense than you do."

"I've never seen . . ."

Aemyra ceased being smug the instant Fiorean's eyes drifted to Terrea's tail. Noticing the number of spikes. The double-crested horns.

He swung around to face Aemyra, blinking rain out of his emerald eyes.

"The Terror is female?" he gasped.

Unable to deny it, Aemyra set her jaw. "Need another sign, Prince?"

She watched him soften, those emerald eyes searching her face as the rain lashed down through the winter-worn trees as two dragons rippled with power in the meadow beyond.

"I will not betray my family," Fiorean said, taking a firm step backward. "No matter what my brother has done, he does not deserve to die."

Temper breaking as lightning illuminated the sky, Aemyra pursued him.

"How many more people will die if Evander remains king?" she shouted over the next clap of thunder. "My father will bring war to the gates of this city whether you like it or not," Aemyra shouted over the storm, struggling with her rain-soaked skirts.

Fire illuminated Fiorean's hair as he walked downhill away from the posturing dragons, boots sinking into the rapidly softening mud. "It's already too late. Leuthanach has mobilized, and they have a larger force than any of the other clans combined."

"They have no magic," Aemyra scoffed, wiping rain from her eyes. "And we have dragons."

"The Covenanters have more weapons," Fiorean bit back.

A fork of lightning split the sky.

"Fuck the Co—"

"How many Dùileach are even willing to fight?" Fiorean asked as the caisteal came into view. "Clan Leòmhann will lurk in their caves until one side is almost victorious, and the vast majority of Dùileach who will fight for you are un-Bonded," Fiorean continued, his face set.

The rain lashed down like it was trying to beat her into submission. There was truth in Fiorean's words, even if she didn't want to hear it.

"The river lairds have declared for me. My father has gathered an army ten thousand strong and Clan Iolairean is sending a thousand phoenix warriors north as we speak."

Another thunderclap had them both hurrying their steps down the hill.

"By the time they arrive, the battles will be lost. Evander has an army of thirty thousand men encamped at Fyndhorn," Fiorean said.

Aemyra stepped directly into a puddle but barely noticed the water soaking into her boot.

Thirty thousand battle-hardened warriors against ten thousand soldiers, less than a quarter of whom would be Dùileach. If Alfred sent for more Covenanters from Tìr Ùir, they would wield the binding agent as a weapon, she was sure of it.

Winning Fiorean to her side might be her only chance.

Reaching the secret passageway that led into the caisteal, Fiorean held the slab of stone open for her to slip through.

Hating herself for it, she stepped back into her prison.

Brow furrowed, Fiorean ushered her up the roughly hewn steps and through the door that led to the walled garden and back into the pouring rain.

Unable to contain her temper any longer, Aemyra spun to face him. "I should have killed you hours ago and left with Terrea tonight."

Fiorean stiffened. "So, what are you waiting for, Princess?"

Losing all sense, knowing a priest or a guard could walk into the garden at any moment, Aemyra pulled the dagger from her pocket. "I am *queen* of this territory and my duty is to my people. What happened between us yesterday changes *nothing.*"

Fiorean's eyes darkened as he stalked toward her.

"Didn't seem like you hated me so much in that cupboard earlier," he said.

Aemyra clenched her jaw as desire pooled deep within her. She should not want this. She *could not* want this.

Lifting her chin, she tightened her grip on the dagger. "Take me to the dungeons to free Sorcha and let me return to the meadow for Terrea."

Fiorean shook his head. "I can't let you do that. There are people in this caisteal I care about. Your father needs a leash, and you are the perfect thing to stop him from putting Àird Lasair to the torch with Gealach."

Aemyra scowled. "That's all I am to you. A piece in this infernal game. I am not some object to be manipulated, I am the *queen*!"

With her last word, Aemyra let the dagger fly, launching it by the hilt toward Fiorean's face as lightning cleaved the heavy clouds above them. He was only a few feet in front of her, and yet she missed.

With catlike reflexes, Fiorean expertly caught the hilt of the weapon and fixed her with a glare.

"That is what it means to be royal, Aemyra. We are all being used by somebody, all we can do is anticipate their actions and make countermoves." He spun the dagger, the blade glowing with heat, his magic barely under control. "In order to keep those you love safe, you need to become what they fear most. Are you prepared to do that?"

Aemyra glared at him. His words were eerily reminiscent of her father's, but was that how she wanted to rule her people? To be a queen they feared?

"So you became a conceited, swaggering, prick of a prince," she spat.

A muscle was straining in Fiorean's jaw. "Careful, Princess."

His proximity was unnerving, and Aemyra's chest was heaving with her rapid breaths as the rain dripped in rivulets down his scars. She wasn't sure if her physical reaction to him was born of fear, anger, or something else. Fiorean didn't give her the chance to figure it out as he glowered down at her.

"My entire life everybody told me that I was fire," he said, his voice barely audible above the rain.

Aemyra huffed a laugh. "Of course they did. Your brothers can barely summon a spark between them. I bet Alfred hated you as a child."

Fiorean's eyes shuttered, his expression downright furious as he took one more step toward her. Close enough now that she had to look up into his face. She refused to back away even as flames licked at his fingers, Fiorean's magic crackling out of him as he struggled to control his temper.

"When I met you, I suddenly understood that I wasn't fire at all. I was ice. Decades of living within this court had me crafting an un-yielding, impenetrable façade that only your infuriating and down-right excruciating presence has been able to crack," he growled, towering over her.

Aemyra was shocked into silence as his presence overwhelmed her senses, steam curling from his shoulders as the rain hit his shirt and evaporated against his power.

"Until I met you, my life was free from torment. Free from your hateful face across a table, free from the anguish of hearing your voice in my halls. Warring against my better judgment every time my blood was set alight by a simple brush of your skin."

Fiorean leaned in closer, anger etched on every sharp edge of his face.

"But from that very first moment in the forge, when you blazed through my glacial pretenses, I knew I never wanted to be free of it. Of you. Because the intensity with which you burned simmered through my soul and left me forever changed. For weeks, thoughts of you have suffocated me, like the cloying smoke of an inferno I will never escape." He paused, his eyes roving across her face as his voice quieted. "I never knew what it felt like, to burn."

Aemyra was lost in his emerald gaze as he spoke the words she didn't want to hear, and yet needed desperately. Heart pounding in her chest, she was soaked to the skin but did not feel cold.

"So how can I be fire? If the only thing that makes me burn . . . is you."

Aemyra's mouth dropped open as Fiorean passed the dagger to her. As though seeking to arm her in case she still wanted to kill him. The second it was in her grip, Aemyra knew she would never use it. Hating herself for what he was making her feel without even touching her, she could sense his magic begin to envelop her. Teasing her already overheated skin to the point of distraction. Breaths erratic, she stared at the droplet of rain on his Cupid's bow and let the dagger clatter to the ground.

The moment she released the blade, Fiorean grasped the back of her head and pulled her lips up to his in a kiss so overwhelming, she melted.

Forgetting her weapon for the second time while in his presence, she found that she didn't care. Not as long as Fiorean kept doing *that* with his tongue.

Maybe a smarter queen wouldn't want this, perhaps a more sensible ruler would have thrust the dagger through the heart of their enemy at the first opportunity. This had never been part of her plan, and yet it felt like the only thing in the world that made sense.

Fiorean's hands dropped from her face and his arms wrapped around her body, pressing her farther into him as if he couldn't bear any distance between them.

"Aemyra . . ." Fiorean moaned into her mouth as she dragged the tip of her tongue lazily across his bottom lip.

He pulled back just enough so that she could read the desire in his emerald eyes.

"Is this what you want?" he asked quietly, his face illuminated by another lightning strike.

Aemyra spoke her answer onto his lips as she crushed them to his once more. "Yes, but we've already established I don't have much common sense."

His low chuckle turned into a growl as Aemyra met his kisses ferociously, just as desperate to taste him as he was to taste her.

She had no idea how they made it back to their chambers without being spotted. Lost in a haze of stolen kisses and passionate touches against stone walls and in shadowed alcoves, Aemyra only became aware of their surroundings when Fiorean set the hearth ablaze.

As if suddenly willing to take his time now that they were in private, Fiorean pressed his thumbs underneath her jaw and tilted her head back. He trailed a passionate line of kisses from her jawline to her neck in a way that made her knees go weak.

This was nothing like the sloppy kisses she had exchanged with men before. Growing irritated with the way Fiorean seemed to master the map of her body in such a short space of time, Aemyra drew her hand back and punched him on the shoulder.

He stilled against her, his lips pausing at the base of her throat. "Something wrong?"

When he flicked his tongue against her clavicle, her words came out significantly more breathless than she had intended.

"Is there anything you *aren't* good at?" she muttered.

She felt one strong hand fist in her sodden curls at the nape of her neck and Fiorean pulled her head even farther back, exposing her throat to him. He nuzzled his nose across her jaw and brought his lips up to her ear.

"I can't carry a tune to save my life," he whispered.

It would have been funny, had he not sunk his teeth into the soft flesh of her earlobe and she spasmed in his grip. He clamped his other arm around her waist to stop her from falling and the hand in her hair loosened to skim down her spine.

"What about you? You've been extremely confident about your forging skills, and even I'll admit that you're not a terrible sparring partner."

Aemyra bent her leg to try and kick him in the balls, but he was too fast for her. Before she knew what was happening, he had twisted so that her back was pressed against his chest. He bent his head over her shoulder and clamped both of her arms against her sides. She became aware that they were dripping all over the lavish carpet.

"Hmm?"

His fingers popped the buttons on the back of her dress, and she let her head rest against his shoulder.

"Horses. I'm a terrible rider," she admitted.

Another dark chuckle met her ears. "Oh dear. That isn't what a man wants to hear before he beds a woman."

The second she thought about striking him, he ensnared both of her wrists.

"Careful, Princess," he whispered wickedly into her ear. "You're playing with fire now."

Maintaining eye contact, Fiorean released a flicker of delicate magic that dried them both in seconds. Shivering with the delicious heat, Aemyra squirmed in his grasp until he let go.

Tendrils of flame snaked out from the hearth to attach to Fiorean's shirt. His auburn hair gleamed as the fire burned away his clothes, leaving him wreathed in flame.

Then he reached up and tied his hair into a knot behind his head, baring his scars proudly for her to see.

Heat prickled across Aemyra's skin that had nothing to do with the fire that licked wickedly around Fiorean.

"You looked just like that the first moment I saw you," Fiorean said, his emerald eyes alight. "Cheeks glowing in the light from the forge, eyes blazing with your inner fire. Even before I knew who you were, I wanted you."

Aemyra's breathing hitched as the fire began retreating from Fiorean's skin, baring the lean muscles of his chest.

"If you had asked me, I would have ripped that dirty shirt off of you, bent you over the anvil, and fucked you until you screamed for more."

Fiorean stepped closer to her, the tendrils of fire slipping away to reveal the smattering of hair on his lower abdomen, his muscular thighs.

"I didn't understand it then. But I was drawn to your magic. The magic that fueled the forge was calling to me. *You* were calling to me."

When Fiorean finally stepped completely out of his flames, Aemyra forgot to breathe. It had been a long time since she had been with a man, but she wasn't nervous.

Quite the opposite.

"Come here," Fiorean said, his voice low.

By the Goddess, Aemyra did as she was told.

His hands pulled the dress down to her waist, the fabric fluttering over her wounds. His eyes dipped to her unbound breasts, and she watched his teeth sink down on his bottom lip as if he wanted to bite her.

"Do it," Aemyra whispered.

Fiorean drew his gaze back up to Aemyra's face. Too slowly, as if he hadn't yet looked his fill. Heart pounding and heat pooling between her legs, she clarified. "Touch me."

He was so close now that her peaked nipples brushed his skin and she sighed at the utter agony when he still refused to grant her wish.

Then Fiorean broke.

His lips met hers as his hands branded her skin, and for a moment she wondered if he was still harnessing his magic. It took her a minute to understand that his touch was setting her skin alight without the help of his gifts. It burned through her like a fever, incinerating what was left of her hatred for him.

One hand skimmed over her buttocks and when he cupped the generous curves, he groaned into her mouth. Aemyra arched herself into him, her nipples seeking friction as Fiorean's hands explored her body like he was committing the shape of her to memory.

"The sight of your arse is enough to drive a man to distraction," he muttered as his hands skimmed the soft underside of her breasts, cupping their heavy weight. "And these . . ."

He pulled back again to watch his hands knead them, his mouth dropping open slightly.

The lust on his face was undeniable as he gazed upon her, and Aemyra arched into his expert touch, needing more friction.

Before she completely lost all sense and began to beg, Fiorean dropped his mouth to her nipple. The moment his teeth made contact with the taut bud, a strangled moan escaped her lips and she bowed into him.

His tongue rolled over her nipple, deliciously warm, and when he sucked it right into his mouth . . .

"Fiorean . . ."

With her breathy moan, Fiorean seemed to lose whatever control he had and got to his knees. She looked down at him, his auburn hair already escaping its knot, as she stepped out of her dress. He pulled the soft cotton down her legs slowly, even though she had been sure he was going to rip it off in haste.

"You are flame given flesh, Aemyra," he said when she was completely naked save for the garnet necklace. He spoke her name reverently as his long fingers trailed the back of her thigh, making her shiver.

His hands continued their path, tracing the outlines of her calves, the arch of her foot, until she nearly kicked him in the stomach to let him know where she really wanted to be touched.

She almost came apart when she found his gaze trained on the smattering of auburn hair between her legs.

Aemyra would have blushed if she had been ashamed of her body.

Instead, it pleased her to see him so entranced by her nakedness. Indeed, no lover had ever looked upon her save for in the moonlight, when the hair between her legs was bleached of color.

Fiorean rose to his feet in a show of self-control, his arms coming around her waist as he carried her over to the bed. He placed her carefully on the quilt covers, and Aemyra gazed up at him as he wrapped one hand over himself and began pumping.

Aemyra arched off the bed in invitation and Fiorean loomed over her, pressing her down into the mattress. His lips found hers again and she felt him pull back. Confused, she looped her hands around his neck to pull him closer.

She wanted this. She needed this.

He broke away from her insistent kisses, their noses still touching. "This might hurt," he said, his voice gentle.

Aemyra bit her lip to contain her laughter. "Trust me, it won't," she said, digging her fingers into his hips to move him closer.

He narrowed his eyes at her.

She arched an eyebrow. "I will admit that I often prefer the company of women, but tonight I'll make an exception."

Fiorean reached down and tweaked her nipple in retaliation for her cheek.

"You let me cut myself on our wedding night for no good reason?" he asked, incredulous.

This time Aemyra did laugh. "Your brother seemed to need proof. We gave it to him." Remembering how Fiorean had rhythmically moved the bedposts, she tilted her head. "Although if that was an indication of how you fuck, perhaps I've changed my mind."

Fiorean growled low in his throat before pinning her to the bed again, his sizeable erection pressing against her pubic bone.

"I can assure you," he said, voice low, "I fuck like I fight."

Aemyra felt herself grow slick with his words and her legs parted underneath him. He dipped one hand to his cock, working himself against her already soaked entrance.

"I won't be gentle," he said warningly.

Aemyra met his eyes with a savage expression.

"Fuck gentle."

Her words broke through whatever was left of his restraint and with one hard thrust, he sheathed himself inside of her.

They both uttered a cry, her at the intense stretch and him at her tightness.

Groaning through his teeth, he slowly eased himself back and then in again, the ridge of his cock dragging deliciously against her inner walls.

Fiorean began moving, insistent, rhythmic strokes that landed deep inside of her.

"You are mine," he whispered in the Seann.

Aemyra would have argued the sentiment if she hadn't also felt exactly what this was—a claiming. To disagree would have been a lie . . . from this moment, she was his.

Wanting him undone, Aemyra rolled her hips and pushed her hands against his chest. Her wound protested under the strain, but she managed to flip him onto his back without breaking their joining.

Fiorean's eyes widened in surprise as Aemyra began grinding herself down onto the length of his cock. She bit her bottom lip with a groan at the feeling of fullness.

The possessiveness in his eyes was enough to light a fire in her blood and she undulated her hips, taking every inch of him inside of her.

Losing herself to the rhythm, she placed her right hand around his throat and pressed down hard.

"I don't need you to play nice," she said. "I want you exactly how you are. A scarred, dangerous dragon rider who isn't afraid to play with fire."

The flickering embers of her magic had begun to return thanks to her sparse diet and she summoned what she could to her palm while she rocked her hips back and forth, feeling him touch the most intimate parts of her. Fiorean reached up, his own flames flickering as he locked their fingers together. Both of them letting just enough of their shields recede so they felt the pain of the burn.

"You are mine," Aemyra said into his mouth, echoing his earlier statement in the common tongue and he snared her lip in between his teeth hard enough to bruise.

Fiorean thrust his hips up to meet her with every stroke, one hand clutching the flesh of her thigh, his fingernails leaving half-moon marks in her skin.

Aemyra arched into him again and suddenly Fiorean let go of his fire to pin her once more on her back.

She could already feel herself quickening, and the look of pure fire in his eyes could have turned her body to ash.

Before she had time to breathe, his cock was buried inside of her again. Claiming her body relentlessly, with hard, strong strokes that caressed that delicious spot at her core.

"Fiorean," she gasped, feeling that great wave about to wash over her.

He buried his face in her auburn curls, biting down hard on the space between her shoulder and neck, his hands still restraining her wrists, rendering her completely powerless beneath him.

"Say my name again, Aemyra," he commanded, the pain of his claiming bite enough to send her over the edge.

As her entire body shuddered with the intensity of her climax, Fiorean swallowed her shout of his name with his mouth.

Fiorean's tongue encouraged her through the shocks of her orgasm as he stifled his own final cry, working her through wave after wave of pleasure.

The only sound was their heavy breathing, and the utter intensity of what had just occurred between them. It had been nothing like her few tumbles in the sheets with stable boys and farmhands. Those couplings had been more like animals rutting on a farm. Aemyra had quickly learned that women took more time with their pleasure and had avoided anything with a cockstand ever since.

But she didn't think that she would ever get enough of what Fiorean had just given her.

Fiorean broke the silence first.

"You're wrong."

Confused, she turned to look at him, barely noticing the scar on his face, she was so entranced by his other features.

"What?"

He smirked. "You definitely know how to ride."

Aemyra's mouth dropped open in surprise before she found her lips turning upward in a smile that mirrored Fiorean's own. A true smile that illuminated his whole face, and soon she found herself laughing until her stomach hurt as she lay beside her husband, the two of them forgetting the troubles that awaited them outside of this bedroom, if only for the night.

CHAPTER THIRTY-THREE

THE SUN WAS HIGH BY THE TIME AEMYRA BLINKED HER EYES open, her body pleasantly achy, and she stretched luxuriously. She could feel Terrea through the Bond, soaring somewhere in the Deàrr Mountains, pleased that Aervor had submitted to her.

The storm had cleared the sky and Aemyra blinked into the sunlit room. Fiorean was sound asleep, his chest rising and falling rhythmically, and Aemyra felt like a traitor to her own cause when she felt no hatred for him. The distrust lingered, and likely would until she was sitting on the throne with Lissandrea's crown decorating her brow.

Pushing her conflicted thoughts to the back of her mind, she slipped from the sheets, grabbing a robe and opening the veritable apothecary Fiorean had outfitted her with yesterday.

Enjoying the sunlight warming her back through the window, she withdrew every vial, jar, and instrument. The selection of herbs was impressive, and Aemyra quickly found what she was looking for.

As was her habit, Aemyra filled the teapot with clean water from the ewer, which no one would have laced with the binding agent. She wrapped her hands around the teapot and heated it with her magic.

Delighting in the sensation of having it returned to her, she set about mixing the right herbs.

"You look beautiful in the morning."

Fiorean's voice made her jump, and she almost dropped the raspberry leaf she was shredding. He was leaning against the bedpost, observing her with a smile.

Putting the lid back on the teapot, she poured them both a cup, making sure not to confuse the two.

"Drink up," she commanded.

He looked down at the liquid but did not lift it to his lips.

"If you wish to experience a repeat of last night then you will drink the tea," Aemyra said firmly.

The expression on Fiorean's face was conflicted, but she saw his eyes dart to her lower abdomen.

She took a long draft, the bitter taste pursing her lips.

"I will have control over my own womb," Aemyra said.

Fiorean lifted the cup to his lips. "I have been taking a tonic daily for years, Aemyra. My father might be gone, but I would never subject my child to the kind of upbringing I experienced."

Setting her cup down on the table, Aemyra thought of their half-finished conversation from the night before.

"You can help me make this territory better," she said.

"Mhm."

"My true inheritance is a quick temper, the ability to forge steel and cure minor ailments. Beyond that, I keep nothing of what I have been given." Aemyra spread her arms wide. "My power belongs to my people."

Fiorean's expression softened. "I'm listening."

"We must root out the stain of the Chosen from Tìr Teine, starting from within this caisteal. I wish to free Sorcha from the dungeons as soon as possible. Then we will figure out how to get Evander to abdicate," Aemyra said.

Fiorean's jaw slackened. "That will be far more complicated than you think. My brother will never willingly step down as king, and

Athair Alfred has hundreds of priests and Covenanters at his disposal. Even if I could convince the royal guard . . ."

Aemyra moved closer to him "We have to try. We both know that the real people making the decisions are your mother and Athair Alfred. Remove them, and Evander will listen to you." She pressed her palms to his bare chest. "You once told me that you believed your brother could become a better ruler than me. Do you still believe that?"

Fiorean didn't answer.

"I'll take your silence as confirmation that your feelings regarding your brother have changed, and I already know you do not share your mother's faith."

Fiorean set his empty teacup down and took her hands. "People will still die, and I cannot guarantee that I can make my brother see sense. This plan is hardly foolproof."

Aemyra nodded. "Which is why you will help me escape when the time is right."

Fiorean paled.

"You don't have to be implicated if you don't want to be. Tell Evander I knocked you out while you were sleeping and I discovered the secret passageway myself."

"Who would believe that?"

"I would," Aemyra retorted with a smile.

Fiorean pulled her closer. "I make no promises, but I will help you for as long as it best serves Tìr Teine. As long as the safety of my family is not in jeopardy."

Aemyra nodded; it was better than she had dared to hope for.

If Fiorean could plant a seed of doubt, start to turn them against the Chosen—Athair Alfred's regime would crumble from the inside. And Evander . . . well, perhaps the dragon madness would take care of that problem for them.

Looking pointedly at the tea she had brewed, Aemyra said, "Part of my plan involves ensuring that every woman, migrant or magical or otherwise, has the right to choose what happens to her body. Has a say in who she marries."

Fiorean smirked. "You didn't seem to have a problem with me telling you what to do last night."

Aemyra wasn't prone to blushing, but thoughts of the third ravaging that had taken place after they had tumbled out of bed and onto the rug heated her skin.

Before Fiorean could distract her, she placed a hand on the solid planes of his chest.

"You said that you invited the Ùir women here to marry your brothers because you saw it as a way out for them?" she asked.

Fiorean nodded slowly. "Yes. However, none of them were required to make the journey, and both Elear and Nael made their matches for love. You haven't had a chance to get to know Charlotte, and I know you think Elizabeth insipid, but I assure you they are very well matched with my brothers."

Aemyra patted his chest reassuringly. "That wasn't what I meant. It's hard for me to understand why you chose to offer an escape from oppression to women outside of this territory when there were women here, in Tìr Teine, suffering right under your nose."

Fiorean frowned. "I can assure you that had I known ab—"

"Those who worship the Savior in this city are few, but the Chosen have views toward women that are entirely backward. I witnessed men commit atrocities and attempt to justify them by saying they were working in the name of the Savior. I saw villages burned to cinders by the Covenanters."

"There is a limit to how mu—"

Aemyra interrupted, her temper spiking. "If I was able to save people from the evils of the priests as a blacksmith's daughter, think of what you could have done as a prince."

Fiorean stilled, and Aemyra sighed.

"When Sir Nairn was appointed to captain, punishments for criminal activity became severe."

"And you view that as a bad thing?"

"When children are being thrown into the dungeons for stealing food they cannot afford thanks to the taxes of a mad king, yes," Aemyra said, her voice rising.

Fiorean's expression darkened. "I never heard about any of this."

"I'm not telling you this to blame you." Aemyra sighed. "I'm telling you so we can agree that this will never happen again if we rule together."

Those emerald eyes snapped onto hers, a promise lighting their depths.

He was easily as powerful as she was, and a prince of Clan Daercathian. Even without the unsettled succession, a match between Penryth and Àird Lasair would have made sense.

"My first commission in this city had been to forge manacles for the caisteal dungeons. I never questioned why the shackles were to be made so much smaller than what would traditionally fit around an adult wrist."

Fiorean paled.

"Where are they now?" he asked, after a moment. "The children you saved?"

Extracting herself from his arms, Aemyra looked up at his face. "They are all priestesses in Brigid's temple. Five of them are anyway. I have never been able to shake the guilt of crafting their manacles with my own hands."

Fiorean's calloused fingers stroked the smooth skin of her cheek. "They were the first to oath themselves to you, after Kenna?"

Aemyra nodded, a lump appearing in her throat as she thought of them. "I know you can't let me visit, but can you please tell me if they are safe?"

"They are confined to the temple but living comfortably. I can send a guard down later this afternoon to inspect."

Aemyra relaxed slightly. "Thank you."

His hair was falling out of the knot he had slept in, auburn strands framing his scar.

"Why do you keep it covered?" she found herself asking.

Fiorean swallowed. "Because it is a mark of shame."

Aemyra traced the outlines of the puckered skin with the tips of her fingers until she noticed Fiorean shudder.

She dropped her hand, and he caught it in his own.

"They are from my father," he finally replied.

Aemyra's heart jolted. Three distinct lines ran down the side of his face, deep enough that the original wound must have been open to the bone.

"But—"

Fiorean squeezed her fingers gently. "I told you that you still have much to learn about my family."

Aemyra knew enough to fit some of the pieces of the puzzle together. The king had been drawing too much of Kolreath's power into himself and it had driven him mad. She wondered briefly if his other sons bore similar marks. If his wife did.

"It is only a mark of shame if you let it be so," Aemyra said quietly.

"These scars are from my father's hunting knife. Given to me the night I tried to stop him from whipping my mother to within an inch of her life."

Dropping her eyes to their entwined hands, Aemyra worked hard to keep the revulsion off her face. Whatever she had been imagining, it hadn't been that.

"When I lay bleeding on the floor, he made me watch as he gave her ten extra lashes for the trouble. I Bonded myself to Aervor the next day," Fiorean said bitterly.

He had been thirteen years old. For the first time, Aemyra truly believed that things were perhaps more complicated than she had realized. This man who had become her husband was far more than the hateful prince she had assumed him to be.

"At least when I Bonded to Aervor I became more powerful than my father. It was enough to get him to stop abusing my mother, but I couldn't bring myself to . . ."

The words hung in the air between them.

"That is not something to be ashamed of," Aemyra whispered as she finally met Fiorean's gaze.

She gently tucked his curtain of auburn hair behind his ear and knew he was wondering if Evander would grow as violent as his father.

The scar was brutal, that was true. Puckered, and still angrily red after all these years.

"I cannot erase what was done in the past, or the mistakes that my father made, but I can promise you that I will do whatever it takes to protect the people of this territory. And you," Fiorean said.

Silently, Aemrya allowed her husband to pull her back to bed.

This time they simply lay under the covers, holding the broken pieces of each other together.

CHAPTER THIRTY-FOUR

THEY MUST HAVE FALLEN ASLEEP, BECAUSE WHAT FELT LIKE mere moments, but was obviously hours later, the sun was shining as Aemyra was jostled awake to find Maggie bursting into the room.

"Edwyn is well!" she cried.

Not waiting for them to dress, Maggie threw herself back into the corridor, her light footfalls disappearing up the stairs. Aemyra and Fiorean wasted no time in following.

Not caring that she was wearing nothing but a crimson robe, she tied the fastening tighter as Fiorean threw on a shirt and breeches.

Moments later, they were in the nursery.

Elear was guarding his son's cot like a chimera.

Sunlight warmed the space, the fresh air drifting in from the window making all the difference.

"Isn't it wonderful news, Brother?" Nael called out warmly, eyes widening as he saw Aemyra. "And sister?"

Aemyra was assessing Edwyn's appearance. He was still shockingly weak, but he had some color back in his cheeks.

Ignoring the glare from Elizabeth, who was squashed onto the cot beside her son, Aemyra settled into a chair beside Maggie.

"Did you eat after prayers yesterday?" she asked.

"Fasting allows oneself to guard against gluttony and impure thoughts. It inspires deeper connection to our prayers," Elear said pointedly.

Aemyra ignored him.

Where grief seemed to have broken Charlotte and Evander, it had hardened Elear and Elizabeth.

Fiorean lay a hand on his brother's shoulder. "Aemyra is the reason Edwyn is recovering. I brought her to the nursery yesterday."

Elear's eyes widened, and Elizabeth clutched her son so tightly against her chest that Aemyra feared for his circulation.

"How dare you go against my wishes?" Elear said, his sleek queue of auburn hair seeming to bristle at the thought.

"Because her mother possessed knowledge from Clan Beaton. Knowledge that she passed down to Aemyra," Fiorean said gently.

Her chest ached at the mention of her mother, but Aemyra was glad that some parts of Orlagh lived on through her. She hadn't been able to save Lachlann, but she had managed to save Edwyn.

Elear's face was turning puce and Aemyra couldn't resist.

"Your brains may have been addled by the Chosen into thinking women are less intelligent than men, but I can assure you that is most certainly not the case," she said.

"Do enlighten us with your theories," Nael interrupted before Elear could snap.

"That because the male organ demands so much blood, men couldn't possibly possess more room for critical thinking than women?" Aemyra asked innocently.

Elear looked close to apoplexy and Elizabeth covered Edwyn's ears until he squirmed.

Feigning innocence, Aemyra stood from her chair. "Ah, you meant regarding this mysterious illness?"

Nael bit his lip to stop himself from grinning as he shared a look with Fiorean.

Crossing to the tureen of porridge, Aemyra spooned out an enormous helping.

"You need not worry about contagion, it is not borne of natural causes," Aemyra said, adding a pinch of salt to the bowl.

Turning, she found the eyes of everyone in the room on her.

"Your children are being intentionally poisoned," she said, shoving an entire spoonful of porridge into her mouth.

Cheeks bulging, she watched Fiorean's concerned gaze.

"But who would want to poison them?" Elizabeth asked worriedly. "Our children are not in line to the throne."

Elizabeth was right, poisoning Evander's eldest son could be interpreted as an attempt to prevent the throne from passing to another male after him. It had been what had made Aemyra suspect her own father at first.

But then the other children had sickened, and she had been forced to consider other options. Having learned of Alfred's particular hatred of Dùileach, Aemyra had wondered if he was attempting to cull magic within the royal line. All of the royals were Goddess blessed, even with only an ember.

But surely he wouldn't kill children. Certainly not when they were all male. That alone would shift the balance of power away from the Goddess and the matriarchy.

All Aemyra could do was shrug. "I know the antidote, but not the identity of the poisoner. I am sorry."

As she watched the siblings share worried glances, Aemyra knew that empires had fallen for less.

"Perhaps they should Bond fire salamanders," Fiorean suggested.

Elear looked offended. "Says the man with a dragon."

Helping herself to another mouthful of porridge as they began prideful bickering, she thankfully tasted nothing amiss.

"I believe little Edwyn should have his breakfast now," she interrupted.

"I do think you would be more welcome in the pigsty," Elear commented as Aemyra made a show of sucking porridge off her thumb.

Fiorean's eyes followed her lips, and her cheeks flushed.

"A princess should not be tasting food for poison," he said, his tone clipped.

"There is only one room in which I take orders from you, dear husband, and it is not this one," Aemyra replied, thrusting the bowl into Elizabeth's hands.

Tension thickened the air between them as she made her way to the door. From the way Fiorean's eyes were lingering on her muscular thighs, Aemyra knew he wouldn't be far behind.

She didn't make it out of the nursery corridor before Fiorean caught up to her.

Like a starving man, his fingers sought out the softness of her skin, the lushness of her curves underneath the robe.

After almost tumbling down the stairs in a tangle of limbs, Fiorean dragged her into the nearest room. Which turned out to be a privy.

Aemyra barely had time to catch her breath before he thrust her against the wall.

"Hardly a romantic location," she said against his lips.

Fiorean growled deep in his throat as he pinned her wrists above her head. "You aren't the candles and flowers type."

Aemyra grinned ferally, her teeth clashing against Fiorean's with the intensity of his kiss. She longed to drag her fingers through his hair, but his grip on her wrists was unrelenting even as she pulled against him.

Frustrated, she bit his full bottom lip and he drew back to look at her, his gaze heated.

She raised her eyebrows. "What type am I, then?" she asked.

Fiorean smirked before removing one hand from her wrists and unsheathing his dagger. His gaze dragged across the curves that were barely concealed by her robe. When he spun the blade expertly in his hand, Aemyra couldn't help but whimper.

With his feral grin, she felt heat pool between her legs and she forgot to even struggle.

"You like to get revenge," he whispered, dragging the edge of the dagger across her jaw. "But I make it a fucking art."

Her mouth dropped open in anticipation as the blade skimmed the hollow of her neck. Fiorean was applying expert pressure, enough for her to feel the threat of the bite but not breaking skin.

Aemyra spread her legs and Fiorean chuckled huskily before taking a step back. Instantly enraged, Aemyra used her freed hands to aim for his throat.

Expertly ducking under her arm, Fiorean pinned it behind her back before thrusting her against the door, pressing her cheek to the wood.

She could feel the hard length of him pressing into her backside as he pulled her curtain of curls away from her neck.

"Did you think I would let you have all the fun with a dagger?" he whispered into her ear, the blade skimming down her spine.

Her breath hitched as she arched her arse against Fiorean's erection.

His lips replaced the blade and her skin prickled in goosebumps as he nipped her neck with his teeth, the heat of his tongue sealing the marks into her skin.

"Fiorean . . ." she breathed, writhing against the door.

Another dark chuckle from behind her as a hand fisted in her curls. He pulled her head back to press his lips against hers in a branding kiss. Her mouth was open, her tongue claiming his as Fiorean tugged her hair to the point of pain.

When he released her again, Aemyra turned, her satin robe slipping down one shoulder. Dagger still in hand, Fiorean's gaze darkened as he found her breasts heavy and swollen.

Aemyra was no longer restrained, but she didn't move.

Another dagger twirl was all it took for the space between her legs to grow slick. His mastery of the blade was nothing compared to the way he had expertly coaxed pleasure out of her the night before.

The anticipation was killing her.

"Fiorean, please," she breathed.

"Aren't you glad you didn't succeed in killing me?" he whispered with dark intent. "You never would have felt this."

The dagger traveled from her collarbone and across the sensitive skin of her left breast. Where the cool metal skimmed her skin, her breath hitched and she did her best not to move. His eyes never left her curves as the dagger circled one nipple, the taut bud hardening further as Fiorean caught his bottom lip in his teeth.

"You like danger, Princess?" he asked.

Emerald eyes met forest green and Aemyra felt beyond words. Nevertheless, she nodded.

Before she could flinch, Fiorean swiped the dagger and made a shallow cut just underneath her nipple. The moment she began to feel the bite of pain, Fiorean's mouth clamped down on her skin, and she arched into him.

His tongue swiped across the tiny bead of blood, the slight pain only heightening the pleasure as he suckled, kneading the other breast.

Aemyra strained against him, needing more, needing everything he could give her.

When he passed her the dagger, she didn't hesitate. His rumpled shirt was on the floor without a second thought, and she grazed the sharp edge of the blade against his chest. The cut was a mere echo of what she was capable of, but he didn't protest as she bent her head and licked the ruby line of blood from his skin.

This time, their kiss tasted of iron and ancient promises.

Not an offering to a Goddess, but an offering to each other.

It broke their restraint instantly.

Before she could get Fiorean out of his breeches, he was already palming her slit.

"You are fucking soaking for me," he muttered into her mouth.

Hooking her leg around his waist, Fiorean drove two fingers inside of her and circled her clit with his thumb until she tilted her head back against the door and cried aloud.

Fiorean chuckled, the fingers inside her beckoning pleasure from her core.

"Careful. I'm not sure my brothers will appreciate your cries of pleasure as much as I do."

His fingers betrayed his words as he did something to her clit that had a garbled moan escaping her lips.

"Fuck them. If their wives don't make the same noises, then they aren't doing it right." She gasped as a third finger joined the other two and she began tugging on Fiorean's belt, needing more friction.

With a groan, he buried his face in her neck and bit down in frustration.

"One day I'm going to take my time with you," he promised, pulling his fingers out of her. With his eyes on her face, he licked the sheen from the digits that had been inside of her.

"Fucking delicious," he muttered.

Aemyra felt no shame when she throbbed at the words. Goddess, she wanted his face between her legs. She wanted to clutch the frame of their four-poster as she rode his face, to see his cheeks grow slick with her . . . but not today.

Fiorean seemed to sense her urgency and had his breeches off in a moment. His strong arms came around her waist and he pushed her back against the door. Hooking her legs around his hips, Aemyra tilted her pelvis up and he thrust into her in one hard motion.

She couldn't help but cry out as the ridge of his cock granted her the friction she desperately needed.

Fiorean's thrusts were unrelenting, hammering her against the door hard enough to make her healed head injury protest. But Aemyra didn't care, she needed more, wanted him completely undone by her.

"Don't you fucking dare stop," Aemyra groaned between ragged breaths.

His hands clutched her waist hard enough to leave bruises as he drove into her, his pace punishing.

"I should have known your need for control would make you a perfect lover," Aemyra gasped bitterly as he dragged his cock out of her before slamming back in at exactly the right angle.

Fiorean bit his lip again, his eyes on her exposed breasts as he worked her closer to the edge. "I'll do the gentlemanly thing and pre-tend I didn't hear you call me 'perfect.'"

Aemyra soon lost the capability of speech as the sensations cours-ing through her body rendered her incapable of forming a coherent thought. All she was aware of was the way his hands were grasping her, and how his cock felt within her.

"Give yourself to me, Aemyra," Fiorean said through clenched teeth. "I want to feel you come apart around me."

The strain in his voice made it obvious that he was trying to hold himself back until she had found her pleasure, but it was his command that was Aemyra's undoing.

As much as she wanted to defy him in all other things, when he was buried within her, all she wanted was to obey.

So she did.

When Fiorean tried to clamp a hand over her mouth to stifle her cries, she bit his finger hard enough to draw blood and sincerely hoped that Elizabeth and Maggie were getting a good earful.

They should know that they deserved to feel this too.

CHAPTER THIRTY-FIVE

FOUR DAYS LATER, AEMYRA TURNED THE CORNER FROM VISITING little Edwyn. Her fingers smelled pleasantly of mint and she was delighted with the improvement in the boy. He really was an agreeable child. She had no idea how Elear and Elizabeth had produced such a well-tempered son.

"We must fly, Brother."

Evander's voice rang out through the throne room, causing her to halt.

"We should wait until Clan Leòmhann chooses a side. If the chimeras declare for Draevan, the west will be lost to us," Fiorean replied.

The two brothers stood before the throne, torches flickering in their sconces, and for once Alfred was nowhere to be seen.

"You mean declare for your *wife*," Evander spat.

It was too late for Aemyra to back out of the room, so she stood tall. Evander's skin was sallow, his eyes bloodshot, and there were open sores on his forehead from where the crown had been rubbing against his skin.

"Why is she wandering the halls without an escort?" Evander asked, gesturing wildly toward Aemyra.

Fiorean laid a hand on his brother's shoulder. "She was taking herbs to little Edwyn. He is much improved."

"Yes, well, how convenient the heir to the throne was not so lucky," Evander spat, shoving his brother's hand off him and storming from the hall.

Fiorean made to chase after him, but Aemyra stepped into his path. "He wishes to fight with Kolreath?" she asked worriedly.

"Your father has made camp at the southern tip of the Deàrr Mountains. We believe he means to march on Fyndhorn," he replied, rubbing a tired hand over his face.

Aemyra stiffened. "Without the backing of Clan Leòmhann?"

Fiorean nodded grimly.

"My father will try to cut off the Leuthanach army before they can defend Àird Lasair," Aemyra said, spitting a filthy curse. "If only he had waited a few more days."

In a swift motion, Fiorean grasped her fingers and kissed the back of her hand. "I must go after Evander. Let me do what I can."

"Of course, go," Aemyra said, watching him leave.

Praying that Fiorean would be able to talk some sense into his brother before he set off with Kolreath to burn her army, Aemyra stilled when she found herself alone in the throne room.

The space was large, dark wooden beams crossing the ceiling, with stone pillars lining the space. The stained-glass wall was nothing short of spectacular. Even at night, when the flickering torches illuminated the painted crystal from within.

But it was the golden throne on the raised dais that commanded attention. She wondered if her feet would even touch the ground when she finally sat upon it.

Fingering the garnet necklace that hung around her neck, Aemyra turned her back on the throne that was hers by birth.

She would sit the throne when her people were safe.

Making up her mind, she left the great hall and hurried back to their chambers to change into her breeches. The time for playing the part of princess was over.

If Fiorean succeeded in calming Evander, they could stick to their original strategy of ousting Alfred and freeing Sorcha before liberating the priestesses and bringing the royal guard under Fiorean's command.

It wasn't a plan to be enacted overnight, but if Draevan had her army encamped less than fifty miles south, they would have to expedite the process.

Perhaps she could mix a sedative for Evander. The man drank so much wine he wasn't likely to notice until he was asleep in his neeps.

Lifting her skirts, Aemyra walked as quickly as she dared up the two flights of stairs to her rooms. If she broke into a flat-out run, it would only cause suspicion.

But time was of the essence.

Lost in her thoughts, she pushed open the heavy wooden door without knocking. Coughing slightly at the smell of incense, she wafted a hand in front of her face.

Stumbling on her skirts, Aemyra came to an abrupt halt as she realized who was sitting at the table.

Athair Alfred.

"What are you doing here?" Aemyra asked.

Alfred crossed his hands over his stomach. "Waiting for you."

Aemyra took one step toward the table. She had him alone with no Covenanters protecting him.

"Did Katherine send you here to distract me while Evander summons Kolreath for war? Here to blackmail me into joining him?"

Alfred's smile widened. "No."

She barely had the time to glare at him before she heard the door opening behind her. To her surprise, Sir Nairn stepped into the room, leaving Aemyra standing between the two men she desired most to kill.

"Rather an obvious trap, don't you think?" Aemyra asked with more bravado than she currently felt.

Neither of them replied.

"All right, boys, how are we doing this, then?" Aemyra asked, rolling her shoulders.

"Careful," Sir Nairn said in a scathing tone. "That is not how you address the leader of the faith."

"That pendant makes you far too confident, Captain," Aemyra gritted out.

Alfred skirted around the table, the long chain attached to his belt clanking. "We wish for your cooperation. Convert to the True Religion and accept your role within this family."

Sir Nairn placed his hand threateningly on the hilt of his sword. She would need to incapacitate the captain first, disarm him, and then use his sword to eviscerate Alfred. If she could rip one of their pendants off their necks with the blade, all the better.

"I refuse."

The priest pretended to laugh. "You would rather face the consequences?"

Aemyra shrugged, keeping one eye on Sir Nairn. "I wouldn't deny the existence of the Goddesses even if it was with my last breath."

Both men smiled.

"We thought as much."

Before Alfred had even given Sir Nairn the signal, Aemyra was moving. Ducking under the first swing of his broadsword, she aimed a kick to the back of the captain's knee, and he went down heavily to the rug, before she had to jump back to avoid her guts being spilled across the floor.

Alfred had wisely backed up against the far wall. "The demonic magic polluting your blood makes you so eager for violence," he reprimanded.

Sir Nairn rose and swung again, and she was forced to retreat toward the fireplace. Fiorean's chambers were large, but the reach of Nairn's sword meant there were not many places Aemyra could go where she wasn't in range.

She feinted right. When he clumsily tried to intercept her, she grabbed the poker from the fireplace on her left and brought it up to meet his hasty swing.

Sparks flew and Aemyra smiled to see the white-hot iron inches from his icy eyes. Her magic couldn't hurt him directly while he was wearing his pendant, but this poker would burn just the same.

With an indulgent smile, Aemyra summoned her magic. "I'm going to enjoy this."

But when she connected to the well of power in her chest, nothing happened.

Sir Nairn smiled again.

Her magic was gone.

How?

There was a clanking sound and the smell of incense wafted over her once more. Aemyra cursed herself for being so stupid. Alfred indulged in a smile as he let the chain drop from his belt.

"Did you really think our only conduits were food and water? We have been observing you for days. Clearly Prince Fiorean has fallen for your manipulation. Come now, Aemyra. I assure you that cooperation will be far less painful."

Heart pounding, Aemyra swung the poker desperately toward Sir Nairn and managed to move his sword. Ducking a punch from his gauntlet-covered hand, Aemyra struck again, attempting to pierce his armor where it was weakest.

A grinding noise came from behind her, but she had no time to discover what Alfred was up to, as Sir Nairn seemed determined to add to the growing number of wounds on her body.

"Rolynd." Alfred's warning tone cut through the room.

Nairn halted his advances, and Aemyra lunged for him. Unfortunately, the movement left her back exposed and before she could skewer Nairn with the poker, hands grabbed her.

Panicking as her makeshift weapon was pulled out of her grip, she found herself being dragged toward the table by two black-robed priests. A small opening in the wall told her that Alfred had opened a secret passageway.

Another trap.

Cursing her stupidity once again, Aemyra briefly wondered if she was even fit to be queen with the amount of mistakes she was making.

She thrashed in their hold, snapping with her teeth and kicking with her feet. Anything to make them let go of her. They couldn't kill her while she was being used as leverage.

She managed to grab a small tureen from the table and launched it toward the window. The glass broke with a satisfying crash, the incense dissipating slowly through the hole.

When three more priests appeared through the secret passageway, it became clear that she was far more vulnerable than she had believed. Not wasting any more time, she used the one weapon that was left to her.

Aemyra screamed.

A shattering sound erupted from her throat and echoed through the room before one of the priests clamped a cloth over her mouth and nose.

The fabric had been dipped in something, and Aemyra shut off her airway the minute she felt her senses dull. The cloth was removed, but before she could muster the energy to scream again, a gag was forced roughly into her mouth by Sir Nairn.

She felt hands encircle both of her ankles, restraining her on the table. Sir Nairn stepped back to give the Chosen space and a white-haired priest began chanting from the Tùr.

Athair Alfred had disappeared.

Hands and feet throbbing painfully, Aemyra wondered what was to become of her.

She didn't wonder for long.

Aemyra's vision blurred as one priest withdrew a curved instrument from his bag.

True fear shot through her entire body, and she fought the sedative with all of her might. She knew those instruments. Orlagh had used them when a babe threatened a woman's life. But in the wrong hands . . .

Her shoulders twisted painfully as she fought desperately to escape the priest's hold. Tears were burning her eyes as her muffled cries fell on deaf ears. She could not let them mutilate her.

They didn't want her siring female heirs. It didn't even matter that Aemyra might never want children—the Chosen were not going to give her the option.

One of the priests was fighting against her bucking legs, trying to get a grip on her skirts.

"Help me!" Aemyra screamed as loudly as she could through the gag, setting her pride aside with the garbled plea.

With one last disdainful look, Sir Nairn walked out of the door, closing it softly behind him.

Nausea churned in Aemyra's gut when the priests began chanting, and her entire body shook with acute terror.

She had boldly claimed a dragon with less fear. Had rescued children from the guards and faced down priests in the tavern without a shred of concern for herself. But this? This was entirely different.

The priests rucked up her skirts, exposing her to the room, and she let out another petrified sob.

Hela herself barred the gates of the Otherworld to those who violated women. It was a crime punishable by death, a direct offense to the Great Mother.

But what was about to happen to her was unheard of. Unthinkable.

She loosed a scream of pure fury through the gag until something tore in the back of her throat and one of the priests pinched her nose shut. With access to her airway cut off, Aemyra silenced herself before she fell unconscious. She didn't want to acknowledge the part of her mind that wished to welcome the darkness.

The graying priest was observing her privates clinically and Aemyra tried to remind herself of Orlagh's words.

I am the light. I will shine.

Bucking and writhing on the table, she tried to tug one of the priests off balance. They gripped harder until she risked her knees snapping and the graying priest spread her legs wider.

Unable to watch what they were doing to her, Aemyra hated herself for closing her eyes. For giving in.

"The sins of the Dùileach shall not be passed on to the innocents," the priest said, pausing his prayers. "Savior, we ask you to cleanse her body so the evils of magic remain with her alone."

Aemyra couldn't believe what she was hearing and called out silently to the Goddess who had gifted her. Swore that she would do anything, would be anything, if only she could be spared.

I am the light. I will shine.

With nothing else to do, Aemyra prayed. Not only to Brigid, but to every one of the five Goddesses.

That these priests would burn, that the air would be stolen from their lungs, that their cocks would shrivel and their bodies become dried-out husks.

As she felt fingers poking and prodding between her legs, Aemyra cried into the gag and suddenly knew what it was to be truly alone. No one was coming, not her dragon, not her husband, and certainly not the Goddess she believed in so fiercely.

Aemyra felt cool metal slip inside of her and she prayed that the wickedly sharp instrument was at least clean. Then she resigned herself to her fate. Coming out of this with an infection would kill her if the mutilation of her womb didn't.

The priests began chanting in unison.

"Savior, we pray. Root out her wicked ways and renew a right spirit within her heart. The stain of the Dùileach must be ripped away from the women who are possessed with evil power. For they cannot resist the demon's call as men can. Cleanse her, Savior, and spare her scourge on the next generation."

Aemyra screamed through the dirty rag that was stuffed to the back of her throat, as the first lance of pain speared through the most intimate parts of her.

The door slammed open.

"Get your filthy hands *off* my wife!"

Before Aemyra could register what was happening, a sword sliced through the face of the priest standing between her legs and Aemyra felt the hot spurt of blood over her thighs.

The hands restraining her disappeared, the sharp instrument sliding out of her to the floor with a clatter. Aemyra ripped the gag from her mouth with trembling hands and breathed through choking sobs.

"Your Grace, forgive us. We were only . . ."

The priests were pleading for their lives as Aemyra's vision finally cleared to see Fiorean withdrawing his sword from the back of her would-be surgeon's head, cold murder in his eyes.

Katherine was leaning against the doorframe, looking like she might be sick.

Fiorean's face was a mask of death as priests scrambled for the secret passageway. "Find Evander. They will all die for what they have done to my wife."

One priest dropped to his knees, pleading mercy as Katherine hurried away.

Why was she with Fiorean? Had she known of Alfred's plan and suddenly developed a conscience?

Aemyra fought with the tangled skirts of her dress, trying to pull them down over her knees. Pain lingered within her.

His hand glowing red, Fiorean grasped the kneeling priest by the neck and the smell of roasting meat met Aemyra's nostrils, turning her stomach. There was a disgusting gurgling sound before a sickening pop, as Fiorean burned the priest's throat away with his magic.

Then he threw the body to the floor.

Chest heaving, Fiorean rushed to the table. His boot connected with the surgical instrument and his face paled.

"What did they . . ." Beside himself with fear, Fiorean reached up to cup Aemyra's face, as if making sure she was alive. "Did he?"

There was a lingering trace of fire in his hand, stuttering slightly as he breathed in the residues of incense. But when Aemyra felt the smear of blood from the priest's throat on her cheek, she leaned over the side of the table and vomited.

Fiorean did not move from her side.

"They tried to cut out my womb." Aemyra had to force out the words from behind chattering teeth. "Or at least damage it beyond repair."

As if speaking the words suddenly made what had happened to her more real, Aemyra grabbed Fiorean's sword and wrestled it from his grip.

Throwing herself off the table, Aemyra sprinted for the door, ignoring the throb of pain deep within her core.

"Aemyra!" Fiorean called after her, but she was already tearing through the corridors in pursuit of Sir Nairn.

Her mother's words rang in her ears as she ran, her feet surprisingly steady.

I am the light. I will shine.

She would burn the darkness from this world.

Aemyra fixed her grip on the sword, its hilt slippery with blood, and she pushed herself faster.

She would not show mercy. Not tonight.

"Aemyra, wait!" Fiorean called after her, but she was quick. His legs might have been longer, but she was fueled by hatred and the torches flew by in a blur.

Finally, she saw a crimson cloak billowing around the bend.

She made it to the courtyard where the guards held sparring practice. Sir Nairn stood beside the weapons rack, looking for all the world like he was supposed to be there.

"What is the meaning of this pursuit?" the captain asked, sword sheathed, standing comfortably.

But Aemyra noticed his eyes darting around as if looking for a sign from his beloved Savior.

He would not find one.

Fiorean skidded into the courtyard just as Aemyra launched herself at the captain, sword held aloft and a scream of rage on her lips.

Sir Nairn met her blow with ease. With each thrust, Aemyra felt herself growing more grounded. This was what she knew—swinging a blade reminded her that she was in control. That even without her magic, she would decide her own fate.

Nairn sidestepped her, trying to make it look as if she were attacking him for no reason.

"My prince, please control your wife," Sir Nairn said as the sound of shrieking steel rang off the high walls surrounding the courtyard.

"Aemyra?"

Fiorean phrased her name like a question as he stalked toward the two of them, plucking a sword from the weapons rack. Aemyra bared her teeth at the captain as she hooked her sword between the pendant and his neck, ripping it from him.

If the binding agent hadn't been in her system, he would already be burning.

"He was part of it," she called out to her husband between labored breaths.

Sir Nairn flourished his blade as if trying to stop the fight. Aemyra dared a glance toward Fiorean.

He had been poised with his sword held aloft, ready to intervene, but now the point was in the ground and his hands were crossed over the pommel.

Sir Nairn was looking grateful. "Thank you, my prince, now—"

Fiorean held up a finger.

"You mistake me, Captain." His eyes tracked toward Aemyra, who was standing in her bloodstained dress. "I respect my wife enough to know when a life is hers to claim."

Sir Nairn's eyes widened as he turned back to Aemyra.

"Please," Fiorean said, his voice dangerously low, "resume."

Aemyra grinned ferally and swung her sword again. The captain barely got his weapon up in time to block her.

"Your Highness, this is absurd." Sir Nairn's eyes were wide with fear.

Aemyra parried his blows, keeping him on the defensive.

Evander stumbled into the courtyard, dueling three guards who had nothing to do with Alfred's plan, his sword dripping gore. Katherine was nowhere in sight, no doubt she had gone scurrying back to Alfred.

"What did I miss, Brother?" Evander asked, a terrifyingly jovial edge to his voice. "This is excellent fun."

Fiorean's face was taut even as Evander gleefully stabbed an innocent guard in the gut, refusing to take his eyes off Aemyra.

"Rolynd Nairn decided to take the law into his own hands."

Evander's face darkened and he finally stopped swinging his sword, allowing the two uninjured guards to drag their companions off in the direction of a healer.

When Aemyra ducked under Sir Nairn's blade and managed to pierce through the weak spot in his armor under the armpit, Fiorean nodded his approval.

As Aemyra jerked her sword out of the shallow wound, her lip curled at Nairn's cry of pain. She spun around and held her position.

"Cailleach is very clear about what should happen to those who defile women," Aemyra hissed. "Perhaps you have been listening to the Chosen for too long and have forgotten? Why else would you have dared?"

Drawing her arms back, pressing her palm flat against the pommel of the sword, Aemyra thrust the blade deep into Sir Nairn's crotch.

His roar caused the birds gathered on the roof to take flight as the front of his breeches flooded red.

Fiorean had his eyes fixed on the captain with an expression of fury. Evander seemed to be searching for his next victim.

Aemyra threw her sword down on the ground and crossed the courtyard to her husband, the gravel crunching under her velvet slippers.

Fiorean had already unsheathed his dagger from his belt in anticipation of Aemyra's next move.

Flipping the blade when her husband passed it to her, Aemyra turned to finish what the Goddess demanded as payment for Nairn's crimes. He was begging for his life as he bled out on his knees.

Aemyra made sure he saw her face.

She grasped a handful of his light hair and wrenched his head back, exposing his throat.

"The Athair isn't here to protect you now, you traitorous, hypo-critical filth," Aemyra hissed down at him. "This is for my mother. The gentle, kind soul whom you murdered. This is so you remember that a woman has her own power, and that you do not have any right to take it from her."

Aemyra's eyes sought out Fiorean's face and she found him in the darkness. His fire barely constrained with his anger, tongues of flame snaking down the sword he held.

She tightened her grip on the dagger and drew the blade deep across the skin of Sir Nairn's throat. Digging it in until she felt it hit bone, she at last loosed a relieved breath.

Her mother was avenged.

When she felt the last choking gasp leave his lungs as Nairn drowned in his own blood, she pushed his body onto the gravel.

Fiorean was looking at her like she was the most beautiful thing he had ever seen.

Evander was slowly clapping his hands together even as his expression grew volatile. "What an invigorating sport, shall we continue?"

The guards fled the courtyard before Evander could corner them.

Fiorean ignored his brother as he folded Aemyra protectively into his arms. They turned their backs on the body of Sir Nairn as Evander began lopping the captain's head off, wielding his sword like an executioner's axe.

Aemyra allowed Fiorean to lead her back into the caisteal. An assortment of bloody weapons in their hands, hair burning as brightly as their inner fire.

CHAPTER THIRTY-SIX

"I NEED TO ESCAPE TONIGHT," AEMYRA SAID, HER VOICE ECHOING in the empty corridor.

Fiorean stayed close to her side. "Ssh, we need to clean you first."

Aemyra pushed him away. "Fiorean, I can't stay in this caisteal any longer. Nairn is dead. Your mother and Alfred will come after me and they will make sure my magic remains bound as long as I am a prisoner here." Her hands were shaking, but her voice was steady. "I need to get Sorcha and leave tonight."

Instead of restraining her, Fiorean blocked the door that led down to the dungeons. Blood crusted his scar and Aemyra had never seen him look so fearsome.

"The Athair will not live to see the sunrise, and I will get Sorcha out." His fingers reached gently for the sword she still clutched in her hands. "But right now you will only attract unwanted attention."

Aemyra's gorge rose at the smell of the blood crusting her dress and hair and she relinquished the sword. She tried not to think about the sharp ache between her legs as Fiorean led her gently up the stairs.

"There is more darkness in this court, in this territory, than I thought. I need to make it right," Aemyra whispered. "Goddess knows what the princesses have gone through at the hands of Alfred, what they are *still* going through."

Fiorean's emerald eyes were far away. "T-they are safe within these walls."

Aemyra laughed, an edge of hysteria within it. "You cannot tell me you still believe that? How can you have witnessed what just happened and think that any woman is safe in this court? The captain of the guard and the leader of the Chosen just sanctioned this assault within the caisteal walls."

"I never thought——" His words choked off as he opened the door to their chambers, his expression one of utter agony.

The room was empty, but the door to the secret passageway was still open, blood covering the floor. Aemyra could suddenly *feel* it all again. The act of dueling Sir Nairn had taken away most of her panic, giving her a sense of control. Now she was just a victim standing in the evidence of her assault.

His expression taut, Fiorean led her into the adjacent bathing chamber and bolted the door closed.

As soon as his back was turned, Aemyra felt herself start to shake. She was escaping tonight. As soon as she was on Terrea's back, she would be safe again.

Fighting not to let a whimper escape her lips, she wrestled with the laces of her corset, needing to get the dress off her body. Fiorean spread his palm flat on the surface of the bathwater until tendrils of steam curled lazily into the air.

She needed this filth off her skin.

The wound on her chest was pulling uncomfortably as she struggled. A band of panic tightening around her lungs the longer she fought with the dress. She could feel the congealing blood coating her skin, and a deep ache was resting in between her legs that made her want to scream.

Her breaths became erratic.

Fiorean looked up from the bath, and his eyes widened as Aemyra's heaving breaths turned into choking sobs.

"*A ghràidh* . . ." He murmured the endearment in the Seann, dropping the soap into the bath and rushing to her side.

Aemyra was still manically pulling at her dress, teeth clenched against the uncontrollable tremors.

"Get it off me!"

Her husband's fingers slipped on the laces and Aemyra felt like she could endure no more.

"Get it off!"

Fiorean's emerald eyes were shining with tears as he pulled at the knots Aemyra had accidentally created. Her own nails were scratching his skin as he tried to help her, desperate to rid herself of the stain.

"Get it off *NOW*," Aemyra roared, her already raw throat cracking on the last word.

Fiorean unsheathed his own dagger, swiping it through the laces with one swift movement, and ripped the ruined dress from her body.

Aemyra flailed, trying to get her arms out of the sleeves, but the blood made the fabric heavy. In her panic she sobbed hysterically, hardly wanting to touch the dress to strip herself of it.

Fiorean's eyes were pained as he reached for her, but she backed away. A second tear followed the first, his cheeks glinting in the light of the fire he had ignited in the brazier, and he raised his palms.

The gentlest brush of magic enveloped her, twin tongues of flame that made contact with the dress, burning it to ashes until the only thing touching her was the garnet necklace.

There was still dried blood crusted on her skin and hair, but she quieted. Sinking to the floor, curling into herself, Aemyra cried.

She cried the tears she had been valiantly keeping in for Orlagh, Lachlann, and Pàdraig. She cried for the two small princes who she was sure had died because of her, if not by her own hand. And she cried for what she had endured within these caisteal walls in just a few short weeks.

How could she ever hope to change the world if this was what had become of her?

Cheeks wet, she felt the gentlest brush of Fiorean's magic and she looked up. He was kneeling beside her, his white shirt stained red, tears tracking through the blood on his face.

He held her gaze as the sobs subsided.

"You survived," he said firmly.

Aemyra hated that her bottom lip wobbled.

"I am here. You are safe. You survived."

"I need to be stronger than this," she whispered, her voice break-ing. "I need to be better than this."

Fiorean was shaking his head as Aemyra began rubbing her blood-stained hands together in disgust. With a rush of heat, Fiorean sent a cleansing fire skittering across her body and the blood was seared from her skin. When he entwined their fingers together, not an outer trace of what had happened remained.

"You are the strongest woman I have ever met," he said, pressing a fervent kiss to her knuckles.

Before she could so much as shake her head, he grasped the sides of her face with his now clean hands.

"You are my queen."

Aemyra's eyes widened. He had never called her that before. Not all the times she had corrected him, not even when she had held a dagger to his throat.

"I don't feel much like a q-queen," she managed to say.

"Did any of our ancestors? What is a ruler supposed to feel like?" he asked.

Wrapping her arms around her knees, Aemyra fought not to look at the door as she knew what lay beyond.

"I don't know," she muttered.

The way everyone still spoke of the ancient queens with such rev-erence had always made Aemyra believe they had been born knowing how to rule. The warrior Lissandrea, her daughter Aesandra, Faeona the Gentle, Isabael the Peaceful . . . Aemyra had modeled herself after those queens. Promised herself she would not let the people of Tìr Teine down.

Now look at what had become of her.

Stripped of her magic, violated in her own caisteal, denied the throne that was rightfully hers.

"Let me wash it away," Fiorean said, pulling her gently to her feet.

She allowed him to guide her to the steaming bathtub.

When her legs submerged into the scalding water, she almost started crying again, this time in relief.

Aemyra closed her eyes as Fiorean rubbed delicious circles into her scalp, his lithe fingers gentle on her skin as he erased the stain of the assault from her curls.

"I don't know how to be a queen after this," she whispered as he poured a jug of water over her head.

"You don't have to, Aemyra." Fiorean sighed. "You just have to be yourself. The rest will follow."

Biting down on her kneecaps, tasting the coppery tang of the water she sat in, she allowed the tears to spill over as Fiorean rinsed her hair.

"Even without your magic, you burn like wildfire. Before I knew who you were, I could see that. It is not your magic, or your blood, that makes you the right ruler for Tìr Teine. It is your heart."

Aemyra couldn't see his face, but the sincerity in his words was unmistakable.

"You are the light, Aemyra," Fiorean said, risking the tenderest kiss to her bare shoulder. "Shine for us."

Her trust in Fiorean was new, and still fragile. She desperately needed to surround herself with those she knew would never betray her. Feeling the separation from her twin ache profoundly, she suddenly needed Adarian beside her.

Rising from the bath, Aemyra stood still as Fiorean's magic dried her off before she could ask. Her skin was still tender but now pleasantly warm, as were the curls spiraling down her bare back.

She pulled on the breeches and clean shirt Fiorean had fetched from the other room.

"I will shine," she said, her voice miraculously steady. "I will shine brighter than the fucking sun for my people. With me as queen, with our dragons fighting together, we can make this right. Brigid will guide us."

The water in the bath sloshed as Fiorean quickly scrubbed himself clean, rivulets cascading down the hard muscles of his torso. He stared into the water, contemplating what she was asking.

"I am risking everything for you. My own life, my *dragon's* life. You expect me to betray my mother, and be prepared to kill my brother if he will not relinquish the throne?"

There was no malice in his tone, the words were hollow, his decision already made.

Aemyra crossed her arms over her chest as Fiorean rose from the bath, squeezing water from his long hair.

"You've seen Evander's behavior grow more impulsive. How long until he becomes a danger to his wife, his children? Himself?," she asked.

Fiorean closed his eyes, bracing himself on the edge of the bathtub.

"This madness, if it truly comes from Kolreath, cannot be reversed. A Bond can only be severed in death. You and I both know this," Aemyra whispered.

She knew she was asking the impossible. The Chosen had used the mental instability of former kings to their advantage. Kolreath had been Bonded to five different Dùileach. Had the madness begun with the dragon? Or with the king who had killed four of his brothers to ensure he sat the throne? Perhaps with the death of each Bonded Dùileach, Kolreath had lost a little more of himself.

"We are all villains in somebody's story, Fiorean," Aemyra finally said. "I am the villain in your mother's. As no doubt you are in my father's. But it is how we view each other that matters."

Fiorean trembled, like he was warring against his instinct to hold and protect her.

"Do you think my mother knows of Alfred's true inclinations?" he asked.

Aemyra didn't want to believe that Katherine was capable of orchestrating such an assault, but Alfred had been her closest companion for years.

"How else would she have known to bring you to our chambers?" she replied.

Fiorean's eyes were unfocused. "No. She was at prayers. She told me she heard it from another priest."

Recognizing when Fiorean was reaching his own mental limit, she placed a hand on his chest. Feeling the beat of his heart under her palm steadied her.

"Nothing stays secret in this city for long," Aemyra replied diplomatically. If Katherine had been involved, they would hear of it soon enough.

"You did," Fiorean said.

His voice was laced with emotion that he couldn't put into words, but he lifted his eyes to her bruised face. "But now it is time to show the world who you are."

AEMYRA PULLED HER CLOAK TIGHTER AROUND HER NECK, LEATHERS squeaking as she shifted from foot to foot. Her emotions were still raw, but it felt good to be in motion.

Terrea grumbled at her back.

"Hush," Aemyra whispered. "They'll be here soon."

Her words betrayed the twitching in her fingers, her restless legs. It was taking everything inside her not to climb onto Terrea's back and leave this court far behind. Her dragon was on edge, having sensed what had happened to Aemyra through the Bond. It was only the fact that innocent people slept within the caisteal that kept her dragon from burning it to the ground.

The caisteal was surprisingly quiet, eerily so.

Fiorean had set off for the dungeons what felt like hours ago and dawn was fast approaching. They needed to be far from Àird Lasair when the sun finally crested the horizon.

Fiorean's first task would be to find Athair Alfred and kill him. Her husband had granted her request to kill Sir Nairn, she would allow him this part of the revenge.

Then they would weather what came next on different sides of the war, in the hopes that they could unite what had been broken decades before.

Another low growl came from her dragon, and Aemyra squinted through the darkness until she saw Fiorean and Sorcha sprinting through the meadow and she sighed with relief.

Fiorean's stride was long, and Sorcha was stumbling slightly with the effort of keeping up with him. She was thin, and her raven hair was matted to her scalp, but she looked mercifully uninjured. Aemyra's heart squeezed painfully as she felt the guilt of leaving her former lover to languish in the dungeons instead of rescuing her immediately.

Her feet stumbling, Aemyra closed the distance between them. Part of her knew that a daring rescue would have only ended in her own capture and Sorcha's death, but the sight of the filth covering Sorcha's olive skin had Aemyra praying to Cailleach for forgiveness.

No bells were tolling from the caisteal, no shouts rent the air. Fiorean had done as he had promised and gotten Sorcha out safely.

"It's all right, you're safe," Aemyra promised, reaching for her.

Evidently exhausted from the headlong sprint, Sorcha collapsed into Aemyra's arms. The familiar scent enveloped her, still there underneath the grime, and Aemyra struggled to control the emotions that rose to the surface.

She was no longer the same woman who had worked in a forge and enjoyed trysts with the tavern owner.

Sorcha stiffened as if she realized it too, and she pulled back. Having expected some degree of resentment from her, Aemyra was still stung by the look of pure venom in her eyes.

"You *lied* to me," Sorcha seethed, the conflicting emotions in her voice evident even to Fiorean.

The barkeep looked as though it was only the presence of the dragon stopping her from striking Aemyra. Knowing what Sorcha was capable of, Aemyra kept a healthy distance from her former lover. It was too soon after the assault to be touched in violence once more and she didn't miss the concern in Fiorean's eyes.

But she could not go to pieces, not again.

"I had no choice," Aemyra said, keeping her tone flat. Not willing to let Sorcha see how close to breaking she really was.

"You should have told me who you really were," Sorcha said, a pleading note entering her voice.

Aemyra crossed her arms as if they would protect her heart. "We don't have time for this. Let's go."

"What the fuck are you doing with him?" Sorcha's dark eyes, welling with furious tears, spared a quick, hate-filled glance at Fiorean. "They killed Orlagh!"

Aemyra flinched and Terrea peeled her lips back from her teeth. Her dragon wouldn't tolerate much more.

"Given that I just rescued you, wouldn't that put us on the same side?" Fiorean asked, taking one step forward as if to protect Aemyra.

Sorcha glared at him. "You are the one who kidnapped me in the first place, Prince."

Aemyra's eyebrows rose and she turned to her husband. Fiorean simply shrugged.

"Villain in someone's story, remember?"

Sorcha scoffed when Aemyra did nothing. "Unbelievable."

Temper flaring, Aemyra reached for Sorcha's wrist and held fast. "Believe it or not, you are *lucky* that Fiorean is the one who captured you. Had it been Evander, or that bastard N-Nairn, you would not be standing here right now."

Aemyra shuddered as she spoke the captain's name into existence, reminding herself that his corpse was rotting up at the caisteal.

Sorcha stopped struggling.

"I am sorry," Aemyra said, relenting. "I'm sorry that I couldn't tell you who I was, but doing so would have only put you in more danger. We were involved for years, Sorcha. I had no idea when my time would come to make a play for the throne, and I wasn't about to put you in such a dangerous position."

Sorcha's face crumpled. "Why make a play for the throne at all? You had a good life, Aemyra." Her voice broke. "Orlagh and Pàdraig had good lives too."

Fiorean's hand went to the sword at his side when Aemyra's lip wobbled. The words hurt more than if Sorcha had slapped her.

After a moment, Aemyra found her voice. "Orlagh and Pàdraig understood my reasons. This fight is about more than just us. Tìr Teine needs a queen."

Sorcha's face shuttered.

Aemyra sighed, exhausted. "We have to go."

Sorcha eyed Terrea warily. "Go where?"

"South. My army is camped in the foothills of the Deàrr Mountains and it is time I rejoin them," Aemyra said, turning back to face her husband.

Fiorean drew close to her, cupping the back of her neck with one hand, letting his thumb graze her lower jaw.

"Thirty thousand Leuthanach clansmen are on that plain," he warned. "If you cannot convince your father . . ."

Aemyra lifted her chin. "I'm the queen, remember? I don't have to convince my father of anything. My army fights for me."

With the moonlight staining his skin bone white, Aemyra crushed her lips to his in a kiss that tasted of farewell.

Aemyra pulled away from him to chivy Sorcha toward an irate Terrea.

"I've seen you face down sailors more threatening than my dragon, get up her leg," Aemyra said to Sorcha when she balked.

Terrea growled low in her throat as Sorcha climbed the scaly limb with trembling hands. Aemyra made to follow.

"Wait," Fiorean said.

Her husband pulled his cloak aside to reveal the weapon she thought she would never see again.

"Where did you get that?" Aemyra gasped.

He was holding the sword she had forged with her own magic, the carved runes thrown into sharp relief by the moonlight. As her hand gripped the leather of the scabbard, she felt a piece of her soul return to her.

"You were in rather a rush to get away from me after our first fight," Fiorean said with a gentle smile.

Aemyra drew the blade with a shriek of steel. To give him credit, Fiorean didn't back away.

"You're lucky I didn't run you through with it," she said, eyes on the spectacularly crafted weapon.

Fiorean snorted. "You tried and failed, Princess."

With the ghost of a smile on her lips, Aemyra slid the sword back into its scabbard.

"So, we're back to 'princess' now, are we?" she asked.

Fiorean shrugged. "Old habits."

Feeling like she had shed an old skin and was being born anew, Aemyra stroked the hilt.

This was the sword she would free her people with.

"Does it have a name?" Fiorean asked, his eyes on the weapon.

Aemyra had spent years trying to think up something appropriate. A name that would be worthy of great stories. She had never seemed to find one that fit.

It surprised her that now, when she had so recently felt what it was to break completely, she knew what her sword's name was.

Remembering Orlagh's last words, Aemyra smiled.

"Fearsolais," she said in the Seann, the blade heating in her hands as she spoke its name into existence. "Lightbringer."

CHAPTER THIRTY-SEVEN

The two armies came into sight just as dawn broke over the horizon. Terrea had flown swiftly and they had left Clan Daercathian lands behind within hours.

Her father had picked a strategic location, allowing ten thousand soldiers to keep the advantage of the high ground. With the mountain peaks at their back, Gealach and Terrea would be able to launch aerial attacks while staying out of range.

Aemyra hadn't been able to fathom how large the opposing forces of Clan Leuthanach might be, but as Terrea descended from the sky, the breath left her lungs.

"Great Mother have mercy," Sorcha muttered behind her.

The hilltop fortress of Fyndhorn was surrounded by black tents spreading across the plain.

A cry went up from the scouts as the black dragon descended from the clouds. Terrea landed atop a high hill just behind where the largest tents were erected, the flattened trees and scorched earth telling Aemyra that Gealach had been here recently.

Groaning as her abused muscles protested the movement, Aemyra slid off Terrea's back, her feet hitting the ground with a soft thud. Helping Sorcha down, Aemyra tried not to notice how the barkeep skirted out of her hold as soon as she was back on solid ground.

Aemyra shouldered the insult and started walking toward the camp. They hadn't made it far before Adarian appeared, sprinting as though Beira's wind bore him hence.

A small cry escaped her lips at the sight of her twin and she started running.

"Aemyra!" Adarian cried, managing to make her name sound like both an admonishment and a relief.

Her field of vision was suddenly blocked by Adarian's chest as her twin enveloped her in a crushing hug. She wrapped her arms around his broad shoulders, reassuring herself that he was still in one piece. Aemyra had lost too many people, seen too much violence and death since they had parted, to take this moment for granted.

"Thank the Goddess you're safe," Adarian muttered into her hair.

Pulling back, Aemyra noticed his dirt-streaked fighting leathers. He had grown his hair out, but those sapphire eyes shone brightly within his now tanned face.

Aemyra searched for the words to explain all that had happened since they had been separated. Grief clouded his eyes and she felt dangerously close to tears.

"I'm so sorry, Adarian," she whispered.

His jaw clenched as he pulled her in for another crushing hug that spoke of loneliness. It was her fault he had been forced to grieve their family without her.

"You are an idiot for flying off and trying to avenge Lachlann without me. What were you *thinking*?" he ground out.

Fighting her exhaustion, Aemyra clutched her brother's arms. She had already endured too much over the last couple of days, she needed her twin to be on her side.

"I will explain everything. Where is Father?"

"Scouting with Gealach," he replied. "The Balnain fleet needs reinforcements. They came under attack two days ago, falling prey to some kind of magic-stripping mist. Thanks to the phoenixes, the battle was won, but barely."

Sorcha shifted her feet and Aemyra fought against her weariness. "Take me to Father's tent. Sorcha needs sustenance while you check her for injuries."

"I don't nee——" Sorcha began to protest.

"You were in those dungeons for weeks. I was unable to help you then, but I will do what I can to ensure you have no lasting effects from your imprisonment," Aemyra interrupted, her tone firm.

To her surprise, Adarian bowed to her like a soldier following orders from his commander, and Sorcha followed as meekly as she was capable of into camp.

Aemyra noticed the confident set of Adarian's shoulders. His was the stance of a man grown accustomed to leading soldiers. She wondered which company their father had placed him in charge of. From the smell lifting off his clothes, she would guess cavalry.

Sorcha never said a word as they walked toward the largest tent. Murmuring and whispers met Aemyra's ears, soldiers on all sides praising their queen's return. Some even going so far as to marvel at her escape.

She ignored them all.

Sorcha sniffed derisively.

Reaching the tent bearing the Daercathian royal crest, Aemyra squashed down her nerves and pulled open the canvas flap.

"Your Majesty?" Maeve said, rising from her chair, shock plain on her face.

Aemyra held up one hand as if to protest a bow the general hadn't been inclined to give. At least she had stood upon the queen's entry.

"Adarian tells me my father is scouting. While we wait for him, please update me on the progress of my army," Aemyra said, remembering Fiorean's words.

She would trust her intuition and learn how to lead these people.

Looking like she was biting back some choice words, Maeve gestured to the maps spread across the table in the middle of the tent.

"We are outnumbered by the Leuthanach army three to one. It is likely that more Covenanters have traversed the Blackridge Mountains and are hiding in the tree line. We had been planning to launch an attack from both sides, but this unnatural mist they wield has given us cause for concern."

Nodding her head, Aemyra weathered the distrust on the general's face.

"I have experienced firsthand the effects of the binding agent. The Chosen used it on me when I was prisoner in Caisteal Lasair."

A muscle twitched in Adarian's jaw, but Maeve remained stoic.

"We had heard rumors . . ." Adarian said, his words trailing off as Aemyra's eyes closed wearily.

Her brother looked about as exhausted as Aemyra felt and she wondered how hard Draevan had pushed her army to reach the Deàrr Mountains in only a few short weeks. Maeve was still in her armor, some of it dented, and had a new scar across one cheek.

Aemyra dragged herself over to the nearest chair and sat down heavily as Sorcha gave another contemptuous sniff.

Adarian turned to her. "Would you like me to examine you?" he asked gently.

Sorcha shook her head, clutching the cloak Fiorean had given her around her shoulders. "No. A good, stiff drink wouldn't go amiss though."

Maeve reached into a wooden crate, armor clanking. Pulling out a half-empty bottle of Truvo red, she winked at the barkeep.

Despite Maeve's intimidating persona, Sorcha crossed the tent and took the bottle from the general's hands, upending it and taking several large swallows. When Sorcha handed it back, Maeve was slack-jawed.

Adarian turned again to his sister. "Well?"

Resolving not to look at Sorcha, Aemyra reminded herself that she was their queen. "You are no doubt aware that I left the Sunset Isle to seek vengeance for Lachlann, Pàdraig, and Orlagh."

Adarian immediately jumped down her throat. "It was reckless, and stupid, and you put yourself directly into the path of our enemies."

Running her hand wearily across her face, Aemyra looked up at her brother. "Please, do me the courtesy of letting me speak without interruption. I haven't slept well in days."

Sorcha snorted. "No, I bet you haven't."

Aemyra bristled at the insinuation as she tried to hold the broken pieces of herself together.

Lifting her chin, Aemyra pulled off her thick cloak and moved the necklace to the side, exposing the jagged wound across her chest. Adarian's eyes bugged and even Maeve let out a low whistle between her teeth.

"Sir Nairn gave me this when I saved you from his knife," Aemyra said pointedly, her gaze fixed on her former lover. "I may be the reason that you were imprisoned, but I am also the reason you escaped with your life. Others weren't so lucky."

Adarian's face was pained.

"We saw you being brought into the dungeons," Sorcha said, her lips making a sucking sound as she lowered the bottle again. "Nairn threw you in a cell and left you there for a full day. You were turning blue without a cloak or a blanket before the dowager queen ordered you removed upstairs."

Sorcha's voice was dripping with resentment.

Aemyra rubbed her temple against the headache forming there.

"I'm sorry that Fiorean could not get you out sooner. I promise that you were never far from our thoughts."

"You sound awfully familiar with your kidnapper," Adarian said, leaning back in his chair.

Sorcha snorted again. "Well, she was fucking him."

Adarian's always carefully contained fire flared outward. "You were *what?*"

"Sorcha, please remove yourself from this tent. Find a healer if you need one and tell one of the camp aides that you need clean clothes and something to wash with," Aemyra said, ignoring the way her brother's face was turning puce.

Sorcha didn't move.

"That is an order from your queen," Aemyra said firmly, staring her down.

The barkeep gave Aemyra one last, loathing look before striding from the tent. Maeve looked inclined to follow her.

"I wasn't just fucking a prince, I *married* him. Congratulations, Prince Fiorean is now your brother-in-law. Deal with it."

Adarian stood from his chair. "Father's spy said you were forced into it and tried to escape shortly after. Unless you're telling me you willingly married the man who killed Lachlann?"

"Fiorean didn't kill him."

"Lies!" Adarian yelled, fist slamming down on the tabletop, the muscles in his forearm straining.

Aemyra was grateful she wasn't in possession of her fire, she didn't have the energy to control it. "I swear it on my own life."

Holding his gaze, Aemyra recounted how their family had really died. As she had predicted, Adarian seemed altogether less inclined to forgive Fiorean.

"The fact that it was an accident will not bring our brother back, but I will not condemn an innocent man because of one mistake," she said.

Adarian's face was furious, his eyes betraying the conflict happening within.

Maeve crossed her arms. "For all we know, you are now here spying on us. You have no way to prove otherwise."

Even Adarian's eyes widened, and Aemyra gritted her teeth. "You seem to forget to whom you are speaking."

Maeve had the sense to look contrite.

"As your *queen,*" Aemyra stressed the word heavily as she glared at Maeve, "I have been working for our cause from within the walls of Caisteal Lasair. I did what I could to destabilize Evander's rule and gain the trust of potential allies. Fiorean helped me escape. He remained behind so that when we launch our attack on the city, the gates will be open to us. I just won us the war. A thank-you would be nice."

Aemyra grabbed the wine bottle and took a generous gulp.

"We did once talk of marriage alliances strengthening my position. I believe mine worked quite well in our favor," she said, the Truvo red sliding pleasantly down her throat.

The silence within the tent was broken by the sound of a dragon coming in to land outside the thin canvas walls.

The wine was helping to steady her nerves regarding leading her people, but first Aemyra had to make sure her father would allow her to.

Maeve stood from her chair, spine straight as she awaited her commander. Aemyra tried not to bristle with irritation that she had not shown her queen such courtesy.

Turning expectantly toward the tent flap, she lifted her chin as Draevan shouldered his way inside. His hair was unkempt and his face streaked with dirt, but he didn't look surprised to see her. No doubt Terrea had been relaying everything she had seen to Draevan via Gealach.

He walked with the confident swagger of a man who thrived in wartime.

"As much as I would have preferred you to come back to us with your traitorous husband's head, I find myself grateful to have you returned in one piece," he said.

Coming from Draevan, that was practically a hug.

Aemyra swallowed nervously as her father accepted a goblet of wine from Maeve.

His eyes were bright underneath the grime, and his face weather-beaten. War seemed to suit him.

"Tell me, did you enjoy the luxuries of court life while your army marched north through winter?" he asked after taking a large gulp.

Trying not to think about the treatment she had endured, Aemyra steeled herself. "I escaped at the first opportunity, when it most benefited both my throne and my people."

"Sorcha didn't seem to agree with that," Maeve interrupted unhelpfully.

Aemyra glared at her.

"I have laid Àird Lasair open for our attack."

Draevan narrowed his eyes. "You mean you laid your legs open for the enemy."

Adarian bristled beside her and Aemyra summoned whatever courage she still possessed. "I did what I thought was best given the circumstances I found myself in. One of your own spies assisted me." She seethed. "I must now ask if any of your allies at court carried out orders to kill the young princes."

Maeve raised her eyebrows, but Draevan stared down his long nose at Aemyra.

"I do not mourn the loss of the traitor Evander's child," he drawled.

Aemyra clenched her fists. "*Children*. Fergys and Hamysh are both dead, they were members of our clan, how can you not mourn them?"

"Did you?"

The words were a test, Aemyra heard it in his voice. Drawing herself up to her full height, she replied, "Yes. I mourned the loss of both boys just as I mourn still for Lachlann. I might have inherited my violent inclinations from you, Father, but Orlagh taught me that fire can heal as well as destroy. I will not lose more of my people so you can play at war."

Draevan did not waver. "You acted foolishly. Without considering the consequences. Your actions were those of a child, not a queen." He dragged his eyes up and down her disheveled frame like he didn't recognize her. "I expected better of you."

Her father's words cutting her to the core, Aemyra's tone turned venomous. "You clipped my wings for twenty-six years and yet you expect me to know how to fly."

Everyone knew that she wasn't talking about dragons.

"I will be the first to admit that taking off with Terrea to seek revenge was foolish. But I never planned to abandon my army. Ever since I woke as a prisoner in Àird Lasair, I have tried to put the needs of my people first. You should be thanking me. If it wasn't for my marriage, we would be facing a long-drawn-out battle on the plains."

She watched Draevan's eyes linger on her chest wound as if considering her words.

"What's the problem, Father? Unable to believe that your daughter might have won this war with words before you were able to do it with your sword?"

Draevan drew Dorchadas, the dark steel glinting in the gray light of dawn. "I will allow no daughter of mine to sit the throne with a usurper by her side. I do not care if you married him in the sight of the Goddess or the false God. Death severs all vows. I shall see him gone from this world, or I shall renounce you as my heir."

Shocked into utter silence, Aemyra watched as he grabbed another goblet of wine and strode from the tent.

Aemyra tried to weather the fear that speared through her. Her father was proud, and stubborn. If he was determined to kill Fiorean, then he would stop at nothing until he had achieved that goal.

She would not let it come to that.

Swallowing her pride, she refused to be ashamed of anything she had done in the last few weeks. Her father would change his mind about Fiorean when he heard their plan. He had to.

"I want half of the army ready to march by tomorrow morning," she said to Maeve. "I need detailed lists of camp provisions, numbers, and strategy. Bring them to my tent at dusk."

Her twin squeezed her shoulder.

"I can't pretend to understand why you let Fiorean escape with his life, but I will be here when you are ready to talk about it," Adarian said softly.

Maeve stood by the open tent flap, the clattering and shouts of the soldiers reaching Aemyra's ears.

"You inherited both the best and the worst of him. Your father loves you, no matter how he behaves. But Draevan was not born to rule Tìr Teine, and as such, he cannot take away your inheritance," Maeve said.

Aemyra inclined her head as graciously as she could manage. Having fought beside Draevan for decades, perhaps Maeve understood parts of her father better than Aemyra did.

"He will refuse to cooperate with you until you apologize," the general said simply.

Wringing her hands together at the unfairness of it all, Aemyra looked toward the tent entrance. Her father had refused to save her, and she too had her pride.

A queen should never have to apologize to a prince, but sometimes a daughter did need to apologize to her father.

Winding through the maze of tents, Aemyra ignored the pain in her body and headed for the ridge overlooking the plains. Sighing as the wind whipped her hair around her head, Aemyra saw her father standing on the precipice. His arms were tightly crossed over his chest and his head was bowed.

She approached him slowly from the side, not wanting to startle him in case he went toppling over the edge. The rush of the wind was loud in her ears and she could just about hear their dragons calling to each other high above. When Aemyra drew level with her father, she expected anything but what she saw.

Draevan was crying.

All the fight went out of her at the sight.

He was aware of her presence but did not turn. He only raised his head slowly and allowed the last droplets to be ripped from his cheeks by the wind.

"I was the first person to hold you," Draevan finally said, clearing his throat.

"What?" Aemyra asked, her hair streaming behind her.

"When you were born. You came into this world by my hand, not Orlagh's."

Draevan glanced toward her and she willed him to keep going.

"Orlagh did not approve of her friend Elsie's relationship with the Prince of Penryth. I would never have been allowed to marry her while my father still lived, not that your mother ever asked me to."

Draevan was searching Aemyra's face, as if trying to match her adult features with the screaming, pink-faced infant he had held in his arms.

"You arrived first. Orlagh was concerned with how Elsie was coping with the second delivery and left me to guide you into the world.

I clutched your tiny body to my chest as your mother weakened. My first child, and I had already failed you as a father. I could not give you my name, nor could I declare you my heir for fear of what the king might do. So I did the only thing I could. I placed you into the arms of the midwife and prayed to Brigid I was doing the right thing by only knowing you in secret."

Draevan lifted his hand and tucked a strand of Aemyra's hair behind her ear. Rather a fruitless endeavor, given the wind.

"When I saw how Adarian had grown to look so exactly like Elsie, how you somehow seemed to have more of my spirit, my heart broke for not knowing you. So I had you trained with the sword and taught the Seann. I tried to give you every advantage I could to make up for my failings as a father, even from a distance."

The wind blew his hair back from his face as Aemyra stared up at him, her heart near breaking.

"But somehow, I forgot to give you the one thing that you might have needed. Not a sparring partner or a teacher. A father."

Aemyra felt the tears fall unbidden down her cheeks as Draevan turned to her.

"So now you are a woman grown. One who reminds me so much of myself that it hurts to set my eyes upon you sometimes. Knowing that it is too late for me to shape you into something better than I ever was."

Aemyra knew now that he did not blame her for seeking revenge. He would have done the same thing had their places been reversed. But the lines around his mouth were tight, and for the first time Aemyra realized that her father had been afraid for her.

Draevan lightly touched the wound on her chest, knuckles brushing the garnet aside.

"Sir Nairn," she said.

His hand contracted into a fist.

"He is dead," she clarified.

Her father still did not relax and Aemyra buttoned the shirt. She would not allow herself to be defined by the violence of men.

The howling wind brought the scent of camp up the mountain.

"Half of my army will remain here to hold off the Leuthanach forces, should they attempt to follow us to Àird Lasair. The other half will march northwest through the foothills. We will follow with Gealach and Terrea in two days' time. Fiorean will ensure the city surrenders to us and then he will journey here with Aervor to order Evander's army to stand down," Aemyra said, eyes on the thousands of black tents below them. Even though they were fighting for Evander, she did not want them to die.

Draevan cleared his throat. "You should not be so quick to trust any of the royals. Not even one who helped you escape."

"Will you carry out my orders?" Aemyra asked, refusing to back down.

Glancing up at the green and black dragons who circled high above, Draevan nodded his head. "The Balnain fleet has recouped their losses and sails north with the Iolairean phoenix warriors as we speak. The Leuthanach army will not dare attack once they are surrounded."

Aemyra nodded stiffly.

"Has Evander gone as mad as the late king?" Draevan asked quietly.

After a moment, Aemyra nodded again, and she saw true pain on Draevan's face.

"I should have read the signs," he admitted. "I never would have encouraged you to Bond to Kolreath had I known for sure."

Aemyra tried not to think about the fact that he had still suspected it. That it had been yet another risk he had been willing to take.

"How do you live with the guilt of your decisions?" she asked, her voice barely audible over the wind.

The lines on her father's face were more pronounced, his lack of response answer enough.

"I do mourn them," Draevan said eventually. "The children. I am not so heartless that I would wish the pain of losing a child on anyone."

The relief she felt was palpable.

With a swift prayer to Cailleach, Aemyra hoped Fiorean would find the culprit soon.

When she remained silent, Draevan made to leave, his tunic flapping in the wind.

Turning, Aemyra called out to her father. "You are a better man than people think."

Draevan's back stiffened, but he couldn't bring himself to face her. "Get some rest. Our forces march for you come daybreak."

With that, Aemyra's father left his firstborn on the edge of a cliff with nothing but the howling wind to fill her heart.

CHAPTER THIRTY-EIGHT

AEMYRA WOKE FROM DREAMS OF DRAGONFIRE AND ROARING screams for the third morning in a row with a jolt.

Tossing and turning on top of the mess of sheets, she wished for a distraction from the impending conflict. Her skin was burning and she wished her husband was not so far away. The ache between her legs built at the thought until she pressed her fingers to her clitoris and began working herself in furious circles.

Still certain she was half dreaming, visions of dragonfire poured through her mind as her toes curled and she fisted her other hand in the sheets to stop herself from crying out. The ache between her legs began spreading to her lower abdomen, down the tops of her legs, and even to her lower back, and she plunged her fingers inside of herself, imagining it was Fiorean. Her vision flickered until she swore her body was covered in scales and embers were crackling their way up her throat.

Practically writhing on top of the cot, such was the intense agony of her pleasure, she turned and buried her face into the pillow as finally, finally, she felt the ache inside of herself build to a crescendo.

Her ears echoing with the roars of a dragon, she finally found her release, spiraling through one of the most intense orgasms she had ever had without Fiorean's help.

Afterward, she lay drenched on top of the mattress, her hands splayed out on either side of her, and was almost glad they were launching their attack on Àird Lasair later that day if it brought her closer to being with her husband.

Her army was progressing maddeningly slowly toward the capital. Thanks to the heavy rains that had swept through the north of Tìr Teine, the ground underfoot had turned boggy. The only positive was that it also trapped the Leuthanach forces on the plain.

Sitting up, Aemyra rubbed her gritty eyes. Her skin was feverish, and she was drenched in sweat despite the cool temperature inside the tent. Reaching for the stale water in the jug, Aemyra gulped it down, wondering if she was suffering an infection or aftereffects of the binding agent.

She had been prone to sudden surges of magic that had already resulted in three tent fires, one burned buttock, and a singed pair of eyebrows. Thankfully, none of them Aemyra's.

When her legs felt solid enough to support her weight, she heaved herself out of bed. Her inner thighs were cramping from Draevan's aerial training the day before. Connecting to the Bond, she knew Terrea was feeling equally achy.

Washing her hands in the basin, she cooled her clammy skin after stripping off her sodden nightclothes.

Hands busy braiding her tangle of curls, she didn't bother to cover herself when the tent flap opened and Adarian stepped in with a muttered curse. "Fucking Hela, cover your tits."

Aemyra smirked, lazily securing the end of her braid as Adarian averted his eyes and flushed to the roots of his shaggy crop of hair.

"Maybe announce yourself before storming into my tent first thing in the morning, then," Aemyra said smugly, pulling on a clean shirt.

Adarian cleared his throat. "It's almost midday."

This was a surprise to her. She had begun drifting off the night before in their father's tent as the two of them talked strategy and barely remembered Adarian putting her to bed.

"The clouds are heavy with so much rain it might as well be dusk, for all I know," Aemyra retorted.

Her twin was scrutinizing her. "Goddess knows you went through enough at the caisteal to sleep for a week."

Pulling on the shirt, Aemyra frowned. "Don't breathe a word of it to Father. He will be unpredictable enough as it is. I shouldn't even have told you."

Holding up his hands, Adarian looked sincere. "I wouldn't dream of it."

Buttoning her breeches, Aemyra went over their plan again in her head. Draevan had been scouting back and forth through the Deàrr Mountains with Gealach for four days and her army was almost within sight of Àird Lasair.

Aemyra would have scouted herself, had Terrea not disappeared hunting in the mountains, no doubt gorging herself on goats.

Hauling her armor off the stand, Aemyra held it up to her brother. "A little help?"

Pàdraig had taught them both the finer aspects of equipping soldiers for battle, and the twins had crafted each piece of their armor themselves.

"It would be my honor," Adarian said, crossing the small space to take her breastplate.

Under normal circumstances, Aemyra might have ridiculed him for his lofty tone.

The armor was a burnished gold, lightweight, and the pauldrons spiked at the shoulders to depict two roaring dragons. They were the only embellishment Aemyra had allowed, given that if all else failed she could impale someone with them.

Adarian's expert fingers had her outfitted in less than ten minutes. Despite the breathable undergarments and fairly sparing armor, Aemyra was overheating.

"Something wrong?" Adarian asked.

Aemyra shook her head as she dusted off her boots. "No. Well, I don't think so. I might be having some withdrawal effects from the binding agent."

Adarian looked concerned. "Has it affected your magic?"

Testing it out, Aemyra lifted her palm and crafted a rose out of flickering flame in her hand. The stem burned white hot while the flower was a deep amber color. Each delicate petal drifted on a phantom wind before fading away in a puff of smoke.

"Sometimes it flares unexpectedly." Clapping her hands together, she extinguished the rose. "I'll be fine after breakfast. Maybe I just need to get my strength back."

Adarian didn't look convinced. "Or maybe the Chosen did more damage than you thought?"

Aemyra's blood ran cold, but she shook her head. "No. I bled afterward, but I'm certain there is no infection. Nothing to be concerned about," she replied, holding the tent flap open and striding into the damp afternoon with her brother.

As they hurried toward Draevan's tent, Adarian rushed to keep up with his sister.

"But you mi——"

Aemyra held up a hand wreathed in flame to silence him. "Not one more word, Adarian."

Her tone begged no questions and her twin dropped it.

After four days of sleep, decent enough food, and the connection to both her dragon and her powers restored, Aemyra felt more like herself again. The steady weight of Fearsolais on her back helped, as did the dagger on her hip.

The knowledge that her husband would have Athair Alfred under lock and key, awaiting their siege of the city, buoyed her. Today she would win back her territory.

The few air Dùileach who remained in the emptying camp were using their magic to blow smoke from the breakfast fires out of Aemyra's path. She nodded at them in thanks as she passed.

They met Draevan outside his tent as he pulled on his gloves.

"What's the report?" Aemyra asked, swiping two bannocks from a basket.

Draevan pointed his chin in the direction of the plains. "Maeve has gone to hold the slopes with five hundred men. Dianne has her scouts well in hand. If the Leuthanach army thinks to advance when they realize the dragons have gone, they know what to do."

Aemyra frowned. "Fiorean will have sent a swyft to Fyndhorn. Clan Leuthanach will not engage."

Draevan and Adarian shared a look.

"You don't have to trust Fiorean. You just have to trust me," Aemyra said firmly.

Smiling ruefully as he straightened, Draevan replied, "It is best to be prepared for any eventuality."

Aemyra acquiesced. Draevan knew far more about war than she did. Together, they would ensure the safety of her people.

"Your cavalry?" Aemyra turned to ask her brother.

He fiddled with the hatchet on his belt. "Guarding the flanks as you instructed. Three thousand foot soldiers make up the vanguard, five hundred mounted soldiers on either side, a further three hundred at the rear."

Aemyra nodded, everything was in order, then. "And the others?"

Draevan rested his hands on Dorchadas's hilt. "Five hundred Dùileach at the center, two hundred more scattered throughout our other troops. The city will be ours by nightfall."

Deciding that her father's tone was a touch too bloodthirsty, Aemyra protested. "The city is already ours. Fiorean will have seen to it that Evander is contained and the streets empty of civilians. The Àird Lasair guard is currently without a commander."

Draevan looked almost disappointed that it was going to be so easy.

It certainly hadn't been easy for the five thousand soldiers who had marched through torrential rain and thick mud. The weather was getting marginally warmer but wetter.

"When will we reach the city?" Aemyra asked her father.

Draevan looked north. "The dragons could reach it within the hour, but the army most likely not until mid-afternoon. Once Adarian is mounted, we will remain out of sight until the army is within range."

"Still no news from Clan Leòmhann?" Aemyra asked.

Draevan cleared his throat. "No. You can make that bastard Lonan regret his hesitation when you are queen."

"I'm already queen," Aemyra countered.

Draevan bent his head to survey her face, eyes skimming over her golden armor.

"Indeed, Your Grace," her father said formally as they left camp.

It wasn't a surprise that Laird Lonan was hedging his bets. No doubt he was waiting to see the outcome of the battle on the plains before pledging the might of his chimeras.

Little did he know that Aemyra was going to win this battle and end the war before it began.

Gealach landed first, Draevan striding eagerly toward his dragon, while Aemyra was left on the ground with her twin.

Clicking her tongue in frustration, Aemyra began pacing, her skin prickling with heat again.

"I thought you said this was going to be easy?" Adarian asked, adjusting his own armor as Gealach took flight.

"It will be," she bit back.

"Then why are you nervous?"

Aemyra let out a few tongues of flame just to take the edge off the magic that was coursing through her.

"I'm not nervous," she replied, wiping the sweat from her brow. The hastily eaten bannocks churning in her stomach, Aemyra continued pacing.

The garnet necklace was a familiar weight under her breastplate, acting as a reminder of what she was fighting for. Nerves kicking in, she sent up a prayer to Brigid that everything would go according to plan.

"No heroics, do you hear me?" she said to Adarian.

Her brother smirked from where he leaned against the mountainside. "I do believe that you're the one who inherited the arrogant tendencies from our father. Worry about yourself."

Hating that he was right, she looked up at the dark clouds above them, feeling Terrea approaching.

Fat droplets of rain had already begun to fall, but with her magic returned, she wasn't chilled.

Shadowy wings tucked in tight, her dragon dropped to the ground, claws crunching against the jagged rocks of the mountainside as she clambered down the last few feet.

"Took you long enough, Beastie," Adarian said fondly.

Contrary to the dragon's fearsome reputation, Adarian seemed to be the only person able to make Terrea act like a house cat. Rolling her eyes as Terrea began emitting contented puffs of smoke from her nostrils, Aemyra snapped her fingers at both of them.

"You can romp in the meadow behind the caisteal with Adarian and Aervor tomorrow, for all I care. Today we have a throne to win," Aemyra said.

Adarian flashed her a grin as Terrea bent her leg carefully for him, ensuring he had the easiest path up toward the hollow in her back, and Aemyra scowled as she followed him.

"Sure you Bonded to the right twin?" she asked her beathach.

Terrea shifted, and Aemyra suddenly had to lunge for one of the black spikes or fall to the ground.

A feeling of surety shot down the Bond before Aemyra could get her feelings hurt, and she hauled herself into place in front of Adarian, patting Terrea's violet neck.

"And don't you forget it."

The dragon rose to her feet beneath them and spread her wings, testing the air currents as the rain intensified.

"Fly," Aemyra said in the Seann.

Before the word was out of her mouth, Terrea was in the clouds, bearing the twins through the sky toward their destiny at last.

CHAPTER THIRTY-NINE

THE MOMENT THEY DESCENDED FROM THE CLOUDS, AEMYRA knew something had gone wrong.

The city gate was barred, archers were positioned on the battlements, and Kolreath was perched atop the highest turret of Caisteal Lasair, barbed tail lashing.

Her heart was pounding as they landed with a crash beside the lines of cavalry and Adarian flung himself off Terrea's back, hitting the ground running. Her dragon was writhing her serpentine neck skyward, where Draevan was pursuing Kolreath through the sheeting rain, long streaks of fire lighting the dull sky. Aemyra's army battered themselves against the nigh impenetrable walls of Àird Lasair, their screams chilling her blood.

Aemyra's heart twisted and fear shot through her. With Evander's instability, and the Covenanters within the caisteal, she prayed to Brigid that Fiorean was alive. Aervor was nowhere to be seen.

Terrea loosed a tongue of flame, roaring her challenge to the two male dragons who dueled high above the city.

Still, Aemyra did not let her fly.

"Adarian!" she screamed above the roar of dying soldiers, another volley of arrows felling more than she could count.

Her brother grabbed the bridle of a gray destrier, swinging himself expertly up into the saddle, and reined around to face her. They didn't need words to convey their feelings. With a heavy nod, Adarian spurred the horse into a gallop, already re-forming the lines of foot soldiers and gathering up his cavalry.

She hadn't planned on Fiorean failing.

Suddenly glad that her father had taken precautions for her troops in Fyndhorn, Aemyra knew what had to be done.

"*Sgiath!*" she cried, and Terrea gladly spread her wings wide, leaping from the ground in a dark blur.

Aemyra buried her fear for Fiorean deep within herself as the wind stole tears from her eyes. In an instant, she merged her consciousness with Terrea's.

Aemyra felt as if she were soaring on wings of her own, the muscles of her back and shoulders contracting with each strong push through the air. Parting her lips, she could taste the fear of the men and women far below.

Fire hot enough to melt bones burned in the back of her throat, but she would not loose it. Not yet.

Keeping low to the ground, her violet underbelly skimming the heads of Aemyra's soldiers, Terrea surged upward to avoid the next volley of arrows.

"Take cover!"

The shout sounded across the battlements as Aemyra and Terrea advanced on the wall. If the gates would not open voluntarily, they would create an opening. Àird Lasair could withstand a siege for months if necessary, but without a proper army, it wouldn't last long against dragons.

Opening her mouth, white-hot flame crackling in her maw, Terrea prepared to throw the full force of her fire into the city gate.

Aemyra roared her challenge as they neared the battlements, gripping the two onyx spikes in front of her tightly.

Just as Terrea parted her teeth, Aemyra felt the world tilt on its axis and she almost impaled herself as an immense force collided with them midair.

Shaken back into her own mind, Aemyra tried to make the world stop spinning, stomach swooping as she almost lost her grip. Terrea's midnight wings flapped furiously to keep them airborne, and Aemyra swiveled around to see Kolreath advancing on them.

Evander was brandishing the first king's sword above his head, wearing a maniacal smile.

Terrea managed to twist and aim a stream of fire directly toward Kolreath's face, but the golden beast soared right through it.

A desperate spiral in the air allowed Terrea to escape his jaws, but only succeeded in exposing her soft underbelly to the male.

Pain shot through Aemyra as Kolreath's claws sliced through Terrea's scales. Dùileach and dragon screaming through blood and fury as Terrea whirled away.

Aemyra fumbled the wet spikes in front of her and was left clinging on for dear life as Evander raised his sword, slicing it through the air as Kolreath brought his Bonded Dùileach within feet of her.

Summoning her magic, Aemyra dared to let go of one spike as Terrea leveled out and threw a jet of fire toward Evander.

Kolreath swerved, his barbed tail swinging for Terrea's side in retaliation.

"Where the fuck is Aervor?" Aemyra screamed into the rain, as if her dragon could tell her.

Before Aemyra could summon another flame, an emerald dragon barreled into Kolreath, spikes missing Terrea by inches. Thankful for the brief respite, Aemyra panted as Terrea leveled out. The wounds from Kolreath's claws were long but superficial.

Terrea shook her neck in agitation, but Aemyra could only watch as the male dragons tore at each other with teeth and claws, wings flapping as they fell through the air. The Dùileach on their backs battling with their fire.

The males went careening into each other, tumbling wing over claw, and Aemyra felt terror grip her heart as an auburn braid whipped around.

"Father!" she screamed, sure that the dragons would hit the ground.

Gealach was the first to level out, using his claws to push Kolreath closer to the ground as he swooped upward on shimmering wings, hovering below Terrea protectively as the golden dragon plummeted toward the army fighting beneath them.

At the last moment, Kolreath righted himself. Wing membranes straining with the effort of slowing his massive body, he narrowly avoided squashing the soldiers on the ground. Kolreath stroked for the sky with a roar of fury, heading straight for Terrea.

"Fuck," Aemyra swore, blinking rain out of her eyes.

Terrea quickly got into formation beside Gealach. As they turned, Aemyra glimpsed Adarian far below. Astride his gray charger, sword held aloft.

Unable to watch her brother fighting within range of the arrows still raining down from the battlements, she focused instead on the mighty golden dragon bearing down on them. Terrea loosed a roar toward Kolreath, her tail lashing angrily.

Hair plastered to her scalp, Aemyra saw the fury in her father's face, the desire for vengeance.

"With me!" Draevan called out to her.

Aemyra followed him, Kolreath hot on their tail. Quite literally, as the enraged golden dragon was shooting streams of fire toward them both.

As the three dragons flew through the rain-drenched sky toward the open fields beyond the army, Aemyra noticed the blood streaming from Gealach's neck. Kolreath had injured him during their fall. Deep puncture wounds parted the emerald scales and her father's dragon was flying stiffly. Before Aemyra could see how bad the damage was, Terrea banked sharply.

Kolreath, still determinedly pursuing them, shot in between the black and green dragons.

Evander's maniacal laughter died as he understood he had flown straight into a trap.

Aemyra hadn't spent four days in the Deàrr Mountains sitting on her arse.

As Terrea and Gealach closed in on the golden beast, Aemyra and Draevan united their magic into a firestorm that engulfed the pretender king.

Gritting her teeth as she heard Gealach crunch into Kolreath's side, Terrea kept her distance and Aemyra felt Evander's magical shield buckle against her power.

Kolreath's wings were so large that they eclipsed everything else, only allowing her to see glimpses of her father. His braid was whipping out behind him, his fire stuttering as he held fast to his dragon with one hand.

Evander's shield broke just as Kolreath swerved to avoid Gealach's spiked tail and he flew directly into Terrea.

It didn't matter that it had been accidental, Aemyra almost impaled herself again as she hurriedly let go of her magic to concentrate. Terrea's fire seared Aemyra's cheeks as her dragon roared her displeasure into Kolreath's face.

Enraged, the male dragon opened his enormous jaws and Aemyra glimpsed death at the back of his throat.

He was too close for Terrea to turn in time. Her dragon might not perish in the fire, but Aemyra surely would. She unsheathed Fearsolais as if the sword would help her.

Terrea looped her neck around, trying to outmaneuver the male, but before she could get underneath him, Gealach slammed into the golden dragon with a bone-shaking crunch.

Aemyra fumbled her sword but managed to keep her grip on the rune-carved hilt.

The she-dragon hovered midair, powerless, as Gealach clamped his emerald jaws down on Kolreath's neck.

"No!" Aemyra cried out instinctively.

Hot blood rained down upon her, mixing with the rain, and she watched as the larger dragon plummeted to the ground. Evander scrambled in panic, Kolreath's blood spraying across his face.

Aemyra's heart twisted, urging Terrea toward the ground after them.

The wind was fierce in her ears, the shouts of the soldiers drowned out by the roars of the dragons. Kolreath screamed and thrashed in Gealach's jaws, their wings and tails lashing as they tried to stay airborne. Until Gealach splayed his wings and the son of the mighty Kolgiath hit the ground.

The impact made Aemyra's teeth shake and even Terrea balked. Gealach barely had time to slow his momentum and landed hard on the ground beside the crippled dragon. He roared his triumph into the sky as Draevan leaped lithely from his back.

The battle still raging before the walls of the city, Aemyra could only stare at the devastation. Terrea's feral roars joined those of Gealach as her claws finally sank into the muddy field.

Aemyra's heart was pounding as she looked upon the twisted and broken giant. Kolreath's wings were twitching, a pained growl escaping his blood-soaked lips.

"Father?" she called out, limbs shaking as she lowered herself from Terrea's back. Mud sucking at her boots, Aemyra scanned the blood-soaked earth around Kolreath's body. Skirting the broken wing, she found Evander clawing himself out from underneath his beathach. Draevan was waiting for him.

It was a miracle that Evander hadn't been crushed in the fall, but bubbles of blood were forming at the corner of his mouth. Blood painting his auburn hair crimson.

Breaking into a run, she made it only a few feet before Draevan drew Dorchadas.

Evander tried to use his magic, but it faltered and died in his palm as his energy reserves depleted.

Aemyra saw it then, the haunted look in his eyes. The madness that had taken root in his mind upon Bonding to Kolreath.

Aemyra slowed from her run.

What Draevan was about to do was a kindness.

Her father pointed Dorchadas toward Evander's chest. Aemyra uttered a hasty prayer to Cailleach and Hela for Evander's soul; he wasn't far from the Otherworld even without Draevan's help.

"We have come to remove your festering carcass from the throne and restore the rightful line of succession. You sought to take what was never yours," Draevan growled.

He paused with his sword held aloft. It took Aemyra a moment to understand he was asking permission from his queen to behead a traitor.

Evander smiled, a hacking cough choking up his throat. "The crown is heavy. She can have it." He turned his eyes on Aemyra and peeled his lips back from his bloodstained teeth. "It will break her neck."

Reminding herself that all the Seers had perished when Tìr Sgàile fell to the curse, Aemyra muttered another hasty prayer.

And nodded her head.

Draevan swung Dorchadas and severed Evander's head from his shoulders.

Despite his injuries, Kolreath loosed a bone-shaking screech as Evander's head hit the ground with a sickening thud. Another Bond broken.

Knowing Evander had given the order to behead Pàdraig, and likely Kenna too, Aemyra felt a distinct lack of remorse.

Turning, Draevan locked eyes with Aemyra, their dragons roaring their victory into the rain-soaked sky above them.

"That was for your family," he said firmly. Lifting his eyes behind the dragons, he looked toward Àird Lasair. "Now we take back your city."

CHAPTER FORTY

Leaving Kolreath behind, Aemyra peered through the rain for any sign of a cobalt dragon. Anxiety banded across her chest as she thought of what might have happened to her husband within those walls for him to fail so spectacularly.

Draevan was already striding toward Gealach, knowing the real battle was yet to come. The green dragon was stretching his neck experimentally; his injury didn't seem life-threatening.

"Cailleach spare us, Beira lend us courage, Brigid grant us your strength, Cliodna we invoke your grace, and Brenna steady us," Aemyra intoned as she mounted her dragon, weathering her fear.

The two dragons rose into the air in perfect synchronization.

The army was amassed outside the city gate. Orderly lines of men storming the walls where hundreds of their companions lay wounded in the shadow of the battlements. Adarian shone like burnished copper upon his horse as he roared orders at the front lines. Dùileach wielded their elements alongside their weapons. Roots sprang from the ground and crawled up the battlements, jets of steam shot up the walls, and archers were blown clean off their perches.

"Fall back!" she screamed as Terrea flew over the wall, picking up two archers with her claws.

Aemyra tried not to watch as the dragon released them, and their bodies broke apart on the rooftops.

She spared a glance for the caisteal, where no doubt Katherine, the princesses, and the children were gathered. Was Fiorean with them? Was he even still breathing?

Her heart clenched painfully at the thought of what Alfred might have done. Fiorean was a talented fighter, but if his magic was bound he was still just one man trapped inside a caisteal with hundreds of Covenanters.

If that was true, Aemyra couldn't understand why Aervor was nowhere to be found.

Gealach aimed for the city gate and the archers atop the walls loosed their bolts, spearing through the membranous green wings. Draevan's beathach let forth a frustrated roar as Terrea banked over the city.

The Covenanters were fighting in the streets with the city guards. Athair Alfred wasn't hiding them inside the caisteal any longer. Despite the size of the force Evander had unleashed within the capital, Draevan did not balk as he pushed his dragon toward the battlements.

Gealach loosed another jet of flame upon the city gate. Huge chunks of stone flew into the air, tumbling to the ground on both sides of the wall.

Her army didn't hesitate, even as the city guards abandoned their posts and fled from the fire. Through the sheeting rain and clouds of dust, her soldiers advanced toward the ruined gate, the Dùileach at the center protecting them from the smoke. Adarian was leading the charge with his golden armor gleaming and hammer held aloft.

The emerald dragon landed atop the crumbling battlements, and Draevan dismounted. Where Dorchadas swung, death followed.

"I need to get down there!" Aemyra shouted to Terrea.

Her dragon growled in bloodthirsty agreement. Her people needed to see their queen fighting for them. It no longer mattered that the original plan had been for Aemyra to remain safely on dragon back.

With Fiorean nowhere to be found, their plan was already fucked.

Terrea let out a menacing roar as she aimed for where the dust was settling. There was just enough space for the dragon to land before the vanguard reached the broken gate.

Her heart pounding as Terrea hit the ground with a thunderous crash, Aemyra slid from her dragon's back and unsheathed Fearsolais.

Today she would not fail her people.

"With me!" she roared, sprinting ahead of the advancing army and scrambling over debris. Flames licked across her armor, lighting the way through the smoke.

With a decisive rumble, Terrea took to the skies after Gealach, her violet underbelly the same color as the bruised clouds pouring rain down on the city.

Despite the danger that awaited her on the other side of the wall, Aemyra was not afraid. She had never been more aware of her heartbeat as she clutched the runic hilt of Fearsolais and wreathed her left hand in fire. She had never felt more alive.

A cry rose up behind her, barely audible above the roars of the dragons and the screams of dying men. But as she crested the rubble and flung herself into the fray, the rain could not drown out what her soldiers were chanting.

"For the true queen!"

Almost rolling her ankle on a large chunk of what had once been the wall, Aemyra jumped into the street that was as familiar to her as the back of her hand.

The city gate was splintered and broken, dragonfire crackling from nearby buildings. Draevan, clad in obsidian armor, was climbing freshly dead corpses to reach the soldiers of Àird Lasair battling behind the shattered wall.

Appearing out of the smoke, Aemyra watched her queen's guard fight their way toward her. Laoise brandished fire and fighting knives with impressive dexterity. Nell wielded their vines like whips as Clea blew smoke to blind those who would wound the queen. Iona was ice personified, her eyes glacial as she froze the very blood of any city guard who got too close.

Aemyra pushed her greatest fears about Fiorean to the back of her mind.

"With me!" she yelled again, her voice carrying over the heads of the men and women fighting for her.

A fearsome cry went up from her army as they attacked the city with renewed vigor.

Despite all of Aemyra's training, she hadn't realized that battle would be pandemonium. Men and women were fighting on all sides, in such a crush of bodies that she could barely tell who was friend and who was foe.

She clutched her sword more tightly as they advanced past the gatehouse. For an indeterminable amount of time, they progressed at a crawl as those fighting in front of them tried to push through the rubble-strewn street.

Cutting down a woman in front of her, Aemyra lifted her chin to look through the wreckage and saw the reason they were struggling to gain ground.

Covenanters were blocking the street.

The soldiers of the True Religion were advancing, pendants around their necks and swords in hand.

Aemyra's limbs began tingling, and fear speared through her core so acutely it made her stumble. The memory of the last time she had seen those pendants flooded her mind and suddenly she felt as though she were choking on incense.

"Brigid, Goddess of strength, power, and hope, be with me," Aemyra muttered desperately.

With a heavy exhale, she allowed flames to snake up the blade of Fearsolais. She would not let the Covenanters lay hands on her today.

Propelled by the soldiers, Aemyra saw the walls pass on either side of her and suddenly she faced the enemy.

Heart in her mouth and chest tight, she slipped into the automatic rhythm of swinging her sword. Ears ringing as steel met steel, she parried and thrust against each person who turned against her. Aemyra lost herself to the rhythm of death.

Many of the Covenanters underestimated her strength because she was a woman. Several of them even hesitated before swinging for her. They all died for that mistake.

Her father was only meters away from her, felling more soldiers than anyone else. She ducked and swerved, dispatching one enemy only for another to advance before she even had time to breathe.

Aemyra twisted her blade and gutted a brown-haired man where he tried to strike her left side. He fell with a cry, his hands automatically cradling his stomach, trying to keep his innards from sliding out.

Aemyra didn't spare him a glance before sprinting off into the alley that led up the hill toward the caisteal in pursuit of her father.

Gealach flew steadily through the air high above Àird Lasair. Never straying far from Draevan but high enough that no more crossbow bolts could reach him.

Terrea clearly had no such qualms. Her dragon landed with a crash upon houses and towers, her jaws crunching around any Covenanter she could find. Soon stray limbs were raining down upon them as Terrea flung dismembered bodies from her mouth, her screeches of bloodlust filling the city streets.

Breath coming in great gasps as she sprinted, Aemyra swung her sword toward anyone who got too close. Her fire took care of those without pendants.

Halting her swings, she peered down the street, to find Màiri wielding what little fire she possessed, blowing smoke to blind soldiers, using her magic indirectly to get around the protective pendants.

Pàdraig's friend Colm was farther behind, pulling water up from the well and fashioning it into shards of ice, which he shot toward the soldiers with a flick of his finger.

The people of Àird Lasair were fighting for her.

The street was a crush of bodies. The blood that sprayed from the soldiers she killed reminded her too much of the last time she had smelled the bite of iron on her skin.

Despite this, she fought on.

The soldiers who battled beside her were determined, their swords unwavering. Like they believed Aemyra would be the queen to save them.

Out of nowhere, a hand closed around the end of her braid, yanking her back. But before her assailant could thrust his hammer through her head, she dropped her dagger and loosed a jet of fire from her left palm that burned through his face. The man dropped like a stone and Aemyra gave thanks that he hadn't been wearing a pendant.

"Adarian!" Aemyra shouted as she spotted her brother, his hatchet buried in a man's skull.

Sprinting for him, she became aware that the priestesses had launched themselves into the fray. Several soldiers had managed to break down the temple doors.

Searching in vain for Eilidh, Aemyra made her way to her brother. There was a cut across Adarian's eyebrow that was dripping blood, but he seemed otherwise unharmed.

"We need to get into the caisteal," she gasped as her soldiers fought around them, guarding their queen.

Ducking automatically as Terrea swept low over the rooftops, her black wings spread wide, Aemyra connected to the Bond. Her dragon was on the cusp of razing the entire city to the ground. Pendants were no protection against dragonfire, but Aemyra wasn't yet desperate enough to burn half of her army, or the innocent people trapped within the city.

With a rueful glance toward the bridge, Aemyra knew that their only hope to take the city without mass casualties would be to find Fiorean.

Aemyra shoved her twin in their father's direction.

"For the Goddess," Aemyra said to her brother.

"For you," he replied.

Adarian assumed his position beside her, and the twins charged through the battle toward their father, who was an obsidian shadow as he cut a path through the Covenanters into the caisteal, already one step ahead of Aemyra.

Finding her path blocked, Aemyra launched herself at a large Covenanter swinging an axe.

"Hello, Queenie," he said, licking his lips.

He swiped at her and she had to throw herself backward, landing heavily on the cobblestones with a cry.

Aemyra scrabbled for the hilt of her sword, having dropped it as she fell. The Covenanter's heavy boots thudded behind her, and she turned in time to see a Savior's pendant around his neck.

She just managed to clutch her sword and roll as the axe fell to the ground where her head had been mere moments before.

Adarian was battling three soldiers, his hatchet and sword swinging in tandem.

"Adarian!" she screamed.

Scrambling to her feet, Aemyra ducked as the axe flew over her head again, several strands of auburn hair falling to the ground.

"I wasn't planning on cutting my hair, you dirty great oaf," Aemyra seethed, launching herself at the giant of a man with renewed vigor.

Her arms shaking, she met his swing, catching the wood of his axe with the blade of her sword. The handle splintered but held fast. Using Aemyra's momentum against her, she was flung away from him.

Aemyra landed on her back again, too winded to get up.

She gasped for breath, fingers stretching for her sword. She blinked the blood of the people she had killed from her eyes and watched as the man above her smiled. His teeth were stained red, and Aemyra felt her bowels turn to water.

The axe glinted as it fell, and Aemyra lifted one hand in front of her face fruitlessly.

Suddenly, a warrior wearing jet-black armor slid in between them. Knees braced under him, a magic-forged sword sliced directly through the wood of the axe.

The weapon clattered to the ground and Aemyra rolled to avoid losing a limb.

With a vengeful cry, Draevan stood and thrust Dorchadas right through the Covenanter's belly. She felt faintly sick as she watched him pull it free, the blade covered in gore.

Her assailant dead, Draevan had his hand outstretched, and concern laced his bloodstained face. She gripped his fingers tightly, choking back a frightened sob as he pulled her to her feet.

Adarian hobbled over and without a word covered her back as their father half dragged her over the bridge to the caisteal.

The queen's guard faced down any Covenanter or guard who tried to follow.

Ducking to avoid a jet of water thrown by Iona, Aemyra watched a great bubble form over the mouth and nose of a guard, and he clawed at his face, desperate for the air he could no longer reach. The water Dùileach wasted no time, and fashioned two icicles in her palms, which she wielded like daggers. Nell expertly snapped their vines around the guards, breaking bones like they were twigs.

Could Aemyra dare to hope that they might win even without Fiorean's help?

The thick walls of the caisteal swallowed the horrific noise of the fighting outside, and Aemyra's breath was loud in her ears as she followed her father up the eerily quiet corridor.

"They will have gathered in the throne room," Draevan said. "With whatever guards and protection they could muster as a last defense."

Adarian and Aemyra followed their father through the corridors at a light jog, weapons held aloft, peering carefully around corners lest any of them come face-to-face with a crossbow.

Draevan was gaining speed, almost accelerating into a sprint as they approached the throne room and Aemyra hurried after him, Adarian following behind.

"Aems, you should—"

Aemyra didn't listen to her brother as she sprinted ahead of her father, desperate to arrive in the room first. She had to know if Fiorean was alive or in chains.

But the large doors weren't barred and Aemyra skidded to a stop, her heavy footfalls echoing through the cavernous room as she suddenly understood why the city had not yielded to their queen.

Sitting on the golden throne that she herself had yet to even touch, looking for all the world like he was supposed to be there, was Fiorean.

CHAPTER FORTY-ONE

Aemyra's legs buckled and it was only Adarian's reflexes that had him catching her elbow before she fell.

Taking stock of the scene before her, Aemyra saw Elizabeth and
Maggie standing with their husbands and several priests on the right
side of the throne. Katherine was clutching Charlotte against her, gray
eyes fixed on Athair Alfred, who stood beside Fiorean.

Draevan strutted into the room, Dorchadas dripping blood onto
the flagstones, and ignored the twenty or so Covenanters who lined
the walls.

The back of Aemyra's neck prickled, this felt uncomfortably like a
trap.

"If they throw something toward you, hold your breath," she whispered to Adarian, remembering the cloying scent of the incense.

Fiorean's hair was tied back, his scars visible for all to see as he
lounged on the throne, hands resting on the golden frame. Aemyra felt
the heartbreak like a physical pain.

"You're in my seat," she called, her voice flat.

This couldn't be happening. This final, terrible betrayal had to be an
illusion. Some trick.

Athair Alfred laughed. "There is nothing that is rightfully yours. Only what the Savior grants us shall we take."

"Hela will enjoy taking her time with you," she promised Alfred.

The priest paled.

Draevan lazily brought the tip of Dorchadas up to point at Fiorean. Aemyra noticed the purple shadows under her husband's eyes, the rigid posture. Ducking out of Adarian's hold, she advanced toward the throne.

"Why?" Aemyra asked, her whisper carrying throughout the room.

Fiorean's green eyes met hers. "How can you call yourself a queen when you are merely your father's puppet?"

Surprised, Aemyra turned to look at her father.

Draevan shrugged as he observed the prince. "Evander's army walked right into a trap. I would have been a fool not to take advantage."

Fiorean clenched his fists. "Our forces were trapped between a thousand flying phoenix warriors from the south and your infantry columns bordering the Deàrr Mountains."

"What a pity," Draevan drawled.

"You slaughtered thousands of soldiers!" Fiorean ground out.

Aemyra felt the world tilt on its axis as she looked between the two men she had trusted to help her win her throne.

Aemyra spun to look at her father. "Is this true? You ordered Maeve to attack on the plains?"

Draevan shrugged. "They were our enemies. Now they are gone."

Aemyra's nostrils flared with suppressed rage.

"You betrayed the orders of your queen. I told the army to remain *neutral* and not to engage with Clan Leuthanach. Our plan was faultless. How many are now dead because you couldn't put your pride aside?"

There was no remorse in Draevan's eyes. He had seen the perfect opportunity to reach for power and he had taken it.

"Was it part of your plan for Fiorean to take the throne for himself?" He drew his eyes off Aemyra. "Or are you simply keeping it warm for your wife?"

A muscle was twitching in Fiorean's jaw, and with a jerk of his head, two Covenanters dragged a man before them, bound and gagged.

Aemyra's blood ran cold. It was the spy from the cèilidh.

"You expect me to believe you do not know this man when I saw you dance with him? That you did not know *he* was the one mixing bitterberry juice into sweet pies for the royal children?" Fiorean said, his voice taut.

The spy had worked his mouth free of the gag. "My loyalty is to the true queen of Tìr Teine."

Cold fingers of fear wrapped around her heart, and Aemyra's grip on her sword faltered.

"I swear I knew nothing of this," she said, shaking her head.

Fiorean's glare was murderous. "Evander tried to tell me how suspicious it was that you knew the cause of their sickness so quickly. Whether you sanctioned it or simply used it to your advantage, I do not care."

Unable to bear the looks of grief from Elizabeth and Charlotte, Aemyra felt as though everything she had worked for was slipping away.

Rounding on her father, Aemyra hissed, "You said you had given no orders to kill the—"

Before she could finish, Fiorean thrust his hand out toward the spy.

He collapsed with a thud to the floor. When she saw the melted eye sockets, her jaw slackened. Fiorean had boiled his blood, cooking him in his own skin.

Elizabeth was crying audibly, and Katherine looked green, but Aemyra's eyes lingered on Fiorean's hand.

"Your magic isn't bound," she whispered as he resumed his seat on her throne.

Fiorean could have incapacitated every Covenanter in this room singlehandedly with access to his magic.

But here he was, willingly siding against her.

Then Athair Alfred spoke.

"We mourn the untimely death of King Evander and trust that the Savior will reward his self-sacrifice in fighting for our cause. Prince Fiorean will assume the throne and the responsibilities of king. Prince Draevan Daercathian will be executed for his crimes against the late king, the present king, the people of Àird Lasair, and the royal children. Prince Nael will assume the titles of Penryth. We have agreed to allow the Princess Aemyra Daercathian her life *if* she remains in exile."

Draevan had the audacity to look mildly amused by his list of transgressions, but Aemyra was frozen in shock.

"You will accept these terms now, or you will be forced to surrender to the grace of the Savior," Katherine said, her voice disconcertingly calm.

Aemyra looked between the faces of her captors. Had they been conspiring against her the entire time? Had Fiorean been relaying the details of their most intimate moments during council sessions? Had they toasted his ability to lay open the little queen's heart and hold it perfectly poised to be broken?

Despite his lack of a crown, Fiorean looked entirely at ease on her throne.

Aemyra's knees almost buckled as she finally pieced it together. It all made sense to her now, how readily Fiorean had agreed to their marriage, how he had manipulated her into helping him connect to Aervor and leading her army here. He had played her like a fool.

"You wanted the crown for yourself," she said.

Still, Fiorean didn't look at her.

The Chosen had finally stepped out of the shadows in Tìr Teine, and Aemyra had played right into their hands.

"I will never give up my birthright. As long as I breathe, my people will have a queen," she spat.

Fiorean rose from the throne, his lithe body unfurling with deadly grace. "Your only birthright is a talent for hammering steel and a hasty temper. A legacy as unremarkable as it is forgettable. Do us all a favor and give up the crown before anyone else you love dies."

The Fiorean who had dueled her in the harbor had returned. His truest self. The one he had been hiding during her time in the caisteal until she was sufficiently broken.

Then Alfred cleared his throat. "Aemyra Daercathian, you are a curse upon this territory. After today, your people will know it."

Aemyra's heart turned cold. Relinquishing her throne to Fiorean now would mean handing over Tìr Teine to the manipulation of the True Religion. The Dùileach would never be safe.

"You forget that I was chosen by Brigid herself," Aemyra spat.

With a great rush, she summoned her fire. Flames licked eagerly up the blade of Fearsolais and she advanced toward the throne. The Covenanters lurking on the sidelines cringed away from the heat of her flames as Aemyra locked everything she felt for Fiorean behind a wall of impenetrable ice.

She would not give him the satisfaction of seeing her break.

He was on his feet in an instant, a magical shield thrown up to protect his family from Aemyra's magic.

Which left him open to Aemyra's attack.

Feeling her father and brother summon their own magic, protecting their queen, Aemyra strode toward the dais as her torrent of flame struck Fiorean in the chest.

The force was enough for him to stagger backward even as he summoned a whip of fire that snapped toward her. It lashed around her ankle, burning through the leather of her boots until she smelled her own flesh cooking. With a yank, Fiorean pulled her off her feet.

With a scream of rage, she shielded desperately as Adarian and Draevan dueled the Covenanters with fire and steel. Adarian was bravely swinging his hatchet, and Draevan was brandishing Dorchadas with bloodthirsty intent.

The whip of fire disappeared as Fiorean was forced to shed his tunic before the flames attached to his skin.

Katherine, Elizabeth, and Maggie had run from the dais and were sheltering behind the throne as if the hunk of golden metal would save them from Aemyra's wrath.

Fiorean was all rippling muscles and fire-streaked skin as he stood before it, chest heaving.

Aemyra turned her gaze to Alfred. The man she hated even more than her husband.

"I will burn you piece by piece. Just a little bit at a time so you feel the pain but will not die. Your body will rot at my hand until it resembles your soul. When your skin is charred and you cannot breathe, perhaps then I will finally send you to Hela."

Fury the likes of which she had never felt flooded her system when Alfred failed to look afraid.

"We have two dragons and an army of Dùileach inside the city. You cannot win," she shouted over the clash of steel.

Draevan was dueling five Covenanters at once, his fire unable to touch them thanks to the pendants, but rivers of blood painted Dorchadas. Adarian sank his hammer into the skull of another Covenanter and he let out a roar of triumph at his sister's words.

"I assure you, we can," Alfred said, accepting a strange clay pot from a trembling priest.

Immediately on the defensive, Aemyra retreated closer to her father and brother.

"I think it is time the Savior evened the playing field," Alfred said with a sick smile.

Fiorean did nothing to stop him as Alfred raised the pot above his head and threw it to the ground in front of Aemyra.

The clay split open with an unearthly crack, smoke and liquid exploding from the inside. Instinctively, Aemyra threw up a wall of fire and held her breath.

Oily liquid burst from inside the pot, splashing in all directions as though seeking flesh. Where the droplets landed on her skin, she felt like she was burning.

Releasing her fire instantly, Aemyra choked on the noxious fumes and desperately tried to wipe the droplets off her skin. The moment she had released her magic, the pain had stopped.

Alfred was smiling. "Now you will learn why power such as yours should be extinguished."

With a snarl, Aemyra made to throw a jet of fire toward him. Her fingertips warmed, the fire cascading through her veins as she made ready to bring it into the world. But as soon as the flames appeared, what usually felt like a pleasant heat began to burn.

A scream of pain tore up her throat as the use of her magic made it feel as though her skin was melting. Extinguishing her fire hastily and clutching her arm against her torso, she glanced up at Alfred.

"Quite the breakthrough we have been looking for, wouldn't you agree?" Alfred asked.

Draevan summoned his own magic, as if unwilling to believe such a thing was possible. Panic took Aemyra when she witnessed her father fall to his knees from the pain.

"Your Uisge experiments will never break Dùileach spirit," Draevan hissed, as three Covenanters wrestled him to the ground.

Before Aemyra's eyes, her twin was restrained and a vengeful Covenanter embedded his dagger in Adarian's thigh.

"Adarian!" Aemyra screamed.

Her twin let out a strangled cry and blood streamed down his breeches as he was forced to his knees.

Knowing if she continued to fight they would kill her brother immediately, Aemyra gritted her teeth as she was forced to the ground.

Maggie's brown eyes met hers and Aemyra silently begged the woman to intervene, to make Fiorean see sense.

The princess looked away.

"Surrender," Alfred said, his hands calmly folded on his stomach. "Or die with your people. You can hear their cries even now."

Shoulders spasming from being restrained, Aemyra heard the sound of explosions coming from the other side of the bridge. The screaming intensified as every Dùileach in her army was struck with the noxious liquid and felt the pain it brought.

Alfred continued speaking calmly. "Thankfully, your people have the benevolence of the Savior's light to protect them from bloodthirsty Dùileach. Just as we restored peace to Tìr Ùir, so too will we unify Tìr Teine."

Aemyra's face paled as she realized how the Chosen would turn the people against her. For the first time Aemyra did not know how she was supposed to win her throne. All of her father's scheming, all of her attempts at building alliances, would count for nothing.

She had to get everyone out. Both her army and the innocent Dùileach Alfred would round up and either execute or torture on his crusade.

The faces of the people she had lived alongside for ten years flashed through her mind, Dùileach and non-Dùileach alike. Her quest for the throne was secondary to their safety.

Before she could make her next desperate move, the wall to Aemyra's right exploded as a black dragon burst through with claws and teeth.

With only two legs and half of her neck able to fit through the hole she had blasted in the wall, Terrea loosed a bone-shaking roar that had everyone running for cover.

Everyone except Aemyra.

Mercifully, whatever had been inside that pot didn't affect the Bond like the binding agent had—only her magic pained her.

No longer restrained, Aemyra was on her feet in an instant. Terrea's mouth was open, flames licking over her tongue as the dragon debated setting fire to the room.

It was only the small hand laid protectively over Maggie's growing bump that spared them.

Concerned with getting him to safety, Aemyra slipped in her brother's blood and pulled him to his feet. Adarian's leg shook, the knife protruding from the muscle, as she dragged him toward Terrea.

Her dragon was growling loudly enough to shake the very foundations of the caisteal as Draevan helped Adarian up the spikes.

With the dust settling and Covenanters fleeing the dragon, Aemyra pointed her blood-soaked blade toward Fiorean, who was helping Katherine to safety.

"I vowed to kill you once before and failed." She raised her left palm and sliced the meaty part of her hand on her blade. "By the Goddess, I will not fail next time."

Aemyra felt the tug of the death promise settle behind her navel as her blood spilled and Fiorean stiffened as he felt it too. Katherine's cry of fear was swallowed by the roar of a second dragon outside the window.

Terrea's claws were cracking the marble floor, huge chunks of stone falling to the loch far below. Sheathing Fearsolais across her back, Aemyra scrambled onto her dragon's back in front of Adarian.

The minute they were secure, Terrea flung herself from the caisteal and into the air.

"Father!" Adarian shouted, twisting around to look.

Aemyra did not spare a glance for Draevan knowing Gealach was already on his way. She had to get her people out of the city before she lost everything worth fighting for.

An outraged roar sounded directly above them and Aervor's cobalt scales replaced the rain-soaked sky. Adarian's grip tightened in fear.

As Aemyra prepared to turn Terrea and engage the male, a feeling of surety shot through the Bond.

Terrea refused to fight Aervor.

"What is he doing?" Adarian asked, yelling over the roar of the wind.

Aemyra shook her head incredulously. "He is covering our retreat."

Even as Fiorean sat on a throne that did not belong to him, his dragon landed in the middle of the lower town, blocking the Covenanters from pursuing the lines of Aemyra's soldiers fleeing the city. Evidently Aervor still deferred to Terrea's dominance.

Hearing another set of wings, Aemyra wished that the men in her life could have been half as convinced of her ability to lead them as these two dragons were of Terrea.

Ignoring the anguish threatening to choke her, Aemyra urged Terrea away from the city.

"Retreat!" Aemyra yelled.

The three dragons herded the Dùileach away from the clutches of the True Religion.

Adarian's grip grew weak, and she twisted around to look at him. His wound was leaking around the blade and running in scarlet rivulets down Terrea's scales.

"Fuck, Adarian, this is bad," she whispered.

Gritting her teeth, she attempted to summon her fire for a hasty cauterization, but almost lost consciousness from the pain that flooded her veins. Whatever had been inside those pots was lingering like the binding agent. Squashing her panic, Aemyra could only hope that it would wear off.

"I need to get you to a healer," Aemyra said.

"'M fine," Adarian muttered sleepily, resting his cheek against her back.

Aemyra reached around and thumped Adarian hard above his wound.

A strangled cry left his lips.

"Stay awake," Aemyra threatened, her voice wavering. "I refuse to lose you too."

He didn't reply, but his grip tightened as Aervor snapped his jaws toward the Covenanters on the ground and Gealach razed the fields between the army and the battlements.

Aemyra looked down at her city and felt a sob choke up her throat.

It was burning.

Houses and buildings were destroyed, and people lay bleeding or dead in the streets. The line of soldiers retreating through the main gate was a trickle compared to the flood of fighters who had stormed Àird Lasair only hours before.

The forge was gone, rubble and burning wood were all that was left of the market. Charred husks of bodies littered the streets. Aemyra had only witnessed such destruction once before.

At a small village on the Sunset Isle, after The Terror had descended with fire and fury.

"They will blame me for this," Aemyra breathed, tears ripping from her eyes with the fierce wind. "And they would be right to do so."

As they flew out of the billowing smoke, sparks of dragonfire and glittering embers cascaded around her. Terrea's wings rose with determination, and Aemyra knew they would stop at nothing to free Tìr Teine from tyranny.

The cut on her palm burned with the death promise she had made to Fiorean.

Aemyra had been forged in fire, but a queen would rise from the ashes.

ACKNOWLEDGMENTS

A Fate Forged in Fire is such an apt title for this book because so much of the journey to publishing seemed like fate. I owe everything to my wonderful agent, Ciara Finan, for changing my life with one email. Thank you for being just as unhinged over fictional men in white-blond lace fronts as I am. To my UK editor, Alexa—thank you for believing in this book just as much as I do and for putting up with me constantly talking about future books and bringing my focus back to this first one. Thanks to my US editor, Mae, who understood these characters from chapter one. Thank you for allowing Aemyra to shine exactly as she was supposed to. I am so blessed to be able to have such a fantastic team of women working with me on this book. Thank you to the wider teams at Dialogue and Dell—Christina, Saida, Emily, Taylor, Brianna, and Mille especially—I couldn't have asked for a better home for this book. To Alessia for your invaluable insight and initial developmental edits—Adarian is forever yours. Huge appreciation to my foreign publishers and translators; you guys don't get enough credit for how hard your job is! Dewi Hargreaves for taking my terrible sketches and making the map of my dreams. Lauren for going through and fixing my rudimentary Scottish Gaelic to really bring the language to life within the story.

I would also like to thank the baristas at Gianotten Mutsaers for fueling my writing with flat whites and croissants. To my mum who sat on a boulder on a freezing cold Scottish beach and listened to me explain the entire 100+ page worldbuilding document—you have always been my biggest cheerleader and I would never have ended up with this much delusional confidence if it weren't for you. To my husband and dog, thank you for the forest walks that gave me a break from writing, even if I complained about the rain and the mud the entire time. My wonderful gran gets the credit for turning me into a bookworm; how I wish we could take one last trip to the library together. To the unhinged AO3 community and specifically Aaliyah, who asked me to write about a sapphire, this book would not exist without you. To my friends named and unnamed (Dee, Nadine, Emily, Alex, Ri, Manda, Dana, Mimi) I appreciated every phone call, podcast-length voice note, and message. Last, a huge thank you to every person who has picked up this book and read it. I am so unbelievably grateful for the time you have taken to get to know my characters, and I truly hope this is only the beginning of the adventures we will take together.

About the Author

HAZEL MCBRIDE is originally from Scotland but lived in the Caribbean, Spain, and France before settling in the Netherlands with her Dutch husband. As a former animal trainer, Hazel loves writing about magical and fantastical creatures, and as a bisexual author with anxiety, she focuses on writing queer characters and exploring topics such as mental illness within her work. When she isn't writing, Hazel can be found eating chocolate (Galaxy only) and watching shows that fuel her daydreams about morally gray villains. At least until her incessantly energetic border collie forces her to get off the couch.

Instagram and TikTok: @hazelmcbrideauthor